W9-DJJ-772

SHIPPING ONLY

Rainbow
on the Road

BOOKS by ESTHER FORBES

O GENTEEL LADY!

A MIRROR FOR WITCHES

MISS MARVEL

PARADISE

THE GENERAL'S LADY

PAUL REVERE AND THE WORLD HE LIVED IN

JOHNNY TREMAIN

AMERICA'S PAUL REVERE
(with Lynd Ward)

THE BOSTON BOOK
(with Arthur Griffin)

THE RUNNING OF THE TIDE

RAINBOW ON THE ROAD

. . . .

Rainbow
on the Road

BY ESTHER FORBES

HOUGHTON MIFFLIN COMPANY · BOSTON
The Riverside Press Cambridge

LIBRARY OF CONGRESS CATALOGUE CARD NUMBER: 53–9248

FOURTH PRINTING   R

PRINTED IN THE U.S.A.

To
Cornelia and Katharine

Rainbow on the Road

One

My Aunt Mitty was as good as gold. If she hadn't been she wouldn't of taken me in after my parents died, and then, my own relatives proving a mite reluctant, kept me and raised me until I was old enough to go for an apprentice and work like a man. But she had her failings and they were of the sort that would make a young rapscallion like I was sort of sorry for an uncle.

First time I ever saw him who was to be my uncle in time (and in jig time too, for when Mitty put her mind on a thing it happened fast), I couldn't have been more than six or seven. But I remember it was spring and on a windy rackerty warm day they met. They were married three weeks later.

I had been told off to help my aunt carry out and hang up winter woolens, extra blankets, the moth-eaten old bear rug (and not a bear had been shot around Hampton, Connecticut, for nigh on a hundred years), which we used to shut out the cold on the north side of the kitchen floor where it always came leaking in. Likewise it covered the cat-hole. I beat these things with a stick as they hung on the line and my aunt checked everything on her list and what was no longer service-able and should be given to the poor, and what needed mending and so on. But I proved that fiddling and feeble (feeling, I guess, that such women's work was beneath me) she sent me to the kitchen for a dose of sulphur and molasses.

She kept a jug of it mixed up against spring fever, like what had overcome me. It was on the kitchen shelf and under the Farmer's Almanack which hung there on a nail.

Now I saw plain as the nose on your face that I could pour one finger of the puking stuff (that was the dose) down the sink's gullet instead of my own and who'd know? Same time I realized she'd sometimes set these little traps for me. I mean she'd trust me to do something "on my honor," and me, unsuspecting, wouldn't — and all the time she hiding up and watching me. So she'd catch me and I'd catch it. Maybe this was good for my moral training but it often riled me considerable.

So there I stood by the sink and darst I or darsn't I? Then I heard a step out at the back door and it was not the step of my aunt.

He rapped a tat-a-tat, although the door stood open. He was standing there among the milk pails turned up and sunning, waiting for evening milking time on the bench set out for us to wash up on, now winter was over and warm weather ahead.

He was a pack peddler. I saw a monstrous big square pack on his back. He had no horse and buggy in those days. Men like that we called "walkers" and looked down on a little. Important peddlers had horses to do their lugging for them. Yet I knew he was important.

I'll say now what he looked like and be done with it. He was very tall and so narrow seems you could of dropped him in an eel skin. I think he was over twenty but not much over. His head was a shade too big for his body or at least for the width of his shoulders — which wasn't much. He was a touch gawky and he had too much, too dark and too tously hair and that gave him a foreign look. When he was happy he carried his head fine and high. When he weren't it sank some, and you noticed his neck was a touch on the pipestem, white and slender like a girl's, and so were his hands. He

had a short square chin with a cleft in it — mighty hard to
shave. A wide mouth, brown rather than red. It was sort of
a tomcat face, broad in the jaw and flattish and he had a
cattish secrecy and serenity to him — that is, most of the
time. His eyes were fine, bright and wide open.

He was a touch winded, for the pack he carried was hefty
for him — hefty for any man. He barely wished me good
morning and then he was inside and slung it right off on our
kitchen floor. As if to explain his panting he glanced appre-
hensively behind him like he was pursued.

"Safe here — for a moment," he said. I had visions of
sheriffs, constables and such, posses and hue-and-cry, and I
was for him and against the law or whatever might be after
him. I'd heard tell of old times and folks hiding in great
stone chimneys like ours.

"They after you?" I asked.

"They always are."

"If you hid up I could stand watch for you — if I knew
what to watch for."

"Lions," he said, so I knew he was play-acting. And
then I saw the mud he had drug in on his boots, not having
bothered to wipe off on the cornshuck mat set out for that
purpose. I knew Aunt Mitty would be after him and the
thought of her righteous indignation was more terrifying
than any lions.

Cool as a cucumber, he was unstrapping his pack and
setting up on chairs, table and sink about five or six pictures.
They were portraits of people, nice-done and terrible pretty,
but not the one of them had a face as yet. It was like that he
worked. For winter he'd hole up somewhere — or anywhere.
He'd paint up the bodies and the backgrounds. Come
summertime he'd go out and peddle them. From nature he'd
put in a likeness. Whole thing cost $3.00. He was talking all
the time to me and pretty fast, I suppose wishing to keep me
from calling my elders and betters before he had his goods

temptingly displayed. All the time he was telling me mostly
of a lion he had once seen in a caravan (as we used to call
what's now called a circus). And he talked of elephants. You
couldn't of pried me loose from him until he was ready. He
was like a magnet and me an iron filing, then and I guess
always.

But it was of course just business to him. How that man
could combine business and pleasure was just about sinful.
Then he stepped back and shook his head in admiration of
his work (that too was business).

"Any of these resemble any of your folks?"

"That there looks like our minister."

"Where he live?" I told him.

"And that there one," I said, "does look like her."

"Like who?"

"My Aunt Mitty."

"Sure enough?"

"For a fact it does."

It was the prettiest of them all. Prettiest thing I'd ever
seen and I couldn't figure how he did it. He had painted a
young woman — all but the face — with pale straight hair.
Just by the set of her neck you knew how she kept her chin
up and her little shoulders back and that nothing much could
faze her. She had a white dress on, and it besprinkled with
nosegays. Before it was part of a table. On it part of a teaset
— white and gold banded — the spitting image of her best
china. Most genteel country ladies had china like that but I
didn't know that then. I only knew that was she, and that
there crockery hers. Even the fact this lady wasn't sitting back
and doing nothing (even in a portrait), like the rest of his
ladies, convinced me this was my aunt. She was pouring out
tea and I could almost hear her voice saying to visiting ladies
"Weak or strong?" and apologizing like ladies always did for
anything nice they set before you. The cream had turned or
the sponge drops hadn't sponged or the jelly hadn't jelled and

so on. Nice company talk like that. Didn't mean shucks. And it wasn't genteel to go clutching at teacups. Little finger out, was the fashion. He'd got that in too. He knew a terrible lot about people.

Then I heard her and was fearful for him because of the mud he had tracked in. She never saw it. She didn't even see the picture which was to be her. She saw him. It was like that and on both sides and at once. I think it's a fine thing to be able to be knocked galley-west like that all of a heap and all of a sudden. Most people can't be. Not me, for one. But I guess it was hoping for this great experience that made me put off settling down and marrying until sort of late. I was not, of course, of a knowledgeable age, yet I felt a something in the air right then, and I never forgot. So I guess for years I was waiting for a girl just to stand in a doorway and look at me and me at her and both of us know before a word said. And like Submit Pratt she would smell of sunshine and cedar chips and maybe camphor. It was a long time before I was ready to accept the facts. First, I wasn't the sort of man to rouse such emotions. And second, if I were, the kind of help-meet I really wanted (and got) didn't decide so important a decision with less good sense, intelligent appraisal and prayerful thought than she would use in selecting a bonnet.

He was that sort and so was she. They didn't always get on too good, and sometimes not so well as that, but they were bound close to each other — maybe it was the memory of that first moment before either had spoken that bound them. She had her lists in her hand. That should of warned him. All those lists of her things that she was putting away and caring for. For these things belonged to her — even her brothers' long woolen underdrawers were her drawers — if you follow me. She was made that way and she took mighty good care of anything that belonged to her. That went for me, and her brothers and Laban's sickly wife, Dorinda, and Jude when she married him and the children they had. But

like all those woolens — she wanted to list them and put
them away where she'd know where they were and have them
stay there — where no moth could get at them nor rust
corrupt.

That's how they met. If there are any Pratts or Reboughs
left around Hampton they may still have that picture and get
some idea of how she looked then. It was a good likeness.
She was a little woman without much hips. And she had long
pale yellow hair. She screwed it back tight, for of that be-
setting sin of women — personal vanity — she had none. At
first he'd get her to let it hang, and then you'd hardly believe
it. She was a pretty pink and had the only blue eyes I've ever
seen that could really snap. I don't believe any misfortune
nor age either could ever alter that. She'd be above all that.
Women — ladies at least — set an awful lot on carriage in
those days. Your real lady used to scorn the back of her chair
and the backs of pews on Lord's Day. Yet I've seen her do
the most distressful hardest work — like say at hog-butcher-
ing time. For anything that had to be done she'd do and no
fuss. I don't think Mitty ever in her life thought whether
she wanted to do a piece of work or not. She just sized up
what was to be done and went ahead and did it. Overdid it
maybe. For even her fancy work, embroideries and such as
ladies like to leave about for pick-up work she'd get her teeth
into and stay up late to finish, although the pleasure of such
work is the feeling of leisure it gives. That wasn't like him
any. He was terribly picky and choosy about the sort of work
he'd do. Yet she was too proud to nag him. Nothing could
humiliate her. Not even Jude. And she was too proud to
complain any. Or to have backaches and vapors, and go lie
down like other women. Perhaps she overdid it, for she did
age young and grew too thin — and taut as a fiddle-string.
Of course they weren't what's called "well-suited" — he a
real careless wandering sort and she so sot. And they hadn't
the same moral code. For instance he'd never have put me on

my honor to do something and then spy on me — she would. And she had the strictest regard for the absolute truth — while he enjoyed trimming things up a little. She never would have pretended, even to amuse a child, she was chased by lions. He pretended worse things than that even to church deacons and selectmen. She was a little deficient in the saving grace of humor. And he could find something to amuse him wherever he looked — even useless things he'd look at, for the amusement they gave him. I mean things like an ant trying to carry off a dead caterpillar too big for him, or courting cats, or the expressions on the church members' faces that time Mrs. Deacon Forbisher put vinegar in the sacred vessels at Lord's Supper for wine. And another thing. Anything that happened Mitty wanted to do something about it. Seems like sometimes Jude didn't want to do anything about anything. I imagine you have caught my drift. No, they were not "well-suited." But they didn't bore each other any, although they bothered each other some.

By the way, Mitty is short for Submit. It is a mistake to give such names, considering the contrary, unpredictable nature of mortals. Littlest fellow in my district school with me was Hercules Hubbey. I knew a Noah once too scared of water to take a bath. And when it comes to Lucrece Chambers I won't soil my pen telling of her. So it is right down the line. And Submit Pratt didn't submit to anything.

. . . .

Two

. . . .

H<small>ER BROTHERS</small> didn't quarrel with her when she told them flat out she was of half a mind to marry Jude Rebough (and that's the way Yankees used to say they were a-going to do something come hell or high water). They were pretty self-controlled men, not given to shooting off their faces, but Tite (the most emotional of the two of them) did go down cellar to fetch up a pitcher of hard cider and I guess also to count ten before he was ready to speak out.

In the meantime Labe said mildly, like he always spoke, "Well, Mitty, you are pretty well fixed, financially speaking. I guess if you want a husband merely to give yourself something to look at, you can afford it." That was about all Labe himself got from Dorinda and she wasn't much to look at either. Mitty always did all the woman's work on that farm. As for Tite he might of married a woman who would of helped her out. So I guess both of these men knew they were living in glass houses. If their sister wanted to take on this sort of lazybones (as they thought him) they were in no position to throw any bricks.

So Tite and Labe sat there by the checkered kitchen table, drank their cider, thought, and said nothing more for quite a spell. And I guess each of them was thinking honestly about their own sins, Tite's of omission and Labe's of commission.

Now it's pretty easy for folks who have lived away from where they were born and reared — say, New England — to think New England just about perfect. Why, I've heard ex-Yankees out here in Kansas going on about what strict, God-fearing moral lives everybody lived back home where they were raised. Fact is, this wasn't always the case. Take my Uncle Tite, for instance. There he sat and darsn't criticize his sister's little peccadillo because he had a worse one himself. He had been in love with a married woman for years. He was about twenty-eight at this time and I guess it was about six years back old Mr. Frank Ryder brought a young woman home from Abington to serve as his third wife. Polly Ryder was her name, as I recollect it. No sooner had Tite laid eyes on her than he began a sort of courting of her. He called twice a week — on Tuesday evenings and Sunday afternoons. Of course her husband was always present and some people said it made the old man feel real good knowing Polly would be well taken care of after his passing. And others said the only thing kept him out of the grave that yawned for him was his determination to spite Titus Pratt. Of course this situation made some talk, but after all it wasn't anybody's business except the three of them. People took it for granted other people did queer things in those days, and it wasn't anybody else's business — long as they kept some show of decency and didn't disturb the peace any. Those old-fashioned Yankees used to be as independent as so many hogs on ice.

So Tite and Labe sat there, each in his own glass house. Laban finally said, "How about a bit of gingerbread, Mitty, to sop up all this cider with?" The kitchen smelt of the gingerbread she had been baking. She fetched it out, and went on standing where she had been standing all the time

with her chin up and her body stiff, challenging them to
object — if they dared. Then I guess she would of told them
plenty. But not otherwise. Not unless they drove her to it.
Laban, you might say, had already given his permission. And
she stood there awaiting Tite's approval. She wouldn't go
begging for it or anything. She was too stuck-up.

"Sure you prefer that painting feller to Dr. Crompton?"

"Yes," she said.

"Lost your taste for Eli Roper?"

"Never had much."

"Well, I guess you're your own boss, Mitty — and worst of
it is, ours too." She was always sharp after them if they
messed up the house any. "Maybe if you take on a yoke-mate
(and that painting feller is an off-ox if ever I saw one) you
won't have so much energy for goading and galling us." They
laughed hard, laughing at her I guess for being such a derned
fool, but they were real fond of her and proud of her too.
She laughed too but only to show gratitude, for her brothers
had just promised her to take on Jude Rebough like a brother
— and for better and for worse. After this talk with them
she could go ahead with confidence as far as they were
concerned.

Best as they were able, those two young fellows lived up to
what they promised her. Sometimes they weren't entirely
able. I got to be sort of thin-skinned about my new uncle's
dignity, for not everybody in town respected it. Once I
remember, soon after the marriage, I was standing around,
with the men at the carriage sheds behind the church. It was
Lord's Day and word had sort of got around that Loomis P.
Beaver was going to swop for Mr. Shedd's old trotting mare
and Mr. Shedd would get stuck on the bargain. It was fifteen
years back Mr. Shedd had played it just a mite fine in a horse
swap he had done to Loomis. But as we waited the men were
talking and sort of marveling at the wonderful stories and so
on this new fellow just settled among them (and married to

a Pratt) had been stuffing them with up at Baker's General store or at Blacklock's.

"How you feel about the veracity some of those yarns, Tite?"

"Well," said Tite, "They reminded me of the biggest liar I ever knew personally. Was a farmer, too. Reputation of pretty good farmer at that, but he lied so he had to hire another man to call his pigs."

For some reason this hurt me so much I remember it to this day, and me walking home hanging on to Jude's hand. By the way. He always looked like he didn't belong at Meeting. I can't describe why. By this time Titus was first selectman and Labe town surveyor, and they looked it, at least in their Sunday clothes. Although oil and water didn't mix, I give all three of them credit for doing what they were able. That's all I ask of anybody these days. I asked a lot more when I was young. You must of gathered I was from the beginning on the side of the off-ox.

.   .   .   .

Three

.   .   .   .

You might say Jude didn't quite show his spots that first summer, although to a discerning eye it would have been pretty apparent where they would come out in time. Eventually he learned how to handle Mitty, going edgewise around her. No frontal attacks ever. But he made an error when he

admitted to her that he was well taught in interior house
painting as well as the fancier sort of thing he liked best to do.
She had him painting the whole insides of our house. I
remember how much skim milk went into the lime and the
linseed oil, and for tinting one room he used beet-root juice.
For the best parlor he cut and added a stenciling of maidenhair ferns. Already I was helping him, for school was out, and
after and before chores I had the time. He and I hit it off
good.

Then seems every housewife for miles about was dropping
in to stare and admire, and Mitty was taking orders for him
and writing them down in a little book. She was pleased to
see she had married a respectable tradesman and no mere
peddler like it had looked first. He was given the ell chamber
for a shop. He called it his painting room and he holed up in
there, nice and comfortable. But he didn't put up the sign
she urged him nor advertise in any paper. He didn't want to
run a real business and have to think seriously of dollars and
cents and bore himself with flat walls and stop traipsing about
and seeing the world.

She did admit he had better first of all sell off the bodies
and backgrounds he had all fixed up. And then he actually
convinced her that interior painting made him cough. He
had a consumptive look to him — being so narrow and he
could (at will) cough more pathetic than any grown man I
ever heard. She couldn't henpeck him any — like she would
of any other man. He just wasn't there (I mean spiritually)
when she tried to. I think Jude's elusiveness, and the way he
got his way in spite of her, tickled her brothers. Men are apt
to stick together. If he hadn't loved her and been (in his own
way) good to her it would have been a different story.

Then that first summer she suggested to Mr. Blacklock who
kept the local ordinary that he take down a new-fashioned
sign — just Blacklock Hotel on it — and let Jude do him a
pretty one like his grandfather had had — a black lock on a

blue ground. He told her it would insult his patrons, for illiteracy was that far licked practically everybody could read and they didn't want picture-writing any more. Still he had always wanted (although of course he couldn't afford it) a nice overmantel for his barroom — say a pretty view of Hampton Main Street. Something quiet and refined.

She came home looking as proud of herself as if she had got him the job of painting the whole State House. Jude shot right over, and me at his heels. He liked doing overmantels, but didn't often get an order for one, for at this time they were passing out of fashion.

As we walked the mile to town he began telling me the first time (that spring three months back) he had come into Hampton and seen its main street. And what a fine April day it had been. The wind had been whipping the greening fields and the flickers yelling their heads off. It was so happy and rackerty a day it made him want to laugh, and then he saw how all the women's skirts were going up, and the minister had almost lost his wig, and so he had laughed out loud all by himself. It might not be too easy to paint a high wind in spring, but he was ready to try it.

Mr. Blacklock was rubbing his hands with excitement, although of course pretending he couldn't afford it and didn't want it if he could. That sort of talk didn't bother Jude any. He understood. Instead he asked me to run back, harness up Goldie and fetch up his painting gear. For he saw Mr. Blacklock was in such a state of anticipation it would be cruel not to begin right away. That painting equipment, by the way, weighed between thirty and forty pounds. The colors came powdered, packed in bladders of various sizes, and had to be mixed with oil by grinding on the stone. He had already shown me how to do that.

It was July, and haying time. I wasn't permitted to waste my time up at Blacklock's grinding paint but Jude came home every night happy as a clam. It was only his own natural

abstemiousness that made him come home sober. Mr. Blacklock was so excited over his work he was ready to furnish any
amount of liquor to act as a primer. Jude never did drink
much. He had his troubles and his faults. Liquor was not
one of them. While he had been working on that overmantel
there in the barroom of Blacklock Hotel he had been getting
and listening to a lot of advice from the usual habitués of the
place. And from Mr. Blacklock himself. Mitty always
blamed them more than Jude that that picture didn't add a
thing to his reputation as a sober citizen.

He had begun all right with a sort of over-all of our main
street. Church and elm trees. Squire's house, minister's
house, and of course bigger than life and plum in the middle
was Blacklock's Hotel. And it was a spring day and mighty
windy and he'd got flickers in the sky just like he had told
me of. And everything had really happened which might have
happened. I mean, the minister's wig had blown off and he
was chasing it, and the women's skirts had risen up over their
heads and some people thought past the bounds of common
decency, and of course they were skretching and trying to
hold them down. Some of them were bowlegged and some
were knock-kneed, some had pipestems and some piano legs.
Jude hadn't particularized any. They were just women, but
right off people were saying that there was Mrs. Grant and
anybody could guess by the way Miss Olly Perkins came
sidling into Meeting that she had knock-knees. And those
striped stockings couldn't belong to anyone except the doctor's
wife, for she was so economical she always used up all the
odds and ends of yarn no matter the color, knitting stockings
for herself. So pretty soon there was a name attached to every
last one.

In the Squire's yard was a wash line flapping with nightshirts and underdrawers and all pinker than a baby's bottom.
This was a reference to the fact a year or so before, his wife
had taken all his worn woolen things and dyed them bright

pink to use up in the rug she was hooking, and people seeing
them out there had twitted the good old gentleman plenty
(and still did — if a town has a good joke they don't give it
up easy) about his pink underwear. Jude had got those things
to look paunchy and pompous, more like Squire in fact than
he looked like himself. So, with the help of Mr. Blacklock
and some of the more frivolous citizens, he touched on quite
a lot of little things of considerable local interest. But it was
the women's legs got under the most skins.

So, as a committee of the ladies asked Mr. Blacklock to
cover up that overmantel, he rigged a sort of theatre curtain
across it on pulleys. Guess that made a bad matter worse. For
now people were coming for miles, knowing if they sat there
running up a big enough bill against themselves Mr. Blacklock would oblige and show this scandal to them. Why, some
people say that picture was why one of the stage companies
next year made Blacklock's a regular stop. So all in all the
overmantel was good for his business and good for the town.
It didn't, however, help Jude's reputation any. Mitty had to
face the fact that people (especially men) liked Jude mighty
well and didn't respect him any. He wasn't a solid citizen by
nature and he didn't look it. Nor act it. And she couldn't
believe how little pay he took home with him, for the hours
he had worked. Interior wall painting was actually more
profitable.

But it must have reconciled her some to Jude's practicing
his trade a little further off from home. She did a number of
things that most brides don't do quite so soon. Like fancying
a shorter haircut on him, and a new, more honorable-looking
hat, and not going to sleep during sermon. He thanked her
for her consideration of him and did as she said. She gave
him a horse for a wedding present, for she owned one third of
that fine farm. Goldie was young but too fat and close to
butter-yellow. She was kind of comical. There was an old
chaise it was agreed he could fix and paint up for himself.

Evidently she had decided if he wouldn't give up his wandering ways he wasn't to be any more a humble pack peddler. If he wouldn't stay home and put some flesh on his bones she wasn't going to have him wear off the little he had by hoofing it.

Or perhaps she'd already seen in his eyes that look of the born wayfarer. I've seen it again and again on the faces of westering men. First time I saw it was on Jude Rebough that summer — only summer he stayed mostly to home.

By the way. He built a kind of coffin to the end of his chaise to carry his gear in. He painted that and the chaise — leather top too — all buff. He said, to match his horse. The effect was far more striking than it sounds. Nobody else would have thought of such a queer thing.

. . . .

Four

. . . .

THINGS WENT ON about as you might expect. They had two children. The oldest was a girl. Mitty let Jude give her the flibberty name of Leaf. But it was agreed between them the boy was to have her old family name of Simon. Titus kept on paying his attentions to Mrs. Polly Ryder. Never thought to look elsewhere. Laban's Dorinda kept more and more to her chamber. She had always had her asthma. Now she had added dropsy and besides her teeth hurt. However it weren't in Laban to think to look for a younger and healthier woman.

All three of those Pratts were terribly sot. Whatever they had made up their minds to they stood by. Laban was always patient with his sickly wife and Mitty bothered with calves-foot jellies and junkets to tempt her.

Mitty worked too hard. There should of been a hired girl to help her, but she'd just try one and let her go. She said she got more tired watching someone else doing things wrong than doing it right in the first place herself.

Every spring, soon as mud was out, Jude and that fat Goldie of his left for the road. Every fall just about the first spitting of snow they came back. Wintertimes he spent preparing more of those backgrounds and bodies of his to peddle off next summertime.

Luckily for Jude, his wife didn't "understand" him. If she had of, she could of got her fingers into all sorts of crannies and crevices in him and just about wrecked their marriage. For instance she honestly thought wall painting and such dull stuff made him cough, and if he coughed, a consumption would follow. She hadn't a notion that he got no more for a portrait with a beautiful background that he had spent hours or days elaborating on than for one with no more than a pair of curtains slapped in. It was their faces people paid three dollars for. Not fancy work — no matter how painstaking and pretty. She simply admired all the flowers and birds, and bugs even, he'd sometimes waste so much time on. And he was encouraged by her admiration. If she had understood what a waste of time it was she wouldn't have.

Some time I'll go a bit more into what these pictures of his were like. Now I'd just like to say a word (having so recently mentioned that picture of his at Blacklock's) about what he liked best to do — that is, fantastic painting upon pine panels. They ran about five feet by two and a half. And so as far as size was concerned they were suitable to be sold and set up in taverns and mansion houses over the fireplace. Now they weren't stylish any more and his subject matter was not well chosen. And he a grown man, with a growing family, did them for no more than the fun of it.

I remember how long he spent on a parcel of crickets. He had them all dressed up in little clothes and playing on little fiddles and such. No expectant mother making little things for her first baby ever fussed more than he did making garments for those insects. Just remembering that picture I can feel how hot and still were those August nights when the crickets played. Even today I'll never hear crickets but *know* they've got little fiddles and a nice pair of pants on.

He did a fine one of a scarecrow left out on the lonely fields. He painted scarecrows (and he was very attached to them) not as they look to a man — I mean no more than a senseless stake and your old pantaloons and your wife's discarded bonnet and perhaps your aunt's old basque for the middle part and straw. He painted scarecrows as they looked to crows — and that is pretty terrifying.

I remember a picture he started after he came back from Pomfret Factory. He called it The Weavers Woven In. The new power looms were spiderwebs. The girls were the flies and the superintendents rich spiders. Or his Thanksgiving at the Poor Farm, you could guess the turkey was a stuffed pauper. And the overseers of the poor gathered about "the festive board" looked real heedless of Christian charity. Whoever would buy things like that?

Mitty thought he carried these out with him and sold them for a pretty price. He didn't disillusion her but he left them hid away to home, for he knew nobody would buy them. Sometimes she would purse up her lips and shake her head over what people would buy. A real scarecrow not being worth five cents she couldn't believe there was anyone so daft as to pay twenty dollars (that's what he got off Blacklock for the overmantel he did him) for pictured ones. And as for crickets! Who would want such in a house? They chew up woolens.

Such work of his didn't strike her quite respectable. But if strangers off in strange parts would shuck out hard cash for them she wouldn't complain. As I have pointed out, she cared most for having him respected, and right here, round about Hampton, and to that end she showed the most courteous respect for him always. I remember how other women would come in to set and drink tea, get on with their hand-work and gossip with her. She always referred to Jude as "Mr. Rebough" and was saying that Mr. Rebough doesn't think too highly of Daniel Webster or of the Republican Party. Things like that that he had never given a thought to. Or that Mr. Rebough prefers his tripe pickled when really he never cared what went in his stomach just so it was full. I don't think she fooled anybody. She'd quote him and his opinion on what the selectmen ought to do about the bridge over Bark Meadow Brook or whether it would be a good or a bad apple year — and pat up her back hair like women do, boasting about their husbands.

So as far as I can see it wasn't up to her to object quite as much as she did when Jude, on his part, enjoyed pumping up actual facts and chinking the gaps between logs of truth (so to speak) with a little imagination. Or as we used to say, "cutting the hem off truth's garment." So he didn't used to fib like that to home — much. But he was a terror at it up to Baker's or at Blacklock's. Then, too, he liked to preambulate with his sketchbook. If he hadn't been out a-drawing and a-drawing in his sketchbooks — chickadees and scarecrows and oxen breaking snowbound roads, crows and such, how could he of painted them so nice when time came to use them? She'd try to put his maunderings to a practical use. Would he look over a certain stand of chestnut to see if it was wise to cut it that winter (it was things like that she pretended to defer to his superior masculine wisdom — things he had no opinion on) or would he leave a nice jelly with old Mrs. Corey? Or pick up mail at Blacklock's or match this sample

at Baker's? Well, he'd just forget — unless I was along with
him. Here I was, coming along say, seven or eight only, and
yet my feelings for him were somewhat paternal. He didn't
need any of that from me nor anybody else. He was the most
completely independent married man I ever knew, for he
knew how to keep his mouth shut and do as he pleased —
without letting small disagreements blow up to big.

Sometimes, something would arise which the three **Pratts**,
as good sensible farmers, would all be for, and he secretly
against. I guess as good an example of that as I can think of
was this farm's long warfare against a certain fox. Naturally
Laban and Tite and Tite's savage old dog Brutus, and
Mitty and even Dorinda, were all on one side. Secretly Jude
and me were on the other.

This here special fox had split his front left paw some time
back. I suppose in a trap. So he signed himself in snow and
mud wherever he went. Old Split Foot, by the way, is a
country word for the devil. That's what we called him. You
could not shoot him, trap him, hunt him down with dogs. Or
poison him. Tite took this almost personally. Sometimes
he'd get four, five other men and their dogs to join up with
him. And Tite's Brutus killed a beagle. Owly Parker broke
a leg. Trying to smoke him out they set fire to the Patching
woodlot. Poison set out to get him was said to have caused
the death of a neighbor's cow — although I'd say a carniv-
orous cow that would touch carrion deserved to die. But
that such an accusation could arise shows how great was the
confusion.

Far as we could figure, Split Foot never raided any henroost
but us Pratts'. I guess others weren't so smart to recognize his
signature. So people said there weren't no such animal and
Tite got razzed plenty for this private fox of his. He was
running for selectman again and his opponent got some good
jabs in on him. So he got sensitive on the subject and madder
all the time.

Then (Mitty being out the room) Jude would settle back and tell him one story after another of phantom foxes — one, say, he'd heard of up in New Hampshire. And get Tite so wound up he'd be talking of trying a silver bullet on the varmint or even to admitting only time he'd got a good look at him he had looked right through him. Titus was plumb knocked off his perch what with the fox's and Jude's antics. But if Mitty came in on them and caught Jude's eye he'd deflate a little, and agree, yes, it was about time to go to bed.

I remember Tite's sitting at our red and white checked kitchen table after supper and swearing he'd get that fox if it cost him his life and pounding the table until the cruets jumped, and swearing he'd get him a new dog. Brutus was too old. For Split Foot had come only the night before and Brutus had been off his chain, roaming and supposedly guarding the place, but had given no alarm. Then Tite began demanding who had left the privy door open? For Brutus was well on in years and he'd snuck in there and gone to sleep. And Tite was lambasting Mitty who liked everything nice, and had padded up the seats with old carpeting, thus making it irresistible to old Brutus.

Brutus was a terrible big fierce old dog. He was brindled and supposed to be death to foxes. He snapped at strangers and even after all these years he still looked on Jude as a stranger. And he was so mean he'd kill little dogs. Luckily, he was fearful of our cats.

Every night he was loosed. Foxes aren't supposed to raid in daytime much. Split Foot would. So if you heard Brutus begin to roar that he smelt foxes you were to hasten out and unchain him. Split Foot knew this. He'd come when, say, all of us were to church.

Like when once the Pratt men were going to Town Meeting and Mitty was on the Ladies' Committee for noontime refreshments. Although Jude was a registered voter by now I don't think they especially wanted him at Town

Meeting, for he never seemed less valuable anywhere than
there. So he stayed home and naturally I did, and so did
Dorinda — naturally. If Brutus barked Jude was to loose
him. But he did like what I hoped he'd do. Took his sketchbook and me and went for a walk.

There was a rocky hummock before the house and to the
right of it. We called it Pine Hill. It wasn't a hill really but
I guess out here in Kansas they'd call it a mountain. It had
been too rough ever to pay to clear for farmland and it was a
very pretty place. When we came back, we came back over it.
That winter Jude had been terrible het up over chickadees.
He'd been filling books full of them. Evidently it was up here
he'd been studying on them and feeding them crumbs, for no
sooner had we got to the top of the hummock, where the old
pines made a circle about us, than he was tossing out bread
to them. He had them about half tame.

Must have been late winter or early spring, for I remember
how they had begun to fib a little — saying they was Phoebe
birds as they do come March. There was crust on the snow
strong enough to hold a man but cracking all the time under
our feet. Jude motioned me to sit on a rock and keep on
throwing crumbs. He sat too, and got out his book.

We neither of us saw nor heard the fox when he came. It
was the birds leaving told us someone had come. He came
trotting on the crust, airy and graceful with his tail afloat
behind him. I never saw a human being look as you might
say so elegant, nor so well dressed. He wasn't hurrying nor
hunting, just obviously a gentleman of leisure out looking
over his estate, keeping an eye on things, you know, seeing
that his hired help had done their work properly. The fact
he had a little limp added to his distinction. Made him seem
even more genteel.

He was so close you could see every hair on him glittered
with good food and the care he'd given to himself, and the
way his russet, black and white were distributed just right to

make him pretty as a picture. We could see the yellow of his
eyes and also that he wasn't quite as nonchalant as he
pretended to be. Obviously he had to keep up pretenses even
before nothing more than chickadees. He was listening so
hard one forepaw drew up. He was listening for a sound from
our yard.

The wind was setting from Pine Hill to the farm. We too
were down wind from him. I could smell him a little. It's an
evil smell somehow. Then of a sudden Brutus got a nose full
of him and such a roaring and a rattling of the chain went up,
and howls and growls thrown in.

Old Split Foot's hackles went up at that, but I guess the
sound of the chain reassured him, for he sat down to pure
enjoy himself, smiling slightly the way dogs do when they
are pleased, and his red tongue going in and out and his lips
curled back, pulling his whiskers up like he was laughing.
And when he had laughed enough he scratched behind an ear
with a limber hind paw. You could see his belly was white
like snow.

I can tell you Jude and I were quiet. We had seen a
wonder. We didn't breathe hardly. But Split Foot turned
his head, saw us, and the jig was up.

Jude addressed him. "Now's your chance, boy. You go get
yourself a nice hen now. Help yourself to that damned old
rooster."

I never knew a man so fond of birds in my life. Except
that he looked down on hens, and especially on our old one-
eyed rooster.

The fox listened with his bright head atilt. And then
bang! Like that he was gone. It was like he never had been
and the crust was so hard he left no trace.

We heard a door bang open and we run and slid off Pine
Hill to get there before Dorinda. We hadn't counted on her
getting up to loose Brutus. She was struggling out over the
ice and very fearful of her footing, with a quilt over her head

and shoulders because her teeth hurt her. But she was approaching the frenzied dog warily, saying, "Nice doggie, nice doggie," which he certainly wasn't. But she tottered and keeled over on the ice. Of course our first duty was to make sure she wasn't hurt and get her into the kitchen and build up the fire. Jude left me to make her some tea. But when I went out to bring in some more fresh water (that was my job and the buckets were getting low), I found Jude a-setting just beyond Brutus's reach and he was ridiculing the dog, teasing him with words only and I guess telling him he would never get Split Foot who that very moment was going off with the old one-eyed rooster, and if he didn't get him Tite would shoot him and get a younger dog, etc. First and last time I ever saw a dog so reduced. He was simply speechless. He'd frothed up all over like he was going mad. And I knew this had been going on behind everybody's back for some time and it was easy to figure why Brutus was so heart-set on biting Jude. Now Jude wasn't cast in any heroic mold, but he certainly sometimes played with fire.

It spoils my story a little to admit old Split Foot didn't raid the hens that time. In fact he never came back again for weeks on end. Instead of being glad to see us, as I had liked to think, I guess he was so terrified he about decided never more to chance it. Now I know better, but I was at an age when I liked to imagine that Jude often met him on Pine Hill and advised him as to the lay of the land.

Neither of us mentioned this little affair to anyone. Jude didn't have to tell me to keep whist. It does show something of his character and mine too — I being at the age I was. As I see it now it was all right for a boy my age to feel that way about a wicked piece of varmint, which after all was all Split Foot ever was, but not for a grown man like Jude was.

The fact was, Jude and I was on the side of the foxes. I grew up and out of such foolishness — I don't think he ever did.

. . . .

Five

. . . .

I WAS THIRTEEN when the next part happened. I can say this positively because it was the last year I spent with them all. The situation was this. The Pratts had taken me in when, about eight years before, a private chaise from no one knew where had turned over into the chasm of Brokington Brook, killing my mother outright, hurting my father so bad he only lingered a little and joined her. The Pratts' house was the nearest and Laban Pratt first man to get to us. By the way, that brook ever since has been called "Broke-Axle Brook" on account of that accident. New England was still naming and renaming things. Maps hadn't yet settled down real steady. So there were two funerals from this house and me too shook-up to attend. Mitty often took me to see where they lay. That graveyard at Hampton is bare of herbage and pointed up like a pyramid. I thought it looked like a Babylonish ziggurat (the Pratts had an illustrated Bible). For round and round, up and up, the feet of the mourners (cows too) had worn an outside stairway. Although horse-drawn hearses had come in, no such modern conveyance had ever ascended that holy hill. The dead rode to their last resting place on the shoulders of men.

I've stammered some all my life, but when they picked me out of the brook I was stammering so bad I was no help for

identification. I could say my name was Eddy but I couldn't
get out either Creamer nor where we was from, which was
Waltham. The Pratts didn't push me. It was weeks before
the mystery was solved and by then it was like I belonged to
them.

I've said those Pratts were good men. I never saw a farm
animal abused nor neglected. I've seen them up night after
night with a sick ewe or an orphan colt — and it wasn't just
the money end, but the loving care they gave did make them
money too. Mitty could no more of shoved me off on an uncle
in Waltham (who didn't want me) than she could of shoved
Jude out after he'd got himself tucked in there. This Uncle
Gore of mine was well fixed with this world's goods and a
harness maker. I suppose he paid them for rearing me. I
know it would of made no difference to them if he hadn't.

Letters now and then went back and forth between them.
He never wrote me, nor sent me a message nor a present
either. He was an old skinflint. But right off he promised the
Pratts as soon as I reached a proper age for indenture (that is
thirteen) he'd take me on as an apprentice.

And now I was thirteen and a letter had come from him.
Next fall, come November, he'd be expecting me. For the
boy that had been serving him would be through his indenture by then.

Sometimes I'd hear them talk of this and it near broke my
heart. Of course I didn't fuss any, for I'd always half known
this was going to happen sometime. The result was they kind
of favored me. I didn't have to go to school quite so regular
that winter, for I had already received all the book learning a
man would need to make harnesses with. Of course I'd
always done the chores — night and morning chores. Late
that winter chance offered a good stout chore boy from the
poor farm. He was Sampson P. Foote, as big for his age as I
was smallish, and he and me shared the attic room and bed. I
didn't care much for him. He could get all the blankets off

me with one roll. He could spit through his front teeth and I was his favorite target. Seems right off he did chores better than I. If any one thing reconciled me to leaving home for Uncle Gore's it was Sampson. Of course nobody knew. Mitty was talking of it being nice for me to have a boy my own age about.

It was Jude suggested that this spring when he left home I should go with him and help him grind paints and even put in a little something of background and such, and in general help him. Mitty agreed right away, for travel, she says, broadens the mind. I guess she knew I wouldn't have much pleasure once I tied up with Uncle Gore, and guessed from his letters there wouldn't be much but work ahead of me the next four years, nor was there.

I was almost sick with joy, but of course I'd learned not to show too much emotion. As I remember it, all I said when asked if this summer trip with Jude suited me was, "I don't mind if I do," which was just what I had said when told come fall I was to go to Uncle Gore and learn the harness maker's arts.

It was March when Jude said he intended to walk over to Norwich (a matter of over twenty miles) one day, and back next. The road wasn't fit for wheels yet. There was an old apothecary shop there where he had often bought his colors. If I were now, of a sort, his apprentice, shouldn't I go with him and help lug? You bet I rose to that for I would have gone to Hell and back only might I go with him.

Walking down to Norwich I don't remember much but how happy we were. And the first bluebird or robin or "look at those pussywillows." He told me a great deal of new and improving "facts." I remember especially he told me about the house of the "boiled man" way up somewheres in New Hampshire and the sort of ghost he made, and he'd certainly have had me sitting on the edge of my chair — if I had been sitting in a chair, but fact is, we were sort of scrabbling along on the high bushy sides of that road which I don't think a duck could of managed to walk on. By the way. We saw lots of wild duck and far up, way overhead, the Vees of the wild geese flying northward. And we heard them too. The Little River was to our left hand most of the way to Norwich.

The old apothecary was standing right under his own sign — a golden mortar and pestle. He was peering and blinking about him as though like the rest of the woodchucks he had just crawled out of hibernation. He had long yellow chisel teeth in front, and that was all the teeth time had left him, and he had on a dirty, sleeveless fur surcoat of extremely antique fashion, so except for spectacles he looked about as much like that rodent as a man. He smelt terrible and I was amazed to see Jude embrace him and he him, for (as I'll explain later) he had been educated somewhat in Italy and had Italianate ways.

I had never heard a limner called an "artist" until Dr. Bloomer (as he was called) said how glad he was always to serve "artists," although he could make more money selling drenches for kine, etc. He wasn't a real doctor, of course. He was what nowadays would be called a quack.

I might add here that this was the only place for hundreds of miles you could buy artists' colors in any purity or perfection. It was this man's grandfather had started the trade. Ships from Europe could get up the Thames as far as Norwich Landing — where the Shetucket and Yantic come together. So for towards a hundred years certain ships had been bringing in painters' colors from London. And in London were merchants who collected colors from all over the world and got them ready to reship. Jude said American paint-makers' paints were not suitable for more than painting a barn, an Indian or a lady's face.

Dr. Bloomer had an old-fashioned scary sort of shop. Dark cobwebs you could all but swing on hung from the rafters,

and a stuffed alligator was up there too. The biggest rattle-
snake killed in those parts in a bottle and a human embryo
in another, and a kitten with two heads in a third. He offered
right off to fix a shake-down in a corner for Jude and me and
he called me "Sonny," which I didn't like.

Jude and I carried our own blankets with us and food
enough. He had been here many times before, and knew
what to expect from Dr. Bloomer, and the old apothecary
knew what to expect from him. For instance Jude furnished
the food and Dr. Bloomer a bottle of wine. He gave me a
pewter cup to drink out of that had an asafetidal smell to it.
And Jude something made out of a horn — or a skull, for all
I knew. Himself drank out of the bottle. This was my first
introduction to wine, for ordinary people didn't drink it
much, and I was too young for Lord's Supper and even if I'd
been older chances are it would be hard cider instead. The
wine, or the long walk or the blustery spring day or the fetid
suffocation of the place, made me sleepy, so I sought out the
shake-down and lay on it soon after supper.

Then Jude asked him if he had any new engravings — for
the shop did a little business in prints as well as drugs and
such. Dr. Bloomer hung the lamp that had been on the table
on a hook. He went back to the room where he slept and
stored things, and brought back with him a large portfolio,
mottled like a frog's entrails outside.

This he opened on the table and let Jude pore over them,
studying one and passing on, then going back to the one
before to study on further. I've an idea here, and nowhere
else perhaps, Jude was seeing imitation of the works of the
great old masters. No color, of course. Just black and white.
The old woodchuck was naming the names to him. "Guido
Reni," he'd say, or "Rubens" or "the divine Raphael," names
I know now, but didn't then. Seems he himself as a boy had
been sent to Rome as an apprentice to an apothecary there by

his grandfather. So he was in a position to explain to Jude how these pictures lived and glowed with color, in their natural state and beauty.

"They don't do things in Italy," he was saying, "as we do over here. A man like you, Mr. Rebough, isn't a limner over there, he's an artist. And he has a north light and a studio."

"Fact is," said Jude stubbornly, "I am a limner. I couldn't ever do what those old fellows did. And if I did who'd buy them? Not enough Catholics in all New England to absorb so many Holy Mothers — and as for naked women like those there — only customer I could hope for would be a whorehouse in need of a sign — and the selectmen wouldn't permit such goings on." He was picking up another one. "Wherever did these fellows find so many obliging ladies ready to stand up naked to them? Not all their wives, are they?"

"Mr. Rebough, in Italy where the arts flourish, including the art of living to a degree unknown in this Godforsaken corner of the so-called United States — in Italy there is a respectable class of beautiful females known as models. Any artist — of equally well-known moral nature — can hire one to sit for him. Nothing wrong with the human body. Nothing wrong in flesh."

"Some of these ladies have God's plenty of it piled on them. Especially to sit on."

"But look at that Venus," says Dr. Bloomer, almost gnashing his long yellow teeth. "Isn't she the beauty! Look at that bosom. Women don't come like that in New England." He was rocking himself back and forth so the greasy-gray pothooks of his hair swung below his velvet skullcap.

"Like this here naked woman on a bull —"

"Europa."

"You couldn't get a Yankee woman up on one of the creatures."

"Guido Reni . . ."

"Even with her clothes on."

"I got it wrong. That's Rubens. You must realize art here is in its swaddling clothes."

"Not much this trollop is. A wind come up, and she'd be naked as a jay bird."

"Why not? She ain't afraid like Yankee women, who got none of that pagan worship of their own beauty, for the body does respond to the mind. Our women don't have enough self-worship, and they come out flat as boards and scrawny, or if fleshed up, fleshed up wrong and look like pears. You've never seen women like these women in New England have you?"

"No," says Jude. "Not with their clothes off I haven't. Clothes on, maybe. A man can speculate."

I didn't see any of these engravings. But I did see what it came into Jude's head to paint after he had pondered on them. And I will here use a word of which I was then ignorant. Those pictures were voluptuous. And although at the time I had never heard the name, I know now it was Emma Faucett had come into his head right then — her form and face but her name as yet unknown to him. She too (for I did see her later) was voluptuous. Which isn't a common New England female weakness.

. . . .

Six

. . . .

THE MORNING wasn't like the evening, for it was all business-like. The first matter after breakfast to come up was how many and how good brushes Jude had made during the winter, the value of which would be set down in his favor against the colors he would buy.

Don't think I've previously mentioned the fact that during winter evenings Jude used to sit in the kitchen making brushes whilst Mitty and Dorinda mended or knit, and the men often read aloud from real good books like Gibbon's Decline and Fall or Bunyan, or they'd whittle things useful to the farm, like, say, a butter firkin or pegs for an oxbow. Jude had taught me the art too, pretty well, and sometimes Mitty helped him. Tite and Labe admired to see him do it, for it was pretty work and him so ready to stop and tie them trout flies if they asked. They all thought he used up his brushes mighty fast, nor had he ever told them nor me neither (but now I saw the facts for myself) that very few of them were for him. They were mostly to be traded against Dr. Bloomer's colors. No Pratt could have believed colors were so costly. I said Jude sort of lived in the crevices of this family, going around through them and behind them, a little like a crab. I think he enjoyed it, for instead of humiliating him that he had to do it, it let him feel alone a bit which was what he liked — even in the presence of many.

You can never trim a brush after it's made. And you must use the natural ending of a hair or it won't be controllable. The hairs were shaken up in a tiny cylinder called a cannon. Then tied. He used rabbit fur and squirrel tails, and the hairs from foxes or dogs. Mink were fine, perhaps the best he could get his hands on, yet Dr. Bloomer was saying nothing over here was so good as Russian sable. Each type of hair made a very different sort of brush.

After tying the hair you set it in a quill and this established the size of the brush. It was customary to use the old English bird names for the size of your brushes — for instance, lark was the smallest, and it went up through crow, duck, goose and swan. Swan was the largest but we really used turkey quills for "swans." Then the quill had to be set in wooden turned handles. It was neat, cute, patient work and all of us had to work a little on it so I was aghast to see Jude not keeping them for himself. Brazen as a monkey he was selling about all of them to Dr. Bloomer. It was pretty sly of him and I couldn't help starting to think maybe when he was away from home, there were certain sides to his nature unbeknownst to his own family.

I guess I've made it clear by now that these days were before the time an artist (and seems like everybody is an artist now) could buy paint in a compressible tube with the oil and the pigment already mixed together. The powdered colors, each ground to the proper coarseness or fineness best for it, came to Dr. Bloomer in containers about like what rare teas come in. On selling them they were transferred to bladders of small animals. When Jude wished to use a certain color he'd prick the bladder with a bone tack, sprinkle out the amount he'd need, and mix in the linseed oil. But I associate the smell of oil of lavender with his work, and turpentine as well. From then on, the bladder having been breached, the tack served as a stopper. Of course even as the size of the bird determined the size of the brush, the size of the animal whose bladder served as container determined the amount of color bought. As Jude read from his list and Dr. Bloomer measured the amount of powder on his steel yard and discoursed, I blew up the bladders with my lips and funneled it in. Then Jude tied them up tight.

The biggest bladder used was that of a rabbit. If you wanted more, instead of going into sheep or swine bladders, you bought two rabbitsful. As I remember, this was about an ounce. A rat's bladder was smaller. These were commonest but other animals served. A mouse's bladder was the smallest unit.

Some colors weighed more than others — like the beautiful blue or green verdigris — heavy as copper. Ultramarine was powdered lapis lazuli and heavy too, but various earths and volcanic ash were light. Lamp black, by the way, was the only color Jude could make for himself and that was light.

The old man kept talking all the time like this —

"Vermilion — you say one ounce of vermilion — blow out that there rabbit bladder, Sonny. That's quicksilver and sulphur. If you mix it with red lead it blackens — and Sonny, t'will kill you if you eat it for your breakfast."

"Burnt terra di Sienna," and he stopped to talk about a volcano in Italy. Cobalt came from Germany. And had Sonny ever heard of Cobalts — ugly little gnome people? Lived under ground and helped miners to mine.

"Paris green — that's poisonous. No, Mr. Rebough, I'm not stocking malachite any more. Paris green is just as good — and a lot cheaper. I doubt if there's another artist in America but you would pay the difference in price." It had a vinegary smell.

Alizarin — from the madder fields of southern France.
Brazil-wood, from Peru.

Logwood, Mexico.

Gamboge from Ceylon, India, Siam — places like that, and everything ending in "lac" came from those far parts of the earth and made out of insects common there.

Cochineal too, from insects.

Chinese red and Chinese white — from China.

But two of them stood out in my memory forever.

Jude wanted four ounces of mummy — a good, dull warmish color, what you might call a born background color. Seems it came from grinding up the old dead people of Egypt with their spices and tarred wrappings and people who'd been dead way back in the Old Testament days. There were so many of these old relicks in Egypt they could be got to London and ground and sold pretty cheap. Mummy wasn't an expensive color. But when Dr. Bloomer saw I was shying away from it a bit — and not anxious the powder should get up my nose — he put his hand in his big canister and hauled out a curiosity. The London color makers had skipped a little thing. It was the vertebrae of a child that they had failed to grind.

Another color gave me the creeps and with better reason was King's yellow. Most beautiful yellow I ever did see. Somewhat lemon-color, only there's no richness in lemons, and this was marvelously rich. It was coarse-ground. Overgrinding would reduce its glitter and glow. This stuff came from the mountains of Persia, a natural vein of sulphide of arsenic. It was the most poisonous thing in the world. Then Dr. Bloomer settled back to tell me and Jude of the wicked Borgias. It was arsenic they had used. And he told of all the people who had probably died already getting this stuff out of the ground and handling and grinding it.

"Now don't you go sniffing of it, Sonny," says he to me, noting my timidity, "for here in this rat's bladder is enough arsenic to kill every man, woman and child in both Norwichs. But a little of it, Sonny (come now, and take a sniff), clears and brightens the skin." I didn't like the idea my skin (like most boys that age) could stand a little clearing. I was glad to get away from the old man, out of the shop and out upon the road again.

Come noon Jude slipped his pack and indicated to me a stone wall. Now we'd eat, he said. I told him everything left over in the food line he himself had given to Dr. Bloomer.

Then he took off his coat, for although the spring sunshine was thin, it was warmish, and the air over us blowing up so soft from the south — that too was warming. It was a sweet day though so sodden. The black satin-shouldered crows were out looking things over. All about us the fields were rough-hided and yellow yet. Then one after another he set his round balls of color out on his coat. The pigments glowed through the thin membrane. They looked like soap bubbles. One after another he'd pick up to admire. The four ounces of mummy had not fitted exactly into three rabbit bladders. What was left over had gone into the smallest container he had. He held it in his strong, delicate hand, toying with it, and saying it was strange how at last a mouse's bladder might hold a Pharaoh. But I hated to think on it: the spice and the unguents and the grave clothes, and the revengeful, spiteful little ghost coming to haunt us.

When through admiring his baubles he said he was afraid we would have to sing for our dinner. He packed himself up and we went on. That road up the Little River valley was a forlorn road, but what farmhouses we did pass Jude never stopped at until that happened which I knew he had been expecting.

A woman out by the woodpile with her husband's coat on over her housedress was picking up kindlings. When she saw us she gave a hurried glance towards the barn and ran across the gummy field to meet us. Jude looked to merely touch his hat and pass on. But mud or not she stood in the road to block our passage. She was panting hard from her running and the excitement she felt at seeing a man with a pack.

"You a peddler?"

"That I am, ma'am."

"Well, I declare if winter isn't over — "

I guess country people did look on the first one with same pleasure as the first robin. She had a flabby white face, white like a potato sprouted in a cellar. She had plenty of heft to her but was pear-shaped just as Dr. Bloomer had complained New England women were if not scrawny.

"Fix clocks?" she said. This was just about always the first question people asked. New England was flooded with clocks and seems none of them ran.

"No."

"What you travel in?"

"What you see — 'cept underwear."

She made a fly-brushing gesture with her hand before her face. "You rascal, you. What line of goods?"

He explained he had no goods — only the supplies out of which to make them. But it was a new face to look at and a new tongue to listen to she was pining for. The Pratt farm being so close to a town I'd never before realized how mighty cut off and lonesome-like life was for many a farm woman.

Where was he heading for?

Hampton.

Where had he come from?

Norwich.

And what was the talk of in Norwich?

The old minister had died, he said, last February. "Now half his society wished to go Unitarian. Other half stay with the old faith. That church had about split itself in two." I'd heard Dr. Bloomer say something about that. "And the spring ice has knocked the paper mill at Norwich Landing into a cocked hat."

"Do tell," she breathed. And was it old Dr. So-and-so died or someone else? And he didn't quite remember but was honest about it, although I could see that spoiled the story a bit for her. Then he began adjusting his pack and indicating to me we was going on. She was like a starving person who'd only been given a scattering of crumbs. She couldn't let him go, so naturally she thought of food and drink, and wouldn't bother us to step up to the house so we knew she had a cross husband — she'd run up and fetch something to us if we'd stay right where we were. She came back panting again and glancing over her shoulder all the time at the barn. As she was running some risk for us, I guess Jude thought he'd better give her both barrels.

There had been a great deal of talk, he said, in Norwich — both of those towns, the old one and the young one. For late the fall before, a sea serpent had swum up from the sea that far up the Thames. Then the ice had closed in on him. Jude had his mouth full of ham and cornbread and didn't speak too clearly.

"My landy sakes alive! True as I'm sitting here? A sea serpent! I've heard tell of such things, but to think it got to Norwich! What did it look like?"

"Much like a centipede — only of course of a monstrous size. I gathered that taken and spread out it might well have reached from this stone wall we are sitting on to yon barn."

"Land alive!"

"And it had fifty legs to a side. One hundred all told. Just think how terrifying such a sight must of been to all the good people of Norwich."

"And could it break out the ice and get to sea again?"

"No'm. It was thrashing about, but the ice formed faster than it could thrash. You remember how powerful the cold was last winter — and early to come? And the town — that was Norwich Landing and not to be confused with the town of Norwich proper — was in a terrible concern lest it die right there off the wharves. It was not that they pitied the poor varmint but think of the stench that would rise up from its carcass — and maybe a death-dealing miasma as well. There was a town meeting called special and it was voted thinking-this-out was up to the selectmen. The selectmen got together and requisitioned (as they had the right, seeing it was a time of public calamity) all the skates, every last pair of them. And these were cheerfully given although they do say some of the unthinking little shavers cried a-plenty." He took another enormous mouthful of cornbread and ham the better to think with, I guess. "They say that sea serpent got the idea right off, soon as they began strapping those skates on his feet. He took right a-hold of skating too, although a bit clumsy at first as you can imagine. Was going real good by the time he got to New London."

You ought to have seen her face. It was like ecstasy and she couldn't keep it to herself, for we heard her charging up to the barn and yelling for her husband to come and hear what she had heard, even if he scolded her for talking to peddlers.

Jude walked along, me tailing him.

At last he said, "You got to give Yankees something to think about, and it don't matter much, if any, what it is. They've got real active minds and without enough to think about they go sour as chokecherries."

I couldn't help but feel uneasy, thinking all the time what Mitty would have thought of that sea serpent — skating so nice down the Thames. And she would have been surprised that Jude habitually sold those brushes to Dr. Bloomer and how much he paid for his colors. Where they came from — and from what and how mighty dangerous some were. She couldn't of believed Jude to be so vulgar as to mention his underdrawers to a strange lady or look at pictures of naked ladies.

We'd only been gone two days and a night but I'd learned things about my uncle I'd never have known staying home.

. . . .

Seven

. . . .

Hᴇ ʜᴀᴅ ɴᴏᴛ ʙᴇᴇɴ no more than to Norwich and back and I could feel the sap rising in him. He was still inflated when we got home, pushing his hat back on his head but not removing it, tossing off his pack like he owned the place and kissing his wife like he owned her too.

Leaf was six by now and looked just like him. She was whimpering because she couldn't do her stint of so-and-so-many rows on the dish clout her mother had set her to knit. He kissed the top of her sad little head but she went on with her crying. Soon as Mitty left the room he had the little girl in his lap and was clicking off the rows fast. He was handy at any little thing you do with your hands.

"When I was a boy in Hubbardston," he began softly "that great-uncle that fetched me up after my family broke up — my old Unk Ike — had a tomcat."

Leaf had a suspicious look on her face. Her mother, fearing she might grow up like him because she was so tall, dark and skinny, was always telling her not to exaggerate and so on. So now Leaf looked as though she couldn't believe anyone had a great-uncle nor a tomcat either.

"Was double-pawed all around. And then all around again. That made him double-double-pawed . . . if you follow me. Quite a cat."

He went on with his knitting, his pack at his feet and his hat and overcoat still on him. I could see Leaf's face and now she was believing him. Mitty had come back into the kitchen in that oversoft way of hers and stood perfectly still listening to him.

"He was what you might call a mitten-handed cat. Best mouser ever was. Could take a mouse and bat it against the old barn door and catch it on the *re*-bound. He practiced and perfected himself. Old Unk Ike set him a daily stint. So many mice and bounced so many times against the barn door. Practice is the only thing ever does make perfect. And . . . dammy if I haven't dropped a stitch!" He went back to correct it. "Well, now the fact about that cat is . . ."

"Oh Jude," said Mitty wearily, "please *don't.*"

"Don't what, ma'am?"

"Everything. You shouldn't of left your hat on. You shouldn't of done Leaf's stint for her. How'll she grow up to be a good industrious woman if you come in and do the stint I set her? . . . Why at her age I was knitting my own stockings. And then that there mitten-handed cat! I do declare!"

"What's wrong with him?"

"Nothing, but please stop it."

"Stop what?"

"Filling up little pitchers with what isn't so, and if it was so, why whatever of it? I know some people do like to hear you going on but I'm fixing to learn Leaf early what truth looks like and these fancies of yours aren't a-helping me any."

"Well," he says, "peddlers are supposed to be the purveyor of news. Fact is, coming up from Norwich Town . . ." I was scared he'd go off on that sea serpent of his and knew how hard she'd step on it. Fact is I was getting sort of fond of that unlikely thing.

"Please don't ever refer to yourself as peddler. If you haven't any pride I have. Nobody's going to be saying Leaf and Simon are peddler's brats. And there you are, dear," says she, handing back Leaf's clout to her. She'd raveled back all Jude had done for her. Leaf began to sniff again and looked to her father for support, but he didn't look at her and he gave her none.

Of course Mitty was right and Jude was wrong. She always was right. This was hard on Leaf sometimes and on him too.

But she was non-interfering with his work. This being along the line of "if I don't respect him who will" that I have referred to before. She would of preferred it that he open a nice interior house-painting shop and stay to home and make more money. But she had said her say on that years before. He coughed and wouldn't. And like a good wife she dropped the subject. She would of been a nagger except she used will-power not to be. And she wasn't.

Experience had taught him about how many canvases (he used blue striped bed-ticking) to take out with him. Of course he always took a good many more, now he had Goldie to haul them for him, than he expected to sell, so as to give people a nice choice. And he would paint up a person from scratch if they preferred it that way.

He also on the road sometimes got orders for inn signs and occasionally for overmantels or even something very special like a map. Or botanical drawings for a botany book even.

Mitty had given to me one of her notebooks telling me besides grinding paint and so on I was to serve as my uncle's clerk. I was to number every one of those bodies and back-grounds and write down to whom they were sold and for how much. The little book of hers did help us out of one terrible predicament but I guess Jude saw to it that we lost it before we got home. I studied so faithfully on the collection he took along that year I can pretty well describe them now. Not how many of each but it will give you a general idea.

He had plenty of grandmothers, with spectacle cases in their hands or knitting in their laps, and beside them on a table flowers going by a little, rose petals dropping, or perhaps some of that shadowy gray herb we call "Old Woman."

Left over from a not too profitable summer on Cape Cod the year before were a couple of sea captains he'd prepared and not sold. They had blue jackets on them and brass buttons, a spyglass, the sea and a ship showing behind them. He told me I'd be surprised how many old captains retired to the hills of New Hampshire and Vermont where we were heading out for. So he was of a mind to take these unsold sea captains along.

He had clergymen in black silk, but they could easily do for the principal of an academy or a doctor or prominent lawyer or judge. For such scholarly gentlemen he'd paint shelf after shelf of books, and one usually open in the elderly gentleman's hands. On this he could add any title any sitter wished. He said for ministers it usually would be published sermons.

To match these gentlemen were some fearsomely respect-able-looking torsos suited for wives to them, with fine lace and jet brooches, capes and tuck-ins, brown false fronts. Usually in black satin or dark damson, gray or maroon color.

There were hearty middle-aged couples, in rich and brighter color, maybe he holding a gold-headed cane or pulling back a curtain to show the source of his wealth. Jude explained he'd be painting in for such "Squires" these days, a factory or a water-power site or a toll bridge or a stagecoach — that being their line, or maybe a broad fine farm with the prize Merino ram peering round the curtain at us. Tavern-keepers too, he said, liked this particular design, and then he put in the tavern for them to be indicating.

The women to go with these, he said, were apt to be a little portly, and the more elegance he had time to add to their clothing the better. As they always felt the heat more than some folks he usually gave them a feather fan to hold.

Likewise it covered up for them a little how stout they were.

He had some scholarly-looking young fellows with books or a flute, and some sort of dandified, with horse whips or patting the head of a hunting dog. And he said sometimes the dandy would choose the background with the book, and the bookish fellow the hunting dog. He said it was enough to put a serious limner right through the roof — the way people chose, and he couldn't stop them. He said his only reward (besides the three dollars of course) was the insight it gave him on human nature.

It was with young women and children he excelled, and for these he never tired painting in flowers, or maybe a rabbit or a puppy for a little boy, or a pet bird for his finger, and the little girls had wild flowers and dolls and kittens, and dresses on them prettier than any I ever saw in life. And lace edging on their pantalettes.

But maybe saddest of all his commodities was dead babies. He usually could sell three or four of these to bereaved mothers, who would get to crying as they told him the lost child was fair or it was dark — or it favored its Great-Aunt Tabitha — and they'd get the old lady in for him to study on. He'd show the poor mites lying in their coffins with the coral dropped from tiny hands. And about the whole thing a wreath of the weakest and frailest little wild flowers — hepatica and spring beauty, tiny ferns or white swamp violets. It was like fairy painting and it took hours. He charged no more for such fiddling work than, say, books on a shelf that he could slap in in jig time.

It got me at last where I was staying awake nights dreaming of all these people a-waiting for us, as it were. For, knowing I was going with him, I had studied and studied them so in my mind's eye I could already see the very face for each, and each was to me a real person and as I say waiting for me and Jude.

Some I thought of more than others. One in particular. It

was a young girl and you knew (although he rarely painted below the waist) that she was sitting on the ground, and she had turned her head to admire a bush full of birds. He'd started with only one or two and kept on adding more and more to amuse me or himself. Never knew which. No two were alike, but all were singing birds. Summer yellow bird and scarlet tanager, a bluebird and a wren, chickadees and song sparrow, hermit thrush and so on until there wasn't a twig on which to sit another bird. Seems like I could hardly wait to catch up with the girl he was actually going to paint in — and she would sit forever with her pretty tip-tilted profile, admiring and listening to what I considered *my* birds. She was already *my* girl. I couldn't imagine feeling like that for any of the actualities I went to school with. Girls with chapped red hands, and cold-sores and head colds. And giggling when even yet I sometimes stammered, or didn't know my lesson — and they did. I wasn't too big for my years and seems like they all were. Seems to be nature's way in the earliest teens.

So, the attainable being for me unattainable, I — like many another boy that age — fastened my dreams on the nonexistent — a picture with no face to it — except in my mind's eye. That sort of daydreaming seems to me now acceptable in a boy that age. But it was folly in Jude, a sensible married man pushing for twenty-eight, who ought to have outgrown youthful foolishnesses. He hadn't. But before I begin on the next picture he painted I should say a word about the weather.

It was the darn-blastedest spring. You should of heard Tite going on about it, and Mitty vowing she'd wash out his mouth with soap. If New England weather isn't always just what the doctor ordered, at least the Lord has given the people strength to swear back at it. It rained blatherscats on top of all the mess we already had. Froze up and rained some more. Spring ploughing was delayed three weeks later than the last date

recommended in *Old Farmer's*. Mitty couldn't get on with
spring housecleaning. Nor Jude and me get off on the road.

It was in fact what we used to call in New England "mud
time," and some years it hit us early and some years late. And
no wheels could get anywhere. The stagecoaches, for all their
boasting, got mired down and stopped. Nothing else ever
stopped them for long. Mud time did. School shut down and
you'd hear children (I guess all over New England) yelling

Mud time, mud time
Six weeks to bare feet!

So there was unexpected time on Jude's hands. And you
always hear how the Devil will find somewhat for idle hands
to do. And I guess he was inspired also by Dr. Bloomer's
engravings to try a little something of a more voluptuous
nature than he had before attempted. Now I know (didn't
then) he had no more to go on than the memory of a woman
he had seen no more than five minutes the year before the last,
and she looking out a window at him.

So he painted her (Emma Faucett) leaning nonchalantly
and a little heavily out an open window. Woodbine grew up
about her with gray-blue berries on it. He had morning-
glories too, for the color of them and their heart-shaped
leaves. But most of all trumpet vines and their copper-
colored trumpets. Somehow he got in ripe wheat. The
woman's dress was pale yellow. And coming in supposedly
after the flowers were birds and butterflies, bees even, and
hornets, but you knew it was the woman they were after.
Some women are like that, and she was that sort.

She looked at ease, comfortable and bold too. And she was
a buxom woman of an obviously careless disposition, for she
had no decent tuck-in for the front of her dress and she
showed plenty, but not, I guess, as much as those goddesses
and such of Dr. Bloomer's. And even where she had clothes
on her you were mighty conscious of a body warm underneath.

I should have begun with her hair. It was russet and a lot of it hanging down about her, and every other color in the picture was put in to make that hair live. It did. It was also a sort of peaceful, slumbrous picture with a feeling of late summer in it — the still warm days and the thunderstorms. And good harvest and ripeness — and yet almost over. Already doomed. You knew this woman wasn't real young any more.

Every year, around this time of the year when Jude would be setting out, Mitty tended to sharpen up on him. I guess she had always wondered if perhaps he didn't enjoy those four or five months away from her a little more than a married man ought. I guess she never could figure it why he was so set on being off so long. He brought back little ready cash. But I do think she was unreasonably upset over this picture. She certainly never had been over all those wooden young girls and aging female forms he had done before, and modest buttoned-up matrons.

I remember her standing there before it in Jude's painting room with her dust cloth in her hands and a dust cap on her head. And Jude watching her, hopeful of her approval. He set a good deal on that.

At last she said, "Mite fleshy, ain't she?"

"A mite, maybe."

"The flower part is monstrous pretty. Have you spent *all* of these last three weeks on it? How many hours by the clock?"

"Oh, I just paint along."

"I hope you get a real rewarding price for all that pretty-pretty stuff — almost like embroidering. But . . ."

"Yeh?"

"Jude, I wouldn't think any woman that plump would want to be pictured so."

"Some women ain't ashamed."

"Should be. And no tuck-in nor fichu. I call it a disgrace. And if she had ever done an honest day's work she wouldn't be that plump. And even if a woman is built like that and runs around with her hair dribble-drabbling down her back like that, and her clothes not fastened nice, she oughtn't to be painted like that. Don't set a real good example for young girls growing up." She laughed awkwardly, trying not to make too much over what after all she knew was a trifle.

"Oh, Jude — that picture isn't nice and I'm ashamed of you and I won't have it in the house!"

"It's going off with me any day now. She and me off together, eh, my honey?"

"And Eddy there to chaperone you. Now one thing you can't do is make me jealous!"

That was only whistling in the dark. He'd done it. I guess she always had been a little somewhat that way before over his traipsings. Most women would of been.

.   .   .   .

Eight

.   .   .   .

APRIL IS THE waitingest month. First flowers, first birds, first warm day have lost their novelty. But real spring dawdles at a snail's pace. The earth stretches and yawns and goes to sleep on you. Yet all the time fields are drying out, soon fit to plough. Mud receding and roads hardening up.

Then one day (right after we came back from Norwich) I heard Mitty speaking sharp to someone at our back door. First peddler of the season. He was a very catch-penny person. Mitty would of sent him about his business if Jude hadn't been there right away, inquiring as to the state of roads. He said it might be another week or two before wheels could navigate in any comfort. He told fearsome tales of bridges knocked to jackstraws in spring freshets and not repaired as yet. And of "squags," as we called mud holes, big enough to swallow up a coach and four.

You could feel Mitty not liking him, nor to think, as Jude's questions suggested, that there was a professional bond between her husband and him, but she bought needles off him (they proved rusty) and pins (mostly bent) to repay him for the information Jude had got off him.

Second to come was a tinker from no further off than Pomfret. Not so knavish-looking as what you might call our first dove out of the ark, but consumptive and real whiny.

Then the third came and it was like he brought real spring with him.

He came lightfooting it down our lane, singing as he came. He seemed to sing as birds do, because it is their nature. You could almost see the maples redden, and the catkins tumble out. Now the bittern would begin to boom for us, morning and evening, and roughly one million hylas tune up. White birch would stand on tiptoe and, what was more important for us, roads harden up at the sound of his voice.

He came swinging up to our front door like he knew he was too important to go to the back door like other peddlers. I saw him. Sampson and I were overhauling seed potatoes, having got them up off the cellar floor and outdoors.

I saw old Brutus merely rattled his chain and whimpered at him.

Dorinda was up out of her bedchamber, thinking, I suppose, he might have patent medicine for her.

Leaf, terrible shy of strangers, popped out, the hemming she had been set to do in her hand, her big eyes dark with wonder.

Mitty left her washtub, rolling down her sleeves as she came — like she would of done for the minister, and for not much of anybody else.

Tite and Labe appeared standing side by side in the big barn door, just determined they weren't going to give in. They looked sort of yoked together like a pair of oxen.

Jude was off with his sketching. Didn't arrive right off, like the rest of us, to gape at this marvel.

He was a staunch little fellow, muddy and free-looking, legs apart, grinning, looking mighty battered but unbeaten.

"Broadsides and ballads, ladies and gentlemen!" he was saying, and his sharp sidelong eyes sized up Mitty and Dorinda. It was mostly ladies bought his stuff.

"I've got the 'Pesky Sarpint' folks. Sad story of how Molly Bland sucked snake poison from her young man's heel. Died. Both of them. Yep. Deader than door nails. Now listen . . ."

He plucked across his belly like he was playing as melodiously on his own live guts as he might upon those of a dead cat. He went "herup" and then again that lovely voice floated out of him and joined with the floodtides of spring.

> "On yonder mountain there once did dwell
> A farmer boy, I loved him well.
> This farmer boy went out to mow,
> He went out in meadow fields to mow"

and so on, leaving out the "tur-li-lees" and "tur-li-lays" which look foolish in print but are the making of such songs when sung.

Dorinda said feelingly, "True story, mister?"

"True? Lady, may I fall dead at your pretty little feet if every word isn't truer than Gospel. Only cost you a penny. Now I bet you got a nice singing voice — couldn't imagine a lively young lady like you without."

And Dorinda did look livelier than usual as she shot back to the chamber to get some money.

"Tell me what interests you," he begged, "and if I haven't

a ballad on the subject I've got a broadside. My collection of last words and dying confessions goes back all the way to Bathsheba Spooner. Dumped her husband in the well ('Ding dong bell. Mr. Spooner's in the well'). Ever heard the ballad of the Murdered Stranger? Bloodstains never would wash off. West Stockbridge man — I believe."

"Whatever they murder him for?" Mitty was asking, utterly spellbound by the fellow in spite of herself.

"For gain, Miss. Cut his throat — Geek! Like that!" And his quick little hand slashed at her neck. You could all but see the blood spurt!

"Mercy on us!" She jumped back two feet. "You don't say!"

"That's just what I *am* saying. But when Murder *and* Love are combined into one song, then you get a humdinger." Dorinda was back now but he knew he had her in his pocket, so he called out to his most difficult customers, Tite and Labe.

"Gentlemen, I got a true and most speaking likeness of the biggest ram ever raised at Wethersfield Bow, Vermont. Below is printed the heft of the beast. How much he cut up to. How much wool came off him each shearing time."

They inched and lurched a little nearer, still side by side, saying no more than a yoke of oxen — which as I indicated they then resembled.

"And if your interest is politics . . . I got an extremely arresting ballad (hot off the griddle) how Ezekiel Jackson, Esq., was about to assume governorship in the State of Maine (I believe) when it was discovered he had sold his soul to the Devil — in exchange for votes. This then laid upon the electorate of Maine a problem . . ."

"Oh fiddlesticks," said Mitty, laughing.

Then Dorinda asked the stranger his name.

"Phineas Sharp is my name," says he, "but if you don't like my singing you can call me Phineas Flat. Some do."

Jude had joined us. Mr. Sharp was dang-blessing himself

and not believing his eyes. They were old acquaintances. And now Mr. Sharp pulled his first boner. For, says he, he'd known this young rapscallion when he was no more than seventeen or so and hid out over in York State because the sheriffs of his native Massachusetts were after him. And then he hadn't been too proud to paint barns.

Of course Jude denied this. Especially the barns, fearing it might put ideas in Tite and Labe's heads.

Before this Mitty had asked him for supper and the night, but now she didn't like him quite so well — even if he were no more than joking about the sheriff out after her husband. He came into our house. He was saying no he couldn't stay and then yes he would, and no, but . . . I guess he could feel Mitty didn't want him. He was the most restless little man I ever did see. No sooner had he taken off that raffish hat of his and he proved bald underneath and not young at all, although when coming down the lane singing he seemed young as spring itself. Or like his own ballads he was sad and gay and perpetually young, yet well seasoned in the wood.

So he sat, uncomfortable (because of Mitty) and diminished before our eyes. He was no brass monkey and he had feelings like any decent man. He tried to soft-sawder her up. He said he had always thought Mr. Rebough a touch tony (forgetting the sheriffs and the barns he had mentioned) but had never guessed how tony until he saw him now, with his own folks, living a life of ease on what could only be described as a gentleman's estate. That didn't help any. She made him so uneasy there was no magic left in him. She couldn't bear to think it was happy-go-lucky's like this Mr. Sharp Jude associated with when off and away from her.

If he didn't actually have fleas he had the mannerisms of a man that does. Naturally this would upset a slick housewife like Mitty. And if you believed his philosophy of life, *thinking* a man has fleas is just as "real" as his having them.

Suppertime went, with Jude trying to make him feel comfortable and Mitty succeeding in making him uncomfortable. First he'd be obsequious to her. Next, too forward, calling her darling or honey.

When she said she was going to bed she meant we were all to go. Her brothers and Sampson went, but Jude for the first time I ever remember defied her. For he went out to the woodshed to fetch back a big log and said it was only the shank of the evening, and sent me down cellar for a pitcher of hard cider. Her jaw just about dropped that he dared disobey her, although of course she hadn't and wouldn't give him a spoken command. She said good night with commendable dignity and went off upstairs.

Mitty's worst fault was she was a peeper. It was her way of taking care of the people God had in his infinite wisdom put into her care. She meant no more harm than a mother stealing up to see if the babe in his cradle is asleep. Knowing her, I doubt not but she did come downstairs once or twice and then stole upstairs again.

I hope she didn't hear Mr. Sharp say to Jude he'd been pretty cute to shuck onto a rich wife — so he wouldn't have to work any. Or how he detested the whole boiling of wives, always tidying up a man. Didn't see how a "sensible" fellow like Jude could stand to be married.

I hope she didn't hear the long discussion between them as to which was most apt to be unfidel — the man off on the road alone and meeting beautiful and obliging young ladies in every other house almost, or the wife left to home with nothing more to console her loneliness with than a preacher or the hired man. And that led him to an old song which he sang, nice and low. Frankly, that song may be low but it is not nice. About how a man comes home. Strange horse in the stall. No place for his. Strange hat on the hatrack "where no hat ought to be." Worse yet, that face on the pillow where obviously no face but his own belongs, and although he's such a fool he seems to believe his wife when she tells him it's a kid her uncle sent her, you know it isn't.

Mr. Sharp was a far-traveled man, going south every fall like birds, not holing up over winter, like Jude and most peddlers. He spoke of the cotton lands and black slaves working, and he sang snatches of their songs. He spoke of ships at sea and chanty men and sang of them too, until he got me where I longed to go any or everywhere. For he had me bewitched again even if he had a bald head.

It was long past midnight when Mitty couldn't stand it any longer and walked in on us, like she had a right to — as I suppose she had.

Said she had forgot to set the split peas to soak. That she did and said no more. But it was enough. There was a cold, meager look to her back as she bent over those split peas. Her feet were bare and blue with cold. Her nightcap was so neat it was unbecoming. I didn't think then of the contrast between her and the luxurious fleshly woman in the painting room. One was fact and the other fancy, and a considerable discrepancy between the two. There usually is, although Sharp was always confusing them.

We loitered about five minutes more after she left us, just to show her we were men, not mice, and then turned in.

. . . .

Nine

. . . .

Aᴛ ʙʀᴇᴀᴋꜰᴀsᴛ Mr. Sharp and Jude sat as long at table as though they were at a tavern, and Mitty in her rage at their dawdling acted as though she were no more than a tavern servant. And they smoked cigars. Such a thing had never before happened in that house until after suppertime, and then not often. Of course Tite and Labe, and Sampson and I could get out and go to work in spite of them. Mitty couldn't get on with her work. So she stayed there, champing at the bit.

It was ten o'clock I came in from the barn with the dead hen she had asked for, eggs and milk. And there those two sat, and Mitty was pursing her lips and tossing her head, but handing them out a fresh batch of pancakes and going into the pantry for more maple syrup. Mr. Sharp, of course, didn't know our habits. Jude did, so it is him I blame.

Even before I had left them, three hours before, Mr. Sharp had been talking of Ruby Lambkin, and stopping to hum or sing a little. We never sang much anytime and I can assure you never at breakfast. Conversation was still on Ruby or back at him once again.

Yankees had a sort of belief that there was such a thing as a "good" thief. I mean the old steal-from-rich, give-to-poor sort of a man. And on the side he kissed girls and tricked sheriffs. He always (no matter what name he went under) got away, and he had to be handsome and smart to do like he did. It made it easier for country people to understand his powers if you said he had sold his soul to the Devil.

The summer before when Jude was on Cape Cod (and nowhere near there) such a phenomenon — by name of Ruby Lambkin — had arisen along the upper Connecticut River; that is, eastern Vermont and western New Hampshire. Mr. Sharp, being around those parts, had had a ballad of him printed up and it had sold like hot cakes. Now he was heading back again this spring for that section where he was confident he'd find "plenty of eggs to suck." But surely we, even hundreds of miles away, must have heard tell of Ruby Lambkin?

As we hadn't, he obliged us in spite of Mitty saying "Don't wake the baby — no, nor the dead neither." He was still sitting to table and he sang soft almost whispering.

> "Ruby Lambkin is my name,
> In tales and jails I've won my fame.
> I give to poor and steal from rich.
> No legal-law can hold me.
>
> Sheriff Burnap is my foe,
> He hunts me high and hunts me low.
> He puts me in, I gets me out,
> Because no jail can hold me.
>
> Sally This and Drusey Drew,
> Jenny What, to name a few,
> Girls all love me, this is true,
> And yet no girl can hold me."

There was a terrible lot more to it, and mostly lies. The trimming to it consisting of

> Oh-ho oh-ho
> Oh-high-roller . . . oh

to pad it out and give people who didn't know the words the chance to join in. Jude was joining in.

"Is there actually such a fellow," Jude asked, "or did you just make him up?"

"May the Great Jumping Jehosaphat strike me down dead where I stand" (he was still sitting) "if this isn't the truth and nothing but the truth — although not the whole truth — which would take too much time to recount. And if it came to making him up — I wouldn't have to. Everybody up there — Vermont, New Hampshire — has gone to work on him, letting, so to speak, fancy play. Doesn't every poor man wish someone would steal, say, a pudding out of a rich man's pot and drop it in his — and yet he himself is either too scared or too honest to do so? Ruby (that is, the bolder, badder, better part of him) does it for him. Here's another man I've heard of. Ox died. Only animal family had. Man gets up in night to go out to the barn to hang himself from a rafter — and sees someone has put a beautiful, gentle, brand-new ox in place of the carcass. How much he care if Squire So-and-so is advertising and protesting loss of best ox he has? Poor man keeps shet and thanks Ruby for it in his heart. He didn't steal it, did he? Doesn't every man wish he were so handsome no girl 'ud ever say no to him? And all the female kittle-cattle long for the man she can't say no to? And who hasn't wished to see sheriffs and other pompous asses flabbergasted? Ruby does that for them, too — or they do it to him. I'd call it fifty-fifty."

"No real truth to him then?"

"He's truer than truth. Stronger than fact: for he's what you and me, and Eddy here, and Mrs. too (if she would take down her back hair and unbend) all secretly long for."

"All right then. But tell me this. You ever talk with anyone who has actually laid eyes on him?"

"Last fall I did. A woman of Hanover, New Hampshire. She said he was the handsomest man she ever laid her aging eyes on. She was forty-five if a day. Good churchwoman. Made fine pies, Mrs. Rebough — just like you and that reminds me — how about a little sliver more of the mince? And she said he glittered with good health and bad morals. Teeth, eyes, every hair upon his head and the very fuzz upon his arms. Felt her virtue shaken at the mere sight of him and . . . "

"No more proof of him than that?"

"I'll have to unpack some." Mr. Sharp knelt beside his pack which he had all strapped up neat and ready to go. He fished about and brought up one of those notices we tack up all over New England concerning wanted men. It was dated last August.

$50.00 Reward

STOP THIEF! ! !

"Hum. I'll skip this part . . . what he's been stealing up around Sharon, Vermont . . . and nary a word said of kindness to poor orphans and the lovelight in ladies' eyes . . . all that left out. Listen to this:

" 'Suspicion rests on Ruby Lambkin (Real name unknown. Birth, residence unknown)' — you see he can be most anybody — 'About twenty-five years of age. Is six feet two in height. Quick and lively in motion. Slim but powerfully built. Considered handsome. Black hair, curly and roughed-up-looking. Short, cleft chin . . . ' " He stopped and glanced straight at Jude. "Well, Mrs. Rebough, if this here isn't the spittingest description of your husband you can have me for soup bones. And although frankly, ma'am, I've known a lot of men that cut up plenty when they get free of their good wives, home responsibilities and such, I never knew the one cut up like your old man cuts up — looks like."

"But he was on Cape Cod all last summer," says Mitty sharply.

"That's what *he* said — is it, eh? is it, huh?" He shook his head pityingly at her. Then studying long on Jude, kept on shaking his head. "Mr. Rebough, sitting here and looking at you as for the first time, I do see how handsome and irresistible you might be if you would forget your meechy, narrer little New England ways and just burst forth — like a butter-fly out of a caterpillar, chicken out of an egg or a deacon outer church. I'll give you the magic words. You say, 'To hell with it to hell with it to hell with it' three times and *then* cut loose. You never had any trouble with him chasing girls around these parts, have you, Mrs. Rebough?"

Such vulgarity turned Mitty pink and left her speechless. Her blue eyes were snapping fire. I don't think Mr. Sharp's way of paying her back for her coldness to him was too delicate myself. But Jude just laughed and didn't deny anything.

"Well now, I'm leaving you all. And goodbye, my dear," says the impudent little rascal to Mitty, "and thank you for the warmth of your hospitality." He had his pack on him and his hat, and with no more than that, he was off.

I'll have to say this of Mr. Sharp: as you got to know him he wasn't a bad sort at all, but by golly he was a fearsome troublemaker. He couldn't help it no more than a monkey.

So there was considerable rift in the marital lute and he had done it with his mischievous twitching at facts. Jude could always smooth Mitty down, like a woman smoothing frosting on a cake. This time he went at it wrong, I guess, trying to appeal to her sense of humor and she didn't have much of that to appeal to, although she would laugh when she was supposed to laugh, so that sometimes fooled you. For the first thing he did was grab up a terrible old black hat, left about to support a net for anyone working on the bees, and danced a bit and whistled the ballad best he could remember it. He said he was Ruby Lambkin and just about to kiss her and to leave her because "no girl could hold him." She would laugh and say "stop it" like women do, but it must have come as a shock to her to see how easy it was for him to look like he hadn't ought — I mean like a perfect rake-hell of a devilish sort of a sot. By nature he was gangling and too narrow, but

seemingly not (like now) when he put his mind on it. He
was saying he was the handsomest, spryest, kindest bad man
in New England and he looked it.

Spring, real settled spring, did seem to have ridden in to us
on Phineas Sharp's shoulders. Now suddenly it was ever so
warm, still, dreamy and drying. Now all our gear was packed
up in the coffin-shaped box to the rear of the yellow chaise.
Next morning with daybreak Jude and I would be going.

These last few days not much had been said of Phineas
Sharp (Mitty always referred to him as "that real useless little
man") and nothing of Ruby Lambkin — whoever he was.
Jude was looking spare and a little awkward like usual. I
guess Mitty hadn't forgotten the misfortune of Mr. Sharp's
visit, because when Jude was showing her the map of where
he thought to go and advising her the first place she's to write
to him was Hancock, New Hampshire, and how he'd get there
by crossing the waist of Massachusetts and would be working
mostly, he believed, along the Merrimack River, she cut in on
him sharply.

"Jude — will you promise me just one thing?"

"To write real often?"

"I know you won't do that. Jude, you keep out of the
Connecticut Valley — upper part of it — will you?"

He was terribly puzzled.

"Only summer before last I was there up and around
Hanover, Norwich. So I hadn't thought to go again quite so
soon. But there are a lot of towns along there I've never
fished in. Maybe if the Merrimack Valley doesn't prove too
good for me I will go there."

"Jude — if trade isn't good along the Merrimack, will you
promise me to just come home?"

"Oh Mitty . . . No I won't. You know I won't. But if you
miss me so why don't you come along with me?" She would
of hated it if she had. "And leave Eddy behind?" My heart

sank, for I saw a speculative look in her eyes, but she shook her head.

"But not this time. Simon is too little to leave. And I just couldn't. But sometime . . . " and her voice softened, "you'll come home and stay home — all the time — forever?"

He took her hand in his. "Sometime, yes I will, Mitty. Sometime — but not quite yet-awhile."

There was a certain wisdom in her. She knew his craving for wayfaring had to just wear itself out by itself. There was nothing she could say or do against that pulling him. And she never did anything against it and said mighty little.

· · · · · · · · · · · · ·

Ten

· · · · · · · · · · · · ·

F ROM WHERE I am now, both in time (some sixty years later) and space (Kansas), I can look back and wish them all well — all the hawkers and walkers, peddlers, packmen, wagon men and such that were out upon New England roads soon as going was good and the little leaves came tumbling out — just like Jude and me.

Quite a collection.

Pious oddities, peddling Bibles and tracts and each one a new way to Heaven. Painting God's "Thou Shalt Not's" on pasture boulders so innocent cows could ponder the Seventh Commandment. Every door they entered they entered in

God's name and "Sister are you saved?" Well, I hope each of you plays his harp now — each in his own perculiar Heaven.

God bless the graves of all essence peddlers, sweet-smelling fellows you were, sweet with thyme and bergamot, peppermint and rose water. "Imported Cologne" water too. Naturally everybody knew they printed up those German labels right here. And the water came from the brook nearest the house.

Patent-medicine men in showy wagons and high hats — but some afoot. And the blood let and the teeth pulled. Used to have (that is, some of them) little colored boy to play the fiddle to drown the victim's screeches with his worse ones. And emetics and purges administered on the spot.

Sam Slick, the clock peddler — Sam Slicks by the dozen and by the gross (from Connecticut mostly). You did good service, by and large, you boys who brought to Yankees (and at a very reasonable price) what they most yearned for — some way better than the sun to watch every minute so as to turn it to good account. Waste not, want not and if you look out for the minutes the hours will look out for themselves. Company too — a clock ticking there — and say the children grown up and gone away, and the old woman alone in the house these days almost all day, but the clock ticks off the time for her. Not so lonely as silence. Patient folded hands and waiting. Those little old ladies of New England that I remember, actually they had been born before the Revolution. Seems to me there were a powerful lot of them about. Mostly, if they got to be old at all, they outlived the old men.

And for every clock seller there had to be a clock fixer — right after him and on his heels. Those clocks ran something fierce.

Broom men from western Massachusetts where the broom corn grew best. Tin peddlers rolling towards you with the sun on them and a-blazing like molten silver. Horse and wagon all overhung with pans, skillets, buckets and such.

Men who specialized in wooden ware. Pinchbeck jewelry men (Attleboro, Massachusetts, usually), and the "mock-turtle" combs from Leominster — also Massachusetts. Needles and pins, scissors and knives — terribly high-priced by our standards today. All came from England. So did the finest yard goods, cotton or silk, and fine laces, ribbons and such. Country stores didn't stock such real luxuries much. You got them from a peddler if you got them anywhere, and if you got them from a peddler chances are you got out-smarted.

But when the great four-horse wagons came to town it is to the general storekeeper my heart goes out. These great traveling stores would draw up right close to him, open up the sides — take all his trade away from him — long as he stayed, for the newcomer was full of novelties such as the womenfolk were dying for. Pretty soon, however, word would go about how all this "foreigner's" goods (he may of come from Boston) was tainted with smallpox or leprosy, or it was stolen goods and whoever bought would go to jail. Things like that — depending upon the ingenuity of the old codger ran the general store.

Well, Mr. Baxter and Mr. Baker, Mr. Perkins and Mr. Dolittle and such, all you who kept general stores (and pretty honestly by and large), you had to think fast how to compete with these here fly-by-night, peddling people. Hope you've all got the good, solid, well-cut gravestones you deserved.

And after all these years I write in loving memory of journeymen, too itchy-footed to settle down ever. The down-at-the-heel shoemaker, with a wreath of wooden lasts about his neck. Out-to-elbow tailor, a bolt of cloth on his back, scissor at his belt and a goose under his arm (we called them "goose herders"). The always tired farmhand out looking for hire and never stayed more than three weeks. Preambulating printers, dancing masters, fiddlers. Indians. Just about the last of them, selling baskets, and those worthless yellow dogs of theirs that were supposed to be great rat catchers and weren't.

Traveling peep-show men. "Caravan" men, keeping the side curtain drawn on their wagons so no one could get a look at the lion without paying for it.

Cattle drovers, pig drovers, sheep drovers on their way to Brighton. And the men the coaching companies sent out to buy up the young horses from Vermont for the stage lines. All sorts of "hoss" traders, and the moldy old stories following them. I mean like the blind horse whose only fault was it "didn't look good." The balky one whose new owner would "be pleased to see go." And men who sold wagons and chaises — eight or ten of them, fastened the one after the other, all drawn by one old horse.

I can hope a good end and a dying repentance was granted to all footpads and jailbirds, lads who stole linen off the line. Silver spoons. Thieves, housebreakers, and horse and dog stealers, and other such as our law indicated as "mischievous men." And the sheriffs and the posses out after them. Even "body snatchers" — if any ever existed. You too, Ruby Lambkin — may you rest in no uneasy grave.

Phantoms too would take to the road like Christians. Some no heads. Some you could see through. It was with all such likely and unlikely folk Jude and I now tossed in our lot.

. . . .

Eleven

. . . .

CONSIDERING THE ROADS, the fat lazy lummox of a horse we drove, and the fact we never were in any hurry at all, thirty-five miles was about our outside limit for a day. And it was within a thirty-five-mile radius (Hampton being the hub) that just about everybody knew Jude and his yellow horse and yellow rig, at least by sight. Of course not everybody. That woman he told about the sea serpent didn't. But most people knew he was that off-ox who made his living (if he made a living) in a funny way. He was odd-looking too, and he was Submit Pratt's husband. This preconceived idea of him — what you might call a magic circle of everybody's "knowledge" of him — held him tight in.

Likewise this whole near-by countryside was just infested with Pratt relatives who would be calling to him from the fields or houses as we passed by to hear how the folks were. None of them, you felt, thought much of Jude, and he thought less than that of most of them. And they'd look at me and say, "So this is the orphan boy what stammers?" Then I'd stammer for them although by and large I'd got over it.

Mitty had asked him to leave a fine ham and regards with some real antique "cousins" of theirs at Thompson. Seems he always did this for her every time he started north from

Hampton and, of course being related, they'd ask him in for the night.

Word of mouth had got to Deacon and Mrs. Deacon Thatcher Jude planned starting north this spring, and they must of been on the lookout and sighted his chaise as soon as it got on that long, easy main street of Thompson. By the time we hove to in front of their gate they stood side by side behind their bristly picket fence, ready for us, glum and staring. We were expected. I'd hardly say we were welcomed.

These derned old critters were something like the Pratts' mother's aunt's first husband's second cousins, and why Mitty cherished them I can't figure. They were of identical height, he and she — gaunt and gray alike, and wore similar oblong steel spectacles for their gimlet eyes. But you could tell him from her because he had a beard like a carding machine, and trousers. If they were congenial to each other, I doubt they were to anybody else.

Jude stopped (not presuming to get out the chaise) and said he had regards from Mitty to them. They seemed surprised "poor Submit" had managed to live through the winter — with such a husband, was implied. There was a pause. Mrs. Deacon inquired for Dorinda and the children. Jude looked out to sea and said, "Fine." Then she screwed up her courage to inquire how the pigs had done, for she was about crazy to get that ham. Jude always made her, as he told me, "ask for it." He said pigs had done poorly, not taking her hint. This wasn't so.

Nothing was said about stepping in and making yourself to home. They hadn't even opened the gate as yet, so Jude started picking up the reins. He believed we'd stop off at the Ezra Stiles tavern (right opposite them across the road), and it *had* been nice seeing them both, and they looking so up and coming. Fact is, they didn't look as if the sap had risen in them for thirty years. And he was saying it was a surprisingly chilly day, which it wasn't.

Then Deacon said he was suspicious of the moral tone of all public houses. Jude sighed dolefully and shook his head. The stories he could tell of sin at inns would flabbergast them. Deacon brightened right up, for he'd rather hear of sin than the Promise of the Gospels. Then Mrs. Deacon said flat out she was sorry Pratt Farm had had such a bad ham year. So he gave up and told her Mitty had sent her one. And at last the gate clicked and we were invited in.

I'll admit he told them about sin — that being what they wanted to hear and he always ready to oblige conversationally, and sing for his supper like a gentleman. We were hardly allowed to take our hats off and not even offered the refreshment of a cup of tea. We just sat in the best parlor (they did show him that much courtesy) and he talked and they shook their heads and said, "Tut, tut" and that they "wanted to know." He even got them to believing there was a tavern up around Boscawen, New Hampshire, haunted by a most appallingly immoral chambermaid, dead this hundred years; and how she'd come to a living man by night (you could all but hear the creak of the softly opening door, feel the cold air came in with her, smell her grave clothes), to the utter and forever damnation of the unfortunate man's soul, and so on. He told it so nice (but pretty racy — they being so pious), Deacon was for getting the very name of the place so he could write to a minister up there who'd urge the selectmen to refusing further licenses. Jude sort of slid around out of that. Didn't say there was no such place, but perhaps it wasn't so close to Boscawen as it was to Penacook and, as long as that's where he and I were heading for, he'd bring back an accurate report. And he did give them a real evil, knowing look like he was one among the seduced and the damned.

After supper it was Deacon's turn. He had a tract against peddlers from a Bible society and he read to us from that, exhorting Jude as he read to give up his junketing about — even as he valued his immortal soul. Tract pointed out how,

with a young man so exposed, "sobriety is exchanged for
cunning, honesty for imposition, decent behavior for coarse
impudence." And it was a temptation (so far from home) to
absent themselves from divine service and, in short, cut up.
Jude sat there, head in hands, looking pious as a prune,
shaking his head, and now he was the one to say "I want to
know" and "Tut, tut."

He had told me, before we got there, how twenty-nine
years ago last August a smart-cat of a peddling fellow had sold
Deacon a leaky calf-weaner and instead of taking it like sort
of a joke on himself (he shouldn't have bought it if he hadn't
known enough to guess whether it would work or not), he
had been chewing and chewing on it and repeating and
repeating this story, of his own stupidity really, and so coming
to regard all men selling on the road worse than sin even —
which he, by the way, enjoyed. Old fellow was utterly unable
to digest that calf-weaner and sure enough he was telling it
all over again now.

But this does bring up a point. How honest were those
peddlers by and large? I'd say ninety-nine out of one hundred.
Lots of them had regular customers and went back again and
again every year. They had better be honest. Some of them
were a thought tricky, and of course they were the ones all the
talk was about, for I've heard a hundred stories of a peddler's
tricks to one I've known of personally. I never saw a wooden
nutmeg, nor a basswood ham. That goes for wooden cucumber seeds too. I never saw cocoanuts sold for the eggs of
the "Golly-wopper Bird" ("lady, all you do is set a goose on
them — and will you be pleased when you actually see them
hatch!"). I've certainly heard the story. I never saw an oak-
leaf cigar. But I will admit that pinchbeck jewelry fell apart
fast. Sometimes sawdust was colored and added to coffee.
There were tinkers that mended pots with sealing wax. The
patterns did wash off calico and handles fell off knives. And,
like Deacon Thatcher, patented calf-weaners didn't work —

no, nor a sight lot other of Yankee ingenuities. Apple corers and corn shellers. Washing machines even. Yet I believe most did — more or less.

By and large, when you bought from a peddler you got about what you paid for, but it often was his wits against yours. I've known women make a swap with one, she giving so much paper rag (linen) against, say, so much so-called "imported" black broadcloth. And he, poor fellow, would find center of each rag sack full of ashes and she that that broadcloth was no more than shoddy and turned green in a year and then bust up. No more need to import stuff like that than poison ivy.

For a lot of that sort of trading was a game to them — maybe a wicked game, but no more harmful than western gambling. Yankees never did gamble much.

The sharpest sharping was of course in horse trading. Then it was your knowledge of horseflesh against his, and the Devil take the most ignorant. And yet even there people would say they'd rather be shaved by a sharp razor than a dull one. And actually, if a trick was cute enough and especially if you pulled a pretty smart one on someone that had once outsmarted you, there would be considerable condoning of an evil.

. . . .

Twelve

. . . .

O<small>N OUR FIRST DAY</small> we had gone from Hampton to Brooklyn
to Danielson to Pomfret Factory to Thompson and there the
night. From Thompson we had crossed the state line into
Massachusetts and to Webster (it was one of those raw-looking
factory towns), to Oxford, to Leicester, to Paxton, to Holden.
There we were to spend our second night.

So we had broken out of that paralyzing circle of "everybody's knowledge." No Pratt relatives from now on to know
Jude was no good. You could feel just by the way he waved
his hat at the girl in pink on the stagecoach, and the air he
put on as he answered people who, seeing the box behind on
our chaise, asked him what he was up to, he was collecting
rattlesnakes for their poison — good for gout. Things like
that. By the way, he didn't think to begin selling until we
were further from home. Old adage about greener pastures,
I guess.

We did not go through Worcester, he being leery of the
place. It was just ten years ago last March he had been guilty
there not only of breaking his indenture to his master, Julian
Parker Cove, but assaulting him to boot. And he had to hide
out like a criminal.

He had always been ladling out to Leaf and me parts,

parcels and fancies about his boyhood. Now he told me some straight facts.

He had been born somewhere north of Worcester and his family had been broke up and come upon the town. That town (never said what town) had located a great-uncle in Hubbardston and he was sent to be reared by Unk Ike and old Auntie Lon. Younger than I when my family had been broke. Two or three, for a guess. The schoolmistress was sort of farmed out with these old people two months a year. She liked to dabble in paint and sketching. He liked to watch her and try it himself. So when he was ten Mr. Julian Parker Cove of Worcester had been persuaded to take him in as an apprentice, although he was three years younger than the usual age. It had been agreed that for eight years Jude was to be learned the mysteries and the arts of interior painting, coach and sign painting, stenciling and such. At eighteen Mr. Cove agreed to give him all the paints, brushes, palettes, stone and such necessities of his trade, and a brand new suit, his "freedom suit," new shoes, and turn him loose. Never heard a word from Unk Ike or Auntie Lon.

Mr. Cove had learned him well, and to paint fast. But he taught him as people said tavernkeepers train turnspit dogs (although I never saw one do it). People said they put a pup and a live coal in a wheel together. Anyhow he was taught when he went to work, to work. A fourteen-hour day wasn't nothing to Mr. Cove. Yet Jude said a little sadly he wondered if he had had more to eat, more sleep and play at that age, maybe he wouldn't be so narrow-framed and scarecrow-like now. And he bet fellows like that Ruby Lambkin of Mr. Sharp's hadn't been worked quite so hard so young.

When seventeen (and tall as he was now) he was doing all the freehand work for Mr. Cove, being better at it than his master. Things like, say, inn signs. He had completed for the local rich man and merchant, one Mr. Salisbury, a very

neat sign for his big shop at Lincoln Square. This fine old
gentleman was pink as ham and his hair white as cotton, and
so aristocratic, poor boors like Jude was, couldn't do much
but gape and gag when he spoke to them — let him speak
never so kindly. He said it was his waistcoats did him in. All
over embroidered in tiny flowers from France. Couldn't say
a word to the man, thinking on those waistcoats.

Mr. Salisbury, admiring his skill, asked him to step across
the square to his house and see some real pictures. Jude had
on his dirty painter's frock and Mr. Salisbury one of those
waistcoats.

They were in the dining room mostly, those pictures. It
was the coolest, cleanest, biggest room Jude had ever been in.
Mahogany here, and silver there, French mural papers, and
then the pictures!

Well, he didn't want to see them again. For now he knew
they could never have been so beautiful, radiant, so breathing
of life. So he forgot not only the waistcoats, but his manners
as well, and just gaped at them. Here he had seen a world of
painting far beyond the world of Mr. Cove and he knew it
was for him. He never thanked Mr. Salisbury for the sight
of them.

Mr. Salisbury (and I bet he was gratified by the boy's
speechless amazement — Jude had a mighty expressive face)
fished in a back pocket and gave him whatever he had there.
Never counted it out. Just, "Here, my lad" and thrust it into
Jude's hand. It was a lot. It was seven dollars and twenty-
seven cents. Jude never forgot. He didn't even thank him.

Then Mr. Salisbury gave advice. First he beat about the
bush, saying what a public-spirited and valuable citizen Mr.
Cove was, and then he told the truth. It had been noted by
some of Worcester's better citizens that Cove's apprentices
were apt to run off just before their indenture was completed,
and they never did get their "freedom suits" nor tools of
trade. This not only made the boys criminals (there was a

law against breaking indenture) but saved Mr. Cove money. Now Jude had no more than eight months left to go before he was eighteen. So let him stick it out, no matter how his master treated him. Forewarned was forearmed, etc. If things were too bad Jude was to come to Mr. Salisbury; he was a justice of the peace, and would see justice done. But until an apprentice brought charges against a master his hands were tied. Jude never thanked him.

Then Mr. Salisbury, on parting, picked an early yellow apple out of a silver basket on the dining-room table and the dam inside Jude broke and he thanked him and thanked him for that apple. He'd regret all his life Mr. Salisbury would think the pictures and the money and the advice had been nothing, and a good eating apple everything.

With Mr. Salisbury's gift Jude bought from a peddler's cart colors, oils, brush, canvas and helped himself to a broken grinding stone Mr. Cove had thrown out. The colors were terrible but at least cheap. Secretly he went to work by himself. He especially remembered a lady's hand with a pearl ring on it at Salisbury mansion. He did it from memory over and over.

Naturally Mr. Cove found out. He accused Jude of having stolen these things from him. Maybe the stone he had. Cove cuffed him and pulled his ears and swore he'd have the law on him unless he confessed and repented and gave up the things he had "stolen." And he was sent to bed with only water for supper and hauled up out of bed and put to work lining coach wheels by lamplight. I'm ashamed Jude had no more backbone, but at last it seemed easier to confess and be let alone, and he confessed before two witnesses. Things went worse (naturally no master would treat a confessed thief as he would an honest boy) and Jude couldn't go to Mr. Salisbury. He was ashamed to have the gentleman think he was a thief.

He got to be like a spring wound tighter and tighter. Sometime it would burst, and it did.

Although Sunday was supposed to be a day of rest, prayer, meditation and no work, and custom (if not exactly law) was against putting apprentices to housework, it was Sunday and Jude had been set to wash the kitchen floor. He had his soap-suds in a great old three-legged iron kettle. Not a light pail, for he did think everything was done to make work hard for him. All the rest of the household had gone to Sunday after-noon service so, believing himself alone, he decided to sit a moment and meditate, like the Good Book says to do on Sunday.

Mr. Cove walked in, flung him out of that chair to his hands and knees, and as Jude grabbed his washrag to go on with that floor he (being back to his master) presented a tempting part of his anatomy. Mr. Cove kicked him. He sprawled head first into the fire. He had a bad burn on his face and left hand. Right only scorched, but it hurt worse first. He should of run to a justice of the peace, for the law certainly protects apprentices from things like that. Instead he only saw, felt, thought red. He grabbed up that heavy old iron pot and cracked Mr. Cove over the head with it. Didn't know how he came to hit him, for he never saw him at all — only red.

The red subsided. Mr. Cove was lying there lifeless at his feet, in a great eddy of soapy water and some blood. Now Jude felt as cool and sure of himself as the moment before he had felt wild, but he was shaking all over. He stepped over the body to Mr. Cove's chamber and picked out the newest and strongest suit of clothes he found there — shoes and all, even to the underdrawers. And he stripped and put on everything new and nice. He took the key to the shop from what he thought was the dead body, went to the shop and very deliberately made himself up a pack of the best colors and brushes and everything a journeyman painter needed. He wrote a note for Mrs. Cove to read when she came home. Only that Mr. Cove had slipped on the soapy floor and hit his head on the kettle but, as long as his indenture was up in a month, Jude had decided to terminate the contract right now. And P.S., he had helped himself to what was due him.

He knew enough not to run as long as he was in the sight of a house. Then he ran and ran. Night was coming down (it was March) and a little snow too. He was thankful that the snow would cover his footprints, for he believed hue and cry would be raised against him and the sheriff call out a posse, notices and rewards tacked up. He could feel the deep burn on his face stiffening into the mark of a Cain.

It had been a frightening, lonely thing to be a hunted man, even in no more than your own mind's eye. He'd never forget. Couldn't yet see the notice of a wanted man (like that one Phineas Sharp had of Ruby Lambkin) but he wondered did the poor devil feel the flesh crawling on him and the hair rising up and the terror Jude had felt that night. And maybe poor devil had had just as much provocation for the evil he had done as Jude had for hitting Mr. Cove.

Jude now stopped the chaise. We were in Holden but almost on the town line of Worcester, just north of Worcester. He pointed to a lonely, dirty-looking tavern with pens about it, and the sign it hung from an old chestnut tree — "Cow Tavern."

"This far I run. Couldn't of run another step," he said. "That barn there — I thought to hide the night out in. But landlady spied me and was after me. I admitted I was a runaway apprentice. She offered to hide me. Fetched me blankets and hot food. That sign there, I painted it for her, hid up in the hayloft and my burnt hands bleeding. But I had to show my gratitude somehow. They had no proper sign then — only some steers' horns nailed up."

It was a fat, frowsy-looking red cow with white spots, he had painted, and on its face a look of lawlessness and goodness and half-a-wink. He said he got the expression for the cow from his benefactress. He said it might be called the first portrait he ever did.

Phineas Sharp was partly right. But he hadn't painted more than one barn over in York State (where he had decided to go for a spell, in case Mr. Cove was dead or had brought charges against him) and he discovered he did have a knack for likenesses. It was there he had begun on what seemed to be his life work. And also he had hit on his present method — painting bodies and backgrounds wintertime, selling them off in nice weather. He bet this way he could make and sell twice as many portraits as any other limner. If I had thought he had seemed a little more enthusiastic about Mr. Sharp than the circumstances warranted, it was because while Jude was hiding out over to York State he had been kind to him ten years ago. And it was also because of the gratitude he felt for Cow Tavern that even today, when it came right, he liked to stop off. It had changed hands. Not a person there who even knew he had painted that sign.

• • • • • • • • • • • • • •

Thirteen

• • • • • • • • • • • • •

A DROVER'S TAVERN isn't like any other tavern. It has to have about it yards, pens and such, so each drover coming in can shut a gate on his own herd and know the fodder he pays for is eaten by his beasts. That's one reason why such "cow taverns" are always stuck out on outskirts where land is cheap. Besides, town people won't stand for the smell and the

flies and the mooing and baa-ing and honking and grunting
and the herd dogs barking. Then a third reason why such
places are set away from towns is the reputation drovers have
for swilling, yelling, quarreling and fighting among themselves. I've heard people out west suggest that all New
Englanders are sort of refined by nature. This isn't true.

Mrs. Buffum (a widow lady) was running Cow Tavern
these days. Jude was telling me most of these places were run
by widows, for some reason he couldn't fathom. And they all
looked like that one who had befriended him ten years back
right there. From where we sat in the chaise we could see her,
out among her yards, holding a gate and hollering at two men
coming in off the road with maybe two hundred sheep. She
was bursting with muscle and energy. And she had on a
scarlet petticoat tucked up to her big, blowsy pink knees, a
man's hat on her head and no shoes. Seeing us stopping, she
roared "Coming" at us, as innkeepers yell when they mean
they aren't coming. Her first hospitality being to the animals,
people were always second with her. Goldie dropped her
head to browse and we sat to watch and be patient.

She was gesticulating wildly at the highway and running to
open another pen, for she had seen, and now we saw, her next
guests. A sizable drove of perhaps one hundred pigs. The
boy who drove them had two dogs to help him, a serious big
black dog, and a fuzzy little something, too indignant and
nippy for such work. Pigs are by nature devils to drive,
they being more individualists than, say, sheep. They
handle easier on drizzly days than fair ones. This day was
bright, and I admired to see the way that boy handled them.
He had them trotting as nice as little soldiers, and they turned
smart right about and into the pen. The sunlight flashed as
they turned, on a band of white paint he had put on every
one of them down their ridgepoles. This was done so that
meeting other herds on the road, or even passing a farmhouse,
or at a place like this, but especially in the confusion of maybe

a thousand pigs all roaming about at Brighton, no one could claim one of his.

Then Mrs. Buffum came panting up to us, but arguing all the time with the boy, who kept right on her heels. So much for use of pen and slops for his pigs and, yes, he might earn his own victuals and lodgings by helping her. Her hired girl had run off with the horse doctor and she'd need help in the kitchen and bar tonight. But, by all that was holy (or unholy), she would not feed those two dogs of his for nothing. And "Shubael, you stop your pesterin' of me." Fact is he wasn't saying a thing to her. "For I won't feed those dogs of yours for nothing. They can catch rats in the barn. And now go away, Shubael." Evidently she knew him.

She put on a genteel expression for us, warned us her accommodations might "not suit" but we were welcome and she was making gestures behind her all the time at Shubael to go away.

He had wide-opened, wide-set gray eyes, real trusting, honest eyes. His straw hat was off in deference to Mrs. Buffum's ladyhood and his hair was the same color as his hat. He had sunburned a clear, even pink. Hadn't browned or freckled any. By tradition (and fact too, I guess) Yankee farm boys are supposed to have freckles and snub noses, and if they haven't knocked out a front tooth, why then they were born gap-toothed. Agile as monkeys, of course, but without any of two qualities Shubael had too much of — grace and dignity. He wore the tow breeches and blue smock-frock so common to farm boys then, but actually his were clean.

She, having told us where to put up Goldie, hustled off toward her back door, Shubael saying nothing at her heels and his two dogs after him. No more than a moment I saw him coming out that back door with soup bones and stale bread for his dogs. You knew he hadn't paid a cent for them. Then the three of them settle down together. Dogs eating, he petting them and absorbed in them like he had no other friends in this world. Both he and his dogs looked a trifle jagged out. For it is a fact, to drive pigs, say thirteen miles, the drover has to travel some thirty miles and I guess his dog nearer fifty, because pigs wander so.

Soon enough Jude and I settled in a modest corner of the taproom. There was, of course, no dining room here but Mrs. Buffum, to emphasize the difference in caste between us genteel-looking folk (although we were peddlers) and the drovers, spread before us a dirty white cloth. Those men ate hunched about bare boards — long table and all together. Most of these men had brought their own victuals and were opening up bandanna handkerchiefs to get at hunks of this and moldy pieces of that. Whiskey, rum, cider and such to wash it down they bought off the house. Shubael waited on them.

They said no more than "evening" to Jude and me and turned their backs on us, like they felt we didn't quite belong here with them. They smelt to high heaven of their beasts and of themselves, and they all either knew each other or pretended to. Mostly we heard nicknames called back and forth among them — names like Buck, or Bull. The fellow they called "Dog" I remember most. He was so loud and foul-mouthed and a real mean, born bully if I ever saw one. He was pasty-faced (most of them were fresh-colored men). Now I look back on it and know why he had grown up to be such a bully. He had a weasel face, narrow and chinless, and from childhood he had had to outfight and outbrag every other boy he met to be respected. And here he was now — man of thirty or forty and still outbragging, and his fists all set to begin fighting at the drop of a hat, and cock-o'-the-walking it over everybody else.

The talk was first the prices for meat on the hoof at Brighton and the charms of the place (from their point of view), although fact was, the place smelt so of offal and slaughtering it was close to a public nuisance. They talked

of shipping schedules, for most of the meat prepared at
Brighton was salted and went to sea on Boston vessels. They
had hardly had more than three drinks around than they
were haggling at each other, trying to buy up the next man's
beeves or sell their own mutton. Drovers were always selling
or buying on the road. A man might leave, say, Thetford,
Vermont, with twenty beef steers and swap and sell and swap
again so he'd arrive eventually at Boston with a perfectly
matched carriage pair, and a harness and carriage to boot, if
he was smart. Then he'd haggle around that town until he
had a flock of Merino sheep, just off a Boston ship from South
Africa, and get those back to Thetford with him to sell his
neighbors at about any price he had the audacity to ask —
people round about there being Merino-crazy.

Men like that, unlike, say, parsons, never can drink without
sprawling and they were sprawled on their long table and
sprawled on the benches. Not being able to start a trade
among themselves, it was agreed among them by no more
than a few winks and nudges that Dog was going to get
Shubael's pigs from him at a fraction of their real value.
Vacant minds like that are always on the lookout for someone
weaker than themselves to sharp and bully. Shubael had been
their goat ever since they set eyes upon him. For one thing he
was too clean. He even had tied a clean white rag on his
bunged-up toe (I guess every barefoot boy in New England
had a rag on one toe or another summertimes), and he looked
as though he *liked* to be clean, a point of view not only incom-
prehensible to them but extremely offensive. They didn't
mind it that Jude and I were clean, but this Shubael had set
himself up to be a drover and hadn't learned the first lesson
— which was to be dirty and talk dirty too. Nor did he look
anxious to learn.

When not serving them he sat alone upon a stool by the
fireplace and whittled at his drover's staff — which, by the way,
he had peeled and was covering with pretty carvings. They'd

yell "She Belle" (for they maintained he was a girl dressed up
in boy's clothes). He'd instantly put down his whittling and
jump to serve them, then go sit on his stool, back to them
and very aloof.

And they'd tell him to draw a glass of grog for himself —
they'd pay for it, for he being a drover should sit with them.
Men like that always think it funny to get a boy drunk. He
thanked them very politely. Always seemed on the edge of
accepting, and then finally didn't. It was the same way about
accepting the price Dog was offering him for his herd. By
now Jude and I knew pretty well what was the price he should
get for them — this being freely discussed while Shubael was
out the room fetching for them. But soon as he was back
they'd be talking solemnly to each other (for him to overhear)
about the bottom having dropped out of pork, and pretending to sell what pigs they might have to Dog — who was
good enough to offer this same (fictitious) price to Shubael.
He'd always bite on this — and then not quite. He'd almost
sit to drink with them — and then not quite. But he had put
by his whittling, and turned about on his stool to face them.
There was a lantern hung from the ceiling to light them.
Half the light fell upon the boy's face — so open and trusting,
like he had not only never met with wicked men before but
nobody had told him such existed, and half the light fell upon
the drink-loosened, shifty-eyed, greedy ugliness of his tor-
mentors.

Jude and I sat and the lighting exaggerated everything,
Shubael's innocence and the men's evil. It was like seeing a
play, played on a stage. If ever Jude had seen innocence and
virtue going down before evil, that was it — Jude told me
later. And it (so he told me next day) had made him just close
to puking-sick, and he longed to yell at the "child" (I guess
he was old as I — say thirteen) and warn him. He had to
keep his mouth shut, for there is a strict code that when a
bargain is being struck no outsider can interfere. And if this

boy was old enough to be trusted by various farmers and widows and such in Princeton (where he came from) to take and sell their pigs at market, why he was old enough to care for himself. But he was so pathetically grateful to them for telling him all those lies about the pork-glut at Brighton and the bottom out of pigs. And it was so kind of Mr. Dog to offer to take his pigs off his hands, and maybe suffer a loss himself. For that was the way hook, bait and sinker finally disappeared down him.

Mrs. Buffum appeared all of a sudden. "Shubael," says she crossly, "what you up to?"

"Nothing, ma'am," says he all lamblike.

"You forgetting you're to knead the bread for me?"

"No, ma'am."

"Then you get to the kitchen and at it — and don't you go pestering these gentlemen."

"Yes, ma'am."

He was gone a long time.

Dog had out a greasy stocking purse, laid it on the table amid the spilt liquor already to pay up when he came back, for Shubael had fallen for his offer and agreed to the price per pig before he went to knead the dough. Then the question, how many pigs had he?

They all had noted the pigs with the white paint on them, for they had come in after him, and that they were fat, good pigs. Nobody could say how many.

Naturally Dog wouldn't pay without counting up himself, and he wouldn't take Shubael's word for it. So they waited for him.

"I'm not asking you to take my word on how many," Shubael said, standing against the doorway, the white dough crusting and hardening on his sunburned arms. "Just so you agree any pig with a white streak on it is my pig." They agreed, and all, except two, who were sleeping off their liquor right where it had caught up with them, got up to go see. They all were weaving some, and Dog a-plenty. So it was Shubael unhooked and carried the lantern for them.

We'd of been left in the dark then if Jude hadn't suddenly jumped to his feet, angry they had got the best of him and angrier yet he hadn't been able to do anything to stop such evil. And he yelled pretty crossly at Mrs. Buffum to direct us to where we were to sleep, and she was to call us good and early next morning, and muttering to me all he wanted now was to get to hell out of this den of thieves, and he guessed she was as bad as the rest of them.

As for "early," it was before daybreak she called us. We had two drovers snoring in the other bed in the room with us. She wasn't waking them. She was ready with our breakfast in the kitchen, and the back door was open to the freshness and wetness and coolness of the dawn which was just about to begin. We could smell the cattle and wet crushed mint. The gray oblong of the doorway was paling as we sat to eat by the hearth light and the light of one candle. First she'd say no more than how'd we want our eggs. Then at last she refilled our coffee mugs and she did like Jude told her — filled for herself and sat with us to drink it.

The bounce had gone out of her a little and she acted worried-like.

Jude asked her where was Shubael.

"Went away last night." Said she. "Soon's he got the money he went — and he better had of."

"You previously acquainted with him?"

"Third time he been here. And I'm about ready to say the last. Trouble is he's too bright. Boys that bright ought to be shucked off into colleges or shut up in lawyer offices where they can't do any harm. But I don't want you to get any idea prejudicial to his character. Only if anyone starts cheating him, he'll cheat furthest and first. And Dog is old enough to look out for himself, drunk or sober. Learn him a lesson — I hope. But such goings on don't give a house a good name.

Yet I, being a third party, didn't feel I could interfere to protect an old hound like Dog, so I just left them and went upstairs to rest."

"How Shubael done it?"

"Shifted some thirty of Dog's own pigs into the pen I'd assigned to him. Used my bread dough to stripe them down the spines. If that's not sin I give up, but . . . of course Dog had it coming to him. If he's that dumb it's his loss. Mine, rather, for it was my bread dough. But I just sit here a-dreading and a-dreading the moment Dog come down yon stairs and finds out — he with that narrow little head of his all swelled up with last night's liquor, and swearing to kill that boy. I told Shubael to get out of here and cut for home. He's back at Princeton by now — he and his ill-gotten gains."

"Any idea how much he made?"

"I figure it he got about twelve dollars and forty cents more than he might have expected by going all the way to Brighton and back, and saved himself a tolerable amount of effort."

As Jude was getting usually three dollars a portrait you see this wasn't chicken feed.

"But he's made him a mean, vengeful enemy in that Dog. But what I care most about, giving my house a bad name — if those men ever had an idea that I . . . " This was as far as she went in admitting she had known all along what was up.

As Jude paid up what was owing I went to fetch out Goldie. It was marvelously fresh outdoors and was getting whiter all the time. The sun didn't seem to be rising from any particular spot, but softly the light was breathing up out of earth and air all over and at once. Dawn seems sometimes more miraculous at a rather ugly spot (like I had thought this was) than where things are pretty to start with.

. . . .

Fourteen

. . . .

I CAN HARDLY BELIEVE it now — what it was like there then, in the month of May. For instance, everybody had an apple tree. Every apple tree was blossoming, foaming over stone walls, pink and white against red barns. Some of them so silly and vain as to be standing on one foot, admiring their beauty reflected in one of those short-lived pasture pools of spring. Nobody in New England lived so mean as to be unable to own a lilac. Even old, deserted cellar-holes had a lilac bush. So, to begin with, think apple blossoms and lilacs.

Little leaves and maple keys were sometimes coppery, but greeny-yellow mostly. They smelled like something out of a bottle — a varnish perhaps. Very nice but acrid.

The sky doesn't seem so high up and lonely-like. It comes closer, bluer, warmer, every day. The clouds are innocent lambs of clouds — not like the black and sulphurous thunder-heads of August, nor the iron-gray blankets of wintertime. You can get soaked one minute and next the sun comes beam-ing out to dry you. Jude and I would hardly bother to put up the chaise top for those twinkling little showers.

I've never seen Ireland, but if Ireland is greener than New England in May it's too damned green. And with us every green is different from the next one. Oak isn't elm color, nor willow same as birch, nor the coarse green of hellebore like the downy greens of bracken. And so on. One green pasture maybe sprinkled white with innocence. Meadow next to it, and the green goes golden along the brook with cowslips. Or the wild rhodora moves in and the green all but disappears under their purply pink. The eye never can tire of any one color, any one thing — for as the road dips and moves you on, very next thing you see is different from the last.

Sounds too. Did you ever know a spring ploughman go afield and not be whistling? Jude bet me licorice strips they did, and he won. Spring air carries the sound of the conch shell farm women blow for dinnertime, sweeter and farther than any other time of year. And that's true of their "chick-chick" to their hens, or "pig-pig" to their swine, and men calling "co-boss, co-boss" to the cattle. And perhaps it is the light quality of the fragrant air that makes frogs croaking and bees buzzing and, most of all, bird song seem almost magical in spring. The drumming of the partridge, the self-conscious perfection of the wood thrush's afternoon song, whippoorwills lashing at the night, and as for bobolinks — they sound as though poured out of pitchers. I mean, they are so liquid.

But one forgets the details, which never do add up to much, and remembers the feeling of floating on an ocean of spring. If when I die I go to where I wish to go, I'll go back there to those hills — bouncy little green ones, some of them, others great bald granite. And travel those roads curling about them, and the blue ponds, and the brown brooks and the rock ledges even — fit to break your axle. I'd be there when the apple trees are blossoming and the oriole singing. In other words, back to New England in May. But to make sure everything will be just right, I'll go back over sixty years — and I going on fourteen.

It was like that for days. We crossed Massachusetts right into New Hampshire. Jude had an idea (wasn't much in it) that the further he was from home, the better would be business. He hadn't begun to peddle until we were in New Hampshire.

He had no nice-kept books of where he had been other years, but a fine memory. He had never been around the Jaffreys or the Rindges, nor to Dublin, nor Fitzwilliam nor Troy. All this considerable territory would be virgin soil. Yet four years ago, while he was doing a job at Goffstown, near Manchester, he had come as close into here as Hancock (about ten miles north of Dublin) at the request of a tavern-keeper at that place who wanted about an acre (so it had seemed to Jude) of tropical foliage and such on his walls. So four years back he had stayed about a month, first and last in Hancock, and now he intended to go there — after we had cleaned up on this terra incognita which I have tried to indicate.

I might say that an itinerant painter may gain from retracing his steps. If his pictures have proved satisfactory he may find new people waiting for his return. But if the paint has chipped off or the town has decided against them, or if even he has about skimmed the cream off the place, a return will not profit him. But when he comes to a new place, where he has never been before, he may find the community too poor (like later we found north of Boscawen too poor) in spite of what it may look like on a map. Or, in unknown territory, people may be too suspicious of a strange limner. Three dollars is a lot of money to risk, and so on. Now Jude, being able to show them just what they were buying (all except their own faces), did arouse considerable confidence. They were not buying such pigs in pokes as they would have if (like most limners) he had started from scratch.

The way we worked things out was like this. On arriving, say, at Fitzwilliam, you could guess the town was prosperous enough to buy likenesses by the size and beauty of the Congregational Church, and by the decency of the common and the fence around it. Likewise — look there! If they haven't a

palm-leaf hat factory — now you know citizens here are up
and coming, ready to risk a little money. A place like Fitzwilliam looked good.

At the store I'd jump out and ask permission to stick up
one of Jude's printed-up trade cards. The other one gets put
up at the tavern. Before we leave this place for good I'll
usually go back and get them down, for we hadn't many and
I was responsible for not wasting them. The tavern at Fitzwilliam was good, and a good headquarters for Jude's trade.
The sixth New Hampshire Turnpike ran right in front of it.
We came in on it.

As for where we put up for the night, it was like this —
anybody who employed a craftsman, or anything like an
itinerant woodchopper or clergyman, by custom gave him
meals, lodgings, bait and board for his horse if he had one
and, in our case, the limner's apprentice. That's why Jude
liked to get where he was going early enough so he could talk
himself into a job and free lodgings before nightfall. But
sometimes we'd get in so late he'd have no chance to tree his
coon (so to speak) before bedtime. Then we had to face it,
and shuck out the cash at the tavern usually.

By now I was running the purse. Even then I liked money
and the handling of it better than Jude (never would of been
president of the West Kansas Harness Works if I hadn't). I
was no help to him in actual painting, as a real apprentice
would of been, although I did considerable grinding paint,
cleaning brushes and palette, harnessing up, and so on. It
was decided, to really earn my keep, I was to take charge of all
financial transactions. So I struck the price we were to pay for
meals and nights (when forced to pay), and it was I informed
the public how much for a portrait, and collected from them.
That Mr. Rebough could afford to carry "a clerk" impressed
people with his importance. Another thing I might mention
here. I had pretty well got the upper hand on my stammering
but when, say, some important sort of a judge's wife would

swing at me suddenly and say, "How much for that there —
with my face done in?" I'd get stuck on "three." Jude said it
discourages people, they thinking I was trying to say thirty.
Long as five came easy, that's what I was to say. Nobody
refused to pay five and I doubt if they ever would have. Can
you believe any businessman so simple he could have got five
dollars per item, and could have for years for the mere asking,
and never raising his prices until he had a clerk that stammered?

Of course he shouldn't of been like that, but that was how
he was, and looking back, one thing I'm thankful for was he
hadn't told me to say two. He might have.

I remember Fitzwilliam for the glory of the mountains
about us, and for the first time I smelt that "great forest"
smell. It hadn't taken Jude more than fifteen minutes talking
to the landlord at that big old tavern on the common before
he had convinced him that he wanted a picture of his mother.
She was a real nice old lady. Only trouble with her was she
insisted Jude paint out the Bible open on the lap of the old
lady he had prepared, and put in her own tiger tom. I spent
most of my time trying to hold that cat down on her lap. He
was hawk-wild and had one ear gone. You'd of thought a nice
little old lady would of preferred the Good Book, but old
ladies are deceptive in appearance.

Jude had been given a downstairs room in which to display
his wares at this tavern and had set his easel there and could
put in a face in anything from two to four hours. The tavern-
keeper liked to have him there, for it did attract people in to
watch or buy and was good for his own business.

We sat considerable in the barroom, sometimes drinking
cider or birch beer, sometimes sitting and talking. It was
there I first heard Jude really put sauce, fixings and gravy on
an event that I knew all about, and serve it up palatably to
those who were listening to him.

I said we were on New Hampshire sixth, and a coach had

come in from pretty well west of us somewhere on the
Connecticut River. According to Mr. Sharp it was thereabouts Mr. Ruby Lambkin was winning a considerable fame.
A young man, come in from there traveling in essence, asked
the room at large if anyone had heard of Lambkin round
here? Being encouraged by the general ignorance, he told us
quite a lot of tales about him. Then Jude said wonderingly
that, by the Jumping Jehosaphat, he did believe he had run
across him — and in Holden, Massachusetts. He told about
the boy, "poor widow's only support" (that was Shubael).
Such a simple, trusting boy, being bamboozled and cheated,
and so on, by a set of wicked drovers — this being fairly close
to fact. But a dark, limber-looking mysterious young fellow
sitting silent in a corner with his hat pulled down over his
eyes, like he didn't want to be recognized, had gone to the
kitchen and got dough. And gone to the pens and stuck as
many of the wicked man's pigs into the boy's pen as there was
enough dough to mark, and next moment he was gone — just
disappeared. The essence man swore to it nobody else but
Ruby Lambkin could of done such a thing. And we all got
pretty excited and stayed up a little late, and there was some
fine storytelling that night — first and last.

I was thankful Mitty wasn't there to hear him slinging the
truth around like it was of no more importance than a pair
of old galluses. Then too, I was a little fearful that it weren't
too safe for him to be thus deliberately confusing himself
with a well-known, wanted criminal. Already he was playing
with the idea Ruby was doing for him things he was too tame
to do. Things like that didn't make sense to me, and less
sense as the summer wore on.

Fifteen

THOSE NEW ENGLAND TOWNS we dawdled through all summer long, and come fall too, obviously belonged to the same family. Some were richer, some poorer, some a sight brighter than the next, some older and some too demmed young. But this is what, in a general way they were like.

Every proper town had a Main Street. Main Street had white picket fences, shade trees, nice-looking white houses. The minister, the doctor and the lawyer lived on Main Street, by and large. The big mansion was Old Squire's. High-stepping pair waiting at the side entrance. Finest elms in town. And a weeping willow. You could recognize Old Squire on sight. Plushy high hat. Long-tailed bottle-green coat. Gold-headed cane. He should have a red face and white hair to look right. Jude painted a lot of them, and their ladies too and litters of their children. Never heard of a "young squire." Nothing hereditary about the title. A man won it by time and wealth. And he should be public-spirited (having started banks, or feed companies or a turnpike, factory or some such thing) and be of a benevolent turn of mind. He wasn't always. But he was always rich. In general people tended to follow his superior wisdom, but if he forgot this here was a democracy, and if the two usually antagonistic lawyers got together, they might kick him around plenty — politically speaking. Nothing personal.

The general store was on Main Street. There was everything for sale there — from logging chains to fish hooks. Dress goods and brown hair pieces (called false fronts) ladies could pin to their caps when they started to gray off. Jude painted tons of them. There was everything from brass knobs for the horns of oxen to copper rings for the noses of bulls. Barrels of crackers and rum, molasses, pickled herring. Traps of all sorts, even bear traps up north and mousetraps everywhere. Mostly men wouldn't buy them. Look them over and go home and tinker up a better one — so they said. Those old stores certainly smelt fine of their patent medicines and liquor, the dye off cheap yard goods, cold grease from gun barrels, and of harness dressing and pickles, horehound and peppermint. Tobacco too, of course, and of the people gathered there, especially when they came in out of the wet and dried themselves before the stove.

It was either here or in the tavern barroom men liked to congregate, have "another one," talk, smoke, chew and spit. There was much horse sense in their talk, and terrible tall unlikely tales were told. Not much bad language, for at either place any moment a lady might drop in on them. Real low conversation was traditionally left for "out behind the barn." They did like to sharpen their wits up on each other — like who could tell the most unlikely story or exaggerate worse, usually for the fun of it, but sometimes I'm sorry to say for worldly gain. There wasn't as much betting as in the West — especially on cards — but I'm not sure but all that Yankee swapping wasn't as great an evil. They'd swap anything except their wives, and I've heard tell of that too —

When we got to a new town, I've said how I'd put up one of Jude's trade cards at the general store. Nothing immodest. Just that he had arrived and wished to serve the community. And I'd put up another card in the tavern barroom, where

about the same talk was going on as I have indicated at the
store, but often the men gathered there were a touch more
tony and less local. We saw a lot of the public houses
naturally and their barrooms, it being to our interest to get
acquainted.

If the tavern was on a stage route with a coach coming in
twice or thrice a week and sometimes a lot oftener it was like
this. First you'd hear — half a mile away it might be — far
away and lonely-like, the music of the horn. That meant the
stage had reached the top of Hog Back or Haystack, or was
coming through the Gap. In fifteen minutes it would arrive.
Then the hostler and his wretched small boy (maybe a
bonded boy) were getting out the fresh horses. The staging
companies set a store on the looks of their horses as well as
on the stamina and My, were they beauties! and landlord
yelling at his wife, or his mother or hired girl or maybe the
old pauper woman he'd got from the poorhouse to "Heat the
flip dogs," "Fetch up cold cider," "Spread the cloth," "Count
the spoons" — "Ding blast it, don't you go slicing the ham so
thick. Get the pudding out of its bag and don't spit on the
plates to polish them," and every moment the coach coming
in until at last the clapperty-clack of hooves, and the blowing
of the horses and the horn this time right beside you, fit to
wake the dead, and never so pretty as the first time you heard
it, still far off.

So the mail coming off and going on and tired horses off
and fresh horses in and lickerty-split and the coach was off
again. Seems it was a point of honor with those demon
drivers to give their passengers just time to order food but
never quite time to eat it.

On Main Street, too, was the Congregational Church, with
its icicle spire pointing up through the blue sky to Heaven.
Every town had one. As I said, we judged the possibilities of
a town somewhat by the size, repair, etc., of its church. Also
by the elegance of the gravestones about it.

Every town always had to have a millstream, just sufficient
water power to grind the meal and saw lumber for the local
people. Those old millwrights didn't upset things more than
a parcel of beavers. That was now changing. Now man was
taking and breaking the wild, free-running rivers of New
England, and a new sort of raw town was growing up about
these big heads of water. You could feel the change coming
in the towns, landscape and people. The salmon wouldn't go
spawning up the rivers any more. The alewives would be
leaving. As for railroads, they were in the egg as yet — so to
speak. You could hear a little tapping from the chick inside.
Most people like Jude and me didn't take them very seriously.
Yet most intelligent people did guess there was a change
coming and coming soon over New England — I mean
factories and such. Some were for change. Some against it
(we heard a lot of talk like that on our travels). Yankees don't
like to all think alike. Maybe they are a touch onery. It is
against their principles to go trotting down the same road —
even if that road led to heaven.

• • • • • • • • • • • • •

Sixteen

• • • • • • • • • • • • •

SOMETIMES we'd pick up trade off the road. If it were a big
house and a prosperous farm there was always hope for us.
But there was a lot of poor farmland in this corner of New
Hampshire, round about Mount Monadnock. The landscape

was pitching around all over the place, and so many boulders it takes a sharp-nosed cow to make a living. The people along some of those lonely roads had gone back to log cabins in their poverty. We saw great bunk and toggle fences made of tree trunks like I guess Yankees always have made in places where there's too much timber, and we saw bear and wolf skins nailed to barn doors. Of course such people had no five dollars to waste on a picture. Yet they, as much as anybody else, did need a new face to look at and a new thought — newer than when old Buttercup was going to calve — to think on.

That long box built on the rear end of the yellow chaise did suggest that we had goods to sell. What goods no one could guess without the asking. And so a woman (it was usually a woman) would hail us and come running up to inquire what we were selling. That woman we had met walking home from Norwich, Connecticut, had been the first I'd seen. The backwoods of New England was full of them.

First thing a woman like that would ask was, "Do you fix clocks?" Then the conversation would go something like this.

"You single man?"

"No. Married man."

"Where from?"

"Hampton."

"Hampton, New Hampshire, or Hampton, Vermont?"

"Hampton, Connecticut."

And her eyes would widen with wonder that actually she was standing there in the skinny road before her own house and talking with a "foreigner" from two states away.

"That your boy?"

"No."

"What is he?"

"Nephew."

"How long you been married?"

"Sixteen years," Jude would say, not too factually.

"Eh? Either you must of married real young or are terrible well preserved. How many children?"

"Two."

"Why only two? Wife weakly?"

"My wife is the biggest woman in Wyndham county. Tall as I am. Twice the girth. Twice my heft too."

And as her eyes measured and weighed him you could see the wonder grow.

"How tall are you?"

"Six-two."

"How much you weigh?"

"Don't know."

This is a fair sample of hundreds of conversations we had — us sitting in the chaise and the country woman standing by our step. It's typical too, because after about so much curiosity he'd begin (as he put it) to give the poor thing something to really think about. He was a little too generous along that line, it seems to me looking back.

To unpack our canvases and display them took a half an hour and it didn't pay when you could see what was really wanted was only conversation. It might go on like this.

"What's your trade?"

"Private."

"*Private?* Then what's that big box in back for, if not for goods? Are you in the doctoring line? For if so I've got a gathering . . . "

"No ma'am. It isn't with living flesh I'm occupying myself."

"Undertaker! That box is formed like a coffin . . . Anybody dead up along the road? Do you furnish the minister too?"

"Not exactly. But you're getting warmer." Then he'd give her a glittery, leery look, drop his voice and croak, "Madam, do you know any good green graves hereabouts?" And lean and whisper in her ear, "Any information you give me will remain secret, and there'll be fifteen cents in it for you."

Then she, turning white to the gills, frozen to the roadway, gasped out the terrible word, "Body snatcher." For there was nothing country people feared more than body snatchers who were said to dig up fresh corpses and sell them to the anatomy schools.

I remember a conversation something like this, and that we had been rounding Grand Monadnock and he lying there like a blue lion, it seemed for hours. The top of it was bare stone which gave the sunlight a marvelous surface to play on. A pretty well aged farmer we gave a lift to told us some fifteen years back the people of Dublin and Jaffrey had got together and burned all the vegetation off the top to "roast out the wolves" that had been "nesting" there. This locality, I might point out, was a sight wilder than a hundred or so miles north where the land lay good and easy for farming. In other words, it was the geography of the place, not the latitude, made it so wild yet.

Soon we were hauling up what felt more like a dried river bed than a road, into Dublin. The road was blocked by a funeral in full blast. People had tied their vehicles so carelessly by the entrance to the graveyard we had to just take off our hats and wait.

Standing by an open grave under the great singing pine trees (and the blue lake beyond) we saw the widow, black crape all over her, and the head sexton rattling the gravel on the coffin and the stern word of committal from the clergyman. There was a sweet smell of pine needles and a smell of lake water. It was a pleasant spot.

We gave a stout man, all stomach and a game leg, a ride back to town which wasn't more than a quarter mile off. Mr. Fanin (that was his name) hung his game leg out the chaise and placed his inordinate belly about where I was used to sitting. I was miserably crowded up.

Seems we had been seeing the last of one Captain Dolliver,

who was leaving his widow well-fixed and about to serve up at her house funeral meats such as Dublin had rarely seen, and "everybody" — including us — was invited.

Jude's ears pricked. I told you he had a couple of sea captains left over from the year-before trip down Cape Cod.

"Military or oceanic captain?"

"Oceanic."

So Jude said he was a limner by trade and naturally wanted to sell his goods. Was it likely Mrs. Dolliver might wish a nice representation of the deceased?

Mr. Fanin spit and he gave us a cute look, meaning she was well rid of him. All he said was that nobody would dig him up again for Mr. Rebough to look at — they having just got that skunk planted.

We were on Dublin main street. You could tell which house it was, celebrating (I'm sorry to say) the funeral. It was commodious and yellow with black crape tied to the doorknob and likewise black crape on the beehives. Lots of people believed if you didn't "tell the bees" of a death in the family the little rascals got mad and left.

Jude told Mr. Fanin he could do a likeness of a dead man — without disturbing any grave. All he needed to go by was a crayon drawing or even a silhouette cutout, and someone to inform him of the deceased's coloring and, perhaps, expression.

So we entered in and feasted. As Mrs. Dolliver seemed real reconciled Jude taxed her with his proposition right away.

We stayed with Mrs. Dolliver around ten days, so I'll begin with her. She was "fresh-colored." In other words, if you had boiled a ham with a parcel of beet roots in the pot you'd of just about got it. She was stout and solid. I know she wore corsets, for the creaking of them announced her comings-in and her settings-down. From looking at her you couldn't place the spot where she wore them — she being the same size from top to bottom, neither going in nor out anywhere.

Nature had formed her to be a single woman, of the sort that most New England towns have one of. I mean the active kind that run the town poor, schools, and the selectmen, and the church — everything about the church from the minister's wife's bonnet and his creed to the church sociables.

I guess she hadn't been so bossy-like when, say, she was fourteen or so, for the little boy that had the desk next her in the red schoolhouse remembered her for some fifty years. So she must of been a smart, pretty, taking little girl. He having made his fortune and thinking to retire back to his birthplace (Dublin), it was agreed by letter that at this late day, and both their characters set like cement, they should marry. Captain Dolliver had been a clipper-ship master out of Boston and he'd grown morose and hard (as well as rich). Nobody had begged to disagree with him for years. You know how men like that get as they get older. So the irresistible body met the immovable force.

So he was dead but not lamented. And I suppose he was a real mean old codger. Nobody felt they were going to miss him.

When his widow began thinking of a nice portrait of him, blue coat and buttons, spyglass and the sea, her pride was aroused. New-made widows sometimes ask unattached female friends and relatives to visit them for a spell. It helps them through the first loneliness. But Mrs. Dolliver's friends had obviously come to enjoy themselves, and they certainly did. So then, five middling or aging women, all pleasant women thoroughly happy to be together and having a good gossip, and Jude and me. For Mrs. Dolliver had agreed to the picture.

They made quite a pet of me, although never seeming to take in the fact I was thirteen and didn't want to make rat-tails on a spool — things like that. And of Jude likewise. He was ever so ingratiating and telling them stories of his travels, such as never were on land nor sea, and jumping up and offering chairs in a way that would of amazed Mitty. I guess Jude, like lots of other men of artistic turn of mind, liked women, and when I say women I don't mean just young girls either. They'd draw their chairs up in a circle around where he'd place his easel, with the headless portrait on it, and they'd rock and talk and fan themselves with their palm-leaf fans (we hit a hot spell) and egg him on to tell more stories and admire him in a way that would have made Mitty about sick. And how they could laugh!

It proved there was but one likeness of the Captain for Jude to make a start with. This was a black silhouette — profile, of course. Jude's sea captains had been painted both of them full face, and he was in a quandary how to attach a profile face to those straight-ahead shoulders.

The ladies, sitting there rocking and gabbling, saw no difficulty. All of them were ready to help him on Captain's coloring, paler than you'd expect for his trade, and his expression — sourish. Jude would try and try to do it and rub off his efforts, wipe the sweat from his brow and, as Mrs. Dolliver would come creaking in with raspberry shrub and sponge drops, he'd flop into a chair and tell them a story. I remember one he told which gave general satisfaction, I suppose partly because it suggested women are smarter than men, and pointed out the fact sea captains can be mean.

"Speaking of retired sea captains being a little close, Mrs. Dolliver, like we've been doing. Ever hear of the captain down Truro way (I was painting on Cape Cod last summer and learned a lot of interesting and inspiring facts.) A Captain Jonathan Pettigrew? Maybe an acquaintance of Captain Dolliver?"

"No. Captain sailed out of Boston mostly. Weren't acquainted with this Captain Pettigrew — far's I know."

"He was a pretty smart man. Some might say too smart — leastways for his soul's good, not for his worldly estate. Best-**off man** in Truro when he decided to retire. He'd been left a widower some eighteen or twenty years back, and now he was going to beach himself for good, he felt he needed a new partner. So he decided to have a competition among all the unattached females of that end of the Cape (and that's the far end, by the way — halfway to Portugal) and find out which one among them was the most suitable to him personally.

"I told you, didn't I, that this here Captain Pettigrew was a touch nigh? He had always fancied clams to eat. Cost nothing but the sweat to dig them and he, being a deep-sea man, never had his fill of them. So he invited young ladies and old ladies — all the unattached females, the whole boiling of them — to a clambake."

"Never ate a clam in my life. Not sure I want to."

"Now, it takes three things to make a clambake. Clams, as stands to reason. Seaweed and driftwood. Salt and butter to dip them in. He got forty or fifty of these ladies together, for being a seafaring community the death rate among men is mighty tragic. They all came chattering and protesting, like ladies will, how they all just adored clams, although in those parts you can have them for the digging. Cost nothing. But half of them came dressed in their best Sunday-go-to-Meeting clothes — furbelows, posy-bonnets and such, hoping to catch his eye. They caught it all right, and he crossed them off as too extravagant, wearing good clothes to a clambake. Half of those left, he noticed (for he let them do all the work), were wasteful of driftwood, or spilt butter. He threw them out after the dressy ones. That left only six in the running. Of those six, five ate more clams than he thought they needed to nourish them. The word had gone around that the lady likely to get the prize in this contest would be the one who showed the greatest prediliction for the Captain's favorite diet. One ate so many she swore next low tide she was going to bury herself in the sand and wait for high to come in and cover her. Then too, it ain't real pretty watching women shuck clams, dip them in butter, suck them up and spit out the sand. But he noticed one sort of plain, nice, fearfully modest piece didn't touch one."

"Now if that were the only refreshment served . . . "

"Captain Pettigrew wondered too. So he got up off the sand dune he'd been sort of lolling on all this time, saying nothing but keeping his eyes peeled — and asked her. Seems how she couldn't keep clams down."

"Shouldn't think how anyone could. They sound like worms to me."

"Then he knew she was the wife for him. Cost almost nothing to feed, as long as they had clams three times a day. So they were married. She'd sit there eating nothing but tea, maybe, and a morsel of bread, hoping he'd tire of clams. After six or eight months he did, a little, for he began putting condiments on them to vary the taste. He could eat a bushel of them raw and still breathing, if he put condiments on them. Well, nobody had ever given her credit for much gumption. But she had it. She went to the apothecary and she bought ipecac. Small bottle. She sloshed it up with his condiments that already tasted so fearsome he never noticed one taste more. Well, ladies, after that he didn't want no more clams. And, moreover, it sort of touched even his hard heart that his wife couldn't keep them down either, now they were in the same boat. As salt cod weren't costly he tried that. But when she had had enough of that, you've guessed what she did? Talk of gumption, she had it. The end was that at this present day she sets the finest table on the Cape. Some folks say there is more than one way to skin a cat, and I guess there's more than one way to manage a husband. That's one of them."

Then they agreed that was a mighty refreshing story with a real happy ending. And they did like happy endings.

I give this as a sample as to how pleasant we passed our time, with the ladies creaking their rockers and their corsets, fanning themselves, and hovering about us.

. . . .

Seventeen

. . . .

B︎UT TALK wasn't painting the picture. He had painted out the lighthouse and substituted Boston's golden dome — that being Captain's home port. Mrs. Dolliver had wanted that. Then at last he took a deep breath, shut his eyes, and did it — somehow, although he knew he had to break the Captain's neck. This disturbed him, but not the ladies. They thought he had the spittingest image of the man and, when he apologized for the neck, one of them said, "Looks like he had been hanged, as he ought to of been, and just cut down. I call your work most gratifying."

While Jude had been shilly-shallying over getting this puzzling picture done he had sold five or six of his paintings to customers, largely rounded up by Mrs. Dolliver. In appreciation of this, and the high living we had been enjoying for over a week scot-free, he told Mrs. Dolliver she was to select any body and background she wished. He'd put her in for nothing. And he told me to go to the chaise and bring in more and more, so she might have what she most wished.

She wanted to be done profile too, so the portraits of him and her would make a nice pair. There was only one picture in the whole collection which called for a profile view of the sitter. And, by now, she knew how hard it was to fit side views on top of front views.

She chose the young girl I spoke of earlier, sitting (seemingly) on the ground, turning her head to admire a bush full of birds.

With all the confidence of a good Christian looking forward to Heaven, I'd been looking forward to actually seeing the girl my imagination had concocted for the blank space Jude had left on that canvas. I had actually "seen" the tilt of her short nose, the chin held just so, the childish little neck. I had known that she existed and was waiting for me. But of course I didn't peep.

Jude wasn't bothered any.

"If it isn't asking too much," Mrs. Dolliver was saying, beginning to rock that solid one hundred and sixty pounds of flesh so her chair creaked, and her corsets, "would you mind putting me in my best black satin? Seeing my age, and the fact I am a widow, that wispy white muslin thing don't seem quite proper."

He did. And he added ten pounds and twenty, over forty I guess, to the slim, girlish figure — just as she had been doing since the days Captain Dolliver had sat next her in school. Of course no stout, elderly New England woman would have been found dead sitting on the ground in her best black. He indicated a chairback for her.

She was very proud of her nice flock of white chickens. He asked her, should he paint out the singing birds and put in chickens? He wasn't to bother. She "didn't mind" wild birds, although she had always thought them a nuisance — stealing strawberries and pecking cherries, and so on.

Well, in the end they did make a pair of them, hanging there over the best parlor mantel. The Captain, just cut from the gallows, and his wife with her double chins and homely, decent, beefy face turned to admire pretty singing birds she never in her life had raised her eyes to see nor opened her heart and ears to hear. She didn't even know what they ate, by and large.

Naturally we had some sorrows and disappointments, as well as pleasures on our trip. But this to me was the worst one. It was as if actually a girl who had existed, and had been waiting for me, had been obliterated. Worst of it was, maybe if I had found her, time would of done to her just what Jude had done to the little young thing I had fancied up in my mind's eye. I guess it was the first time I was aware how pretty, delicate-looking young girls do become commonplace, workaday old women. There was a horrible truth revealed to me at the time I have never forgotten.

Then I got to pondering on Captain Dolliver. What had he been like back in the red-schoolhouse days? Bright as buttons he must have been, ambitious, bold and lively. And he ending up like Jude had pictured him, and perhaps sometime someone would be making up a story to explain whatfor he was hanged —

· · · · · · · · · · · · · ·

Eighteen

· · · · · · · · · · · · · ·

IT WAS PRETTY all the way from where we were (Dublin) to where we were going for (Hancock), and it was a rough, twisty road with pines, maples and great grandpa paper birches — we don't have them at home — touching over our heads. So we sort of cork-screwed most of the way through a tunnel of green. There were boulders flung all over the place, in the grassy, rutted roadway even. Yet now and then we went through pasture land and ploughed land and saw a few houses. As we came close to Hancock the farming was good.

We knew just where we were going and what doing. Four years back Jude had painted "acres" of wall painting at the Hancock House which looked like French wallpaper, but was of course cheaper. Winter before, the Fire Society's buckets had drenched down the walls. The fire wasn't nothing, but the water damage considerable. Mr. Billington, proprietor of the place, hearing Jude was again near by, had sent word to him to come over and fix them up. Jude promised me some more high living and that we'd be leaving Hancock as fat as a couple of settled ministers. Fact is, we were both born to be skinny fellows.

On that earlier trip Jude had likewise done a number of portraits. One, in particular, he would like to see again and have me see. None of his prepared backgrounds had seemed suitable to him and this woman he had done from scratch, very plain and very simple. It was of the young wife (third, he believed) of an elderly, but real beguiling little minister. Her name was Evelina.

We pulled up the last steep hill into town and there was the fine, frosty-white Congregational Church, first thing we saw, and the white parsonage beside it. And behind them was a beautifully serene lake called Norway Pond. We turned right and were on Main Street. Hancock has style to it. Bright white houses, neat as pins. Red brick ones, even neater. Great elms clasping hands, so to speak, overhead.

We soon learned from Mr. Billington, keeper of the Hancock House, that Evelina had passed on two years back. When Jude said how come? he compressed his lips and said he wasn't a gossip. When Jude asked how poor Reverend Dr. Perch was sustaining this loss of his young wife Mr. Billington snorted, "Nobly. Marrying again, any time now, and even younger this time." When Jude said, as country people did then, that we "wanted to know," Mr. Billington said he would know fast enough, for Dr. Perch had especially asked him to ask Jude to drop in and talk business as soon as he arrived.

We found Dr. Perch next morning out tinkering at his front gate. He had on an old-fashioned clerical wig (askew) and through it his face sailed like a new moon in clouds. Likewise he wore the silk stockings and black clericals of his calling, but had put on top them one of those heavy blue and white striped aprons, all over pockets, workmen sometimes wear to keep their tools and oil cans in and protect their pants. For he was first of all an ingenious man. Secondly, I guess, a marrying man. And third, only, a clergyman.

Immediately he began explaining to us what he was up to, with all these wires, pulleys, springs, screw-eyes and bells about him, down at his front gate. He was working on the Perch Automatic Gate Opener (patent applied for).

He said, "Daughter Gussie isn't as young as she once was," pitying her old age but not sharing it. "On rising, her legs sometimes remain swollen for hours. She feels safer with the front gate locked, and it is too much for her to come out and open it in person. With this arrangement perfected she can glance out a window, see who's come, and snap it open with no leg work at all on her part. I try to think up little ways to save her steps, for she's been a good daughter to me."

He was taking off his dirty workman's apron, wiping his hands on a rag, asking us in to talk business, cheer up Daughter who was in the dumps, and have a glass of sherry.

Inside the front door, crouching like a bug, was a contraption of iron and leather.

"There," says he, wriggling like a child or a dog with pleasure. "You give a guess, Mr. Rebough."

"Automatic unwanted-guest ejector?"

"No. That's a dog-barker."

"A *what* is it?"

"Perch's Patented Automatic Dog-barker. I intend to put

it on the market. Lots of aging females, like Daughter, can't abide a dog. Hairs on furniture. Bother to feed them. Fleas, rabies and such. Bark at the wrong things and not at the right. Just around Hancock I know several timid females living alone, or like Daughter, often left alone nights (for I do like to go to a convention or a convocation now and then). Now, suppose a woman like that hears a night prowler, or thinks she does, for women that age are always hearing prowlers. All she does is step on a pedal by her bedside. That wire goes from there to here. Then this bellows begins to bark. I got the old pair when the church organ was repaired. All is in working order — except one thing."

"What's that, Dr. Perch?"

"It doesn't sound like a dog."

He sounded it.

"Prowlers might think it a lion," Jude said, to encourage him.

"No. As of today it sounds like a demmed opening hymn. But I'll fix it. Just you give me time."

Instead of stopping us in one of the two big company rooms, very genteel rooms, he walked us straight through the house to the kitchen, for he wished to show us some more of his household contrivances. And there we sort of caught his daughter, Miss Augusta, off guard. And in the dumps for certain. She was sitting at the kitchen table, and the sink was full of dirty dishes, although it was no earlier than eleven o'clock. That kitchen was so webbed up with wires, overhead and underfoot, she looked like either a spider or a fly — I never did figure which.

But she got to her feet on seeing Jude, brushing back her iron-gray hair from her unusually fine forehead as she did. She must have been handsome once (and with sleep and no worries might be again) but, as she was that moment, her face looked like it had worn out two bodies. And she was pale as dishwater. You couldn't believe any woman could look so stately and unabashed when company came and caught her sitting idle in such a messy kitchen. Nothing abashed her much, I guess, for she was pretty high in the instep. Her worn face brightened as she said she was glad to see Jude again. And he her. He had liked her, but the only reason he ever gave me was the fine shape of her skull.

Dr. Perch trotted off to fetch the sherry and glasses.

"Yesterday," she said, "Papa got his apple parer down from the garret and put it in the sink, although I told him we'd have no apples to pare for months yet. And I was trying to figure out how ever I could get those dishes done." She did apologize that much.

"But you always had a hired girl, Miss Gussie."

She never batted an eyelash. "When Father decided to marry the last one I had, I thought it more decent for her to go back to her own parents — until after the nuptials. Considering the difference in age, education, social position, I can say I hope forever."

He back, we drank the sherry and he indicated his potato washer.

Miss Gussie said it took one hand to turn the crank, one to insert the potatoes in the slot, and a third to release the water. And besides (this being only an experiment), Papa had used his old blacking brushes for it, so the potatoes all had to be washed by hand afterwards.

"Daughter has no feeling for machinery or the machine age just around the corner. Now we had a young person . . . a . . . to be specific, a Miss Matilda Povey, helping out in the kitchen until recently, who had a genuine talent for using the equipment I believe I have a talent for thinking up."

"Tilly," said Miss Gussie, "is a hypocrite."

Jude hadn't mentioned Evelina. The old gentleman certainly lived in the present and the future and it would have seemed unkind to pull him back into a consideration of his last wife. He had an off-with-the-old, on-with-the-new temperament and it certainly had kept him from aging up to his years, which were, by the way, eighty and over. Then too, by now we knew that Evelina had drowned herself although the coroner's jury had been so obliging as to bring in a verdict of death by accidental sleepwalking. On leaving, Dr. Perch stood a moment with us down to that gate he was rigging. He was putting back on again his workman's apron as he talked. He asked Jude to "switch faces" on that portrait he had done for him, last time he was here, of his dead wife. He never did mention Evelina by name — not once.

Jude suggested leaving what he had done before alone. As I said, he loved that picture. Let — Miss Povey was the name, was it? — select from some of those fine new ones he had with him. Eddy would fetch over some and she might select. Dr. Perch said no. After all, he had paid for a body and background and it had given complete satisfaction. All he wanted was a new face on it, which couldn't cost him more than a dollar. "Five," said Jude, for he was irked. Well, then, *five*. Fact was, Miss Povey had just set her heart on seeing her own face in that one particular spot. Nothing else would suit her and, as soon as he had heard Mr. Rebough was about, he had promised her. Jude said he'd think. You knew he wanted to think up a good reason why not.

That work on repairing the wall painting Jude and I both worked on. It was so simple he felt he could trust me. I remember we put in foliage with a sponge. Every day Dr. Perch would come and stand at the foot of the stepladders we were on and ask most modestly if Mr. Rebough couldn't get around to him a little faster. You could feel Tilly was pushing at him. He mentioned her name frequently but, as I said, never once Evelina.

Jude did consent to come over, look at the portrait and consider the proposition. I guess he was half hoping that it wasn't as nice as he remembered it and that he wouldn't feel too bad about ruining it. But it really was a beauty, and so

was she. Jude said on seeing her he had felt none of his prepared pictures were right — too fancy, or something. He had
taken her outdoors and sat her under an old apple tree. That
came in from the right side, and he had it all over tiny green
apples. And beyond that there was nothing but the blue of
Norway Pond behind her and a vast deal of sky. There was
more lavender in the sky, and shadows, than you might have
expected and he had given her a lavender dress. Likewise, she
did have lavenderish about her eyes.

Jude had told me that Evelina had been "plain." He
meant undecorated. Her pale hair was straight and pulled
back plain. Her lips didn't curve any. She didn't have
noticeable eyebrows to distract from the purity of the model-
ing, nor did she have what's called a handsome color. But
Evelina's plainness made your average pretty woman look too
fussed up with cupid's bows and spit curls, dimples and stuck-
on-looking eyelashes. She had dark-for-blue eyes, set a little
too close together. A look too intense for comfort.

I remember hearing that she was around middle thirties
when she died, but as Jude painted her, she looked no more
than twenty. This was partly the way he worked, not shading
and shadowing things as school-taught painters were doing
by then. He couldn't suggest age much except by actually
drawing lines in, and this had a way of making a middle-
young sitter like Evelina look terribly old. So he left all that
out. There was sweetness in the face but a touch stern too,
like a virgin martyr. Perhaps she was one of those people
never do grow up and so her face had never lost its youthfulness. She and all those little green apples did go together —
somehow.

If she had been a sensible grown-up woman she never
would have married a man old enough to be her father, in the
first place, and if she had, she wouldn't have fallen so crazy
in love with a divinity student ten years younger than herself.

Miss Augusta had been the one to show us the picture, and

tell us of her. Dr. Perch had sort of slunk off. The portrait had been up-garret ever since Evelina died. She told us her father hadn't been able to bear the sight of it.

"Can't your father forgive her?"

"Worse than that. He can't bear to think back to her." The divinity student was "the meachingest broken reed" she'd ever seen. When her father was off on his junketings this young man used to supply for him, and what Evelina saw in him she couldn't figure. But she saw a lot more than she, for one, guessed there was.

"Could of run off," Jude suggested.

But Evelina couldn't. Not that sort. And at least she was spared the sin of "falling," so I guess she was as pure as the delicate oval of her face.

"Father was a fool," she blazed out suddenly, "to marry her (and she him) and now he's doing it again — only ten times worse. There will be another tragedy. Mark my words. Then, too, his congregation are up in arms. The ladies of his society won't ever accept Tilly Povey as minister's wife. It will lose him his church and that would break his heart. Old hearts are brittle. Mr. Rebough, I'm at my wits end. I was praying to God for light that morning when I looked up and saw you and Eddy coming into the kitchen, and I can't sleep nights."

It ended up with Jude promising her that, soon as we were done at Hancock House, we'd move in here for a space of time. She was heart-set on it.

. . . .

Nineteen

. . . .

N<small>ATURALLY</small> there was talk about the town that Evelina "walked." She was the sort that would, and suicides rest in no easy graves. We heard plenty about the sight of her coming up out of the vapor above Norway Pond and floating along through the moonlight to peer in the windows of the parsonage. However it wasn't her ghostly appearance that bothered us, when we had kept our promise and moved in over there, but the flesh-and-blood appearances of Miss Povey. She was trying to seduce Jude by her charms to do her in where Evelina's face had been.

Now, for what she looked like. She was red-cheeked and darkish, and must of put up her dark corkscrew curls in paper every night. She had wet-looking black eyes — popped some, but pretty. A touch pop-toothed too. Soft little no-chin with a double one under. Creases around her neck which Dr. Perch called "rings of Venus." She was plump as a little pig, active as sin, awkward as a calf, and not much more legs on her than a pigeon.

She was scared to death of Miss Gussie and that made her spiteful and saucy to her, and I guess she looked forward to having the upper hand over her, for any wife in any household would take precedence over an unmarried daughter. By nature she was as cheeky as a man on the town. Indeed, she showed no reverence even to Dr. Perch, treating him, I guess, about as she treated the rest of the "boys." He liked that. It made him feel young, and he didn't mind that she was fresh as green paint to Jude. All he did was marvel at his darling's high spirits. I don't think he had a jealous bone in his body.

Now that she was coming in all the time to sit and let Jude draw her in his sketchbook — he flattered her by telling her that he was studying her — we saw a lot of her. She never lifted a hand to help her future stepdaughter in the housework. In fact, Miss Gussie stayed in the kitchen mostly, which was really where Tilly belonged, and Tilly expanded herself in the company rooms, where she never did look quite right.

When Dr. Perch and Tilly were both out Jude often sat with Miss Gussie. They were trying to figure out, somehow, to stop this thing. She'd wonder if Tilly couldn't be scared off by playing up Evelina's ghost? That lavender dress was still up in her room. It would about fit me, and . . . No, Jude said, that trick was old-hat. And he had never heard of it working, except on drunkards. She thought it might work on Tilly if he would discolor my face with his paints, and she explained why.

Two years back, when Evelina was found missing and the empty dory out on Norway Pond was noted, two and two were put together. Half the town thought it would be more dignified to wait out the nine days it takes for the drowned to rise up by themselves. Other half were for immediate efforts. They won.

It had been ever so pretty a day in late June, like now. There were men out in boats with poles and grappling irons. Most of the women and children stood along the banks to watch. But Tilly Povey, being that fond of gentlemen's company she'd even go out coon hunting with them, was in one of those boats.

It took hours. Then the body came up, shooting straight

up like it had been standing there on the bottom all the time and had just heard the trump of doom. One eye, right eye, had been destroyed by one of those poles. The face had blackened, either with the choking natural to the process of drowning or by staying down too long, or it had been bruised by a pole — although you can't bruise the dead.

Anyway, it rose straight as an arrow, right beside the boat Tilly was in, and flung the girl into a conniption fit. Miss Gussie, who had not had the heart to be out there staring and had been sitting here quietly in the kitchen, had heard her screams. Wouldn't you think Tilly would remember this gruesome experience and concede the fact Evelina had killed herself for not much more reason than having married a too old man? That should be a lesson to Tilly, who was a deal sight younger than Evelina even, and Papa older every day.

Jude had sworn to me he was not going to paint out Evelina, but soon he was doing it. He put a square of varnish over the head, for that was all he was going to alter. Tilly wanted to sit there forever in her old mistress's best muslin dress and, incidentally, considerably slenderer body. Jude offered to change the one and plump out the other. She wouldn't have it.

Tilly was a bad sitter, for she was always jumping off her chair and running to see what he was doing. He scared her quiet by acting like magicians act when they are going to fry eggs in gentlemen's high hats or pull rabbits out of your ears. She was so ignorant she did look at his art almost as a black art. When he'd pretend to go off in a trance she was so scared she hardly breathed and she did stop flirting with him, which honestly had made him nervous.

He took a time when Dr. Perch had taken the stage to Concord to see a bellows maker and to be gone three days; then he did what he did.

"Don't talk to me, Miss Tilly," he'd say, "for I can feel it coming like a dream."

"Nightmare?" she quipped.

"No man knoweth the future," he said, solemn as an owl and gesturing to me what brush he wanted.

We were silent, and then, "I'm having trouble with that right eye. I don't want to go scaring you but, if you ever have eye trouble, I'm betting on the right one."

She was white and staring, remembering, I guess, that terrible sight she had seen two years back.

"Miss Tilly, did you wet your curls this morning?"

"Shouldn't pry into a lady's beauty secrets," she sniffed. "But with me, the fact is, no water, no curls."

"Too much water, then. Too much water uncurls curls, doesn't it? I don't seem able to twist them up right. And what's happening to your color?" It was fading before our eyes.

All this time he was working fast and sure, doing just what he wanted. At last he tossed aside his palette for me to clean up, put a hand to his forehead in an exaggerated way, and gestured to her she was to look. I saw it too.

Tilly's head, dead and blackened. Her hair stringy wet. Right eye gone. Face like a decayed fish. Mouth gaping — and yet it was Tilly.

Miss Gussie, sitting in her kitchen back of the house among all those wires like a spider or a fly, heard her screaming, just as she had heard her two years back. She went at the fainting girl with a pail of water, applying it with some considerable relish.

Jude stood back to, to this touching scene, wetting a cloth in turpentine, wiping off all he had done, right back to Evelina.

We didn't wait for Dr. Perch's return, nor did Tilly. Next day we packed up and headed out for Hillsboro on the Concord road. First we stopped to say goodbye to Mr. Billington. He told us Tilly Povey had taken the early morning coach for Boston (the coach left from his house). She seemed a little distracted but had all her belongings with her. She was so set upon not losing any of them she'd say, over and over to herself, "Big box, little box, hatbox and bag." Still when the coach came in and the driver offered her a seat beside him, as they do offer pretty girls in nice weather, she perked right up and leaped for his little ladder, all ready to begin her flamigigs on him.

Jude never did get one cent for what he had done for Dr. Perch and Miss Gussie, and I guess for Tilly too, and for the First Congregational Church likewise. But he had made a good haul, first and last, on this his second trip to Hancock, and many friends. And I guess we had done more good than harm.

. . . .

Twenty

. . . .

I HOPE I HAVE INDICATED with what respect Mr. Rebough was treated by the cream of society at both Dublin and Hancock. Nobody had thought of him primarily as Mitty Pratt's husband, and he no more than a shiftless peddling fellow. In response he had behaved with an air that his home town couldn't have believed possible. As I see it, this is one of the advantages of leaving home. You are not hampered any by anyone's idea of you.

It took us two weeks to get to Concord, for Jude stopped at Hillsboro, Hopkinton and related spots to do up a picture here and another there. It was a high rolling country, pretty well settled and well watered.

He had never been to Concord, a large place and capital of the state of New Hampshire. I think he had hopes of doing a good business there, at least if no other limner had been by recently and skimmed the cream. We were in Hillsboro when he read in a Concord newspaper that which dampened him. It went something like this.

H. H. Hooper, Portrait Painter of Boston
Has set up a studio opposite the Central Building
Concord, New Hampshire
For weeks or months, depending upon
The wishes of his patrons.
The public is invited to call and view
Specimens of his art
Including a likeness of
HIS EXCELLENCY THE GOVERNOR

Under the threat of such distinguished competition Jude was about ready to by-pass the place. But he had written Mitty to write him there — had told her he'd be there over the Fourth of July. So it was decided we'd go there, perhaps only for the day, pick up her letter and see how lavishly the holiday was kept at a state capital compared, say, to a little place like Hampton. Also he wished to spy out the land. I mean see just what Mr. Hooper was up to.

Everybody, and I mean almost exactly that, had the same idea of getting to Concord for the Fourth. We didn't call it the Fourth then but "Independence Day," and it always seemed to me after the name was changed it never was so good. Lots of people had crowded into Concord the day before, when the celebration had opened with a ball given by the Governor for the gentility. Most of the people we saw on that hot, dusty road were like us, planning to go in and out again same day. There were two-horse wagonloads of brown, homespun boys and pretty girls in sunbonnets, a farm cart full of family, everything from grandparents to babies. Chaises and gigs and high-stepping pairs. Some came on horseback, or ride-and-tie. A lot on foot. There was plenty of conversation and good feeling on the road that morning, in spite of dust, heat and the beginning of drought. I remember a farmer said he was confident there would be enough cannons, oratory and fireworks and brass bands going off, to shake down the rain which was needed.

Although it was imperative, if we were not to miss the exercises, to get into town by nine, two miles before we got there Jude decided to leave Goldie with a farmer, for, as he judged it, Concord was going to be so jammed up with people a vehicle would be a nuisance. Likewise, every thief and pickpocket would converge upon the capital for the day, and a rig tied up, say, on a shady side street might very well get broken into. We told the farmer we'd probably be back that night and he agreed if we were to sleep us, and anyway to care for the horse until we did get back. Then, it was so hot and going to be hotter, we redressed ourselves there in the barn, putting on the thinnest clothes we had and the least the law would allow. For instance, Jude had no proper neckcloth on. We tied up in two bundle-kerchiefs the few prerequisites for a night or two. These bundles we carried on the end of two poles we cut, like flags, as workmen looking for hire carry their possessions. I'm sure if Jude hadn't been dressed like that he wouldn't have carried on as he did in Concord but, as I see it now, he was discouraged about his prospects there (on which he had counted much) and was in a to-hell-with-it-mood before we got there. He'd said he'd get Mitty's letter, show me the sights and get out.

It was one of his limitations that he had no taste for oratory. I myself have always enjoyed it, especially since I have so often been called upon to orate. And the fact is, when we did get to the mob-packed square in front of the State House where the exercises were being held they were half over and we couldn't get within earshot, but even so, I was speechless with admiration at all the red, white and blue bunting, and flags over the front of the building, and the grandstand put up for the speakers.

The Governor gave the principal address, with extremely appropriate gestures which I have sometimes used myself, although what he was saying I couldn't hear. We could hear the full brass band all right, and the militia men doing evolutions and firing off four-pounders, and the hurrahing that went up from his constituents (he was up for re-election), and the catcalls of his opponents. We were by then swimming in our own sweat and, what was worse, in the sweat of everybody pressed against us, for we were all melting together like a box of candles left in the sun. So Jude was for backing out. We went first to the Eagle House where Mitty had written him, took a moment sitting on a curbstone in front of a nice house on Main Street to read her news and then, by the hubbub and clapping, we guessed the exercises were over up at the State House.

Not until they were might the peddlers begin to peddle, nor the showmen (down along the river) begin to show, nor saloons and bars dispense liquor. So all these people we had seen weaving must have brought their own. We bought us birch beer and gingerbread and hunks of molasses candy as soon as the selling of such was authorized. Jude was in a rambling, offish mood. He didn't inquire where the Central Building might be, or try to inform himself as to Mr. Hooper's successes. All he wished was to listen to the peddler's "speels."

I remember one comical fellow who, for a change, was running down everything he offered for sale. This he did with such exaggeration and good humor he attracted quite a crowd about the box he was standing on, and they were buying from him.

He had on a dirty felt hat, broad as a Quaker's and stuck all over with cheap pinchbeck pins, necklaces, earrings, lockets and rings.

He'd take it off, pick off one after another of his treasures, and go on like this, "Fine gold jewelry, guaranteed non-genuine. Ladies wearing these charming objects will run no risk of being murdered for their jewels." Or, when showing knives and somebody asked him if they were steel knives, he'd swear there was "some steal in them, for the sheriff is after me." Or, his tinselly hat back on his head, he would hang himself with bright printed cotton goods. "Lady, were you asking if these colors are fast? If you put them in hot water you'll be surprised at how fast they run." There was something so appealing to Jude's irresponsible nature in such monkeying, I think we stood there best part of an hour.

Next he found a friend among them, a traveling lady who cut silhouettes. Jude said she was the only female he knew who consistently followed the road. She wasn't at all rough-looking. In fact, her being in a semi-respectable trade had increased, rather than decreased, her respectability. She was no spring chicken, but youngish yet. She went everywhere on foot, carrying her pack like a man. As her trade wasn't good Jude and I both sat to have our faces cut so as to start things rolling for her. This not producing results, Jude offered to "bark" for her. And there he stood, no hat on him and no collar, claiming she was the greatest living practitioner of her craft and that she was fresh arrived from Italy, and so on. Then people began to step up. A few little incidents like that makes me realize he weren't so far above other peddlers in his notions as I like to think.

Next we went down to the river.

There was a roped-in platform and a sporty gentleman shooting his cuffs and yelling at the shy-looking, big country boys gathered around him that any of them that could throw the "Champeen" was to have a dollar. And in the corner was a man with little more on him than a towel, looking as big as behemoth, and no brighter.

And a pavilion with fiddlers and dancing.

We came to a great canvas fence set up around the circus caravan. We paid the price and went in. There were trick horses and trick riders, poodles jumping through hoops of flame, and six women, gauzy-dressed like houris, entered riding on an elephant. Everybody sees his first circus sometime. This was mine.

But I remember the sideshows best. Each cost a nickel extra. Jude left me, for it seems the summer before (down on Cape Cod) he had run across this same caravan, which boasted it was the biggest on earth, and he had painted pictures on their wagons for them. I think he had his mind on doing a few more for them. Last summer he had traveled with the caravan for two weeks as he painted, and he had friends among them.

He warned me not to waste money on seeing the lion, for he was moth-eaten, sick, elderly and not worth a nickel.

I saw the girl with no bones, a tattooed albino lady, a fat lady, a giant, a blue man and a dwarf. And a hyena, a leopard and a panther in one cage. Two white bears in another, suffering horribly from the heat. And the smallest horse in the world. But, most of all, I wanted to see the lion. I stood looking at the painted ferocious poster of it, eyes blazing, teeth like scimitars, knocking down black natives of somewheres, like they were bowling pins. But I didn't waste my nickel. I did hear him cough. It was a sad cough and I so pitied it I imagined myself sitting beside it, and it lapping warm milk from a bowl I held.

I found Jude talking with the proprietor, a big man who looked just about halfway between a blackguard and a banker. And the thin man was standing around, and the man who led the elephant the houris rode on. They were all laughing and passing a bottle of rum back and forth, and looked pretty disreputable — and that included Jude.

The proprietor was telling Jude the picture of the tiger eating up a native child had scared a pregnant woman so she had miscarried, and they hadn't settled the lawsuit yet. Soon as they did he'd sue Jude. But he was urging Jude, if he found no better accommodations for the night, to come back and sleep under the canvas that covered the sideshows. Jude thanked him but accused him of every so often, in the interest of advertisement and after dark, permitting the cry to go up that the lion was loose. Then the whole town went into convulsions — women locking themselves and their children in closets, drunken militiamen seizing rifles and whacking at bushes and shooting each other. He wasn't too sure he'd sleep good if that cry went up. But I guess the real reason was the heat and the smell of the place. Likewise, Jude had spotted the posters of another friend, also with a commodious tent and, being in the waxwork line, no smell.

The boy that took the tickets in front of this great tent and the young man who was barking for him were local talent. It was the long painted flyer in front that brought the people in.

Professor Paracelsus World Famous Statuary
See Evil and Learn Good

By that he meant he specialized in crimes of violence, murders mostly, and still pretty hot ones — I mean, not a Cain and Abel among them.

Professor Paracelsus was done up to look like a statesman — dark pantaloons, black frock coat, pearl-gray waistcoat and a high hat. He had a great craggy head, dark, sunk-in glowing eyes, and looked enough like Daniel Webster to arouse considerable enthusiasm and confidence in New Hampshire. Must have changed his gait for southern states.

Where his money came from, as he told us later, was not

in the entrance fee (only a dime), but in the "true stories" of each crime which he had written up, printed and sold. No more than a few sheets each, and for them he got a quarter apiece, instead of the penny that would have seemed reasonable. He would walk from group to group of his waxworks telling to his patrons somewhat of the story, enough to arouse curiosity. He'd peter out at the exactly right moment to get them to buy the printed account.

He had an air of the highest moral probity. As he went about his collection, pointing out their good points, he would seem as pitying and understanding of the murderers as of their victims — patting his bad men on their heads and his bad girls on their haunches as though, even now, begging them to consider the consequences of their evil deeds before they gave way to their lower passions; before it was too late.

Here was Jason Fairbanks, with his withered arm and little penknife, once more stabbing plump Betsy Fales in the back. "And ladies and gentlemen," he would say softly, shaking his head, "to pack a weak vessel like Jason too full of love is like putting new wine in old bottles, as the Good Book has it. For Jason Fairbanks, with all his virtues — he was a beautiful chirographer . . . His story, her story, would ring tears from a stone. In the glory of their youth, etc . . . All printed up in this little booklet. Priced at no more than twenty-five cents."

The women were exclaiming over Betsy Fales's dress, vowing they had never seen one better hung — although she was struggling against her assailant for her very life.

And there, standing on the gallows with a rope around his neck, was New England's greatest highwayman, Captain Lightfoot, his glassy eyes glaring. The fierce expression of his mouth may have been augmented by the intense heat under that canvas, which was sufficient to melt human flesh and pretty tough on wax. Someone asked Professor Paracelsus if that blue suit was the very one Boston had hanged him in, for waxwork men often either made that effort or said they did. He immediately admitted in so honest a voice that, no, it was not — but very like, that when he next said that he had been so fortunate as to procure the hair off Lightfoot's head and, as they might read in his booklet (price 25 cents), at considerable expense and effort, that did start a sale — such is the macabre curiosity of the human race. And I'm sorry to report that no sooner had the Professor turned his back than I saw a lady helping herself to a few wisps for her locket. Of course that would mean he'd always have to be replacing it, but it was good business. Later he told us there was a certain lady in Boston, when he had been pitched there last year on the Common, came back fifteen times, paying admission every time, until she had got enough for a hair bracelet.

The most grandiose display was in the middle. A four-poster canopied bed and, there, in it, already hit once and spouting gore, was poor old Captain White. He had on a calico nightcap, his eyes rolled up at his assassin, looking like he was trying to pull the sheet over his head for the protection he was obviously in need of. Above him was poised that demon in human form, Dick Crowninshield, with a bludgeon in one hand and a dirk in the other, high hat on head. His coattails had been wired out behind to give an effect of action. I think it was the most utterly evil face I ever saw, writhing with evil — like a basket full of snakes.

Professor Paracelsus was shaking his Websterian brow and compressing his big, loose, eloquent lips. Dick was a boy of a very good family — one of Salem's best. Yet he had died a hired assassin. This deed he had done for one thousand dollars, spot cash. How come? Well, it was all in this booklet (price 25 cents). Wine, women and song had been that unrecoverable first step down into this final iniquity. Professor Paracelsus hadn't wanted to soil his pen with such lewdness and impurity (but implied he had), and certainly never would his lips, but here "for only twenty-five cents ... " Dick had had a "den of vice" in Wenham and, seemingly, another one in South Carolina. Professor Paracelsus had suffered, forcing himself to write about such things, but he had felt it his duty as a good citizen to emphasize (especially to all young gentlemen) how the first step leads to second, and so on, until at last you have the sacred life blood of a fellow human on your hands and the gallows yawns for you.

Even Jude bought that. And everybody else, I guess.

Although the Professor had been talking fifteen to the dozen ever since we came in, he had told Jude by all means to sleep the night out here under this tent. We were both most welcome.

So we left our bundle-kerchiefs hid behind Captain Lightfoot's gallows and went to locate a little something for supper up along Main Street.

Twenty-one

ALL THIS CONNIVING and tricking we had been witnessing had come off on Jude. When we inquired for entertainment at two or three places you could see nobody really wanted us, for we didn't look too honest ourselves by then. Or maybe they truthfully were full up. Next place demanded to see "the color of our money" before they'd take us in and this suspicion hurt Jude's feelings, although it shouldn't of, for by now he had his shirttails out, saying it was cooler that way.

The place we found was a private house, licensed for this one big night only. They didn't know how to handle so many.

If you ordered liquor it came along fast enough, but food was slow.

We sat at a trestle board with eight or ten other men who had already got acquainted before we joined them. They were irritated, not only because they had been sitting there an hour already and no food but because, like us, they never had heard the Governor's speech; he being too weak-voiced or the wind setting from the wrong quarter or they too far out on the outskirts. Jude, on being questioned, said modestly that from where he had stood in the crowd he had heard "plenty."

"What he say about turnpikes?"

"Best as I understood him he recommended building three new ones, but abolishing all tolls."

"Heaven sake! How that fool think to finance them?"

"Fire fines. Anyone so careless as to let his property get burned up will be fined equal to the original value of the property."

"He couldn't do such a thing. Contrary to the Constitution."

"May have misunderstood him. I did lose a lot."

"Anything on taxes?"

"Intended, if I understood him correctly, to tax the poor right out of the state. 'Let them go west,' says he. And by going a mite easy on the rich (according to him, most valuable part of any community) all the rich from other states will be attracted in. Thus New Hampshire will be a sort of Paradise on earth. But don't get too excited, gentlemen. I may have misheard some." They went off on telling each other stories of political skulduggery. Some of them were pretty funny. And, like men do sometimes, each man had to either tell a story, sing a song or pay for a round of drinks.

It came to Jude, and they, being substantial farmers, I guess all of them, guessing Jude to be an out-of-work, down-to-heel artisan or factory hand, let the matter drop right there; for he said for the life of him he couldn't think of a story, unless they would consider he'd done his part if he retold the one the Governor had used in his speech. It was about George Washington, and it had a moral to it.

"Cherry trees?"

"A few bushes maybe. No cherry trees. Matter of fact, he had told a new one I have never seen in print nor heard. Moral was, don't shilly-shally."

I had known this story for years, for it was supposed to have happened during the Revolution and somewhere near New London, Connecticut.

Jude set the stage for it at Norwich, the big crackerjack mansion house where George Washington and his staff were being entertained to dinner by the local gentry. And it was hot; haying time. They had drunk plenty of toasts, seated about the mahogany, and that led to those gentlemen competing among themselves as to who could drink fastest or sing loudest, and that led to which one of them could jump highest and furtherest.

The lady of the house realized it was time to get them out of doors. They wobbled down to the river to find out who could swim longest and dive best. The Thames is bushy right along there so they took off all their clothes and hung them on the underbrush, wigs too. And such as had false teeth (like the father of our country) set them out like so many turtles on a flat boulder. Well, there they were; playing about in the refreshing water like porpoises and yelling at each other "Last in smells like sin," with the innocent humor of schoolboys, when a sharp-eyed aide espied scarlet uniforms moving surreptitiously among the bushes on the opposite side. He yelled "Red-coats" and General Washington yelled "Charge," for he was always first in war, even when not appropriately dressed for it. He weren't no summer soldier, in the words of Paine. They all pell-melled out of that river after them skulking redcoats.

Soon the red-coats had outdistanced all but the General and his trusty aide and they were heaving along after them when the aide gasped, "General, we're in error. Those aren't the British. Those are the village girls in their red petticoats."

"Knew it all the time," says Washington, and he kept right on running.

"Now the Governor applied it this way," Jude was saying, "if I got him right. First, your born leader (I think he was referring to himself) is apt to be a little sharper-sighted than his followers and General Washington all along had known what he was going after. And, by gum, he went after it."

"Well," said one of the men, "if Governor's got the gumption to tell about the Father of our Country chasing girls bare-ass through bushes, and he standing up there on the grandstand and ladies present, I, for one, am for him."

But by then it was our table's turn to be fed the salt cod, sass and gingerbread. That was all we got. Although nobody complimented Jude on this story which they had enjoyed, Yankee-like they showed their appreciation in a practical way, for they insisted on paying for our suppers.

By then the church bells all over town were clink-clanking away, meaning all shows and drinking places were to close up for the night. It was ten o'clock, and the town fathers did not wish the hundreds upon hundreds of strangers landed down upon them to go on high-jinking all night.

. . . .

Twenty-two

. . . .

WE COULD SEE Professor Paracelsus' tent was lit up inside. A gummy light shone through the canvas, but it was laced up tight and we had to roll in under the flaps. One lantern was hanging from the center post and by its light the Professor was adding up his day's take.

He looked more comfortable now, but less like Daniel Webster, with his frock coat off and underneath he had no more than a dicky and a pair of dirty galluses. He drew out a bottle of warm apple brandy from under Betsy Fales's skirts. He told us how this year he had cut his show down to one two-horse wagon and was making more money than formerly.

"People always did linger longer over the murderers. Mr. Rebough, do you remember the tasty collection I had of Presidents of the United States? And Fulton with his steamboat? People care for that? Not a tinker's damn. As for George and Martha Washington, I'd of had to pay people to stop and look at them, although they were mighty like. So I decided last fall to renovate. Sold some figures to rival showmen. Some I could make over. For instance, just between us, Dick Crowninshield used to be President Jackson, and Betsy Fales was once Martha Washington."

They both had a pull at apple brandy. He was still counting his take, which was considerable, as he told us things. Seems every section of New England had a different taste in what it longed most to see. Take Captain White; when he got to Salem, Massachusetts (some time a month from now), nine tenths of all those who came would come especially to see that one exhibit, for that had been a Salem murder. While a place like, say, Brattleboro, Vermont, and from there north up the Connecticut River (where he just come from), nine tenths paid the price only to see Ruby Lambkin.

"You got him?" says Jude, pricking up his ears. "For they do say he looks like me."

"Frankly, my representation wasn't any good. But it is an example of local demand, and me supplying best I'm able. That law-enforcement officer to Captain Lightfoot's left, I used that effigy (was Dan'l Boone once)." He took another drink. "Soon as I could post up before my tent that I had a good, true representation of Ruby Lambkin himself you should of seen the suckers falling over themselves to get in. And then the complaints I had! Too many people had actually seen him. Why, he came himself and complained."

"So you seen him?"

"The folks in my tent said it was he. He said it was. But law officials said no, it wasn't; just a stewed-up young riverman. Constable said the very same moment this young fellow was threatening to sue me for libel (down to Brattleboro), up at Sharon the real Ruby was penning up Sheriff Burnap in his own pigpen. But if mine was only an imitation may the Lord spare me a visitation from the real article. There were (always are) God's plenty of small boys outside the canvas trying to get a peek without paying. First thing this fellow did was roll up one side of the tent, invite them all in — free gratis. It was bedlam. Lot of little things got snitched, and me yelling for the constable. But long before any law and order got to my help, that fellow had just evaporated. Which was like his general reputation. Very like."

"Much damage done?"

"Women went off with Betsy Fales's bonnet, and so on. But my, my, what free advertising I did have. Pitch after pitch, everywhere I went for fifty miles around, people came flocking. Why? Maybe not to see my representation of him, but because they were sure he'd come again. Sure as of the second coming of Christ. Financially this was rewarding, but when I left the Connecticut River to come over here I gave him up. He was too poor a representation, for one thing; didn't give me or anybody else any real artistic satisfaction. Then too, he's no murderer; and that is what I'm specializing in — these days. And the fact I tried my hand at a living man made me trouble. So, in answer to your question, Have I seen him, I'd say if I did I had been seeing double. But that's part of the trouble they are having over there; everybody's seeing double."

"You acquainted with Phineas Sharp?"

"Yes. Just saw him. He's over on the Connecticut now. And he about seeing four ways at once."

"He says Ruby is a basic truth, not like any other truth. And if he is, half of him, a figment of the imagination, why, naturally, he can be anywhere and anybody. He could be you, or me . . . " He had been leaning back in his chair, loose, hot and sprawly. Now he did like what he had done to Mitty; assumed a rapscallion grace and glitter and his hand (it would look like a thief's hand to your ordinary working man) stole out towards Professor's strongbox. "Aren't you getting a little too rich for your own good?" he whispered. "Lots of poor people in this world, and sure's my name is Ruby Lambkin . . . "

"Why, Mr. Rebough," and Professor tried a weak ha-ha. "That's very good. Very good, ha-ha. My apple brandy can't be that strong." But I'd seen a look in his eye. For a moment he had thought his old friend had planned to rob him. It would of been easy.

It was a joke, of course, and they were both laughing. But, from my point of view, it had been a bad joke.

"Guess you boys are ready to turn in. You can hardly feel lonely tonight, surrounded by all these good folks, and I'll leave the lantern burning to warn off thieves. As for me, I have a good bed in my wagon and now I'm heading for it. If you'll give me a hand with Captain White you can have his bed, and I guarantee it's restful. Now easy does it . . . There, now."

And we had the poor cringing old geezer out from under his bloodstained sheets a-lying on the ground. The professor must of had some affection for him, for I noticed how modestly he drew down his nightshirt and rolled a little something up to pillow his head. Then he told us if we started up suddenly in the dark, to mind Dick Crowninshield's dirk.

We rolled in and Jude was asleep right away. I wasn't. First, there was the bloodstained sheets and headboard. The greasy light of the one lantern gave movement to Professor Paracelsus' collection. Maybe it was the heat that was melting Dick's knees, but that ghastly, wicked face seemed to be coming closer all the time. The light would shift, catch in Captain Lightfoot's glassy eyes, or on Jason Fairbanks's withered hand. He had to use his left one to get that penknife into Betsy Fales. I kept telling myself she was nothing more than Martha Washington, redone, and that that horror leering over me with murderous intent, was really good Old Hickory — and who could be afraid of a President of the United States, even if he did have a bludgeon in one hand and a dirk in the other?

Then far off, leisurely-like, the thunder (with which Independence Day traditionally closes) began to roll.

I was asleep all right. And it wasn't the rain pelting on the canvas overhead, nor the still distant rolling of thunder that woke me up. It was the yelling from the next pitch to ours, the caravan, and the cry that went up was soon to be spreading from street to street.

"The lion is loose. The lion . . . "

Well, that woke up Jude too, and he was grumbling because now all those drunken militiamen would be out taking pot-shots at yellow tomcats and each other and he wasn't going to let the caravan man's ideas of advertising interfere with his sleep. Soon some men were shaking at our canvas walls. They didn't sound like they were fooling, but real serious. Had the lion crawled in here? Jude did what he rarely did (but could do topnotch when he put his mind on it): he swore. They waited quite a while to see how he was going to finish off and, with no more than begging us to keep our eyes peeled, left us.

It was getting light when I woke next and I found I could look back into Dick's writhing face and yawn and turn to sleep again. But there was a funny smell, a musty animal smell, and then an apologetic little cough. This sat me up so fast I nearly hit my head on Dick's dirk and, pulling Captain White's bloodstained sheets to my chin, I gaped about me through the gray, early light. The sick old lion was waking up too. He looked real peaceful stretched out there, like a lion on a hooked rug. He must have heard me stir, or the chattering of my teeth, for he turned his head my way. The light struck into his eyes; they were white with cataract. Even so, I wasn't taking any chances, but by nudging and whisper-ing got Jude awake, for I had an idea the first thing a lion would think about upon arising was breakfast. We rolled out of that bed and kept on rolling under the side of the tent and, with not much more on than General Washington crossing the Thames, we rolled until we got under the canvas of the caravan tent right next to us.

Yet stronger than the fear I felt was pity for that raddled yet still noble face lifted to me, not seeing me, and the shock I felt when I realized he was blind.

Twenty-three

THE LION, poor fellow, was prodded up off the ground and back into his cage again. The caravan people, even that early, were hitching up and loading their great four-horse wagons. The tents were already down. Great iron pots were set up over wood fires with mush boiling in them, or stew. And everybody, with a tin plate and a tin cup, lined up for breakfast like soldiers in the field. The proprietor invited Professor Paracelsus and us two to join them, but before we were fed a wagon was packed up and off. Then the next and the next. Every animal that could draw, drew something. The one elephant was harnessed to the lion's wagon. The eight trick ponies who, for a performance, wore no more than white surcingles and bells now had on harness heavy enough for a ploughing rig. The clown's white mule wasn't kicking the chaise he was hitched to to pieces, although in the ring he'd kick everything to hell and beyond. It was a big caravan, and in spite of all the seeming confusion, it ran like clockwork.

Jude now was ready to put his mind on his business. He told me he intended to talk to Mr. Hooper man to man, map in hand, dividing up the surrounding territory between them. For this overlapping of rival portrait painters wasn't good business for either of them.

Across from the Central Building was a private house,

made over, with two shops downstairs. Mr. Hooper had
rented the one to the left. All he had in the window was
green curtains, and a palette which was too big to be practical,
with huge brushes run through the thumb hole. And on the
palette, painted in a very refined blue, was "H. H. Hooper."
Then there was a card saying public invited to view specimens, etc. But not one picture shown in that window. The
effect was tony.

The store to the right was Butters's bookstore. It had a big
swinging sign for people to read coming up the street; it was
an open book with cherubs poring over it; their pink hides
were flaking like sunburn. Among the books in the window
was a card. It said "Rooms."

We went in there. Mr. Butters had a great, twitching nose
and on it, jutting out further yet, were warts. He was a quick-
spoken, nervous man. I don't know whether his nose made
him nervous or he made his nose nervous, or enjoying the
single state had had that effect on him, or he had always been
too nervous to marry. He was featherdusting his stock of
books all the time he was talking with us.

Mr. Hooper had already ordered his rig sent round from
the livery stable, said he, and gone out to breakfast, for
although Mr. Butters "slept" travelers he didn't "eat them."
No, he didn't expect him right back. He was doing a portrait
of Miss Sophia Estes. Judge Estes had not wished his girl to
come to a common place like this studio; he had insisted the
artist wait on her under her father's spacious roof. After
breakfast Mr. Hooper would be heading for the Estes'.

"How much he charge?"

"Thirty dollars."

"Are his pictures that good?"

"Well, yes, they are."

Jude tried to persuade him that as long as the public was
invited to come in and see Mr. Hooper's work it would be
all right for Mr. Butters to let us in. He wouldn't, but he said

Mr. Hooper had done one of himself in return for rent of the shop. We could see that.

It was the most amazing likeness I had ever seen. As I've said, Jude didn't use shadows much and he did rather draw in paint. This portrait was two thirds dark shadows and out of it came that nervous face of Mr. Butters, the great nose and the warts jumping at you off the canvas. Jude looked from the picture to Mr. Butters and back and forth. He was impressed.

"I guess he merits thirty dollars," he said thoughtfully.

"He has had the best instruction Boston can offer," said Mr. Butters. "But would you believe it? — he ain't satisfied yet. Plans to go abroad and learn even more. Has studied five years already to learn all he knows, and that's a lot."

"You bet. Your warts are just perfection, even if I do say it, and being in the same trade myself mightn't care to crack up a rival."

"You an artist too?"

"I'm sort of. I'm a limner. And, to be open and frank with you, I had had my hopes to get considerable trade around Concord, but having seen what Mr. Hooper can do, I give up and go elsewhere. Only I want to talk with him — get some idea where he intends to go next. He giving general satisfaction?"

"By and large, except . . ."

"Except what?"

"Almost nobody will pay thirty dollars. What's your charge?"

"Five."

"That a fact, now? Then you won't be above putting a new coat on my shop sign? Mr. Hooper said it was beneath him."

"I'll do it," said Jude sadly. "For I'm not above it."

"There's another stripe against Mr. Hooper. His personality doesn't always go down good. He has an insulting personality."

I went to fetch in Goldie and our goods. It was agreed that
Mr. Butters would "sleep," but not "eat us," for two nights
in pay for the work on the sign. Under this roof, I could see
Jude would get what he was longing for — a good chance to
study Mr. Hooper's work and a chance to just sit and talk
with anyone so well trained.

I got back and we had got a ladder and the sign down and
spread out on a kitchen table under the big ash in the yard
and the paint was ground and the work going forward. The
only hitch was we had drawn quite a crowd of idlers and a
rough-tough gang of genuine urchins. Mr. Butters was
threatening to call the constable on those boys, they were so
mischievous.

Then a slick little rig drawn by a pair of matched little
black horses drew up. On the outsides of the vehicle was
lettered, "H. H. Hooper, Portrait Painter." Mr. Butters
leaped to hold the horses' heads, and he called for one of those
boys to "earn a penny" by now taking them to the livery stable
where they, and Goldie, were being boarded.

They stood about snickering and one threw a stone and one
mimicked Mr. Butters's nervous speech, but their eyes were
peeled for one sight — the desperate agility with which Mr.
Hooper was getting himself out of his rig and balanced on his
crutches. He was older but he didn't look more than sixteen.

"Hip. Hop. Hop," the boys sniggered in a singsong,
"Broke a crutch and went flop."

Mr. Butters was shaking a futile fist at the boys. And there
again you couldn't figure which came first. Was he so nervous
he couldn't handle them, or did not being able to handle
them make him nervous? At last one boy, wanting a penny
even more than his cruel fun, stepped forward, made his
manners and agreed to put up the rig.

Mr. Hooper had a delicate, bedeviled face; two profiles and
no front view. His living red curls contrasted unpleasantly

with the dead white of his skin; they looked dyed, but were not.

Jude had just gone on painting at the inn sign, thinking there was enough cruel curiosity without his staring too. Hooper wouldn't let him be.

"Hum," he said rudely, propelling himself real close to us. "So Butters did find an artist to do up his sign for him. Frankly, one of the worst-looking signs I ever saw. Can't say you're improving it any."

Jude turned to the huddled little figure swinging between the crutches, like a child on a gate.

"It's my trade," he said.

"And I suppose you do portraits too? Dollar apiece, eh? One of those self-taught geniuses?"

"I charge five a head."

"Well, if that is the sort of slopping around you do I need not fear you'll cut in on *my* trade." And he swung himself off to his shop, or "studio," and slapped the door shut.

"That boy," said Jude, "is like a fox in a trap, biting at his own flesh. He can't be more than twenty-three or four. I'll give him fifteen minutes by my watch to compose himself, then you and me will go call on him. His card says the public is invited."

. . . .

Twenty-four

. . . .

I CAN'T SAY our first visit was a success. We found Mr. Hooper flung down on a sofa and he looked like he had been crying. But he put on a composed, sneery face to greet us with, his eyes traveling up and down us like we were riff-raff. We were still dressed like that, and the fact Jude hadn't shaved for two days was appallingly apparent.

Mr. Hooper's face was so brittle you felt that if you dropped it it would smash up, like any other cameo. Set up and hung all around him were examples of his art.

Jude talked softly to me about them, honestly impressed with the young fellow's skill but not saying much. You could feel the fur going down on that crooked little back, but not all the way down. Not even Jude ever got it really down, and Mr. Hooper to purring. And that poor, gifted, afflicted little fellow to the end of our friendship (if that's not too strong a word) never could dull the razor edge of his tongue.

It seemed incredible to me how everything in Mr. Hooper's pictures stuck out. And the light fell on the faces as it does in real life. As for background, a thing Jude was apt to lavish such loving care on, Mr. Hooper dismissed the whole thing with no more than some dirty curtains. And, as we commented on this fact between us, he deigned to tell us that curtains was the modern taste.

His painted hands looked like real hands, each belonging to one particular sitter; portraits in themselves. Of course as Jude always painted them in advance, they never amounted to much, as he was now telling me.

Mr. Hooper liked all this and he mellowed some, but he never mellowed much. He did condescend to give a little speech on chiaroscuro (knowing Jude had never heard of anything like that). But, even as Jude praised him, he'd purse his sensitive white lips and shrug at the presumption of a country limner's daring to have an opinion on his "art."

Hip-hop (as I called him behind his back, like the wicked, mocking boys did to his face) never won my heart, but he did Jude's. And now Jude sent me out to fetch us all bread and cheese, things needing no cooking that we might be spared the necessity of going out someplace for dinner. I got back in time to find Jude had spread out his traveling map and was suggesting a division of the territory, from now on, each should take, but that wretch had the impudence to refuse to admit Jude could be a rival. And he had sufficient confidence in even small-town people's taste that the sight of one of Jude's "daubs" would increase their avidity for one of his "portraits."

I'm putting in more about Mr. Hooper than I might because he became so famous. He must have been pretty well on in life when he did that big one of Lincoln and his cabinet that was engraved and reproduced and went all over the country — at least north of Mason and Dixon's Line. When I saw his name on it, all those years later, I tried to imagine him with those gore-like curls whitening on him, or even he gone bald. But I coudn't. I never even knew whether his wife was née Sophia Estes, but always felt sure she was.

Hip-hop, when a dam broke in him and he began to talk, proved a real kiss-and-teller. He had been hired the year before to teach drawing and art work at a finishing school in Boston where Miss Sophia, like a lot of other young females, had been sent to be finished. Now girls that age, shut up like that, are apt to elope with handsome riding masters or fall in love with French dancing masters. If employing a young, unmarried man, the headmistresses of such schools must select someone so unappetizing there is no such danger. Hip-hop explained this to Jude (and me, modest in a corner) with blazing indignation and, you bet, plenty of hurt feelings. But Sophia Estes had fallen in love with him, and he with her. Naturally they hadn't told her parents of their engagement and, she being finished and back here in Concord, of their surreptitious correspondence. He had been determined not to present himself to her parents as just one more peddler (obviously like Jude), so he had hired that neat rig from a livery stable in Boston (no, he didn't own it, and he couldn't figure how he was going to pay the hire of it when he got back to Boston). He had set his price high to appear successful and elegant, and near gone broke advertising spaciously in newspapers. It had been easy for a beloved daughter of rich parents to persuade them nothing would suit her but this new-come portrait painter should take her likeness. And all had gone, says he, happy as wedding bells and right in that direction until the Judge had stepped in on them the very morning of our arrival to Butters's and, catching them in amorous dalliance, told Mr. Hooper he was never to darken his door again.

"What Sophie do?" Jude asked curiously.

He knew her. She would keep quiet, but really do something. Judge Estes hadn't acted too bad. For instance, he had paid off Mr. Hooper all of that promised thirty dollars, although the picture wasn't quite done, and actually had writ him out a letter, to all whom it concerned, "that he found him a most excellent artist," and so on, and said nothing about not trusting him in the room alone with any presentable young female as he must have thought.

Now Hip-hop was wishful that Jude approach the Judge

and offer to finish off that portrait, and Mr. Hooper was ready to recommend Jude as a craftsman able to complete the dress and crimson curtains. "But God damn it," he exploded, "don't you dare to go touch the face, nor her pretty hair. Don't you go, like your kind, adding on and adding on jewels and laces, just to get people's minds off your miserable painting." For this service he agreed to pay him five out of his thirty dollars. "But five dollars," says he, careless-like, seeming to have forgot what he had told us only the day before about his own poverty, "will seem like real money — to you."

I was bothered Jude had no more pride than to agree to thus picking up the crumbs falling from that insufferable young man's table. It had pleased me no end Hooper was having a hard time to make both ends meet and that he had not found one single sitter the weeks he had spent at Concord, except the Governor, whom he had done for nothing, and Sophie herself. Yet, confound that mean little fellow, he had the nerve to talk to Jude like that. And Jude had been getting plenty of work wherever he went. Likewise, we owned our rig and owed no money anywhere.

Yet next moment he was melting, saying he hadn't ever had many friends like Mr. Rebough, and begging Jude to call him Henry — that was how he pronounced the name (he had a nasty, quick, slick way of talking). Of course Jude really called him "Henery," for so all country people said it.

Well, there we were at the Judge's house and there was Sophia and that almost-done portrait of her. She was sweet-faced, but no beauty; sort of too womanly for her years, with compassionate brown cow eyes. A warm, simple girl to heart. She had been taught to not slump and to be stately. Over-taught, I'd say, but she had the real stuff in her and she'd outgrow those expensive mannerisms. She had a stylish way of arching everything about her that was archable — wrist and eyebrows, instep, neck. She never let her hands fall into

ugly fists. And, whether her corsets were so tight or her back
so well trained, she never touched a chairback, no matter
how long she sat.

Yet this outside elegance and affectation was all Henery had
got down on his canvas. The important part, the inside part,
the fact she could love a penniless, driven, gifted, frantic, bad-
tempered cripple, just wasn't there at all. It would have been,
had Jude done it. With all his sad lack of training he'd of
done something with those loving and forgiving eyes. But
perhaps it was the other side of her, I mean the too fashion-
able, too rich-looking outside of her, Henery longed for.
Maybe those cow eyes never had touched him as I know they
touched Jude. What if Hip-hop could make cheeks bulge and
noses stick out? After all, he'd done no more for her than any
good taxidermist could of done — granted a taxidermist had
had a chance at her.

We stayed in Concord, first and last, two or three weeks.
Henery condescended to pass on to Jude names of five or six
people who had wished their likenesses taken but considered
thirty dollars too high, and whom he believed "did not have
such high standards" as to know the difference between
"daubs and work of serious artistic merit."

Such people we waited on at their own houses. It wasn't
until we were going next day Henery had either the curiosity
or courtesy to say he'd like to see some of Jude's work.

We got them spread out all over the upstairs rooms (with
Mr. Butters's permission). I fetched in every last one of them.
All except that of the woman looking out the window, whom
Jude had told me previously I weren't to show, for he was
holding it for a "special sale." Henery worked and worked
up the stairs with that sad, pathetic patience of his that was
so at variance with the way he would do other things. And he
stepped in to view what we had done. I saw his face, and my
heart went to my boots. Suddenly those things did look funny
enough, with no faces on them. Yet the coloring was so

beautiful and all that pretty stuff he put in so perfect it was almost as if faces didn't add too much. But I saw Henery was trying not to laugh. At least he made the effort and he didn't. This time, by the way, was the nicest I ever saw him. He was feeling polite, for him, and I've a sneaking idea he had somehow got in touch again with Miss Sophia.

He'd say, "You shouldn't think to do things like that, Jude. But, under the *circumstances,* you do very well. Now look at those wild flowers .... Why not even I, with all my training, could do them ever — not like that, so fresh and limpid-looking. And the birds, why, Audubon never did, maybe no one ever did .... It was terrible that a man with your natural gifts should never have been taught even the rudiments of painting, and so everything just thrown away."

Then he explained to Jude, speaking not arrogantly at all, how, by starting first with a body and background he was always getting his cart before his horse. Not a chance in a hundred, ever, that they would come out right. He said he doubted if even Rembrandt could have done portraits like that. It simply wasn't possible.

I guess Jude and I were both thinking about Captain and Mrs. Dolliver. They had been terrible. Jude took all his criticism, and there was plenty, very nicely. But he had his pride and I know some of it did get under his skin, and I think Henery did convince him that he was going at the painting of people wrong way about. I wish we had had some of those overmantels of his to have shown Mr. Hooper. I've a feeling he would have admired them.

Now Jude told me, step over to the livery stable and fetch in that one picture he had previously told me not to show ever. I refer to the fleshy woman. He had been fearful if he set it up for sale someone like Mrs. Dolliver would snap it up, as she had my girl with the bush full of birds.

Henery looked and looked at it. You could see on his face he couldn't believe it and yet he wasn't laughing any, even

inside. "I never saw such color, never on land nor sea . . .
but . . ."

He'd begin again. "It isn't of this world and . . ." Then
he'd get sort of lost in it, but straighten up and say reprov-
ingly, "An artist's duty is to paint the world, just as he sees it,
every day and round about him. Don't you understand,
Jude — this isn't art; this is just day-dreaming, child's play.
Pleasant fooling, but it isn't art."

Then he'd sit down and look. "Wherever in God's world
would you find a face pagan enough to complete such an
effort."

"Could make it up."

This infuriated Henery for he looked upon an artist
making anything up as falsifying, and therefore lying. And
he went back to chiaroscuro again, and the necessity of
shadows and the absolute impossibility of anyone painting
anything worth the looking at that had not (like himself)
been trained. And, in the end, he was rudely suggesting that
Jude just give up, and go paint walls. And, looking again at
that headless woman, this time he laughed the meanest laugh
I ever heard. "So all winter you sit and paint backgrounds
and bodies and dream up the sort of lady you'd like to meet
next summer and, being so thin yourself, you like them
plump. Jude, I'll bet you your wife's thin too." True
enough. "Now, never once in all your life did you ever
actually *see* a woman like that, did you?"

"Once," says Jude promptly. "Once I did."

"Not in these parts."

"Not far from them. Over to Norwich — Vermont."

"If you do see her again I think you'll be surprised how
little she is like your memory of her. And then, for God's
sake do throw away all this you've done, in a dream as it were.
And you look at her honest, and paint her just as she is. No
hummingbirds and no bees. No improbable flowery stuff
around her."

"Curtains?"

"Best background there is; just curtains. Why, man, this isn't portraiture — this isn't more than a God damn valentine."

Even this Jude took, for he had great respect for H. H. Hooper's knowledge, a thing he had none of. But I knew he wasn't going to throw away this "dream." He was terribly fond of it. What if it was all illusion? What did he think men lived by? Mr. Sharp was a deal smarter than Hip-hop, at least someways.

$$\bullet \quad \bullet \quad \bullet \quad \bullet \quad \bullet \quad \bullet \quad \bullet \quad \bullet \quad \bullet \quad \bullet \quad \bullet \quad \bullet \quad \bullet$$

Twenty-five

$$\bullet \quad \bullet \quad \bullet \quad \bullet \quad \bullet \quad \bullet \quad \bullet \quad \bullet \quad \bullet \quad \bullet \quad \bullet \quad \bullet \quad \bullet$$

JUDE TOLD HENERY one unvarnished fact. He was charging too much. If Luke the Apostle appeared driving a coach and the four beasts of the Apocalypse he couldn't expect more than fifteen dolllars a throw, not in New Hampshire.

And at last Henery was in a humble enough mood to agree Jude was a rival to him and they had best divvy up the territory.

Henery chose the whole Merrimack Valley from south of where we were; that is, south of Concord. He wasn't suited to the road by temperament. I've a feeling he shot back to Boston, for that livery stable rig he had hired to impress Judge Estes with, was running up a big bill on him. He better had get them off his chest.

We turned upstream, going north, and the pickings got leaner and leaner as the hills began piling up for mountains. Yet the river Merrimack was good company to us and, further up we went the merrier it ran. But smaller. Smaller all the time. And likewise the towns.

We did all right at Boscawen. When we saw the size of the church we knew we would. Franklin, not so good, but good enough. And here, for the first time, we saw the full force of the White Mountains; wave upon wave before us, and not white at all — rosy and lavender, sort of untouched by man, just as God made them. And he made them good for man's soul, but not for his pocketbook. By the time we got to Bristol we knew we'd come to the end. Bristol looked fair-sized on our map and we had had hopes of it. The road we came in by felt around those crouch-backed foothills and pitched up and over ledges, and the land about us was more fitting for deer than man, and lumbermen than limners. In fact, it was a mistake our coming here at all. And Goldie cast a shoe.

We could have sold axe-heads and logging irons, spirits by the barrel, calico, or Bibles even. It weren't worth to even show our goods. Jude got a smith to shoe up Goldie. Actually he was more used to shoeing oxen than horses and he botched the job, for lumbermen don't use horses much.

To go east from here would mean just a lot more natural beauty like what we were enjoying but no profit for us. We had no choice but turn west. If the district between the Merrimack and the great Connecticut Rivers proved profitless we'd keep on a-going until we hit the rich, fine towns along the Connecticut. Jude had been there two years before and swore he had but scratched the surface. There was every reason for us to go; one thing was a letter Mitty had forwarded to Jude at Concord. It came from a Dartmouth professor (real one; no Professor Paracelsus about him). Two years back Jude had done up for him a series of pen and ink drawings of plants, roots and all. Professor Dwight had written all the way to Hampton if Mr. Rebough could arrange to do some more he'd be gratified. He was working on his big botany and was having a time finding anyone who could draw plants fit for the engraver.

There were two reasons why we hadn't ought to of gone. Ruby Lambkin (or a parcel of characters working under that name) was over there. So also that Emma — a Norwich woman. And that town is separated from Hanover (where Dartmouth is) by no more than the Connecticut River. Already my back was up against this Emma Faucett, and Jude looking so like Ruby made me nervous.

Newfound Lake we left behind us and Bristol too, such as it was. We were warned that to as far as Grafton we'd have little more than a logging road. There were hills and mountains all about us and lake after lake breathing off coolness. We stuck pretty much with Smith River, going upstream. Some places the road (if it were a road) was taken over a swampy spot on corduroy. Goldie (she had fallen down on corduroy five years before and never forgot the experience) wouldn't cross it unless I got out and led her. In fact, Jude and I walked most of the way, for the chaise was pitching about so it was enough to make even a good sailor throw up Noah. For the first time in my life I saw a wild bear.

It all smelled too good and there was too much to see for either of us to say much, but I remember how happy-like we were.

We came into a broadening valley, and the Smith River, by now just about petered out, was trickling through cleared fields. And in the valley beside the remains of the river was the remains of Grafton, straggling and sprawling down its own Main Street and looking like thunder. Later, out west, we'd of called it a ghost town.

Goldie saw a stone horse trough before a falling-apart old

house and beside the horse trough was a mounting block, so we figured this was a public house. She made for the trough and began fingering along the bottom of it with her loose upper lip. There wasn't any water, so we guessed this wasn't a going concern any more.

Sitting there and speculating on what sort of a curse had befallen the place we did see that quite a few of these houses were occupied. At first sight all looked abandoned. Barn roofs were caving in and windows broke, shingles off, chimneys falling, fields and pastures grown up to sumac, hardhack, birch and alder. It looked fierce.

And in what had once been some woman's front-yard gardens, hollyhocks and orange daylilies — magenta phlox. It was so forlorn we just sat and looked. There was no real mystery to it. The land had been cleared a generation or so back (as recent as all that) and it hadn't been worth the clearing. Sheep next, and that about finished off the soil. But already a nice, hopeful well-built town had gone up, before they realized the land wouldn't support one. No new people came and, mostly, people left.

We got a little something of this from a knowing and polite old gentleman who, seeing us without water for the horse, stepped out of the house next to, with a pail in his hand. There was a good well of water, he said, behind the fallen-down inn. He had an old dog at his heels; too old to bark, half blind, deaf and terribly fat. That dog went to sleep again right at his master's feet for the duration of our brief talk, and when he waked up and found the old gentleman gone without him he was funny enough with his looks of utter despair, then he waddled after him.

I remember he told us, first of all, to keep on going for Canaan, no more than ten miles "as the crow flies," and we'd be well accommodated. And he told us how one hundred and twenty-eight families had left Grafton; not a new one coming in. He told us his two sons and one daughter had gone but he, being the clergyman of the place, felt he had a call to stay, for, mostly, those who were still here were old folk like himself and needed the comfort of gospel readings and prayers and someone to run their funerals. There had been one funeral, he said, three days before and another was coming right along. And now, if we would excuse him (and put that pail on his back stoop when through with it), he would go back to the deathbed he had been sitting by.

Jude asked him who the dying person might be. The poor brave old gentleman tried to smile, but it came out wrong, yet he said it real matter-of-fact. "It is my wife," he said. "And she been my good helpmeet for fifty years." Then he left and that's when his old dog woke up sudden and felt he had been abandoned. That old dog was like the spirit of the place.

Having fetched water for us and Goldie, I put her nose bag on her and Jude and I sat side by side upon the mounting block. We heard a cow moo far off and a woodthrush sing, but it was so tarnation still there you began listening for something, unable to believe the world could be so still. We were munching at the bread and cheese we always carried with us, for it looked like we'd be getting into Canaan after suppertime. But it was to Canaan we expected to head for after this little pause.

"Where those people go to?" I asked Jude. He guessed a lot to the ugly new factories, but mostly west — like New York State, or Illinois. Hadn't I heard tell of Ohio? But further out than that — out to the great plains where the Indians and the buffalo were. The Mississippi River; hadn't I learned of it in school? And beyond even that was the Missouri. People, New England people, were going that far these days, and then beyond that. Likely some of the very people whose abandoned houses stood here about us, empty as a snake's skin, had taken up free land out there. It was flat as a table top, rich as pork gravy. A man might set his plough

and follow his furrow a mile and more without hitting rock
or hummock.

It was the stillest of still late afternoons in early August.
The westering, sinking sun came in on us and filled up the
wretched little valley with light. Then it was a miracle occurred, for the hills, mountains, cliffs, rocks about us were
full of mica. Now the light catched it and it began to twinkle.
Why, even the mounting block we sat on and the horse trough
beside us were mica-laden. And before we could get accustomed to the eeriness of this twinkling, the sun was down
and everything was pink. I never saw such pink air anywhere — whole town, us two sitting there, sky. We couldn't
think to remember that we should of started pushing for
Canaan.

We saw Mr. Sharp coming before we heard him, a-walking
towards us from the west. Then we heard him singing soft,
but haunting-like. He lifted a hand in recognition, but never
stopped his song until he came up abreast of us. He timed
himself good.

He bowed with a flourish but did not remove his hat. I
guess he weren't too happy about being so bald. He slipped
his pack and dropped before us cross-legged like a Turk.
He hadn't any food on him. We fed him, but he did have an
old-fashioned leather bottle of apple brandy. Then he told
us a woman had told him there were some old cornshuck
mattresses left upstairs in this inn and any wayfarer could
put up there for nothing, if only he didn't mind the rats. So
Jude and me gave up the thought of Canaan. It was too late
by now, anyway.

I had liked what he had been singing when he joined us,
although I hadn't made out the words, so I asked him what
it was.

He jumped to his feet, poised himself before us just right.
"Ladies and gentlemen," he said as though we were a roomful and, plucking across his own lean little belly as though it

were a musical instrument, "Song of the Western Migrations."

> "John, John, the piper's son,
> Married me when I was young.
> We journeyed to the setting sun,
> Over the hills and far away."

He lingered on the far away and he had a lovely voice; best of all, I think, when soft like this and not at full stretch. It floated off now through the pink air and the forlorn town. There was another verse or two, then the last one.

> "John, John, the piper's son,
> Died out there when he was young.
> And I wish I were where I begun,
> Back in the hills of far away."

"For," says he, very reasonable and still in that addressing-a-roomful voice, "to you, living about here, 'far away' is our great West. And when you get there (like John's poor young widow), far away, likely as not, will prove to be where you came from. In this case Grafton, New Hampshire. When you are young (like Eddy here) 'far away' will be being grown up and your own boss. When you are older (like me) it will be happy boyhood days. For it is whatever you aren't — boyhood for men, manhood for boys. Wherever you aren't, East or West, whatever you haven't. Or," says he, "put it like this.

> "How far is far away?
> Close by as yesterday,
> Near as tomorrow."

And then (it was his voice that did me), and he standing before Jude and me parading his gifts, and the air so pink about us, it was I knew I had to go. It had near broke my heart this spring when Mitty told me I was to go to my uncle in Waltham (come fall) and learn the harnessmaker's trade. Now it didn't matter, for, when my time was up, the great

West waited for me. I felt excited and yet same time terribly content. For knowing just what you are going to do does give you ballast. And I knew, sure as shooting, I'd be lonely out there, homesick and heartsick. But what the shucks? It made no iota of difference, for I had to go.

And I did go. And I never came back.

One more thing about Grafton. When I was out west, and homesick some, I could always see that place (where I never spent more than this one night) more clear in my mind's eye than, say, Hampton, Connecticut, which I knew every nook and cranny of. I could see the slim trunks of pines against the sky, and the twinkle of mica when the sun hit it just right. And that poor, broken-down town that never should of been built. I felt if I ever got there it would be just the same, like wax flowers under glass. So still in that pink, pink air. The broken backs on the barns and the falling-down houses, the old inn (and the rats in it). And the minister's wife dying in the house next to us. But, hung up in the air above all, was Mr. Sharp's song; like an iridescent bubble, if you see what I mean. And, if I ever did return to Grafton, it would still be hanging there waiting for me to hear it once more.

And what Mr. Sharp said about "far away" was correct. When I was thirteen it was the West. Now, me an old man who has lived my life out in Wichita, Kansas, it is New England. Or maybe my dream of it. And then, it was to be grown up. Now it is to be the little shaver I was then, once more.

. . . .

Twenty-six

. . . .

WHAT WITH Mr. Sharp's propensity to chatter, and the rats, we had a night of it. Next morning we offered Mr. Sharp a lift back over the way he had come. Whatever he came to Grafton for first place, I never figured, except he was so itch-footed he'd go anywhere rather than submit to stay where he was. And riding in a chaise made him restless; he always had one foot out on the iron step all ready to leave, or he was jumping out, rocking the chaise like a boy diving off a row-boat, then he'd bounce back in again. And he talked all the time — mostly about Ruby Lambkin, upon which subject he considered himself expert. Ought to have been. He made up a lot of him.

He told us all about Ruby's having bust up Professor Paracelsus' show for him in Brattleboro, Vermont, only in his version the constable did get there in time and Ruby niftily escaped capture by palming himself off as a wax image of himself. Didn't bother him any that the same night Ruby was in Sharon, locking Sheriff Burnap in his own pigpen. He sang us that song. The whole chorus of it was the honk-ing and the grunting of the pigs. Likewise, he had the Sheriff's wife a touch deaf. Hearing her husband yelling for help, she thought the pigs were hungry and she fetched down swill for them and dumped it on him. That was pretty crude country humor, but that's the kind of humor country people like.

And to explain the origins of this fellow who'd come among them, sometimes appearing in three places one night and then not appearing for two weeks to a time, he was attaching to him all sorts of hoary old tales that had always been floating about. Like how, he being an infant and sick to death and doctor having given up, the distracted mother promised if he might live, to dedicate him to the foul fiend, who then appeared and took her up on it. Contract to run for so many years, of course. This time having expired, old Horny came to collect. "You just wait," says the lad, "till I get my galluses up." Horny agreed. So the lad (now it was Ruby) flung the galluses in the fire and never got them up. I heard this one told around Hampton of Tom Cook. And it was off the same bolt of cloth that Sharp told us how last year, when Ruby had been picked up and put under a three-man guard in an upper room he seemed in such a sweat of fear one of them asked him what for. Then he admitted he had sold his soul to the Devil and this was the very night (midnight, of course) the contract fell due. And when that village clock, that now was striking eleven, struck twelve there'd be a terrific flash of fire and a thunderburst. He felt it only fair to warn them of their peril. But as he paced and circled that upper chamber he was strewing gunpowder here and there, unbeknownst to them. When midnight struck he dropped a coal from his pipe and — Flash. Bang. Bang. When the guards recovered and the smoke cleared he must have gone up the chimney in the fiend's arms — at least he was gone.

Although it was around ten miles from Grafton to Canaan as the crow flies, we were no crows. Goldie normally had little heart for a day's work, and now she had none. Worst yet, she was beginning to limp.

Mr. Sharp was so full of his subject or of his apple brandy, or just full of old Harry, that when we stopped and tried to locate the trouble with her off front leg, he wouldn't pay heed to our predicament; only chat on about his own fancies. And, after all, we had had a whole night of him before starting out.

Enough was enough of Mr. Sharp. Too much was terrible. Never could figure it how Mitty got on to him so fast. He had no more sat down in our kitchen and taken off his hat than she had known. Women are uncanny sometimes. Especially wives.

So here were Jude and me, standing on that dusty road, trying to figure out what was wrong with Goldie, and he going on and on about Ruby. Fact and fancy, old yarns and new all garbled up like he liked to.

For instance. Five days before, Lambkin had stolen a horse over to Springfield, Vermont. The horse owner was a farmer known as Old Popham. Sharp was telling us he was the evenest-tempered man in the whole township — for he was mad, all the time. And he had a too young, too pretty and a sight too fly a wife. Because Old Popham was offering the enormous reward of twenty-five dollars for return of horse and twenty-five more for the capture of Lambkin people were naturally saying he had come home and found Ruby in bed with his wife. Sharp had the audacity to begin singing to us that hoary old ballad he had sung the night he put up with us at Hampton. I refer to the old husband coming home and finding first a strange horse in the stall, then a strange hat on the hatrack, a strange coat over the chairback and last a strange face next his wife's on the pillow "where no face ought to be." It had been a little refixed to meet the situation over to Springfield, but not much. For instance the saucy wife gives him the same answer when he objects to that face on the pillow:

> Oh you old fool, you dam fool,
> You doddering fool, says she,
> It's nothing but a little kid
> My uncle sent to me.

He squeaked as he sang it. First trying to imitate the old
man and then squealing more for the unchaste young woman.
He sounded worse then a dry axle and in spite of his efforts
not much funnier.

We weren't listening much. Goldie's off knee was swollen
and hot to touch. Jude was trying to get the shoe off, but
without farrier's tools that's about impossible. He bade me
fetch cool water from the brook to cool it, and he just relaxed
back among the roadside weeds and told Mr. Sharp with
some asperity that he for one was hemmed tired of Ruby
Lambkin, and he hoped the posse over in New Hampshire
would catch him this time, for he was proving no more than
a catch-all for all the moldy old jokes and disgusting songs
that had been lying around New England for the last hundred years.

"They won't catch him," said Sharp, paying no slightest
heed to Jude's boredom, and he went on to say how all
females were for Ruby, and all poor people too. And a lot
others besides. If the chase, say, did get too hot over in Vermont, why you could bet your pants on it people would begin
seeing him over here. Why, even he himself had done that
much to help Ruby out. People were so gullible, and there
weren't a town on either side the Connecticut that wasn't
waiting and sort of hoping he'd show up among them. He
went on like that.

Jude wasn't exactly rude to Mr. Sharp, but he was terribly
tired of him. Finally he broke right in on him and said there
wasn't any point of his just standing there in the road chattering at us. If he wanted to get to Canaan he'd better start
walking. After all, shank's mare was the only one he had any
feeling for. So he shut up his mouth in amazement and some

hurt. We saw him whipping it up that long hill that leads into Canaan. He was whistling.

I don't know whether what he did next was to punish Jude for dusting him off like that, or whether he thought time had come to draw the hunt for Ruby over on this side of the Connecticut. Later, when Jude taxed him with it, he said he thought if people first believed Jude was the great Lambkin himself it would give him and his wares plenty of advertising.

Well, anyway, that little numskull only had to look knowing, cup his hand about his mouth and whisper how he had seen a "stranger" heading for Canaan with what was obviously a stolen horse (although how a stolen horse looks different from another I don't know), and the fat was in the fire. Likewise, just to make sure we'd get a nice welcome when we finally did get to Canaan, he was saying how this time it looked to him like Ruby was disguising himself by pretending to be an itinerant limner. Likewise it might draw the chase away from Springfield.

Canaan is a mile-long, maple-shaded street. Everything is pretty there, and orderly. Why even the lake you look down on from where that high town sits is heart-shaped, like it had been cut out with a cookie cutter. Curiosity we aroused, and no hostility in it. We took it to be no more than the curiosity any man stuck with a lame horse might normally expect. We got plenty of advice. Some said those shoes put on over to Bristol were too small, and some too big. Some that the hoof hadn't been pared enough, and some it had been cut to the quick. You know how it goes. We were conscious of a certain amount of whispering as one person was telling the next, I suppose, Mr. Sharp's speculations. But Yankees are pretty hardheaded, by and large, and not too prone to believe all they hear. I don't think there were more than two or three men there who weren't satisfied but Jude was just what he said he was. But when we got Goldie to the blacksmith shop, that man obviously had been told and be-

lieved the little rumor Mr. Sharp had planted. He had a hot
as Tunket little forge shop with a whale of a big overgrown
sign before it — "Barlow Jones, Smith." He was a big, rough
workmanlike fellow in coarse pants and nothing more on
him but a bull hide, tanned up to serve him as apron. The
shoe was off in a trice. The Bristol smith had pared into the
quick. It was oozing some and the infection had spread up
the leg, but it weren't nothing more than, say, a week in
pasture barefoot would cure. But, believing as he did Jude
was a crook, he attempted to scotch him, for he was saying
our mare couldn't travel for months, if ever, but out of pure
brotherly pity, he'd swap that beautiful, sound-as-an-apple
big bay we could see in his pasture for this wreck of a mare.
So we saw he had no interest in curing Goldie, only in cheating us. As he went out to catch that wicked-looking old bag
of bones of his, offering to trot it back and forth so we could
see its beautiful action, Jude told me what he intended; leave
Goldie here (and us at Pierce Tavern) for, say, twenty-four
hours, then walk her slowly over to the Shakers' Colony in
Enfield. It was no more than eight miles or so. And over
there was Elder Richman (he had done a map for him three
years back) and he was most knowing about all animals and
an honest man.

    Mr. Jones took it ill that no matter how many times he
trotted his scarecrow before us, we hardly bothered to look or
listen to his praises of it. He had been trotting faster than
that horse himself (having to pull it) and, when he came
heaving, sweating and heavy, back to us, he was a touch ugly.

    "Mister, where'd you get that horse?"

    "Connecticut," said Jude.

    "Oh, yes — uh."

    "Yup. That's where."

    "What you pay?"

    "Nothing."

    "Why nothing?"

"My business, ain't it?"

I think he was trying to tell Jude he suspected Goldie was a stolen horse, and yet if he had been real sure I think he was the sort that would of tried to get the reward money. He was what country people called pixilated.

* * * * * * * * * * * * *

Twenty-seven

* * * * * * * * * * * *

Mr. Jones agreed to take Goldie's shoes off and pasture her for the night, but he was muttering about refusing to keep "shet" if anyone came inquiring after her. Jude and I took out our gripsacks and, innocent as two doves, made for Pierce Tavern.

The bell had already rung for supper. We ate that and then went to sit a spell in the barroom.

I remember there was a Bible peddler sitting there who not only didn't believe in strong drink but felt called upon to preach cold water to others. He looked like a minor prophet right out of the Old Testament, with his burning hollow eyes and his shaky long forefinger stabbing at the air as he indicated "tipplers and bibbers" in a voice like doom.

Nowadays, I guess, such a real oddity would be locked up. It seems sort of a pity to me. He wasn't doing any harm and may have done some good. Leastwise he was causing amusement among a group of four or five young men who were badgering him a bit. One was accusing him of selling *Fanny*

Hill on the side. Said he had bought a copy of that shameful tale off him a few days back. The Bible man was getting more and more heated up under their joshing and finally did like they told him — go sit in the ladies' parlor if the sight and smell of liquor offended him so. Some of those religious fanatics had a lot more guts. You ought to have seen some of those I saw later, out in Kansas.

This group of young men were all gentlemen of some fashion and they had the air of old friends. Every evening (having supped at home) they were in the habit of meeting here for conversation, a few drinks, maybe a card game or so before bed. Not a club yet, but what might in time grow into a club. They weren't shut in on themselves; they were ready to enjoy what fun this place might offer them, like the teasing of the Bible peddler, or a little relaxation with us — if we proved conversable. They had spoken courteously when we came in to sit.

One of them, "Gyp" (his cronies called him) Hammond — and a rising young lawyer — all the time had been eyeing Jude pretty sharp. He had a consumptive look to him. Thin face, hectic flush, bright eyes, cough and all. His friends treated him with a more obvious affection than they might have if they hadn't known he was doomed. Seems to me that fell disease was always striking down the brightest and most lovable (if you can apply that word to a man) young people of New England.

He reminded Jude that they two had met three years back at Enfield when Jude had been doing that landscaped map for Elder Richman. Seems the Shakers didn't hold too much with mere pretty pictures. But a map of their great colony was a necessity and they had got Jude to paint it. But in on it were all their great stone barns and four-story buildings and, set out in the pastures, fine examples of their stock. So it was as much of a picture as a map. I saw it later.

There was handshakings and chair-edgings. We all sat

together. Mr. Hammond having been pleased with Jude's work, Jude naturally offered to paint him up, and his wife too if he had one. And Hammond told him not to forget his name if he was ever in need of a lawyer.

They agreed it was a coincidence, their meeting again like this. Then Gyp either got to coughing and covered it up with a laugh, or laughing made him cough.

"Anybody pointed out to you another coincidence, Mr. Rebough?" About the bar were tacked up notices of auctions and vendues. Things lost, found and stolen. And "wanted men." Hammond gestured toward it so we guessed what he had in mind. "And Rosie," he called to the girl. "One more of the same all around on me. And the young gentleman here is having birch beer. And bring along that Ruby Lambkin handbill tacked up on the board."

She brought everything, but when she set Jude's cider before him she was blushing and almost curtsied, for she was of a believing nature. Maybe all summer she had been day-dreaming of meeting Ruby Lambkin. Then before she went on duty this evening she had heard how he had arrived in Canaan. Now all her prayers were answered, for there he sat and she was waiting on him.

Jude read the handbill, laughed, and pushed it to me. It was announcing the misdeeds and the reward for the apprehension of one Reuben Lamb, alias Ruby Lamb, popularly known as "Ruby Lambkin." I was struck with what he had really been up to, from the point of view of the law. Nothing of a supernatural nature at all, nothing of his sensational amatory successes, and nothing to suggest his sympathy with the poor. He had broke jail four times (during the past two years), he had stolen horses and silver spoons, and he had broken and entered; highway robbery. Once routed an old couple (believed to have money hid) out of bed. They either refused to tell him where they had it hid or never had any. Anyways, he set fire to the bed-dress and it was only luck the old people escaped with their lives. Here, in plain print, was just about the sort of things he really did. For the unvarnished fact was, there never was much evidence for the shinigigs people were crediting him with. Lambkin had a perfectly understandable weakness for keeping what he stole for himself.

The reward was already at one hundred dollars, a terrible lot of money for that time and place, especially considering the fact he had never injured anybody life or limb. He certainly stole a lot.

There was a small notice so hot off the press it was smootched almost to illegibility. This was of the added fifty dollars reward by Old Popham. So, may I point out, there was already one hundred and fifty dollars on Mr. Lambkin's head. The description did tally pretty close to Jude. I mean the height and the darkness, the broad face, cleft chin, and hands "obviously unacquainted with honest toil," "gentlemanly appearance and address." Jude weren't what you'd call "powerful" however, and hadn't by nature much of that limber grace. Nobody had ever thought him handsome either, but he could add these attributes, seemingly by just taking thought.

It was getting for ten o'clock and about when most people at taverns think either to go upstairs to bed or back home for the night. Yet more and more kept coming in. Our table where we sat, the local blades and us, was the center of attention, partly because Gyp and Jude got to sort of competing as to who could tell the biggest one (and get away with it). They told ghost stories mostly and, although I knew all the tricks and could see all the strings, I'll admit they just about had my hair standing on my head and my teeth to chattering. Gyp told the one about the woman locked in the church eating the human arm, and Jude a very mild, but even more terrifying one, just about a door that wouldn't stay shut.

You never did know once exactly what did happen. That made it worse.

Barrooms are no place for females, except only the bargirl. Now we noticed that all the female servants of Pierce Tavern were sort of crowding in behind the bar with Rosie, as though just come in to help her, and there were even a number of ladies in bonnets and such, standing about the two doorways. The admiring glances cast toward Jude would have turned the head of Brigham Young. And he was playing up to them a bit, like he often played up to situations. Then he told how, once having been "falsely" arrested, he had done exactly like Sharp had told us Ruby had done; that is, extracted himself by saying the Devil would come for him at midnight, and the strewn gunpowder and so on.

Then one of the girls behind the bar (she had on the starchy cap and apron and pretty calico dress such as a chambermaid would wear) called to him. All her fellow serving girls were giggling and egging her on. She was a pert girl and they were daring her to.

"Mr. . . . Mr. Lamb . . . Mr. Lambkin . . ."

Jude responded instantly, although of course he oughtn't to have.

"Guess you've got my name wrong, miss."

"What you doing night of August second? Last week Thursday that was. Mr. Lamb? — if I don't mistake myself?"

"For the life of me I can't think."

"You that absent-minded? Mr. Rebough — if you like that better."

"Eddy," says Jude to me, "where ever were we five nights back? Oh . . ." says he suddenly, cottoning on to the drift of things. "Ladies," says he, bowing to the bar full of serving girls and two doorways full of ladies, "may I drop dead at your feet if my boy and me weren't, last Thursday night, sleeping under the hospitable roof of one Tabor, tavernkeeper at

Franklin. But now I do recollect I had a real funny dream."

He acted out the part well, and to the amusement of our table mates and the flabbergasting of the ignorant. For here he was, "dreaming" how he'd done everything Ruby had really done that night over to Springfield. Naturally, with ladies present and all he was too modest to give much more than a hint about the young wife. And, so help me, if he weren't sitting there and blushing — and he dark as a gypsy. He weren't sallow by nature, but too pale. That blushing became him marvelously.

There wasn't a one there who hadn't heard some such similar tale — I mean, two natures being housed in one body. And we talked some of such "split-offs." People sort of agreed such things used to happen in the old days, but not now. And Jude was reminded of something along that line of which he had personal knowledge, although he admitted it had happened before he saw the light of day, in Hubbardston, Massachusetts. But he said he had often talked with eyewitnesses.

"This woman who had the misfortune, or at least embarrassing ability to split herself up died the year of my birth, or close on it. So you can put this back just about twenty-seven years or so and decide for yourself whether it was in old days or now. Half the time she was just one more farmer's wife — a real peeler for work. Some said she worked so beyond the usual limits of female endurance to smother up disappointment at having reached a considerable age childless. And even sleeping she wasn't always resting, for there was every reason to believe that split-off of hers, that other shape, would go skittling down the back stairs, whisk out through the cathole and take to evil ways. Ladies and gentlemen, she did what she did (even if this lawyer here won't believe it) furred all over and tailed behind like a fox, and little like a fox — teeth too, and smell. And no more morals than you'd expect, for she'd go raiding all the hen roosts that end of Hubbardston (north end, towards Gardner). But she knew enough not to raid her own roost. This caused certain amount of comment. Her husband, Joe Casserine, some such odd name (real taciturn fellow, never said more to her year after year than 'slide me the pickles'), did wonder some how come there was chicken three times a day on his table without no lessening of his flock, but he thought it nothing to twit her about.

"As I said, they never had had a child, much to the sorrow of both of them. So they were mighty tickled when Mrs. Casserine began to display the well-known indications of a happy event in the offing. Now, the question arises in a situation like this, how much did the Mrs. Casserine (who went to Meeting every Lord's Day, kept her floors so clean you could eat off them) know about what that other half of her was up to? And vice versa. For Mrs. Casserine (if I've got her name right) was just as surprised as he was, and the doctor too, when she gave birth to just about the prettiest litter of fox cubs you ever did see. Real cute little fellows.

"Doctor saw them first and hardly could think how to break the news to them, for they were getting on. Couldn't just say to them 'Better luck next time,' as he might to a young couple. So he says, best medical opinion (that was his, of course) was that in time they'd outgrow their tails and grow up proper Christians. He mopped his brow and grabbed up his black bag and leaped for his buggy, leaving the situation — which had edged him up considerable.

"From now on the wrassling was up to the minister.

"The minister was a Baptist, the Casserines being of that persuasion. Time came pretty fast (they being foxes and quick-growing) to dip them in the river in the interest of their immortal souls, if any. Which, with a prayer on his tongue and his eyes turned up to God, he did. He sure proved butter-fingered and they were such durned slippery little red rascals they swam off and never did come back. Although

it would have been considerably in the interest of science if
that minister hadn't lost his hold on them, it was, by and
large, for the best."

Gyp said, "So that's how you do it, Mr. Rebough. Respectable limner by daylight — Ruby Lambkin himself when
the moon rises."

But it was pushing for midnight. The landlord came in
(for the second time) and he begged us to disperse, for
although the bar had been closed with the striking of eleven,
it didn't give his house a good name that guests sat so late.
And people would be saying that he was serving liquor after
hours and illegally.

Of course, Jude had been doing what he ought not to have.
For one thing he had been displaying something of that feline
grace (by no more than how he sat and waved his hands) so
characteristic of Ruby. And he had been smiling quicker and
wider than there was any real need of. You know how "little
acorns do to mighty oak trees grow" or, to change my imagery,
to beans. A little bean of falsehood gets planted and comes
up and gets nursed, and first thing you know, you've got a
Jack-and-the-bean-stalk   with   an   ogre   fee-fie-fo-fumming
up at top, smelling blood.

Jude was always ready to do his share at planting a few of
these pestiferous bean seeds. So, if called upon later to fight
it out with the ogre, it was really his fault.

Although he slept good I was wakeful, having, it seems to
me now, something of a premonition of danger. And now,
for the first time, I recollect, that year, I heard the crickets.
They seemed as eerie to me as that many disembodied spirits,
more than the melancholy, doomful Katy-dids. And floorboards creaked. A hound bayed.

I guess it was too many ghost stories too late at night. I was
wider awake than awake. My heart was pitty-patting. Jude
was like a log beside me, not moving, scarce breathing.
Suppose it were true? Suppose (like Mrs. Casserine) he had

this dreadful gift? Maybe that real worthless half of him, the Ruby Lambkin half, had abandoned this sleeping body — and me too.

• • • • • • • • • • • •

Twenty-eight

• • • • • • • • • • •

I HAVEN'T TOUCHED much on superstitions thus far, although when Captain Dolliver died (Dublin) it was thought just as well to "tell the bees." At Hancock most people believed that poor Evelina walked. But take all that yarning that night, sitting around the barroom of Pierce Tavern, how much did people really believe all that?

I'd say for a guess less than half of them believed about half what they had heard. But the fact is, those who didn't believe any or all of it came right along to enjoy the ride. I'm referring to Lawyer Gyp Hammond. Real knowing, men like that. Jude too maybe; never was sure of him. I know I believed a lot then I wouldn't have now, because of my youth and gullibility.

I guess most children (real small ones) believed everything they heard told, sitting about the hearthfire wintertimes — times like that. And they grew up and couldn't ever quite get these childish beliefs out of their blood. For instance, I, being Edward by name and Eddy for short, "knew" it was for me the bullfrogs boomed, "Ketch Eddy, ketch Eddy, ketch Eddy, eat him up, eat him up, eat him up." Every child believed that was what they said — but I tell you it was terrifying for all us little Eddies. Naturally by the time I was ten or so I'd cottoned on to the fact those ignorant reptiles didn't know my name. But even to this day when I hear the bullfrogs hooting, I can feel what's left of my hair getting ready to rise six ways for Sunday, for the innermost inside of me, say my bowels, couldn't ever forget. For there's two kinds of knowledge — head knowledge and bowel knowledge. So even with well-educated grown folk heads might not believe too much of the sort of nonsense we'd been indulging in night before, but deep in our bowels, took in with our mother's milk, was belief in the wonders of the invisible kingdom. So when we had been weaned all the way up to hard cider and whiskey, a little somewhat of this earlier "knowledge" stayed on.

Every child in Hampton, and half the adults, "knew" why "Mike" apples had a pinkish heart to them. For very long long ago, over to West Farms, Connecticut, one Micah Rood had robbed and killed a traveler and buried him under an apple tree, nobody the wiser. But next spring the tree told on him, for it put forth blood-red flowers. Thus murder did out. Scions and grafts from that one tree (and it was a fine, tasty eating apple) right down to my day never did forget the murdered man, for every apple from them has one drop of blood at its heart. I'd of no more doubted the truth of this story as a boy than I'd doubt the whale swallowed Jonah today.

And we had haunted houses a-plenty, even haunted cellar holes with chimneys still standing and moaning. We had graves that never could be filled. Every spring more gravel had to be carted in. Every winter, ground sank.

Death did announce his coming with a curious assortment of phantom vehicles, pale horses, howling dogs, screeches and death ticks. And if you "met yourself," you died. Mitty used to tell me of a way-back uncle of hers — a Grafton, Massachusetts, Brigham. He was going to fight the Indians in the days of the old wars. He walked a space down the road from his home place. Then (and it was broad daylight) coming up from under a dry bridge, was his own self to meet him, dressed in a dirty Indian blanket — gave him one terrible look and evaporated. Well, he really did die — just like that, up in Canada.

There was a young woman from no further off than Abington who had gone up to Boston to buy her setting-out for marriage. She was on Washington Street, and it was as full of people as a dog with fleas, and then she seen it. It was her own self approaching, a white nightgown and a most peculiar red and yellow calico nightcap on, no shoes. Her mother beside her, nor anybody else did see it. She screeched and fainted. They got her home to Abington, and she feverish and half dead already. At first her terror of death was so great they couldn't get a nightgown on her. But at last her sufferings were so piteous she, like a Christian, welcomed death as a good friend. But she couldn't die until her poor, weeping mother made her a nightcap out of red and yellow calico, then she passed on easy. I've often read her name on her gravestone. She was Marlena Marvin, age twenty-one years. And they got a weeping willow on her stone.

Most people died, got planted and stayed put. Some didn't. Wronged people were great hands to take up "walking."

Suppose a will gets "misplaced" accidentally on purpose. Naturally, the testator (if able) begins to materialize around where he put it, and you hear considerable rattling of legal papers. Suppose a dead woman knows her child isn't being done right by, now her husband had married again, wouldn't she come back, if able, and scare the living daylights out of that stepmother?

Murdered people walked, especially if unavenged. Or at least gave some hints — like the Mike apple tree, or like the bloodstained floorboards Jude and I stopped to gape at this summer up somewhere (I forget where) in New Hampshire. They were on the kitchen floor of an abandoned house. No sand and no scouring had effaced them. No, even putting down new planks hadn't stopped the curse, for the stains came seeping back.

The secret of that murder never was solved, but people got tired of the place. Nobody would live there. Another example — just from that one summer traveling I did with Jude. It was that fall and we were on the Barrier (as local people called the Berkshire hills). We were told to avoid a certain crossway because a murdered traveler was too apt to appear right there, pointing at his gashed throat, trying to lead you to his hidden grave. Everybody avoided the spot after nightfall — and we did too.

Suicides were prone to walk, and if they proved too pesky there was nothing for it but dig them up and drive a stake through the remains. Then they were ready to call it a day.

Just to vary the pattern some, there was at least one murderer so wicked not even Satan would give him asylum in Hell. He was the doctor of Moosilauke. He had stolen babies and used their blood to make an elixir of life. And it was his doom to wander forever with his long black cape a-flying and a-whipping in the wind, and his gray locks streaming on the air. His eyes gave off red sparks and you could hear the gnashing of his vampire teeth. His coming presaged forest fires. North New England people were pretty scared of him. I was too when we were in his part of the world and the road lonely and cliffy and the wind roaring in the great forests. And I'd hardly dare look up at the cliffs above us, fearing to see his ghastly black form, and he carrying fire in his bare hands.

But descending to everyday, workaday life, if your cow acted queer, it might be bewitched. Cut off her left ear (at least if you were a shade below the Pratts in education), and next day cross old Widow Gooch has a bloody bandage over her left earhole. And she'll wear her cap pulled down on that side as long as she lives and leave folks' cattle alone.

Butter wouldn't come? Plunge a hot poker in the churn, loud scream, then it came — but the witch has a burn on her leg.

Speaking of witches, I heard of one who, being refused victuals by a farmer, twisted the heads of his geese to backwards. He had to feed them by sprinkling the grain on their backs. Small boy as had the desk next me in school always said he had seen them.

And we did wish on a load of hay, and take care to see the new moon over the proper shoulder. If you handled toads you got warts (but that, I think, is a proven fact). And you could make black snakes out of horsehairs — if you wanted more black snakes. If a cow lost her cud she died. See a black cat a-crossing your path, it's better go home and start out fresh. I wouldn't think to go under a ladder to this day.

But even with the perspective of the years, I couldn't say how much of these supernatural occurrences (and tales) people actually believed. Things like Mrs. Casserine and her litter of fox cubs. Or Jude sleeping over at Franklin, New Hampshire, and his infernal nature over at Springfield, Vermont, same time playing ducks and drakes with the Seventh and Eighth Commandments. Half of it, more than half, was for fun. People enjoyed scaring themselves and others. Also, don't forget those old-fashioned Yankees had terrific imaginations (wouldn't of hit on so many inventions if they hadn't), and if you have such gifts they demand exercise — just as much as spirited horses. And it did give excitement to life (like knowing you might meet old Mr. Scratch himself any night you went out to the privy), and a sort of queer, harsh poetry like some of our best ghost stories had. Can't explain better than that.

The Yankee can be rash beyond belief, flinging himself and all his ready cash (and wife and children after) to start a new project — canals, turnpikes, railroads, shipping lines, great facories. And yet, besides, he is just a mite cautious too. Lots of people by my day weren't quite swallowing things like black cats, and yet why not play safe? — go back home and start out again weren't much trouble. I think that was what Tite and Labe did on the farm. They most certainly always planted corn and all grains (butchered hogs too — lest they might "shrink in the pot") at the time of the new moon. And all roots (including potatoes) were planted, and timber cut, in time of the old moon, and they never did start important new work on Friday, although that was a good day to complete what you had already begun. Or, take me and Jude on the Barrier — Jude would say he didn't believe in apparitions, even of murdered travelers, but we avoided that crossways. That seemed sensible.

• • • • • • • • • • • • •

Twenty-nine

• • • • • • • • • • • •

Wᴇ ᴄᴏᴜʟᴅɴ'ᴛ ꜰɪɢᴜʀᴇ how much Goldie's leg hurt her and how much she was limping for sympathy, as pet horses are prone to do. But it wasn't far to the Shakers' Colony at Enfield; there we could get honest help for her.

These Shakers had the finest farms, and probably the biggest, in New Hampshire. Their lands, lying between Mont Calm Mountain and Mascoma Lake, were rich as Croesus. A man in Canaan, on commenting on poor hard-scrabble

Grafton, had told us once he had met a rabbit over there, sitting on a mica-rock and weeping because his father had died and left him the entire township of Grafton for him to get his living off of, and he couldn't do it. Same man told us that the Shaker lands were so rich that if they planted corn and took first-rate care of it they got one hundred bushels to the acre; if middling care, seventy-five, but if they didn't plant at all they got fifty. Yet these two places weren't more than twenty miles apart. New England has always been a notional giver of her gifts.

So, there was the mountain and the hills beyond, looking like pink-to-gray-blue porcelain, and the lake — dark bright blue and rippling. It was a fine day, blue and sunny. All sorts of mills were set along a brook falling into Mascoma. Not only the usual grist and saw mills, but new inventions they had made, for they threshed, washed clothes, made butter, by water power. No one farmer could afford to rig up water power for the churn and the laundry tub just to keep his old woman out of the grave. You could see right off the advantage of community living. There were at least three hundred men, women and children living here.

Jude said last time he drove in, it was wheat harvest and he'd seen forty strong young scythemen, and every one a Shaker man, and heard the hush, hush, hush of the golden grain coming down before the slow, sweet swinging of their scythes. And that (to his ignorance) had been a handsomer sight and sound than their shaking and singing.

That he had considered childish.

There were acres upon acres of fields — fine fields and persnickety neat. Just a mite too old maidish, I thought — yet their care did pay off. Their seeds were the best money could buy — no weed, no sawdust in Shaker seed. Same with their nursery of little trees. If they sold you, say, a black Spanish cherry tree, that's what it was — not a chokecherry, like some would. Same with their extracts and such. Everything tiptop, violet, rose, and peach water, attar of roses, and a famous medicine called Mascoma Nerve Root. And they made and sold Epsom salts, horehound lozenges, catnip tea, maple and buckthorn syrups, and wooden ware — like ladders and grain measures, pails and such — also best yard goods. Of course there were other colonies of Shakers in other places doing the same sort of things, but the Enfield colony was good as any and the one I happened to visit at.

Their animals too were of equal excellence. For a people so durned celibate and so hard set against procreation for themselves, they certainly put their minds on the breeding of their animals. About this time they paid $1100 for one Merino ram and two ewes (another advantage to community living, for no one farmer could pay that much). But their horses weren't much. Most people used oxen (and theirs were the finest red Devons) for farm work. They had a notion if they put their minds on horse breeding they might get them too fast — and that would lead to racing and that to Hell.

They had as many buildings as many a small town, only better built. Some were stone and some clapboard. There were a lot of them and sort of beautiful in their sparse neatness — dainty-like but strong, like things you see in nature. I'm thinking of deer.

An elderly sister told us where to put the horse and what house and what room in the house we were to have. These people were well accustomed to guests from "the world." The Boston to Montpelier stage ran right through their property. The room we had was so neat even the chairs were hung up on the wall when not being sat on. It smelt of beeswax and lavender and sun-dried linen and just a slight undercurrent of camphor from the blankets. I remember rules posted for their guests:

Breakfast 6.30 summertime, 7.00 winter. These were terribly lazy hours it seemed to me.

All married people must sleep apart.

There was no charge for anything, but people were supposed to pay what they thought right.

Don't leave food on your plate.

And some others.

There was nothing at all about not being noisy, drunken, nor laughing at them. I guess no need for that.

Jude and I went searching for Elder Richman, where the old sister told us to look. We found him in the cornfields — feeling and estimating the half-ripened ears. He was what you might call one of those withdrawn Yankee men, eyes drawn way back in, cheeks sucked in like they'd meet in the middle, and his mouth pulled far in under his nose — and no gush to him, but pleasant. He was said to be the brains of the place and mighty shrewd.

We had hardly come up with him than it was four o'clock and the bell from its little belfry up along the ridge behind us rang, calling in everybody from fields, shops and gardens, for the day's work was over, except of course chores. Shakers disapproved of overwork. They considered that one of the sins of the "world." You were supposed to work hard and "joyfully" while at it, but to have enough starch and ginger left in you for singing and dancing before the Lord evenings.

Saying nothing, he looked at Goldie for us, cleaned his pocket knife with fire and cut along her hoof to let the matter out, then flaxseed poultices. She was trembling with fear and pain, yet he could just do anything to her — although she would hardly let Jude and me touch her leg. Elder Richman certainly had "the horseman's touch."

All he said to us (although he had been cooing at her) was, "Five days."

After a fine supper we went to their meeting hall, sitting in chairs with other guests (for a coach had come in) along one wall. The place was bare as a garret. The brethren came in one door and the sisters in one opposite. The men and boys, even little boys, were all dressed alike — pale blue jackets, white pantaloons, clean shirts, but no neckties. The Devil lurks in neckties. I don't know why.

All womenkind, even some of those little girls no bigger than dolls, were dressed alike — simple dresses of plum or dull blues, white aprons too narrow for genuine work tied about them, and white fichus. Their hair was dressed neater than neat, and on it net caps.

Then (from my ignorant point of view) all they did was to play kid's singing games — girl games at that. Yet you ought to of seen the muscle on some of those young men. They'd circle sing, weave and pantomime. If they sang they were shaking off the Devil, they'd stand on one foot shaking him or wringing him right out of their finger tips. Or they'd reap down sin, or garner in their "gifts," or go jogtrot to the tune of Yankee Doodle. They sang a good deal about their "gifts" and about "love" — their sort of love. And took some pretty outspoken cracks at what the world of the flesh and their own animals might have considered love. By the way, they were the healthiest-looking people, especially you noticed how healthy the children and the real aged looked.

· · · · · · · · · · · · ·

Thirty

· · · · · · · · · · · · ·

O F COURSE, having no marriage and no children of their own, they increased by the children other people gave them. At first these children had come largely from married couples or widowed people who had wished to join them, and not many from, say, the "poor houses." But now overseers of poor, or selectmen having to deal with families that had come upon the town, were getting so trustful of the Shakers they were dumping all the children on them — by the wagonload. Elder Richman explained this to us next morning, sitting in his office, and behind him, painted on paper like it really was a map with black rods top and bottom to roll it up on, was Jude's picture of their place. He'd seen it at wheat harvest and it was golden, and blue, and very still. And he'd got all the neatness and the busyness and the fatness of the land and animals and the austerity of the buildings, and a real true feeling for the place. Hip-hop couldn't have done it.

Elder Richman said that there was too much original sin in some of the poor little lambs now getting carted in on them, and it had been decided that if these town children dumped on them proved genuine limbs of Satan from the start, they were to be returned to their communities right away. He was thinking of the Pease children — boy, four, girl, six. Their widowed mother had come upon the town of West Lebanon. Her brats were real little hellions and he was going to dump them back on West Lebanon. But first place, he was hoping the mother had been able to pull herself together and make a home for them — then he'd send them back with no special qualms.

The town had taken, in lieu of back taxes, a bunged-up riverside tavern and set up Mrs. Pease there to see if she couldn't make a living selling victuals and liquor to rivermen. Elder had tried to advise her, for he himself had been a publican before he had seen the light. He had told her first thing she had to have was a sign big enough to be read the width of the Connecticut River. If she couldn't pay for it and the town wouldn't, nor her church either, then, ding-blast it, maybe the Shakers would, for they were determined to return her children, although they wished well for them.

What he was asking Jude to do was to walk over to West Lebanon, do her a sign (but who'd pay for it wasn't settled yet), look over her establishment and report back to Elder Richman. Also he might prepare her mind for the return of her limbs of Satan and arouse, if possible, an iota of maternal affection within her breast.

We were in no position to refuse any favor to the Elder. We knew he'd got up twice the night before to change the poultice on Goldie's leg — and no charge for anything. He stood at his high desk and wrote out for Jude a letter of introduction, for him to present to Mrs. Pease. We decided to start right out. It was a hot, breathless day. Jude couldn't get his painting gear down to less than a forty-pound pack and, although he theoretically loved to walk, the fact is he hadn't done much of it in the last years — I mean real pack-on-back walking.

It was that time of summer when everything is standing still and one golden day follows the last. Heat waves shimmer on the stumple of the hayfields, birds don't sing much, farmers have a little respite. Everything is growing now, but not like the heady growths of spring. Little apples are getting bigger, and the corn stands higher and prouder every day. Fat animals get fatter. But these things you don't notice just walking past, and things like how the potatoes in their hills grow underground, nobody could guess.

We had walked to Lebanon and were no more than two miles from West Lebanon when Jude pitched his pack off on the roadside in disgust. His blue nankeen jacket was black with sweat and his face dripping. I too was perfectly ready to sit a while by that dusty roadside. Then he began explaining to me how kindly country people were, and all we had to do was sit and look hot and someone would offer us a ride. It was a fact we'd given many a lift ourselves. He said if they looked like they were driving by with no more than a "howdy" the thing to do was ask them how far it was to So-and-so, or did they have the time. He said we'd let pass by farm wagons as too slow, would just tip our hats but make no advances to a lady driving alone — some were timid. As long as there were two of us, the best luck we could have was one gentleman driving a pair of fast ones.

We saw just that approaching, heading right direction for us. "He's coming so Hell-for-leather," says Jude, "he may shoot right by us. I'll just ask him the time. Those Morgans of his are fresh as paint and there's plenty of room in that gig for us."

I never saw a finer span of Morgans — bay, with black points, perfectly matched — real dandified in their manner of going. The young man, too, was a touch on the dandy. Jude left his pack with me and stood on the road. It was so narrow, that just about barred it.

"Fine day," says he, looking very unpresumptuous and touching his hat. Morgans came to a standstill, prickeared, curious and friendly. Never saw one of that breed who didn't expect a pat on the head. "I was just wondering, mister, if you had a watch on and . . ."

Now nothing about that rig would suggest that the young gentleman was driving all the way back from Concord, carrying money borrowed from the bank over there so his father could meet the payroll and other expenses at his factory at White River Junction. Young Johnny Fessenden had on him two thousand dollars. He had heard rumors that Ruby Lambkin had been seen about real near by and he was, when he met us, just about holding his breath and praying to get back to his papa, money and all.

If you hadn't known these facts (we didn't) you couldn't believe how he acted now. By the way, Jude put his foot in it when he asked about his watch.

That dandy's face turned green, not of a sudden but slowly.

His Adam's apple rose, and I guess his stomach with it, and he sat looking at Jude like a house-wren looking at a serpent; even his bill opened, but at first he couldn't get a twitter out of it.

Then he gulped out, "Please . . . Please. I'm not rich. I know this rig looks it . . . but . . . fact is, I'm no more than hired help — out to exercise my master's horses." But he had wit enough to try pull his pretty little creamy-white driving jacket over his flowered waistcoat and the great, fat gold watch chain and seal big as a walnut. "If you'll excuse me . . . please, but fact is I'm due back to White River Junction by three. Now . . . will this do?"

He fetched out and heaved at Jude's feet a knit change-purse.

"What's this trash?" Jude asked with asperity, for the un-manliness of the young man did irk him. The young fellow began taking his watch chain off its buttons and holding up a big gold watch. "This isn't trash," he squeaked, and would have hove that overboard if Jude hadn't stopped him.

"Oh for God's sake," said Jude. "I don't want a thing from you — no, not even the time of day. Get along with you, do. But don't venture so far from home next time without taking your mother with you."

As he stepped back the whip fell across the backs of those little Morgans' round flanks. They broke into a dead run, and with the gig swaying behind them, disappeared in a cloud of dust — heading for the bridge across the Connecticut, and White River Junction.

A lot of that dust settled on us. I was laughing. Then he took in what I'd taken in right away.

"Blessed if he didn't think I was that Ruby Lambkin of a fellow. Jumping Jehosaphat! Wasn't the first thing he said something about not being rich? I was so thunderstruck by his expression I wasn't listening good."

"He said he was just hired help, out exercising his master's horses." This claim fascinated me, for I had never seen such a dandy in all my life as this one was.

Jude pushed back his sweaty hat and scratched his head. "I suppose I should feel flattered. Didn't know I could scare anybody into such a conniption fit without even putting my mind on it. Broad daylight too. Think what I could do nighttime." Then he began to laugh too. He didn't laugh often, although he smiled easy. But when he really laughed like this, he had to sit down and wipe his eyes to do it.

The knit purse still lay there in the dust. Jude gave it a contemptuous kick and we started on again. We hadn't gone far when we came to a tumble-down sort of place. There was a big girl child and two or three smaller ones about her all gaping after what they thought was a runaway. Jude nudged me. "If I'm to be taken for that God-forsaken black Lambkin so that decent people won't give me a lift, I may as well get the advantages of my bad name."

"Miss," he said softly, no more than that, but he gave a secrecy to the word, something wrong. Not having heard us, she was scared. She wheeled quick, and instinctively gathered the children closer. The children had scabby heads and she didn't look much better. They were literally in rags.

"A gentleman," said Jude soft, so wheedling soft, "dropped his purse out of that runaway — up back along the road a little bit. Might come back inquiring for it and, if you returned it, give you a little somewhat. If he didn't come, I'd say finders are keepers. But first could we have a drink out of that well?"

She shot down the bucket and hauled it up and lifted it for us. She couldn't say so much as thank you, but she did long so to serve us.

In the big eyes in the thin little face we saw a look almost like ecstasy. She couldn't say a word, but she "knew" who he was.

We turned to see her starting back along the way we come,

carrying one poor howling baby in her arms and one not much bigger holding on to her tattered skirts. We both were real satisfied the young gentleman had dropped his purse.

.   .   .   .

Thirty-one

.   .   .   .

FROM THE NEXT RISE, for the first time, we saw the great Connecticut — peaceful, confident, sleepy-like under the hot August sun. We saw logs chained together into rafts coming down, big as blockhouses; flatboats riding down so easy, the men setting about playing cards, fiddles and other shinigans. There were cattle and sheep moaning and baa-ing, and baled goods on the boats going down, for it was a cheap freighting. That's one reason the roads alongside this river weren't better. When it came to getting a flatboat upstream with manufactured goods and such, then those rivermen certainly had a time of it — two weeks down from Fairlee, but five to seven weeks up. They took them up with poles mostly. You'd see seven or eight husky fellows push at the muddy bottom and walk forward, and then return to where they started from, and do it over and over again, and day after day — like oxen in a treadmill. Seemed unfitting to use men like that. Jude told me (we sat some time watching the river below us) that the men going downstream sang in little bursts; nice and pretty, but not much, really — usually one fellow at a time. But the men poling all together, working more like slaves than men, sang all together and sang mournful, strong-rhythmed songs wonderful to hear.

It was Mr. Sharp, once, had told him that same thing was true in the South where he'd seen the Negro slaves working in the fields, and the same true on great ships to sea. For when work goes beyond all human decency, you might say, tedious, hard and terrible, then men sing real good. Free men, idle men, maybe happy men, jig about and trill, but you never get that haunting mournfulness from free men.

We were too far away to hear them. But I was to hear them a-plenty later on — coming up and going down — so I put this in now.

Over yonder, over the river, was Vermont, and it was blue and humped-up-looking. We could see White River Junction over there on other side (and the bridge across the Connecticut) and we lolled about, letting the day slip away toward dusk, and the great valley filling softly with rose-color and lavender. Then we braced up and went looking for Mrs. Pease. We knew she was on the riverbank, that her establishment wasn't too good and had no sign, and we could spot the broken-down wharf and the stakes driven into the ooze for rivermen to tie up to.

Jude told me that although drover's taverns (like the Cow, Holden, Massachusetts) were a touch low-down, wait until I saw one set up to attract rivermen, for they and lumberjacks had the reputation of being the roughest men in New England. And often a man would work as a lumberjack in winter and then take to the river summers. They came from everywhere and from nowhere — Frenchies from Canada, Herring-chokers and Bluenoses from down East. They were free-living, free-drinking, free-thinking men, and he for one admired them. Not all people did. For instance, no settled minister did.

Mrs. Pease was a mere stub of a woman. I guess she was sitting in the last row when the faces were given out — vacant-looking, not too bright. She and her place had an air of dejection fatal to publicans and public houses. We no sooner had stepped into her kitchen than she was telling us it didn't pay her to fix up, for nobody ever came and, anyway, next spring freshet would take this whole shebang down to Bellows Falls — as it had four years back. Town fathers of Lebanon weren't very smart to think they could get her started as a self-supporting citizen by trying her hand at tavernkeeping.

Then she got her eye on Jude's pack. Had he snake oil for her joints? If not, something for summer complaint? Anything for female weaknesses? If not, something for bedbugs?

It was some time before she'd let him explain what his trade was and why for he was here and present Elder Richman's letter. The old Shaker hadn't quite said he'd pay for it, although implied it, and she was saying she couldn't any more afford a sign than a pig a pocket handkerchief, and as long as no one came anyway, why waste the money? That woman was born to be on the town.

So it looked like we were stuck there for a night and no financial reward. It was past suppertime, but she had a tripe pudding boiling on her hearth fire and it would be fit to eat in, say, an hour. By the way, she knew we had just come from the Enfield Shakers, but nary a word did she ask us of those two limbs of Satan of hers the Shakers were about to dump back on her, or rather on the town, no more than the old cat remembers last year's litters.

We got away from her and her complaints in an upper room that looked east, not out over the river which would have been a pleasure to us both. Her interest in bug remedies had somewhat aroused our suspicions of the big lumpy bed that about filled the room.

Jude was hanging out the window saying there must be another inn in West Lebanon, but he guessed we were the only people who had stopped there for a long time and he hated to walk out on her, and so on.

"Well, and if here doesn't come a whole wagonload of men. Now, if they stay, I'll feel no guilt about pulling out. Let them eat that high-to-heaven tripe pudding," and he'd be so and so if he would.

I stuck my head out. There were eight men in a wagon drawn by two lean but good fast horses, and they were all roughly dressed and carried guns. Two or three of them stayed outside, the others dove for the inn.

"I'll tell you what's happened," Jude told me. "Somebody has been losing lambs to a bear, and these here farmers are pooling their efforts to go out after it." I'd seen the same sort of getting-together down Hampton way — only there it was things no bigger than Old Split Foot. We hadn't bears, cata-mounts, wolves and such left over down there from the old days; they still had up here. One thing Jude hadn't had the wit to notice, these men had no dogs with them.

Jude was pleased to have a little company, and we were starting down the stairs before Mrs. Pease called to him to come. Six men lounged about the public room, each with his gun between his knees or nonchalantly in his hands — no place for Jude and me to sit.

"These gentlemen," said Mrs. Pease, twisting her hands in her dirty apron, "were wishing for you to sit and drink with them."

"Much obliged," said Jude. "Evening, gentlemen."

"Evening," they croaked.

"Well . . . " he went on, real debonair considering the cold eye they were giving him, "if I'm to sit and drink I'll go fetch me a chair."

"No — stay standing where you are, mister. Mrs. Pease, you get them somewhat to sit on." She fetched from some-where two stools. We sat, feeling like bad children set on stools a-waiting teacher to add a dunce cap.

"And if no one else has a mind to order drinks, then I will," said Jude, "seeing as how your invitation called for sitting and drinking." They perked up at that and gave Mrs. Pease their orders.

They began questioning, one man taking the lead. He was straddled hind side around on his chair, arms on the chairback and chin on his arms — man about fifty. The bare arms and the visible piece of his chest were all fuzzed up, pretty as a caterpillar — but no prettier. He had rather small bones, considering his bulk. A meaty man. He would cut up good — lots of roasts and steaks to make money, in proportion to soup bones to give away. Not much suet nor tallow on him. He had unblinking blue eyes set a bit nigh to each other. The bridge of his nose had either been bashed in or grew that way. His mouth was curly as though he done it with his wife's curling tongs. On top he had God's plenty, and then some, of sandy hair gone gray. He chewed and spit, spit and chewed. This constant exercise had certainly developed his jaw muscles. His skin was a fine bright color. Some people would of thought him handsome. I disliked him on sight. His intimates called him Smokey.

Questions ran like this: "Where was Jude from? What was his trade? Was there money in it? Where had he spent last night? Night before? How tall was he? Where bound?" Just about the usual things.

Nobody had thanked Jude for the drinks he had ordered them. The conversation was repeating itself over and over.

"Where were you last night?"

"Shakers, Enfield — as I told you three times."

"Night before?"

"Canaan, Pierce Tavern — if it is any of your business."

"Ain't it though? Mister, just what time o'clock you say you left Lebanon for West Lebanon? And what time you get there?"

"Wasn't looking at any watches."

"Not even for a gold watch, heh? You were dressed as you are now?"

"Yes. Pepper and salt pantaloons, nankeen jacket."

"Met any fellow travelers on that there road?"

"Yes, Mr. Sheriff. That's right isn't it? I'm addressing a sheriff, aren't I?"

"Yep. That's me. Sheriff Burnap — of Windsor County."

"He's Smokey Burnap," one of the henchmen added.

"If you'll recall," said Smokey, his snake eyes narrowing and narrowing and beginning to glitter with disapproval, "you pulled a neat one on me June twenty-third last, locking *me* in my own pigpen. Cute, aren't you?"

I suppose Jude was getting a touch nervous, for he laughed now. It was the wrong time, but it made me giggle too — thinking of that particular fellow locked up in his own pigpen.

"Oh let's get this joking over with," said Jude impatiently. "It wasn't me ever, although I can see the humor of the situation. About then I was round about Hancock, New Hampshire — nowhere near Vermont, nor you, nor your pigs. And by the way, whatever are you, a Vermont sheriff, doing over here in New Hampshire where you don't legally belong?"

"Legally!" and he spit. "Look here. I go just about where I damned choose to go — and no questions asked."

"Like into your pigpen."

He blinked those icy eyes but made no other response to Jude's prodding at him. "I'll get down to business. Last night you broke and entered the store of Mr. Thomas Archer of White River Junction. You didn't get much ready cash, did you? But it was breaking and entering. This afternoon, say two-fifteen, you held up Johnny Fessenden, not three miles from here. And I'm going to find out from you who it was over to White River told you young Fessenden had gone to Concord to fetch home that two thousand dollars in bank money. Someone put you up to it. But you lost your nerve,

didn't you? Johnny says you shrank right back when con-
fronted with his well-known ferocity. All you got out of that
was his change-purse — which, by the way, you later gave to
one Dorothy Johnson. I've talked to her already. But only
think boys," and he turned to his posse men, "the great Ruby
Lambkin was scared by a thing like Johnny Fessenden. Dear,
dear, dear. And Johnny said as how Ruby was a monstrously
powerful tall man, evil-looking as old Horny and devilish
handsome to boot." They all looked contemptuously at Jude
and laughed. "Well," Smokey continued, "seeing is believing, and now you're seeing."

"Wait a moment." Then for the first time Jude told of his
meeting with Johnny. The posse men, local White River
Junction men Sheriff Burnap had called out special, no real
friends and relatives of his, liked it — evidently looking upon
Johnny Fessenden as a figure of fun. They all really knew
Jude wasn't Ruby. At the time I thought Smokey Burnap did
too, and was only bedeviling him because he had laughed
over him in the pigpen.

"Boys," said the Sheriff, "just take a good gander at this
here Mr. Rebough. If he's handsome I'm John the Beloved
Disciple. As for 'powerful' I could twist his head off 'tween
my thumb and finger. Spavined," and he spit, "knock-kneed.
So, looks like Johnny was too terrified to see straight."

I forgot to say one of the men had been going through
Jude's pack. Burnap had the small account book I'd been
keeping of pictures sold and expenses in his hand. Now he
was running a blunt finger down a column. "Yep. June
twenty-third, Hancock, New Hampshire. The Reverend
Perch. No charge."

Sheriff Burnap stretched and yawned, but it was like the
yawning of a carnivore to show off its muscles and the length
of its teeth.

"Boys," he said mildly to his men, "there ain't a thing here
for us, is there? What's your opinion?"

They agreed.

"Boys, you get into that wagon and wee-waw back over the bridge to White River. Long as I'm here I'll do some business I've long had in mind — up on Main Street. Get my supper up to Palmer for I'm hungry enough to eat the lamb of God."

The men shook hands with Jude real friendly and soon we heard the wagon go rattling off. Mrs. Pease was pointing out nobody had paid for the rum drunk. Jude reached for his back pocket.

"No you don't," said Burnap. He had a pistol in his hands. "Don't you move or I'll drill you — with pleasure."

And looking at him you knew it would be a pleasure to him to drill anything or anybody. That man was a killer by nature, and he had the hard blue eyes. I've noticed out here in the West all the famous killers, sheriffs and bad men alike, have had the same blue eye. Not a dark-eyed man among them. And although mean mouths are apt to be thin-lipped and straight, curly mouths are often cruel. As I said, his was curly as a pig's tail — and no prettier.

"You think fast enough for those dumb posse men," said he, "but now you've got to talk faster and better to suit me — Mr. Ruby Lambkin."

Mrs. Pease squealed "Not Ruby Lambkin! My, to think I was here practically alone and completely at his mercy for hours. My sakes alive." And she patted up her back hair and looked real pert.

"Shut your trap," said Burnap.

"See here," said Jude a touch angrily, "you yourself told your posse men there wasn't any doubt of me."

"Sure. Sure I did, and you made a laughingstock of me. For ever since June twenty-third last I've sworn I'd get you — and I'm going it alone. You'd be surprised, when you are arresting a man alone, how often they resist the officer and have to be shot for their pains. No posse, no witnesses, eh?

There you are, turning white like a girl. Enough to make a man laugh — except I don't laugh easy."

"Oh," screamed Mrs. Pease, "not in my kitchen. Oh, you beast . . . and I'm a witness. So's that boy setting there. And you can't . . . "

"One more word out of you and I'll bust your harslet. Likewise, why divvy up the reward between me and eight other fellows? I can use it all myself. And no need," says he, "for twenty tailors around one buttonhole."

"Need money for a new lock on your pigpen?"

He spit, but didn't rise to that. "Yesterday I'd of got one hundred and fifty dollars for your hide. But Mr. Fessenden upped it when he heard how close he'd been to losing two thousand, and you scaring poor Johnny so. You're worth two hundred today. Glad I didn't go after you earlier. Or," and there was a speculative look in his eye, "I might leave you loose a little longer — let it get to three hundred, say."

I might explain that the sheriffs got no salary, being paid only for special jobs such as a hanging. Then too, they got more than their share of reward money, being in a position to know more of such things than anyone else. But if Sheriff Burnap did actually think he now had Ruby Lambkin and didn't take him because he was waiting for the reward to go still higher, he was doing something I never heard of another sheriff being base enough to do. But he was saying a hunter never did take a pelt until it was good and prime.

Mrs. Pease came in again with her squeaks. "Sheriff, you know Elder Richman over to Enfield?"

"Naturally, I've been selling him lumber for twenty years."

"And his writing? I've got a letter — just thought. Now where'd I put it. Tarnation! Where'd I put the letter? No. There, yes. Here in my apron pocket."

First she read it to him, then he let his pistol slide down and took and looked the letter over himself, not keeping Jude covered at all — which proves he really knew now (if not before) that Jude was what he said he was. He slipped his pistol into his holster.

"Maybe you think I owe you an apology?"

"You do. And I'd like to hear it."

"You're too smart for my taste. You don't get any."

"Your manners are a credit to Vermont."

"Real chatty man, aren't you, eh? And I suppose you looking like him and all that, gives you good laughs. Well, young fellow, let me tell you one thing. If you've any brains at all (which I doubt) you'll keep that 'handsome face, powerful, agile anatomy,' your 'gentlemanly appearance' and 'softspoken ways' out of Vermont — or you're going to meet someone that shoots first and asks questions afterwards. Have done such things myself. Nearly did this time. New Hampshire people are sort of a meechy set, but in my state, where I come from, men certainly are men and not afraid of their firearms."

"Oh, Vermont," said Jude scornfully, "more sheep than people in Vermont. As hard to tell, sometimes, which is which as sheriffs from pigs."

"That there Green Mountain State . . . "

"Forget it. Vermont doesn't mean green mountains. It means Hill of Worms. People who named that demmed place so illiterate they even slipped up on their Latin," for Jude now was feeling pretty good. But Sheriff was thinking his own thoughts and pulling at his lower lip — sort of uncurling it.

"When time comes I'll take Ruby Lambkin's hide — nail it right up on my own barn door."

"You said that before." For he had.

They shook hands at parting and yet there was something a little threatening about the way he said, "See you again, Mr. Rebough — did you say the name was?"

Mrs. Pease shut and bolted the door after him and she was

breathing hard. "If only I'd recognized you . . . Why, I could of warned you the sheriff was coming. You could of dropped out that second-story window and . . . "

"No. First place, Sheriff Burnap had placed his men in the yard . . . "

"You could of done it." She looked admiringly at him. "I guess you can do about anything."

He thanked her for thinking of Elder Richman's letter. We hadn't, and that's proof Jude and I were pretty excited. But she was hardly listening, only staring at Jude, licking her lips and shaking her head. And here note: that there poor woman had no thought of the two hundred dollars she might get for him. Then the smell of that tripe pudding worsened considerable — for the water had boiled away and it, wrapped in its old cotton rag, had caught at the bottom of the pot. We went out for fresh air and to stretch our legs as she aired out and agreed to set out eggs and bread and make coffee for us.

We could see the Connecticut River and the strong, straight white moonlight, "the moonglade" country people called it, like a silver sword dividing Vermont and New Hampshire. And over there, doubtless among those "Hills of Worms," was that other fellow, and Jude was speculating how Mrs. Pease would be boasting Sheriff Smokey Burnap and his men had caught Ruby under her roof, and except for her quick wit, would have taken him.

We walked on a bit. It was a still night, white with that drenching moonlight. "Give the story time," says Jude, and he himself would recover from the knock-knees, or whatever Sheriff had accused him of (and it was not true, as I knew) and would be the handsomest man eyes ever did see. And poor Mrs. Pease, with her stomach complaint and female weaknesses and so on, would grow young again and prettier than ever she had been. For there was some truth in what Mr. Sharp contended — handsome rascals should be loved by pretty girls and Devil-may-care should outwit the sheriff.

The rich should be stolen from, and the poor given to. Jude said he had seen men that could take a stick and whittle pretty things out of it. Out of nothing — something pretty. That's what people were doing out of facts round here. Making facts into art — something pretty.

And he hoped very much sometime he'd actually meet up with Ruby Lambkin. One thing he wanted to ask him — if he had trouble shaving the cleft in his chin. "Maybe by drawing that sheriff over here to hunt me I saved his hide for him. Disgusted me hearing that brute talking about nailing it up on his barn door — and he would of shot first, questioned later."

I said earlier that Jude, and me, too, at that stage were on the side of the foxes. We certainly both felt a sight fonder of Ruby Lambkin than Sheriff Burnap. I outgrew it. He never did.

.   .   .   .

Thirty-two

.   .   .   .

Not HAVING SLEPT MUCH, due to the activities of that bed (and I'm not referring to its camel's hump either), we left early as light came for the cleanness of Enfield and Shakers.

I hoed corn longside the Shaker men and boys. Jude added, to the "map" he had done, a six-story stone building Elder Richman wanted him to draw in, for they already had begun on it.

He had already written to Professor Dwight, the botanist of Dartmouth, that he'd be along real soon and now, Goldie's leg being cured up and she back in shoes again, we started out.

We traveled with the Connecticut River to our left and the road was poor. The great valley, with its purple hills and mountains about it, was green and golden with midsummer — golden as a goddess, and most celestially still.

Professor Dwight was eighty, if a day, but a gay gimmick at heart. When he laughed he tossed his white beard up, shut his eyes and roared. I suppose he was the most famous man I've ever met. Dwight's Botany is still the standard authority, but he wasn't dignified in small ways. For instance, being bald as a baby's bottom, he fancied a red bandanna handkerchief knotted at all four corners for house wear (kept off flies and drafts) rather than the velvet skullcap other old gentlemen wore. But on Sunday he did wear a dignified plug hat. He had no regards for his health, for he ate, worked, laughed, drank, smoked, more than some would consider becoming. He had no regard for his personal safety, and although already a touch too teeter-tottery to go up and down all those fearsome mountains and precipices for specimens, he went up them and he got specimens. It was some years later, and I way out west there, I read in an eastern newspaper how he had fallen to his death on Mt. Ascutney. I was still in Missouri then, and was reading the paper out loud to some fellow loafer before the post office. Seems the old gentleman had gone after an alpine that had never before been collected in those parts — and, if it weren't still in his dead hand. One of those men laughed to think a man would die for no more than a "pukin'-to-hell damn posy." But I thought it was a fine brave death for a fine, brave old man.

They were ready and expecting us. His married daughter, Mrs. Schofield (husband taught mathematics), had the bed chamber she usually put a couple of students in fixed for Jude. The college was closed for a few weeks in August.

She put me in the ell chamber with a couple of her sons. The dining room was to be Jude's workroom. Professor Dwight had all ready and waiting for Jude a stack of pressed flowers, and pen and India ink and the drawing paper he liked best. He said nobody else but Mr. Rebough could get pressed flowers up on their feet and alive again. We ate in the kitchen, which wasn't real convenient for his daughter.

But the whole family, Mr. and Mrs. Schofield, and the children too, all were backing Dr. Dwight's work to the hilt. I think by and large it was the happiest family I ever visited in. It weren't a large house and now it was crowded some, for there were five Schofield children — the three oldest of them and me playing ball a lot over on the short slippery grass of the campus under the still, limp elms. Others must have joined us, for we played three-o'-cat and rounders. Not base-ball, for it weren't invented yet — games we played were baseball's seed fathers.

I never saw a girl that could catch and throw like Primrose Schofield. She was fourteen. She had short black curls, cherry-red cheeks, happy mouth, happy eyes, and real big feet. When the day was ending and it was getting on, too dark for ball games, we played Hoist the Green Flag, Run, Sheep, Run, Relevo — running games, running through the dusk, and all over the campus, and around the empty college build-ings — all over the place. Primrose was fleet as a skeeter then.

Every morning at eight o'clock sharp she tutored her two next-younger brothers, Ernie and Roscoe, in Latin, usually sitting out on the campus under an old elm tree. Fact is, she was already "prepared for college," but at that time there was no college that took females. It saddened me a little that she was no more than fourteen, so all ready and willing to go, and no place for her to go to.

By the way, she was the first young person I ever saw with a pair of spectacles on. She put them on for Latin lessons, and she did look cute in them. I was pretty taken with Primrose.

But even then it pained me that she was learning nothing of housework and woman's proper sphere. That big girl couldn't knit so good as six-year-old Leaf Rebough. I suppose she came to a bad end — like crowing hens and whistling girls. I hope not, for she was a darling.

She knew a lot of botany, having been collecting so much with her grandfather. She knew every last dinged little bird by sight and by sound. Perhaps it is natural that I still sometimes think of her, sitting on the grass, with her bright little head turned to admire the bush full of birds Mrs. Dolliver had taken eternal possession of. And the flower-delicate tip-tilt of her profile fitted in just right. Neck too — just right.

When, after the late War Between the States, an institution for the higher education of females was starting out here, and I was in a position to do a little something, financially speaking, I thought first of calling my modest gift the "Primrose Fund." I thought twice and didn't. But even after all these years I did it for her.

I was taking Latin lessons of her too. Roscoe (he was only nine) and I were just about the same far along. Then Jude asked me would I like to stay here and go to a real tutoring school and then to Dartmouth, rather than Waltham, and learn harness making. I don't know how he figured to pay for all this, but somehow he would of done it. I guess this was the most important decision I ever had to decide. I did want so terribly to stay here and go on being educated, and yet I couldn't. I figured it this way: three years tutoring, four years college — seven years. But if I went to that uncle in Waltham I'd be through my apprenticeship in three years at most Then I'd go west. No, I couldn't of waited. It was as if had no free choice left in me. Maybe I decided right. Mayb wrong. I've thought many times of those empty white build ings, ranged around the campus (they are always empty buildings in my memory), and not far off the river, circling hills and lavender mountains of New England, and the summer sky, blue and high. And Primrose coming up to bat, or running through the summer dusk, "Run, sheep, run." Or turning her quick head, "Hush," for she had heard a hermit thrush. Or maybe with her spectacles on, helping us with the worst part of Caesar's Commentaries. I'm referring naturally to that bridge.

"Tigna bena, susquipidelia." That's how I remember it, but like so many other things way back then, maybe a little wrong.

. . . .

Thirty-Three

. . . .

I HAVE BEEN TELLING more about me and less about Jude for this reason. I want to explain how right here, Hanover, New Hampshire, middle of August, we lost each other off. For on this trip, up to now, we had been thicker than any thieves. Ever since we left home we had (up to now) slept in the same bed. Now I was in with Ernie and Roscoe. I've described my world to you. Jude's world was Dr. Dwight's. True, he'd call me into the dining room where he worked to let me see the wonders of vegetation through a microscope. Then I'd hear the tick-tack, tick-tack of someone playing catch, or a voice my own age calling me out to play, and I itched to go. I did lose track of him. Looking back on that happy spell, I think I had more of real childhood then than any other time in my life. Which seems odd, for I was just leaving childhood.

I have mentioned the fact that right across the river from Hanover is Norwich — not to be confused with her old mother town far off now, in Connecticut. It was in Vermont's Norwich Jude had seen, three years before, Emma Faucett, leaning from her window at him. I know this much of their first meeting. She had been washing her hair and had taken off her tuck-in so as not to muss it. That's why she hadn't answered to his knocking at the door, although she had looked out to see what was up. He had held up two bodies and backgrounds to entice her. She had laughed at them (he told me that). She said those weren't women — those were paper dolls. Then she'd pulled her head in and the top half of her body, and was gone. He just stood there under the huge old pine the inn sign swung on, looking at his own work, and he'd be gosh-darned for a polecat if there hadn't been something in what she had said. He was so bemused he just got in his chaise and drove off, although when he had come up to this place, and noting an inn sign, he had thought to put up there.

Only this spring the apothecary and the engravings at that other Norwich brought the thought of her from the bottom of his mind (where I guess it belonged) to the top. He'd gone to work and, according to both Hip-hop Hooper and my lights, he'd done a wonder — all but the face. No face yet. And he longed for that face he'd seen — but still, I honestly believe, in a very nice way, for I don't say he was longing for the woman herself yet. That came later. You might say he'd been taken by Emma three years back but not hooked. Yet I do think it was smart of Mitty to smell a mouse.

Now how could he wait, wait, wait just those few miles away, over in Hanover working with a microscope, getting red-eyed and headachey? Every day he was putting in from eight to ten hours' work on the drawings. And the children did stand on the rung of his chair and watch him and breathe on him as he worked. They did bother him.

Now I'll have to speculate. I was too wrapped up in my own world, too shut off from him to know much. I was too young to really understand what I did see. In fact, it wasn't until I myself had been married for some years I really understood what Jude went through.

I think he didn't go right over after her because he was afraid. Perhaps he was scared that when he saw her again she wouldn't live up to his memory of her. She had grown so beautiful in his imagination he dared not face disillusionment. Perhaps he was fearful if he saw her again, and she didn't prove disappointing, he might be more taken by her than a married man ought. Wives never seem to realize how hard husbands do try to keep out of trouble. I do know one thing he had no fear of, and that was Sheriff Burnap's warnings that he better had keep himself out of Vermont.

He was just waiting, like other people in his position, for some external force to push him. That force was only this: Dartmouth was opening up. The two young gentlemen who had rented the chamber Jude slept in were returning. Mrs. Schofield told him not to think to leave — a neighbor would put up those two students for a spell. Yet he caught at this as an excuse to leave them and get other side the river.

He told them last time he was hereabout he had noted over to Norwich the quietest, nicest, best place to work he'd ever seen. If they didn't mind, he would leave Eddy here with them, but he was going over to that other place. If Dr. Dwight didn't mind, he'd take a big pile of pressed flowers and a microscope and such with him. Of course he'd be driving back all the time to get more specimens and be checked on his work and see Eddy behaved himself. "I'm afraid the children have bothered you," Mrs. Schofield said contritely, "for six children do make a lot of racket. They can't help it." So, that seeming to be his wish, he went.

He asked me to drive over with him and walk back. I think he took me because he wanted a chaperone although, like me going west, he had to go over there — come Hell or high water. But he didn't want me hanging around with him. Fearful, maybe, that I'd be a constant reminder to him of Mitty's generosity to both of us. Both of us strays and she had taken us in. I felt something was wrong with him. Anyway, he wasn't any of those happy bridegrooms such as you read about in the Bible. He was a little sunk.

We crossed the Connecticut River (and it was our Rubicon), which separated one town from the other and the two states. We were in Vermont — which did prove a veritable Hill of Worms to us, just as Jude had twitted Sheriff Burnap. We went up a rise and were in Norwich. It was white and green and scholarly, like the college town we had just left, for here was Norwich Military Academy. I guess the reason that old bridge we crossed the Connecticut River on was so wobbly was this: from time out of mind the young gentlemen at those two seats of learning had been meeting on that bridge and fighting it out. It was good fun for them, pretending to hate each other, but it was a headache for the towns-people of those two towns. That was why eventually one of the two seats of higher learning had to move out. It was Norwich Military Academy that moved.

We took a sharp right by the Academy and were on a good sandy road running on the second terrace. Those terraces around there were so neatly done you could hardly believe man hadn't done it. It was the river did it.

The second we left Norwich we realized the extent of the "sheep craze" hereabout. Sheep bells tinkling and sheep baaing, sheepfolds and pens and dips, lambing and shearing houses, wool houses. People had gone so far overboard on sheep nobody wanted to stop and milk a cow. Fortunes were being made in sheep. I might add here how that bubble broke. Domestic wool was highly protected from cheaper imports by Washington. Some ten years later the duty was taken off. Wool went from one-fifty a pound to twenty-five cents. The farmers killed the sheep for no more than their hides. Couldn't get a price on mutton. At last they killed the sheep merely to get rid of them. A man from those parts told me the rotting bodies of the slaughtered sheep stank up the whole place, and brought back the wolves. Then Vermont was indeed a "Hill of Worms" and nobody thought it would ever arise again to be the beautiful Green Mountain state. It did take them a few years to get back on their feet. But you know Yankees. They have been taught how to take bad weather, bad crop years, bad luck generally along with the good. They just keep shut about anything nature can do to them, work hard and hope for better. No complaints. But the idea that it was their own government had so greased the ways under them and sent them careening down to poverty did make their blood boil. You ask a Vermont man today what he thinks of federal government — he hasn't forgot and forgiven yet.

But the sheep were doing fine when we were there. When we came to three farmhouses set fairly close together (this was Kitchen Corner), Jude knew we turned right. We pitched off the second terrace and were on number one. Our road was no better than a cart path. Before us bushes and trees grew along the bank of the river. There was a low broad house with weeping willows and old pines about it, and a big red barn to it and the usual signs of sheep keeping. There were cornfields and the fences were well kept up. It didn't look like a tavern except only for the sign hung from a great pine. It read:

F. Faucett. Bait and Board
For Man and Beast

Painted on the sign was a golden faucet dripping in a silver cup. Jude told me that eventually that sign got on his nerves. He'd lie awake and feel like he could hear it dripping and wished someone would give it a new washer.

There wasn't any life about, yet it didn't seem desolate. It only gave off a feeling of heavenly or (by hind-sight) infernal peace. We sat in the chaise, listening to sheep bells and baa-ing, and to the rivermen singing on the river beyond. We thought maybe a stable boy would come for the horse. No-body came. It was like nobody ever would.

Now I'll tell it like I remember it, even if I know I've got it wrong. For I saw her looking out the window — a first-floor window, and the trumpet vines and the woodbine and morn-ing-glories were growing up around it. Just exactly like the picture. She had washed her hair, and as she leaned out the window to smile at us it hung forward and about her and glittered like copper shavings. Too much for good taste. Yet of course this didn't happen (here my memory plays tricks on me). Yet she was there — like that. And I saw her . . . and I know I didn't.

I'll put in here what she looked like. She really was a beauty. It was her own beauty, and nobody else's, which made it a lot more entrancing. It would be easy to say she was too fat, but if she hadn't been she couldn't of looked like she did. Or that she was too old; same answer. Most people don't fancy red hair. Then they never saw Emma Faucett — and hers, down and coiling about her half-bare, plump shoulders, like melted copper. She had freckles. Take one away and you had diminished her. Her expression was sleepy mostly, but when she woke up she glowed like you could never forget and made other women look no more expressive than a parcel of mud puppies.

Many things I noted later I will jot down now.

She had a way of getting up off a chair like she was getting out of bed. Doesn't sound enticing, but it was.

When hot she'd lift her skirts and fan her knees. When chilly, back up to a fire, hist her skirts. Lots of respectable New England women do both those things — yet she did it different.

She had gray eyes with dark fringes to them and a free look in them. It wasn't the look of a wanton who'll give herself to any man, but of a woman who utterly owns herself, bowing to no man, nor law either. Yet not a bit wild-looking, peaceful mostly.

I won't say she was a good moral woman, for she was not. And when she fell she fell in jig-time. But (being her) she didn't fall hard, for she never took anything hard — not even her own departure from the paths of virtue. She didn't take her husband hard — he was the most worthless man I ever met, east or west. Mr. Faucett didn't faze her any. She could take him, or anything else, and make out. Or get along with nothing. If that's where strength lies, she was strong. In comparison Jude weren't no more than an empty shirt, flapping on a clothesline.

Although I'd swear it on a stack of Bibles I saw her look out the window, waiting for us, I know she did not, for I remember rapping and calling at the front door. Then going in, for it was open, and this a public house. The hall run from front door to back and the cool air was moving in off the river. It set the clean white window curtains to breathing.

"You can see," says Jude, "why I thought this would be a good place to work. Always a touch too much going on over to Professor Dwight's." Seemingly nothing was going on over here, or ever would.

We kept on out the back door. There was a big willow there. We turned up toward the barn. Jude helloed softly. We saw a man step out from behind a hay rick. He had a pitchfork in his hands and he came at us sort of sidewise, like a crab. He was a small black man. I don't mean honest black like a Negro — black like a devil.

The way he walked you knew he had something wrong somewhere. A little limp — like Split Foot the fox. Jude always insisted that he had cleft feet. And the reason for his continual twitching at his galluses was Christian pants weren't cut to accommodate a forked tail. He was a powerful little fellow — all steel springs and whalebone. His huge hands, hanging to the end of those too long, black-haired forearms, ought to have belonged to someone else. He looked at us with an air of knowing everything and saying nothing. Then he spat.

Jude said, "Any accommodations?"

"Yep," said the imp.

"My horse is tied out front."

"Yep. I seen it."

"Before you put her up I want to take some stuff out the chaise, for if you can accommodate me I'm intending to stay on a space. I've work to do and I brung it with me."

"Yep." He spat again, more like a cat than a man. He put down his pitchfork and led us back into the tavern. He showed us up to a fine big room. It was spotless. We toted in what Jude needed and the imp waited for us in the public room. He had taken off his blue barn-smock and he'd tied tight about his wiry body a starched white apron. What would we have?

Jude said, "Rum and water — but mostly water for the boy. And mister . . . Happens you are Mr. Faucett?"

He went to the door to spit, for he was cleanly as a cat.

"Not me," he said. "I'm Silas Poke. Not Mr. Faucett — thank God."

He drew deftly. Then took off the white apron, put on the blue smock and went out to put up our horse.

The cool drink tasted good and the cool air drifting in off the river refreshed us. The pine floor was sanded. The peace, the coolness, the cleanliness — everything here seemed so relaxing, if you had one drop of the old Puritan blood in your veins you could guess something was wrong.

"I wonder," says Jude, "if this place hasn't changed hands. Mr. Poke may of bought it, and kept the old name. Never saw a landlord like him — this side of Hell. Maybe he is an imp, come to toss us on his frying pan. Whatever is that shooting?"

"It's been going on for some time."

"Mighty small-bore gun." Jude went out the back door to look. Me too. To our left, on the riverbank, you could see bushes shaking. Mr. Poke was down there, doing something. Even on such short acquaintance both of us believed he was doing something he shouldn't. Then we heard a man's voice down there yelling at him. "Silas, yer derned fool you! You blasted limb o' Satan! Ef ye turns me over I'll get right up out o' here, knock down yer uprights and kick in your slats."

It was a high-pitched, terrible, old man's voice.

The bushes shook. Out of them the imp was trundling a homemade wheelchair, heading it for the front door.

"Gifted," says Jude. "Can't say Mr. Poke isn't gifted. Did you notice how nice he tucked that pillow in? So he's stable-man and farmer, chambermaid, barman, landlord, maybe the Devil — and nurse too. Miss my guess if he don't cook the food too."

We had seen the old man's bald head a-glitter in the sun. It was at the end of a long, wrinkled neck that he kept whipping about like a snapping turtle, and it was the same mud-gray color. Across his knees he had a wee little gun. Then we heard Emma's voice.

"Mr. Poke, I'll help you get him in and to bed."

"Maybe," says Jude, thinking, "that crotchety old man **is** her father."

"Might be her husband."

"Oh don't be a fool, Eddy. She couldn't of. No woman could of."

Jude was listening for her voice. It was low and didn't

come to us again. We heard the old man.

"Ye derned fool, now. Where my birds? Ye stinking idiots! Where you put 'em? Give 'em to me. I'll clean 'em. Emma — you slob of a bitch-sow, you realize we got guests? Tend 'em now. You go tend 'em."

So, by the familiarity of address, we guessed this was her husband. She came in to us. She moved easy and was graceful. The gorgeous red hair was tucked up neat under a white cap. But once you had seen it you never forgot it was there. Her skin was pearly-white — not pink and white — and the freckles on it pale gold. Her hands so white and delicate you knew she had never done an honest day's work in her life.

Her face was open-looking and pleasant, but indifferent. Not like most landladies, who are apt to be too anxious to please. Jude told her he'd come to stay for a week and more, hinting at important work he had to do. I guess Emma Faucett was the only woman in New England with no curiosity — she didn't even ask him what the work was.

Now it was suppertime. But she didn't start to set it out. Jude was right, Mr. Poke did that. And it was he carried Mr. Faucett's tray to him. He was in his white, starchy apron again, slicing rosy ham and the fine white bread he had made, boiling up green corn ears and setting out pickles, jelly, preserves, fresh cold butter (from the spring house). To top all, an apple pie — and that was a high stepper. Pies were his specialty. Emma helped some, but not much. The two of them talked in a dawdling, inconsequential way to each other. Nobody talked to us.

We four sat to eat together. The talk went meandering on between those two — only about work on the place. So-and-so had offered so much for lumber, how the triplet lambs were, how much Mr. Poke had sold to flatboat men that day. Then Mr. Poke was up on his presumably cleft feet and was washing up the dishes. Emma stood by to dry them, but half the time she forgot and just stood by.

Then, from the invalid's room, we heard the old man yelling for someone to take away the tray. So Mr. Poke went for it.

Emma said to Jude at last, "We don't have many guests here. Norwich House is right on the highway. Most those traveling by land stop there."

"You get your guests off the river?"

She shrugged, "We," meaning Mr. Poke and herself, "don't let them come inside the house — ever. They got real dirty ways and make too much commotion for our taste. We do sell them supplies. At least Mr. Poke does. Everybody working the river knows about his pies." She stopped to pick up a dishcloth she had dropped. She couldn't do even that without being graceful. "But if you prefer it here than up to Norwich House you can stay, for Mr. Poke and I don't think you'll be bothersome. So, suit your own mind on that. For as long as you like."

You saw she didn't especially care whether he stayed or went. She was like that about most things.

You may wonder how a tavern like that supported itself. The reason why doesn't speak well for Emma — if she knew what Mr. Poke was up to. and I've every reason to suppose she did. He was honestly selling supplies to the rivermen but also receiving from them contraband — things like French brandies and silks that smugglers got in from Canada. There was a lot of smuggling on the Connecticut River in those days. A good deal of that stuff was taken off here, and hid up wherever Mr. Poke thought to hide it — until rather odd-looking gentlemen came a-driving up with fast spans and so on, night mostly, and took it away. If the place wasn't accepted as a house of public entertainment, the comings and goings of these odd-looking men would have aroused talk. That's why it paid them to pay the license and make an idle pretense at putting up guests. Jude told me he guessed all this before he had been there three days. They never doubted

but what he was a limner, like he said. Never a suspicion he
might be a revenue man. There was something disarming
about their trustfulness. Trustful even in small ways. There
was a slate beside the sink. Any liquor or any victuals he
wanted when no one was there to serve him, he was to help
himself to — and just write down on the slate.

Mr. Poke came back with the tray, then went right to work.
He sifted flour and dotted it with lard, making pie crust.
Before he went to bed those pies would be out the oven,
waiting for next day's sale. He wore a blue and white checked
apron — just like one Mitty had. He was the hardest working
little fellow I ever saw. Anything from pies to lawbreaking he
did so deft and quick it was a pleasure to watch him.

It was twilight, and I was standing to go. Emma came
back from her husband's chamber. Did Mr. Rebough play
checkers?

"I'd be delighted," says he. "Your servant, ma'am," bowing with old-fashioned courtesy. And to me, "You cut
along, Eddy."

His beaming face fell when she said, "My husband fancies
a game or two of checkers every evening." And so Jude was
caught right then and there — for as long as he played one
evening with that ancient horror, why not every evening?
And he couldn't get himself free of this pattern no matter
how he struggled. He knew this was Emma's work — that
every evening she had been playing checkers with Mr.
Faucett, while out in the kitchen Mr. Poke baked fresh pies
for next day's trade. Now, being relieved of her usual
evening occupation, she just sat in the kitchen, relaxed and
doing nothing, except for the unending, meaningless,
dawdling conversation that went on forever between her and
Mr. Poke.

. . . .

Thirty-four

. . . .

Jᴜᴅᴇ ᴅɪᴅ like he said. He was back to Dr. Dwight's with the
work he had got done, looking for more specimens to draw.
He looked good. He said Mr. Poke was the finest cook he had
ever eaten after, and he had brung over two of his pies for
Mrs. Schofield to prove it. He said it was wonderful how fast
and easy the work was coming, now he was never interrupted — ever. May have been the weather, for we were
having a most refreshing cool spell right then. He didn't
come much.

Now and then I'd get restless for him, walk over and see
what was up. Soon I was carrying specimens and such over
and back. Jude didn't come back again ever, and after that
nice cool pause the heat really began in earnest. It was the
hottest spell anyone could recollect around there.

Jude told me some after we got to North Adams. I saw a lot
of things, but piecemeal. There was a rhythm to the place,
once you got on to it. Every other day a pauper woman came
in to clean up. She was all but speechless: a toad of a woman,
no teeth, unblinking far-spaced eyes. Seems she was always
flopping on the floor, with a pail beside her and a wet rag in
her hands. No wonder Mrs. Faucett's hands looked so ladylike
— between that pauper woman and Mr. Poke she hadn't a
thing to do.

Mornings Jude spent in his room working. Dinner was twelve. He, Mr. Poke and Mrs. Faucett ate together and ate good. But they never paid any heed to him. Jude then went back to his room to go on working. The fact is, it was such fine work his eyes were bothering him. He didn't really work much afternoons. Or perhaps it was the heat coming down on them, or he was catching Emma's laziness. Then too, he hated the afternoons.

Every nice day Mr. Poke and Mrs. Faucett got the old man up and out into his wheelchair, gave him his shotgun and the imp rolled him to the riverbank. There he sat, happy, hour after hour, his head swinging at the end of that long cartilaginous, reptilian neck; chewing, spitting, and watching for "game."

Jude and me, people like Dr. Dwight and Primrose, loved songbirds. That is what he shot. He shot catbirds, and bluebirds, robins, warblers, summer yellow birds, woodpeckers. If he got a wren he was up and crowing, it being so tiny was proof of his marksmanship. He was always talking about getting enough for a bird pie; he never did. There wasn't but a small fraction ever of the birds he shot even picked up. But when Mr. Poke came for him, to roll him in for supper, Mr. Faucett would direct him to where he might find a dead bird or two. Never many. He'd take them to his chamber to pluck and draw. Often their poor little remains would come back into the kitchen on his supper tray. The tiny plucked body, bright feathers stuck in the gravy, and a small pile of guts. He used a salt spoon for that.

There was not a cat nor dog about the place you could feed this destruction to. Emma told Jude why. Mr. Faucett would shoot them. Sheep, cattle and so on were so large, people too (luckily), they did not arouse his sporting instincts. She was always sort of hinting that Jude fetch out that tray. He didn't bite on it. He knew now that anything he consented to do

once, he'd be doing forever. Like that checker game — every
evening he went into that invalid chamber and played
checkers with the old man. Anything Emma could shove off
on him, she would shove — for surely it was a wife's business
to care for and comfort an invalid husband. And just once
he had lent Goldie to Silas Poke. Now Poke acted like he
owned her.

He weren't going to let them absorb him further into the
hideosities of Francis Faucett's life. He swore he wouldn't,
ever, either roll him out for his shooting or respond when he
yelled for someone to come fast pick up his game, nor roll
him back in again. No, nor fetch him trays in and out. He
had some sense left.

It was the birds upset him most. Once he asked Emma why
he did it.

She shrugged. "Oh, just something to do."

She didn't mind this massacre of the innocent. He began to
wonder if there was anything she did mind. And he resented
her thick skin — there was something horrible, pagan, about
her indifference. Yet Venus hadn't minded the birds sacri-
ficed to her. And he had to give Emma credit for carrying
the burden of a revolting marriage with serenity and grace.
She was even getting fat on it.

The afternoons when Mr. Faucett was out "hunting,"
Emma rested. She took off her shoes (her bedroom was
exactly under Jude's), and he could hear them drop. She took
off her stays — he could hear the characteristic click of stays
coming off. She lay down on her bed and he could hear the
bed-cords creak under her weight. Then she would stretch
and yawn. And she yawned right out loud.

Now it was getting hotter and hotter — that August. This
was one reason why he never could seem to get to work after
dinner. Then too, he'd hear Mr. Faucett's gun popping.
And once a wounded catbird cried for hours. They sort of

buzz when they are hurt. He'd lie on his bed and think of
Emma. Why ever did she need so much rest? Eight hours
every night in bed, three or four more lying down every
afternoon. Of course she wasn't real young. Was she thinking
anything of him? (He couldn't think of much else but her by
now.) Whatever was she up to? The fact was she was up to
nothing — Emma Faucett was just bone-lazy.

He began to torture himself with the thought of her and the
imp. He didn't have a thing to go on. Although Silas Poke
moved sort of sidewise like a crab, he moved mighty fast and
quiet. Jude was getting impure ideas in his head. Mr. Poke
(like Jude) knew Mr. Faucett was stuck down there in the
bushes by the river — didn't he ever, these long, hot, drowsy
afternoons, come sneaking in to "call" (shall we say?) on Mrs.
Faucett? And now Jude was sure he had heard a whisper from
the room below, the sound of a phantom foot (cleft at that).
He'd even steal to the stairhead, and his heart pounding, to
listen. Or look out his window to see if Mr. Poke was really
up to the barn where he belonged. Not having a thing to go
on made it worse for Jude rather than better, for there was no
curb of fact to bridle down his wild imaginings.

Even mornings he'd be suspicious of them. He knew (after
he himself had gone to work upstairs) Silas Poke habitually
brought up the milk. Then Emma strained it, and put it
away. He'd go sneaking halfway down the stairs to listen to
them. It was always the same diddle-dawdle homely talk
between them — one cow was drying up and one was freshen-
ing, it was hotter today or not so hot. And evenings he'd
finish off his checker game with Mr. Faucett and just about
sneak back to catch them, but at what? in the kitchen. It was
always the same. Emma was sitting, maybe, fanning her knees.
Mr. Poke was making pies. Not a word of love, not even a
sort of knowing word was exchanged between them. Jude
wasted hours of his life eavesdropping on what was probably
the dullest conversations going on in the entire New England

States. Those two may of had their virtues, but they were no wits and conversationalists.

Those long, hot afternoons were the worst, he having just about used up his eyesight and the weather so hot and sticky. He had no heart to walk over to Hanover, nor take his sketchbook and go out drawing. So, like Emma (in the room below), he'd take off his shoes, and everything else that came easy, and fling down on his bed. Now the house was ever so still. He could hear the voice of the imp selling stuff to a flatboat that had come in. What wrong he had done Emma to think there was a thing between them! And yet he got to wondering and wondering. He had caught it again and again — a look, no, more of a flick in her gray eyes. Would she be seriously offended if he just walked down those stairs and into her room? Her door into the hall was always ajar for the sake of the air.

But the more he thought the more paralyzed he got. The whole thing was getting, on his part, to be a terrible waste of time and energy. Now, I've never once in my life said a good word for adultery (if you'll pardon the frankness of my speech), but I'm not sure but what he was thinking, and not doing, was worse. At least it was a lot sillier.

Mr. Poke was off somewhere about his nefarious business and had took Goldie (like he always did when he pleased now). Jude and Emma sat over the remains of their dinner. They were not alone. The pauper woman was on the floor.

At last he was telling her. Some faces, he said, he had to do. She wasn't to pay him a cent. Just sit like that, and he'd fetch down his sketchbook. Would she? Wouldn't she? Please, please, wouldn't she?

The pauper woman stopped flopping and raised her unblinking eyes to stare at him.

"You've been looking at me so much," Emma said, "I'd think you could draw me without any more looking." Then their eyes met and held to each other. Of course she had

guessed how he felt about her. He couldn't help it — no
matter the pauper woman; no, nor God in his Heaven, nor
Mitty to home.

"Emma . . ."

The pauper woman reared up a little — to have a real
good look. Then from Mr. Faucett's chamber, graty as a dry
axle, came that raspy voice, "Emma, dern ye for a blasted old
cow-pumpkin! Emma, I say."

She moved in her chair but didn't respond. One thing
Jude liked about her was that when she sat she really sat, no
pernickety perching about her. "If I hadn't clean forgot
about him, and Mr. Poke away. You took my mind clean off
my duties, Mr. Rebough. But it's terrible hard work for me
alone . . ."

"I'll help you."

He did help her and he hated himself for helping. He
hated the feeling of the old man's flesh, dry as corn husks. But
as they dressed him he had to feel it. And he lifted him into
the wheelchair. He weighed no more than a child.

"Now mister, gimme that gun there. I'll show you young
fellers real marksmanship. Shot a swallow yesterday, right
through the eye, and he on the wing."

So it was Jude rolled him out to his "blind," and he settled
the pillows for him, hating himself all the time. He not only
carefully set the brake on the contraption, but he blocked the
wheels with a piece of wood. The river ran deep and swift,
and the bank pitched downhill into it, then some six to eight
feet drop and you were in it. Anybody wheeling Mr. Faucett
had better be pretty careful.

Then the sweat broke out on him and his hands began to
shake, for his body had known what he was thinking before
his mind had really taken it in. He hadn't been able to help
it, but he had had a wicked thought. All this time the old
man was chattering and boasting, stopping now and then to
dod-blast Silas Poke for not being to hand, but of course never

thinking to thank Jude. And now he knew — he hated Francis Faucett as much as he loved his wife, if you can call what he felt love. I'm not sure.

He told me when this terrible idea came to him it almost blinded him, and he knew he staggered as he turned to walk back to the house. There by the barnyard, grinning from ear to ear and watching him, was Silas Poke. He had a pitchfork in his hand. He always looked more like something out of Hell with one than without, and Jude thought how perhaps he and Emma had fixed it between them — it was going to be Jude's work to roll Mr. Faucett in and out, wait on him, pick up his dead birds; just like checkers.

Mr. Poke came sidling towards him, half laughing at him as if to say, Dare you complain? So Jude said he'd often wondered if you could kill a man with that little popgun of Mr. Faucett's.

"Not likely," said the imp. "But if you are thinking like I think you are thinking, it would be a lot easier to just not set the brake." He nudged Jude with his elbow. "Safer too. No questions asked." And he was off on a spitting sort of a laugh, fairly exuding sulphur and brimstone.

So this wicked thought now joined that other wicked thought in Jude's mind, and between them they just about pulled him to pieces. He was getting run down. Couldn't get any work done at all. But it would of seemed that what was good in him and held him back was stronger than the evil nagging him on. He couldn't get anything done — work, sleep, and neither good nor mischief.

Now you could say it was honor held him back, for honor is no weak virtue, nor is it suited to weak characters. Although Jude was no steel trap, he wasn't weak neither. He was twenty-seven or -eight. That's pretty late to begin taking human life. I've noticed again and again, out here in the West, it's the young ones just growing up takes to it best. And I've a theory he thought too much about these two sins

he was contemplating. If he was going to roll that invalid
into the river he should of done it first time he thought of it.
Same things hold about Emma. Jude was too derned slow
and thoughtful to make a good sinner.

He weren't coming over to us any by now. I'd come to him.
And how cool, empty, peaceful, that house would seem after
the hot, dusty walk. The white curtains breathing, and the
smell of pine needles before the house, and the cold, watery
smell from the river at the back. Emma's door was always
ajar. I'd go upstairs to him — tuckered out and done in, his
eyes red-rimmed, just lying on his bed. Then I'd hear the bed
creaking, under Emma's weight, from the room below, or the
popgun of Mr. Faucett going off. And Mr. Faucett yelling
he'd shot a bird and for Jude to come pick it up before he
forgot where it had fallen. And he was to come double-quick,
ding-blast him for a . . . Only his language was unwritable.

For just what Jude feared had happened. He was doing an
awful lot of trundling and waiting on Mr. Faucett. Now, very
heavily, like he was hauling a bucket up out of a well, Jude
heaved himself up and felt about for his shoes.

"I've got to go, Eddy — go to him. Wait for me. Won't
you wait until I get back, Eddy?" I could feel him almost
clinging to me — spiritually speaking. Then I'd hear Emma
yawn or something, and about see his ears prick up.

First and last, he was real miserable. Personally I think far
too much has been written (especially by the more immoral
poets, like Tennyson) of the joys of illicit love. If Sir Launcelot
felt about the Queen and King Arthur like Jude was feeling
about Emma and Mr. Faucett, may God in his mercy pity the
Round Table.

Many say virtue seems a pretty long row to hoe — but it *is*
hoeing, good honest work and you know where the rows are;
not like getting lost in bogs like Jude was.

. . . .

Thirty-five

. . . .

B UT TO LEAVE, for the moment, Jude frying upon the skillet of his base desires, and glance at Ruby Lambkin and his shinigigs.

Stemming, I suppose, from Mrs. Pease and our experience at West Lebanon, two contradictory stories sprang up. One: Ruby had been cornered over there by Burnap and an armed posse; Mrs. Pease's quick wit had saved him. Two: that brutal imbecile (Sheriff Burnap) had mistook himself and exceeded his authority. He had found under Mrs. Pease's roof an honest young limner, unfortunate enough to tally well with the printed descriptions of Ruby. Burnap had beaten and punched that poor fellow. And had him down on the floor and kicked him, and so on, before he was convinced he had the wrong man. Even then, didn't apologize.

Although Jude had told several people around Hanover of his run-in with Burnap, he had never once suggested Burnap had so much as laid hands on him. Neither of these stories were true, so people were just taking their choice of which lie they preferred to believe.

Lambkin had cottoned right on to the idea there was a limner impersonating him, even if unintentionally. He got his hand on several of those printed trade cards we put up about everywhere we went, advertising Jude's skill — you can't say he wasn't a pretty cool cucumber. Armed with one of these, and assuming a most respectable air of injured innocence, he accosted Johnny Fessenden right in the middle of White River Junction. He demanded an apology from that shrinking violet. He talked about his honor, and duels even. Finally, young Mr. Fessenden persuaded him that one hundred in hard cash would perhaps poultice Mr. Rebough's sensitive feelings.

Another time he introduced himself as Mr. Rebough, and presented a trade card to Reverend Peele, Windsor, Vermont, hoping to have an opportunity to serve him. The Reverend had heard those ghastly stories of how Mr. Rebough had been beaten up by Burnap. He sat him right down and offered to help him draw up legal papers and bring criminal suit against the Sheriff. But this particular "Mr. Rebough" seemed too timid to go against the forces of the Sheriff, so the Reverend patted him on the back and said the forces of God were greater than the forces of the Sheriff and he'd back him. So he was to sit right where he was and think things over. He himself had now to retire to his study and finish off his sermon — next day was Lord's Day.

The Reverend decided to do an entirely new sermon (not just turn the barrel over), and his subject was the wickedness of jumping at conclusions, and I forget what text he chose. He took it back to the sitting room to read over to the injured limner, thinking it would strengthen him to bring court charges against Burnap.

The limner was gone, and half a ham and a bottle of madeira, and the silk clerical gown laid out for the hired girl to press up. But worst of all, the silver communion service. It was the finest one in all Vermont and was in the kitchen awaiting a final shine-up from that same hired girl.

Although everybody, except the Fessenden family, had been pleased Ruby had got that one hundred dollars out of Johnny Fessenden so easy, many were shocked and horrified to think of consecrated silver in the unconsecrated hands of Ruby Lambkin. The congregation added $50.00 to the reward.

So that August Ruby was real active and real close by. And he was sticking right in Sheriff Burnap's own county. Everybody knew Smokey had sworn to "nail his hide on my barn door." Now it did look as if Ruby was saying, "All right — let's see you do it." This caused Burnap to lose his head — calling out posses on wrong scents and losing right ones, accusing wrong people of sheltering him, believing all false stories and refusing to take serious the true ones. He was getting laughed at plenty. Far as I know, nobody liked him. But he couldn't take ridicule, for he was sensitive (in his own way) and ridicule hurt his feelings. His temper was getting up to high G. And Ruby, like he was a bad boy and the Sheriff a cross dog, was teasing him.

Either Ruby couldn't take even his profession of stealing seriously or wasn't real bright, for he was taking chances. If he won, he won no more than the pleasure of thumbing his nose at the Sheriff. If he lost, he lost his freedom. For example, one of those hot, still August days I've already written about, for no more than the heck of it Ruby moved in on Burnap's own town of Sharon. This is about ten miles west of Norwich. He knew Burnap was down to Windsor pestling around over that stolen church silver. So Ruby just came idling in down the main street of Sharon, broad daylight. He wasn't hurrying any, just looking about him curiously, and friendly seeming. It was so hot there weren't many signs of life until he got to J. Robinson's store. There, sitting on pickle barrels and slapping at the flies, were a group of men. So he sat with them. Never denied who he was, just took it for granted nobody could wish him ill. What had he come for? Why, says he, he never had seen Sheriff Burnap's famous stone-built pigpen by daylight and, happening to be going by, and with plenty of time on his hands, he thought he'd like to see it. Will you believe it? — those men (and not just silly girls) got off their barrels and escorted him. Mrs. Burnap looked out her back window and thinking there must be some good legal reason why these men were pondering the scene of the famous crime, called them in for cider and such. So they sat in the Burnaps' kitchen and were waited on by Burnap's wife. Ruby had the best rocking chair. He didn't say much. Maybe Mrs. Burnap knew him and didn't say — she had her own reasons for feeling disgruntled with her husband.

Later it happened Jude and I talked with one of those men. He gave us the best description we had of Ruby at this time — his heyday. After this he began to worsen.

He said Ruby Lambkin weren't so flashy-looking as made out. More modest. He smiled easy. He had a direct, trusting, sort of innocent expression. You no more thought of his hurting you, or you wanting to hurt him, than you would a child. And yet in one way the printed description was right — he was beautifully built and balanced. Couldn't say whether he had a handsome face or not. He'd leave that for the girls to say. But speaking as a man, he had never seen any man with a finer build on him. He seemed real at ease but, like a catamount, you knew if he moved fast he'd go like greased lightning. Not a nerve in him. As for the "gentlemanly address" of the hand-bills, wasn't much to that. You knew in five minutes he was just one more ignorant day laborer, a flatboat man, for a guess, and as shiftless as a cowbird. No more morals than a tomcat.

Why no one took him, right there in Sharon, is a mystery still. There was a terrible lot of money on him by then. Nowadays, they'd say he had hypnotized them; then the talk was he had cast a spell. But it was such a stultifying hot day nobody could think much — nobody wanted to think. If they had begun to think, why they would have had to act. It was too damned hot for action.

One morning, to breakfast, Dr. Dwight was reading his newspaper and began to laugh. He read the piece out loud. This is about how the newspaper piece went:

The citizens of New Hampshire and Vermont, and especially of Windsor County in the second of those two sovereign states, are especially WARNED against RUBY LAMBKIN who, having never before pretended to an honest trade, is now posing as an honest itinerant limner. In fact, as he stole away the black silk clerical gown of the Reverend Peele of Windsor, Vermont, he may pop up among us in the guise of a clergyman. So, once more BEWARE any stranger answering to the following description.

Then there followed about the usual one.

And REMEMBER you'll never have a chance to earn TWO HUNDRED AND FIFTY DOLLARS as easily as by apprehending him and turning him over to the renowned and very active Sheriff of Windsor County, for Ruby never seems to offer violence and does not go armed. But he may out-cute you — he has been taken several times already and broken jail. Or he may MESMERIZE you, as he is said recently to have done to Mr. Burnap's village of Sharon. And, if we are to believe all we hear, he may simply make a noise like a clap of thunder and dissolve into thin air. But, in the interests of law and good order, this INTERESTING OBJECT must be apprehended and brought to trial.

Why do we especially warn our friends in Windsor County? Mr. Lambkin seems to have accepted the challenge of the popular "(that's sarcasm for you)" Sheriff of that County, Mr. "Smokey" Burnap, as he was last reported in Sharon in the Sheriff's own house, drinking his cider and gossiping with his wife. And even requested to be shown the very pigpen where, we have been informed, Mr. Burnap intends to nail his hide, when he catches him. This in revenge for an occurrence last June too well known to our readers to necessitate a repetition here. So he is definitely working right under the Sheriff's nose with the obvious intent of what children would call "double darse-daring him."

In fact, this very active official is so confused and enraged already he is on the point of arresting every young man of six foot two who carries himself handsomely, is of good address and has black hair. Therefor, we further WARN all such to stay in bed until Sheriff Burnap has apprehended the genuine Lambkin, for mistakes are being made.

NOTE: there has been and still is among us a most respectable and honest gentleman, a limner from our sister state of Connecticut. This gentleman, MR. REBOUGH, has already more than once been mistaken by hotheads for Lambkin. And, although using such a word as "hothead" might be thought disparaging for an official of the law, it is not unknown to our readers that Mr. Burnap behaved, while in West Lebanon, to Mr. Rebough in a manner not calculated to make our BELOVED STATE popular with foreign travelers and which suggests a degree of hotheadedness somewhere.

So NOTE: Mr. Jude Rebough is not MR. RUBY LAMBKIN.

Dr. Dwight cut out the piece and bade me carry it over to Mr. Rebough to laugh at. Also he was disappointed Jude hadn't come over for more specimens to draw. Couldn't I politely egg him on a bit?

I found him, just as I expected. He was lying down on his bed. He sat up and told me, go down and draw rum and water for him and birch beer for me. Write it down under his name on the slate and bring it back. And he tore up the newspaper piece. He didn't want to read it.

There wasn't a soul I saw downstairs. I did hear Emma rustling and creaking. She was there, but in her own room.

Jude was yawning and scratching at his chest. It was a close, hot day, like being wrapped in a feather bed and then set in a slow oven.

When I started egging him on to get more work done for Dr. Dwight, he said coming over here and all this peace and quiet hadn't worked. He thought the river air had debilitated him. Hadn't been able to get his mind on anything (except, of course, his sinful desires, which he didn't mention), and when his mind was working his hand wasn't — and if they both were ready to get up and after things — why, his eyes gave out.

"If it don't work here," says I, "come back to Hanover. Mrs. Schofield has located a nice big inn room, and no children to disturb. So come along back."

"I've thought of it," says he indifferently, "for it does seem that over here all my energy seeps away from me at night. Dreaming — some real bad ones."

He was up, tucking in his shirttails and brightening a little, now he had someone to talk to. I said he was to go ahead. I'd like to hear a real bad dream.

He thought some time, then he said, "When I was your age, Eddy," and he was sitting real comfortable on the edge of his bed and finishing off his grog, "I used to believe a witch could come to a sleeping man and bridle him. Then from midnight to cock-crow she rode him where she list. You still believe things like that, Eddy?"

"No," says I. For I didn't — not quite.

"Well, she got the bridle on me all right — although I did fight her."

"Who did?"

"Witch."

"You serious?"

"No. This is a dream. Do you know how they make a witch's bridle — out of what?"

"Hair of the tail of a black horse. Inside bark of a yellow birch tree."

"That's what I used to think. But fact is, this was hair from a chestnut horse. Bright like copper. Funny I noticed that even in a dream."

And I thought of Emma. Obviously he hadn't — if he had he wouldn't have mentioned the color of the horse. I did, and my flesh creeped.

"Sometimes we were in the sky, flying; sometimes hammering the rough roads of this earth. But from beginning to end, I fought her. God! How I fought her. She was of considerable weight — I felt caved in under her. And I knew if only I could cross running water I'd loose her off. I longed to cross say, the Connecticut River, like a Christian longs for Paradise."

"Couldn't you wake up?"

"No. And all the time I did know I was asleep — right here in this bed. But she was sawing at my mouth and clapping her spurs in my flanks. Somehow I hurt one foot, hoof I should say. Like poor Goldie. Guess I was thinking of her."

"Then what?"

"Oh . . . I just woke up — anyhow. And I heard myself giving off little yips and blowing and breathing hard. I was swimming in sweat. There was only one funny thing."

"How funny?"

"All my back teeth have been aching since. Just where a bit would rest. Now, regular toothaches don't come like that — all four points of the compass at once, top and bottom, both sides. And next few days my muscles were aching, like I really had galloped all night. But the funniest thing is this — one foot was cut and bloody, like I had stepped on broken glass. You can't cut your foot in bed, can you? Made me wonder if I'd been sleepwalking. Used to as a boy."

"You never had bad dreams in Hanover. It's so sensible-like over there, couldn't you come back — right away?"

"But some of my dreams are so nice I cherish them. Like a few nights back I was doing no more than taking a walk. Can't figure why it was so pleasant. Just the light feeling of it. I felt I could walk forever. And I felt a pure happiness at just being alive — like I haven't felt since I was your age, Eddy. And I came into the most wonderful little town. No more than a village. All so distinct I could see every detail of it. The moss inside the horse trough, and every shingle and shingle nail on the church roof. Never been there before, but I'd know it if I ever met it again. I looked about for identifying marks. Only one I saw was the name of the proprietor over the general store. And now if I haven't forgotten. Sort of ordinary name, like Simpson or . . . Robinson."

"Oh, don't," I said, for I was sick with fear for him.

"What? Boring you?"

"Not exactly." I was trying manfully to keep a hold on myself.

"Well, there wasn't much more to it. I went in and sat with the men of the town. Guess they had slunk in there to keep out of the heat and wet their whistles until time for evening chores. After that we just preambulated. No more than that. Went up to see a stone something or other one of them was building. For cows, I guess. I never felt so happy — inside and all over, in all my life and . . . Eddy, whatever's wrong with you?"

I was too old for tears, but when they burst out of me they burst with a roar.

Since then I've met up with stranger coincidences. Then I hadn't. And it seems strange enough even now. Jude had been so shut up at Faucett's he hadn't heard any of those tales going around. At this time he hadn't even heard of Ruby Lambkin's visit to Sharon.

It cut him to the heart to see me bawling and, worse yet, I had gone back to stammering. I couldn't get much out. He jumped to the conclusion I was unhappy over to Dr. Dwight's where he had left me, that someone was bullying me, or I was failing in my Latin lessons, or chagrined because Primrose could catch better than I. But my despair did pull him out of his, for this was why he left Faucett's. It is true in life (just as in sermons) — try to help someone else and inadvertently you help yourself.

He didn't know he was leaving that accursed spot forever.

He thought he was coming back, later the same day. For he left all his gear there, and Goldie (as usual Silas Poke was off with her), and his bill unpaid and no farewells. I guess all he thought was to walk back with me, and quiet me down and find out what was eating me.

Yet he did give one little suggestion of independence. For, as we stood under the sign of the golden faucet dripping into the silver cup hanging from that great old pine tree, we heard Mr. Faucett from down by the river yelling for him, and "dern him" (and so on) for he was to come, and come fast, and give him a hand at something. Jude didn't budge.

It was then he told me about wishing there was a new washer for the painted faucet, to stop the imaginary drippings.

We stood a moment as though listening for the little wearing sound of drop, drop, drop. We did hear the shrieks from the invalid, but from here couldn't make out much of his bad language nor could we see him — only the bushes shaking down by the river.

We took the sandy cart path up off the first terrace. Then came those three farmhouses, set sort of nose to nose with their lands and barns fanning out behind them. They were physically a lot closer to Faucett's than they seemed. I said earlier they were called Kitchen Corner. It was here we hit the main road running south into Norwich.

Jude told me these were the Kitchener houses, but country people couldn't be bothered with that final "er." He said they were strange people because for generations, soon as they reached middle age, they all went deaf. And then he added (as though it had no meaning to us) that Sheriff Burnap (from over at Sharon) had married one of these women thirty years back.

"So his wife really is deaf," said I, "like in the stories?"

"Yeh," he said. "Deaf as a stone hitching post." And he told me she was always coming back here to her own folk (afflicted like she was), for those Kitcheners understood each other well and sort of stuck together. Then he said Mrs. Faucett had told him this. Only time this afternoon he so much as mentioned her.

.   .   .   .

Thirty-six

.   .   .   .

WE GOT to Norwich. Jude was amazed to find it filled up with cadets, for vacation was over. They were marching and countermarching and yelling "Hip, hip" to each other and beating on a drum and blowing on a trumpet.

Half over the bridge leading from New Hampshire to Vermont, we paused to idle. Jude was tossing scraps of bark from the guard rail into the strong whirl of the deep, blue water. By now we knew the weather was breeding a thunderstorm, and it would be a monster. We could feel the electricity pricking on our bare arms.

Jude said, "When I think how I struggled and fought only to cross the running water of the Connecticut in my dream and couldn't do it — but now I'm awake there's nothing to it."

We were no more than half over. "Let's keep moving," I said.

By the time we had trudged up into town he was so recovered from his dumps he was whistling pretty and he

asked me which inn and where was it — the inn Mrs. Schofield thought might put him up. I knew, and I took him
to it.

It was on a side street and either the "Blue" something
or run by a man name of Blue. Perhaps both. And there
was a room as spacious and well kept as the one he had
left over to Faucett's. Mr. Blue agreed to lug in a kitchen
table for him to work on. But it was three o'clock and we
had had no dinner. Mr. Blue told us to go sit in the
barroom and he'd send cold victuals in to us. Dining room
was closed.

We came in there. If it didn't turn out that there were
five or six of those Norwich Academy cadets, sweating in
their white duck pants and all-over-buttons blue wool
jackets. They were sitting peacefully with about an equal
number of young gentlemen from Dartmouth College. Yet
they were supposed to fight on sight. But the boys from
Norwich came stalking in the front door like they were gen-
erals already; college boys came sneaking in over a fence,
through the barn and kitchen. This is why: it was against
town ordinances and college regulations any Dartmouth boy
be served liquor in Hanover. Same thing was true as to cadets
over to Norwich, yet neither institution of higher learning
could discipline boys from the other side of the river. So no
wonder they were always longing for each other's terrain.
And when they got together, like at Blue's, they got on fine.

Mr. Blue (pompous ass) introduced "the famous Mr.
Rebough" with a flourish, and reminded all there how they
had read of him in their newspapers. "Alias," says he,
ponderously jokeful, "Ruby Lambkin."

"Hey . . . " yelled the boys, really welcoming. Jude chose
a table by an open window and in a corner. Those boys
grabbed up their liquor and chairs and came piling into
the corner after him. Jude ordered same thing all around
and they yelled, "Hey . . . " again. You could of heard them

a block away. First they wanted to know, had Burnap beaten him up? He said no. That disappointed them, for both sets of young gentlemen hated Smokey Burnap's guts and wanted more fuel for their hatred. They were not only against the Sheriff (and, I'm afraid, all law and decency too), but were passionately for Lambkin although, of course, parents spending all that money on their education would hope they'd of learned more sense. I might admit (although it don't speak too well for them) it was that rascal's success in seducing our pure New England womanhood they fancied most. Mr. Rebough having "so often" been confused with the Lambkin, I guess they thought him an authority. He did tell them some along that line we'd heard of about Ruby and they liked the stories and yelled, "Hey . . ." They told some, but they were dirtier and not as funny. It takes a real mature mind to tell things like that — just right. Some men never acquire that much maturity. But we all politely yelled, "Hey . . . " together. We got on fine.

Two or three of them had good singing voices. They sang all the verses they could think of in regards to Ruby Lambkin, and we all came bellowing in on the chorus. The one about the pigpen was especially good. That chorus was all honks and very taking. I smelt the insidious hand of Phineas Sharp in some of them.

Then a voice outside squealed, "Indians," (a freshman forced to wait out in the street and warn them), and the Dartmouth boys dove for the back street by way of kitchen, barn and fence. I guess it was the constable, and he couldn't do more than shake his head sorrowful at those smart-looking cadets and tell them their colonel wouldn't like it.

They were terribly courteous to him and called him sir and stood up straight when he addressed them. Real little hypocrites, if you ask me. He left and the Dartmouth boys came back.

Jude was in high fettle now — just like his old self, only

more so. It did look like "crossing running water" had
released him. Now the boys had took to calling him Ruby
and Mr. Lambkin and he was looking the part. Don't know
how he did it, but he could — especially if he stayed sat
down.

A man drifted in and, still standing at the bar, said to
the roomful at large that three hours before he had noted
Sheriff Burnap's sorrel pacing mare hitched before Kem
Rupert's woodworking shop (I've said Burnap was a trader
in timber lands and a lumber dealer). She was still hitched
there now — broiling sun and no water for at least three
hours. Worse yet, that mountain of callosity, known as
Sheriff Burnap, had left his old woman out there too —
sitting on the wagon and there was no top to it.

Someone said she was so scared of him she wouldn't dare
jump out the wagon and seek shade until he told her she
might. They said all their children soon as old enough
had moved out as far as they were able. She were pretty
much alone now, in her deafness, and at the mercy of that
man. And what did Mr. Lambkin (the traditional de-
fender of the weak) think of that?

Mr. Freshman again called, "Indians" from the street and
the Dartmouth boys took a dive. It was a false alarm but
the boys didn't return immediately.

They went up to Kem Rupert's and told the Sheriff (he
was having a few with Mr. Rupert in the shop) that Lambkin himself (in his well-known disguise as a limner) was
down to Blue's — just waiting to be taken and skinned. Of
course he didn't fall at first, but I think he was grateful
anybody was on his side, and yet same time suspicious they
were making a fool of him. Well, he agreed to go to Blue's
with them and drink Mr. Rebough's health, so long as they
were inviting him.

This was an error on his part. He never did know who to
believe, nor who to trust.

He came in. There was a howling of "Heys," but real derisive this time. And a catcall or two, likewise a little popping like spitting. And the good singers began to sing and the rest of us tumbling along, but strong, on the chorus, now

> "Ruby Lambkin is my name,
> In breaking jails I've won my fame.
> I give to poor and
> Steal from rich,
> No law of man's can hold me."

Then the humming and the Oh-ho, oh-ho's, oh-high-roller-oh's that came in after every verse.

> "Sheriff Burnap is my foe,
> He hunts me high, he hunts me low.
> He puts me in, I gets me out
> Because no jail can hold me.
>
> Sally This and Dursey That,
> Jenny Thin and Alice Fat.
> The girls do love me, that's a fact,
> And yet no girl can hold me."

And so on and on. With a rum-rum-tid-diddle-dee-ee, and a lot more oh-ho's.

Every one of those boys were on their feet, glass in hand, gesturing towards Jude. He sat in his corner by the open window and had to laugh. Burnap gave him one glance and and no more. The bar girl was putting a glass of brandy and water (she knew his tastes) into his hand, so he stood back-to this concert and slowly swallowed his drink. He wasn't going to let them draw him in.

"Where'd you leave your old woman, Sheriff," someone yelled at that great back — he hadn't much legs on him.

"My business, ain't it?"

"Sure it's your business, Sheriff — and if she drops dead of the sunstroke that's your business too? Agreed?"

"Agreed," says Burnap, but he swung slowly about, facing that light-minded roomful. At this time, I, as well as Jude, was not on his side. We were on other side — side of the foxes. Now I'm not so sure. After all, he was an officer of law enforcement and every decent man should of backed him. And if they didn't think him bright enough for his high office, they ought to have voted him out. At least I know that by the time I was of the age of that man who came in and told us of what he done to his wife and his mare, I wouldn't of just stood about laughing at him. At least I'd of gotten up to Rupert's and led those two poor suffering females out of the sun. And I wouldn't have stood about a barroom jeering at a serious man attempting to do his serious work; I'd try to help him.

Burnap was staring cold-eyed as a fish at Jude and where he sat. Jude told me he noted how those eyes were measuring the size of that open window. Could a man six feet two, and weighing about so much, get out it? It was a small window. And how long would it take a real active man to make it — granted it could be done. Could the Sheriff get out his pistol in time? He read this in Smokey Burnap's calculating, narrowing eyes. Jude said that look convinced him that Burnap did believe this was indeed Ruby, but he was determined not to act fast, and not to lose him either. Jude said this knowledge didn't scare him any. In fact, it made him feel lightheaded and lighthearted. Happy — just as he had in that dream.

Burnap stood back to the barroom going on with all the drinking he had started on over to Kem Rupert's. He staggered some as he walked straight over to join us at the table where we and those boys sat. Just about half an eye once again measured the width of the window against Jude's shoulders.

He spoke to the Dartmouth boys. "What you fellows

trying to pull on me? That man — Jesus, I know him. If his hide, taken off and cured, tanned to finest cordovan, is worth fifteen cents I'm John the Beloved Disciple." He spat.

Jude was back-to to the window. He couldn't help himself; he turned his head to estimate it himself.

Burnap said, "Pretty view, ain't it?"

"Yeh," says Jude, "and wouldn't you think they'd of put in a bigger window — considering the pretty view?"

"Well," says Burnap, squinting at it, "it's big enough to suit some. Me, for instance." He was convinced now a grown man couldn't take a dive for it and get through.

Everybody laughed.

Burnap was leaning forward across the table, with his elbows on it and his chin on his fists. He had made up his mind. That fellow over to West Lebanon and the one he knew had been holing up at Francis Faucett's (but out marauding all the time), and this here man across the table from him, were indeed Ruby Lambkin. But he couldn't go straight at him. He knew everybody in that room was against him.

We heard a bell toll from College Hall. Only one Dartmouth boy got up to go. The others preferred demerits. We heard far off across the river in Norwich a bugle, fairy-like and far away, calling the cadets. Not a one budged.

"Young fellow," said Burnap to the good Dartmouth boy, "as you go by Kem Rupert's will you slip the nose bag on my sorrel mare? You'll find it under the seat."

"Young fellow," says Jude, "while you're at it, take out both the nose bags under that seat and slip one over the old woman. Will you?"

Burnap laughed and (I guess hoping to curry favor) ordered a brandy and water all around. Me too.

Now he chatted sort of easily with Jude. Had he enjoyed

his stay in these parts? How many portraits had he done? And it came out Jude was planning to walk back to Faucett's for the night.

Then it was like he pounced. He said he'd give him a lift. He didn't offer him one; he stated the fact. Then he asked casually if Mr. Rebough, having traveled so widely through these parts, had ever happend to meet Ruby Lambkin.

Jude knew he was going to take that ride with Burnap. He had felt it coming down on him like a lid on a pot. But he had to have a last fling.

"Well," he said in that reasonable voice he used for some of his fanciest embroideries upon the skirt of truth "Like some other people, naming no names, I sometimes find it hard to tell him and me apart. Supposing he were a part of me — and no more than a part of me — if I did meet him (according to our best authorities), why, then whichever was the realest of us would be dead. You ask me I ever met Ruby Lambkin? I'll tell you an experience I had and you can judge for yourselves — if the brandy we are having, on top all we've had before, hasn't upset reasonable judgment." This was a crack at Burnap.

"It was over a month ago. I was on a straight, lonely road — lonely and straight as the road to Heaven. Eddy here weren't with me. Were you, Ed?"

"No sir," says I, fearing the worst and hanging my head and, of course, wishing he wouldn't.

"Was driving in my chaise. Not far from, I think it was Canaan, I saw ahead of me some sort of a man skulking in the bushes to the side of the road. It was on the right side. Every time he appeared it was on the right side. I drove a mile more and there he was again — and the same thing again. This began to get me nervous like witches. I swore next time I'd accost him. And I did. I yelled to him to get out of that there demmed underbrush if he were an honest man and show me his face. He come up on the road limber-light, stepping nice and easy. He was grinning at me so friendly I grinned right back. Then I noted, with a premonition of horror, he had on pepper and salt summer britches — just like me. Had on (and he pointed to his own garments as he talked) blue jacket with a mended-up barn-door tear in it — just like I had. Yellow galluses too. It was like staring into a looking glass, we looked so exactly alike, one to the other.

"Now I wasn't exactly afraid of him. No sir. Not until later. My horse? No, she didn't carry on as horses are said to do in the presence of an apparition. I meant to say, 'Guess you're Ruby Lambkin,' but my tongue slipped and, so help me, I said, 'I guess you're Jude Rebough.'

" 'Yep,' says he. 'And you're that Lambkin fellow they've made up all those songs about.'

"So I offered him a lift of which he accepted. And I had a bottle of rum tucked by — good Jamaica rum. But my horse was trotting along smart, never realizing she now was hauling two of us. Well gentlemen, we two got so mixed up it was plumb pitiful. I'd try to lift my left hand to slap a fly and I'd find I had hit him. He tried to blow his nose and he near screwed mine off my face. And then whose turn was what on that bottle of rum? We never could figure that out. It weren't no time at all before a certain amount of hostility began building up between us, for I've heard people often don't like themselves such a hell of a lot. Then too, there were too many of us. We both knew one or the other had to go — and when I say go, I don't mean out of that chaise and off the road, I mean straight off this earth. We finished that bottle *some*how, not saying much, but each knowing what had to be done. We drank so much (for what he poured down him came out in my head, and vice versa) that by gum! — if there weren't four of us. Horse never took in the fact — trotted lightly, like there

was only one. That was disconcerting. And from bad words
we fell to tussling, and from tussling to blows. He (or
maybe one of those other two fellows) caught me a mean
one — right there, on the point of my jaw. I heard my
vertebra snap, so I have every reason to believe it was me
passed on to my reward right then and there. And so the
honest limner, good family man, kind husband, decent
and respected citizen of Hampton, Connecticut, lies buried
somewhere along that lonely road. My guess is, it's those
three other fellows as has been playing ducks and drakes
with the law — eh, Mr. Burnap?"

Those boys liked this "confusion worse confounded." They
yelled their "Heys!" real hearty. But now we all sensed
this pleasant party was over. There was a scraping back of
chairs and a getting up. Financial settlements and handshakings.

Burnap hadn't looked too amused. You could feel him
waiting for us — after the others were gone. Again he told
Jude he was giving him a lift back home. It was no invitation, it was a threat. Jude said no thanks, he didn't want to
bother him. Burnap said it was no bother, long as he was
putting up at Kitchen Corner himself. Jude said he'd
rather walk. Burnap said his mare was a terrible swift
pacer, he'd guarantee to get Mr. Rebough under a roof
before the storm broke. Once out in the street you could
see the thunderheads towering up and up. When that
storm broke it would be a beaut.

Jude was a hooked fish. He could jump and run with the
line — he couldn't get off it. Burnap would play him a
little and land him when he pleased.

I said goodbye to him up in front of Kem Rupert's. Someone had put a nose bag on his mare, and I guess fed his old
woman too. She was perched up there on the wagon seat
eating a pickle. I believe now if Jude had refused to go
with Burnap he'd of arrested him then and there and shot

him if he resisted. He was armed. I'd noted the bulge on him.

Jude knew Burnap might get ugly. Also he had complete confidence in his own innocence. Never occurred to thrash it out with him right there — and Burnap half in his cups.

I saw him drive off seated between Burnap, big as a bear and no more agreeable, and Mrs. Burnap, little as a mouse. She heard nothing. Said nothing. She went on munching that pickle.

Jude realized his predicament, at least partially, for he turned and yelled at me, "Eddy! Eddy, if I'm not over early, come over to see me. Will you?"

. . . .

Thirty-seven

. . . .

Later Jude told me how he fared. Burnap had handcuffs on him before they crossed the bridge. No apologies either. And already everything was bathed in a sulphurous yellow light. In Norwich even white houses were yellow, and the wash the women were hurrying to get in, and their faces too. It was that queer hush before the storm. Men were hustling through chores and battening down henhouses. There were black clouds, like feather beds full of wind, riding in low and fast from the north. They knew what was a-coming. The thunder rolled and the lightning flashed unremittingly, but still was pretty far off.

On leaving Norwich the first big drops came polka-dotting down, but by the time they got to Kitchen Corner they were soaked and the wind had come in earnest — limbs off trees, even trees themselves coming down. The temperature was dropping a mile a minute.

I remember over in Hanover that great, destructive storm and the roaring of the wind and the rolling of the thunder, like it had just taken the landscape in its teeth and shaken it. The lightning splintered an elm on the campus, right across the street from Dr. Dwight's. And how dark it was! Darker than a wolf's mouth.

There was a fire in the kitchen of Mrs. Burnap's sister (Mrs. Rice), and it felt good. Nobody paid any attention to Burnap and his prisoner. It was as if they didn't wish to flatter him by showing any curiosity as to what he was up to. But they took on over Mrs. Burnap. Jude couldn't help noticing that she seemed to hear her deaf sister and her affectionate brother-in-law even when they didn't yell better than her husband's loudest bellows. Although I'll say this for him, Burnap was a low-spoken man, by and large. Brutal men often are.

Mr. Rice built up the fire good and lighted lamps, although it was no more than six o'clock, and he served out hot toddies. The storm was right on top of them now.

Then men were pounding on the door and yelling for Burnap. The wind had taken the roof off a barn, and such men as lived at Kitchen Corner were now rushing out to save hay and get stock out and estimate damage. You could feel how Burnap was hated there among them, but he'd be a great help at an emergency like this. Mr. Rice scudded out and Burnap told him he was coming in a minute.

He took Jude upstairs into a chamber with one small window. It had been carelessly left open. He shut it. He then turned up the bed and drew out the bed cord and hog-tied him flat on the floor, just about in the puddle of water that had rained in. All he said was if he did succeed in freeing himself (which wasn't possible) the window was too small to get out and, if he did, he'd be keeping an eye on it and take pleasure in drilling him as he came down. And that door was too heavy to kick down, and besides, had a good bolt on it.

Jude heard him bolt it on the outside, then go down the stairs. I've spoken of how slender Jude's hands were for a man, and subtile too. He worked and twisted, and he slipped the handcuffs. Then he spent, he thought, hours (no more than minutes) picking at the hog-tie. The lightning would flash and that helped him some. He was cold in his wet clothes, lying in a puddle. He wrapped himself in Mrs. Rice's blankets and sat in a chair and soon stopped his shiverings.

He told me he felt awfully sleepy, and sort of relaxed. Dozed off maybe, for he felt no slightest fear of his own fearsome predicament — like he hadn't quite sense enough just then. And he wondered how Faucett's and the people down there had weathered the storm. Who had thought to get Mr. Faucett in? Or was he still in the bushes? Had Emma rested all through it? Or had she got up and closed the windows in time? If not, what of his drawings and Dr. Dwight's microscope and specimens; Jude had left the window by them open. Not even this thought seemed to bother him just then. And of course nobody would know where Silas Poke was, or what he was up to. Nobody ever did. He said already people at Faucett's seemed to have moved off and away from him — not in space, for they were no more than a quarter mile from where he was, but in time, like they were people he had met years ago.

His room was getting lighter and lighter and the storm rolling off down the valley. Then Burnap came to fetch him. There he was standing, short-legged and barrelchested, in the doorway. He said nothing, but Jude realized the ease with which he had got himself free didn't look to Burnap like no amateur. He didn't care for Burnap's expression, so, to propitiate him, he began to apologize. Hoped he didn't mind his slipping his handcuffs, and that the bed-cords had hurt him, and it had been too cold on the floor.

Burnap said nothing, but he knew tricks had been played on him and he hated tricks. He stepped over and felt Jude's arm.

"You been out of here — and in again?" He glanced at the window.

"Not me."

"Why you so wet?"

Jude told him. He took up the handcuffs and adjusted one to be real small. "You are in fact, a sort of poor skinny little sprout, ain't you?" He snapped one cuff on Jude's right wrist and other on his own left.

"More or less."

"Come on down now. The womenfolk are setting out supper. And no tricks. You hear me?"

"None."

They sat in the kitchen and, far as she was able, Jude noticed Mrs. Burnap was trying to get the best of everything to him. And she helped him, for it is hard to cut up meat with only one hand, and that your left.

She was the only one there who had met the actual Ruby — and no more than two weeks before. What she knew she was keeping under her bonnet. Jude never could figure why.

The lamps were still burning, but it was growing daylight again, and they could hear men from the other two households outside talking over storm damage — for there was no rain now, just dripping from eaves and trees. And then sudden shriekings. It sounded like "Murder!"

The door burst open; in the background were four or five of those Kitchen Corner men but, bursting right in on the Rices, Burnaps and Jude, was a hunched-up little old man, soaking wet and roaring mad.

Jude gaped at him and couldn't believe it. It was Mr.

Faucett and up on what looked like pretty good legs. His eyes were rolling and shifting all around, like they couldn't stop and focus on anything.

"Where the Sheriff? Where that Smokey. Where . . . "

"My God," said Burnap softly, "if it ain't Francis Faucett."

"There, you — you slobbery damned do-nothing — get going, for it's too late. He's down there yet. It's murder. Catch that murderer. God damn it. I gotter have help to cotch him," and he was ringing his hands.

Then he saw Jude. His snapping-turtle neck lengthened and swung. The only sound he could get out was like a death rattle. "How come, Smokey, you got him — that fast," he whispered feebly. "Fer there he sets, right there. Like magic." He collapsed back into a chair.

Burnap says reasonably, "Now Mr. Faucett, collect yourself and tell a straight story. Who are you accusing of what?"

"That there painting fellow. Rebough he calls himself. And my wife. My Emma . . . "

"Of murder?"

"Attempted, I should of said."

"He attempted to murder Mrs. Faucett?"

"No, no." He woke up and began screeching again, "God damn you fer a tarnation blundering, bumptious, stinking (and so forth) idiot! And that fellow sitting right there, eating your victuals like an honored guest and laughing at me."

"Cut your abusive talk. Begin again."

Mr. Faucett said Silas Poke had rolled him over to the river, then gone off to salt and tally the sheep on Star Mountain. It had been too hot and breedy a day for good shooting. Mostly he had just sat there and watched the storm cooking up at the head of the valley. It rolled slow at first, but it kept on rolling down. Mr. Rebough, he supposed, was in the house. Emma too. And he had been conscious for some time that fellow had been casting sheep's eyes at his wife, but he thought they had bounced right back off Emma, who

had been for twenty years a true and loving helpmeet to him
— Dod blast her filthy hide.

As the storm approached he began to "sing out" for someone to come and fetch him in. It came closer and he was
forced to really screech. "And she left me there, a poor, helpless, paralyzed old man — bedridden at that." For what? (to
put it politely as I can think how — and not at all as Mr.
Faucett put it) — the embraces of her paramour. Well, the
rain came down in buckets on him, bouncing on his bald head
like peas on a hen's back and the lightning hitting all about
him. It was dark as night. All the time he yelling his top off.

Then he saw Mr. Rebough down to the wharf, fingering
at the painter of the old dory they kept tied up there, looking
like he was thinking of stealing it. And he brought home to
him his Christian duty to help a fellow human being in
distress, and cursed the living daylights out of him to think of
thieving. Mr. Rebough was to come — and come quick, not
be so dawdling and slow.

"He come?" asked Burnap.

"Sidewise-like, and real snaky. Yes, he come, and I told
him what was what, right from the shoulder in real outgoing
language, for it sickened me to see a young, able-bodied man
so neglectful of common decency — and the rain bursting all
over me."

"He say anything?"

"No. Mr. Rebough ain't chatty. Not to me he ain't. I was
exhorting and commanding him to get me up out of there
in a hurry and be careful, for the mud on that bank was
mighty slippery. I spoke to him very firmly, first and last. So
he got a-holt of the back of my wheelchair and stood some
time, stockstill, listening to me. You can't believe the inhu-
manity of what he did. He gave me a good sharp push down
that bank into six feet of water — and me paralyzed and bedridden. Haven't set foot to the ground for nineteen years, not
since I fell from the barn ridgepole. I went a-shrieking to my

death. But the Lord was on my side. He wanted me to live and bear witness against them two murderous, fornicating sinners. For no sooner was I in that cold water than my legs began to work, and they took right a-hold. I was swimming, and swimming good too."

He had washed against the wharf and pulled himself up on it, "gagging and gargling and full of river water," but he had managed to drag himself to his own back door. There was a lamp lit. He tapped on the pane, for the door had been bolted on account of the high wind — and he wanted to get in and dried off, worst way.

And there was Emma, "not dressed in any way fittin' to receive strangers," clasped in the arms of his "murderer," and he in hers. He had seen them.

He opened his mouth to curse them and then decided to get to the nearest house and have help in surrounding "them two criminals," but he tripped and lay half conscious in the mud for some time. With the Lord's help he had gotten up and going again and, by crickety, if Sheriff hadn't already gone and got the one of them! But he was going to have the law on both. Collusion — they both had colluded in those crimes. And weren't it a hanging matter?

Burnap looked at Jude with honest respect. "Mister," says he, "what you got to say for yourself?"

"Nothing more than it weren't possible."

"He can't deny any," Faucett put in.

"Yes I do, everything but . . . but . . . " For now he had the feeling and couldn't shake it, he really had done like he'd been longing to. He felt both guilty and sort of self-satisfied, and it all seemed years ago, and he felt everybody had forgotten and forgiven. He had forgiven himself even.

"Well," says Burnap, "you're the brisk lad — and no mistake. And no mistake who you are — for all your mooching around with them dod-blasted posy pictures of yours."

Mr. Faucett was collapsing, breathing hard and yellowing

off. The Kitchen Corner men took him home on a padded ladder. Mrs. Burnap and her sister went along to nurse. Burnap was ordering witnesses and a doctor and a justice of the peace summoned. He was so sure of himself he was acting pretty legal — for him.

A whole lot of people came. And Emma came.

And she betrayed him, not inadvertently, but by deliberate intent with her hand steady on the Bible and her voice steady. She looked very virtuous, and more buttoned-up than when relaxing at home. And she was looking all her age. That increased in Jude the feeling all this had happened too long ago to matter now. He knew by the way her interlocutors addressed her she always had borne a good reputation as a virtuous wife, and a truth-telling woman.

This was the man (and so help her God) that had pushed her poor helpless husband in the river and then came into the house and had made "improper advances" to herself. She had had some reason to be suspicious of him before. He hadn't been doing any honest work, and had a little the air of a man hid-up. Yet he had often been gone abroad, and given no explanations why or where. This was a staggering lie. As Burnap gave her the dates of certain of Ruby's crimes, she admitted right off, yes, those were the very days when he had been gone away. She was such a convincing liar Jude half believed her himself.

She only addressed Jude once. "Sir," she said with modest dignity, "I must beg of you to clear my good name, and set to rest forever the ugly rumors my husband's unjust accusations have aroused." This he swore to.

They got the pauper woman over from the almshouse. She goggled at them. Yes, she had known right away this was Ruby Lambkin, for he had pitied her poverty and given her a coin now and then.

Silas Poke looked like he'd die a-laughing, if he dared. His eyes were brim full of fun and the devil, and he saying he was a Quaker man to heart, and must be excused from laying a hand on the Bible; and looking like he knew the whole room would explode if he did — he was so chuck full of original sin. He corroborated everything Emma had said. He looked to be complete master of the situation and to be enjoying himself to the hilt. Once he looked straight at her. And then Jude knew. He knew slam-bang and for certain Mr. Poke was her lover. He had never got beyond painful suspicions until that one glance. It came almost like relief to know.

Jude also guessed why (maybe) they were lying so. That tavern was engaging in smuggling. Last thing they'd want were the Sheriff's men hunting for Ruby Lambkin down there, and stumbling on French brandy, British cutlery and watches. Naturally they'd be saying the criminal was all caught. And now he was wondering, perhaps it was through Mr. Poke Ruby had been disposing of his own stolen goods. Why, perhaps Emma had known him some time and real well. He hadn't liked the idea of her virtue collapsing quite so sudden to a perfect stranger. Yet half of him was saying to himself — that fellow is a better man than I am, for he up and did, in say a half hour flat, what I could no more than long to do. And I took weeks. I'll take off my hat to Ruby Lambkin.

The justice of peace was satisfied. Papers drawn out. Next morning the Sheriff was to move the prisoner down to the breakproof new prison to Windsor, and under an armed guard of militiamen — say fifty of them. And maybe the cadets from Norwich. They were sharp little razors and would give style. Tonight an armed guard about this house, three men (armed again) in the room with Lambkin. They were fearful that Ruby might be freed, on the road, by an uprising of the population if all precautions weren't taken.

Jude was almost asleep. He was feeling relaxed and content, now somebody had gone ahead and pushed Mr.

Faucett into the river and seduced Emma. Of course he had denied everything, and had known enough not to sign the "confession" drawn up for him to sign. He was satisfied that there would be no hunting that night for Ruby. No one had even looked to see if he had left in the Faucetts' dory. Jude's capture would give Ruby a respite. It was like he really was believing that Ruby Lambkin was a part of himself — and a far more active part at that.

He had heard it settled that three men were to guard him that night. When he saw it was going to be one man, and that Burnap, he felt a spasm of fear. For eight hours now — he and Burnap alone. It made him queasy in the stomach. Yet Burnap never did manhandle him. He threatened, and shoved his great fist in his face, and said how he was going to knock his teeth down his throat, break his nose for him, smash his eyes in if he wouldn't confess. He wouldn't let him drop off to sleep. He talked to him all night through. Every moment Jude was expecting the crash of that heavy fist in his face. And the fear of it was so unmanning to him he wished at last it would come, and be over with. He couldn't put up a hand to fend the blow, for he was in irons.

At last he admitted he was Ruby Lambkin. And signed the confession. And he signed another paper the Sheriff had written up, to the effect he wished to testify to all whom it might concern it was Sheriff Burnap, and nobody else, who had taken him and to whom the reward money was due. It was dawn then, and Burnap let him sleep.

. . . .

Thirty-eight

. . . .

THE NEWS swept like wildfire. People yelling out of windows, knotting up on the street and gesticulating with excitement. I guess it was about like this all up and down the river, as it was in Hanover.

"Have you heard?"

"What?"

"Lambkin's taken."

"No!"

"Over to Norwich."

"Burnap got him?"

"Yeah. He got him."

The bell tolled from the top of College Hall for eight o'clock morning prayers. The students would head that way. They'd stop to yell back and forth and hope to pick up more news before the college shet them up. And everybody was coming out their houses into the fine cool sunshine to learn whatever was happening.

Dr. Dwight pooh-poohed me when I told him how fearful I was it might be Jude Burnap had by mistake. He told me, and Primrose and her brothers, to get inside and after Latin. I stayed on beside him, for I was worried.

You noticed that everybody felt bad it was Burnap would get the reward. And at least half the people out milling around were frankly sorry Ruby had been taken at all. It was known that Burnap feared a delivery on the road and had called out all sorts of militiamen and borrowed the cadets as well, and had warned all the towns he was passing through to have strong guards out.

Then, as I loitered there, a constable came up and politely asked Dr. Dwight to give a bond, or his word or something for my appearance at the trial. This woke him to believing what I'd been saying. He gave up all thought of chapel attendance and, just as he was, with that knotted red bandanna handkerchief on his head, he grabbed my arm and set off on a jog-trot for the bridge and Norwich, to tell Burnap he was making a mistake. But we were too late.

Drawn up on the green before the military academy, stiff as wooden soldiers, were the cadets. They were all spandy in their white duck pants and form-fitting buttoned-up blue jackets. It seemed to be a matter of pride with them to have no feelings and no expressions. A cadet officer "heruped" at them and they clicked into place right in front of Sheriff Burnap's two-horse wagon the second it appeared. Those boys marched good! And held their guns properly.

About the Sheriff's wagon were fifty of the local militiamen, sort of slouching and spitting and carrying their guns whichways and not bothering to keep step much. The reason they weren't trying for any military smartness was because they knew the cadets would beat them at that. So, I guess, they thought it safer not to try any.

Jude saw us and nodded, as though we weren't to worry any. Then someone would yell, "Hey, Ruby. Ruby . . . how's the boy," and he'd turn and smile at them. He looked roughed up, of course, and he was in irons but he was certainly keeping his composure and his chin up. He was giving bold confident glances all directions. He told me later that he had been determined not to disgrace the name of Ruby Lambkin (who, after all, was a brave, active fellow). And as long as he wore his name, he'd play the part.

Dr. Dwight was trying to force himself through the cordon of sloppy militiamen to get at Burnap. They called him "Grandpa" and pushed him aside, so he told me he was hustling home again to write a letter of explanation and send it special messenger, and right away, to Windsor. Then too, he was flabbergasted to notice practically the entire student body from Dartmouth were intending to join the procession, following along after the Sheriff and his prisoner. I guess those boys had figured it if their old enemies, the cadets, were going to have a pleasant holiday junket to Windsor, they were going to have one too. As for me, I caught right on to the spirit of the occasion. I decided I'd tag too. A powerful lot of young women were appearing and coming along. Some folk came on horseback and in vehicles. Most of us on foot. It was higglety-pigglety, but great fun.

The cadets had a little band and they played fine music. Burnap might be fearful of a delivery, but he did like everybody to see him in his glory. The band struck up an old song, wrote first in honor of George Washington. Although custom forbade them to sing on parade, everybody round there knew the words. It goes:

> He comes, he comes, our hero comes!
> Sound, sound the trumpets!
> Beat, beat the drums!

They played it sharp and staccato, with the drums rippling through it and the trumpets tooting. Naturally, soon we were singing it, "He comes, he comes, our Lambkin comes," and making other changes to suit the situation. And all of us taggers-on clapping and swinging to the music.

Burnap was trying to yell at the cadet officer to stop it, but he'd turn and salute and say "Sir?" but somehow mistake the order. It was a mistake in judgment to send those boys off with no older head to command them.

We had the Connecticut to our left hand. Flatboat men and rafters were waving and yelling at us. And some came in, tied up, and jumped ashore to join us.

White River Junction was, from Burnap's point of view, the worst of all. He'd sent warning to the towns we'd be passing through that they had best call out the militia to keep order. We didn't see one of them. But the superintendents of the wool-weaving factories (they had a lot of big ones there) had given their girls a half holiday so they might enjoy a glimpse of their hero. It was girls, girls, girls, lining the streets, squealing and jumping and surging forward and through us. And "Oh my, ain't he handsome!" and "Ruby, Ruby darling." And "You get out fast now, won't you?" But some were crying, they felt so sorry for him. They had nosegays and posies to throw at him. The wagon began filling up with pinks, pansies and marigolds, bachelor's buttons and such. If any one group had been more taken in by Mr. Sharp's lying ballads and the mouth-to-mouth stories of Lambkin going about, I guess it was the factory girls of White River.

Burnap stood up and yelled for the cadets to keep a-going. "Clear a way." The youngster in charge of them saluted sharp as a mousetrap. Should he order his "men" to fire? Sir? So Burnap sat down again and for the moment gave up.

The girls pushed up to the wagon and all over it. And all over "Ruby" too. Some wanted an autograph, some a button from his coat, some to no more than touch him. Most of those bold enough to be this far wanted to kiss him. Jude said he got to laughing, and although he tried to explain, none of those witless females would listen to him. He said some of them kissed Burnap by mistake — but you know he exaggerated.

It is shocking to think that these well-brung-up, wage-earning, respectable Yankee girls could go so far off their rockers that they joined our procession to Windsor. North

Hartland and Hartland too, and the militiamen that had been called out just stood there scratching their polls and no idea what to do.

This spontaneous triumphant procession which was accorded "Ruby Lambkin" does not speak at all well for the law-abiding, serious mindedness of New England. But there is no point to glossing it over. Yankees are said to be too dern sot on doing what they please and this was what they pleased. Then too, the weather. It had been hotter than hot mustard for weeks, and then this drop in temperature, brisk, cool and most invigorating. Sometimes (I've noticed before), times like that, Yankees get too blasted invigorated. You might blame it on the weather.

Now we were fetching into Windsor, and that was different. Windsor men, constables, deacons from the churches, I guess, militiamen, were all out and the joyful Comus crew we had picked up on our travels was somehow disbanded. Main Street of Windsor was just about lined with serious-looking men, and they were yelling (like they meant it) "No demonstration," although even here people were yelling to encourage Lambkin and demanding, "Speech. Speech."

There before us was that great stone prison, and the gate was opening into its courtyard, and the Sheriff's wagon, with Jude in it, driving in. The gates swung shut. And now it was as if I had woke up cold sober. Suddenly I realized how far I had walked, had eaten nothing; no, not even breakfast, and had no money. I didn't want to go back to Dr. Dwight's — not yet anyway. I wanted to be right to hand when Jude was turned loose again. But the great stone prison looked terribly final. I was a little scared for him.

Then I felt a touch on my arm. It was Phineas Sharp.

. . . .

Thirty-nine

. . . .

J UDE TOLD ME later that by Windsor, his irons, both handcuffs and leg irons, were hurting him cruelly. Burnap had
put them on terribly tight, to punish him for having slipped
the bracelets once, and also because he hated him. So Jude
couldn't stand to step out the wagon, and fell out. Burnap
had seen to that. He fell again on the steps. Then Burnap
saw his chance to kick him in the face "accidentally."

One of the jailers and Burnap got him up and pushed
him for the Warden's office. Two days later his face was
swollen and blackened and he had as bad a black eye as I
ever saw, but now he only had a cut lip and a nosebleed
to show for Burnap's cruelty. He said it felt mighty lone-
some, walled in, in that yard — no admiration, no music.
He guessed the bubble of his grandeur was about to burst.

The Warden was sitting at his desk in the Warden's
office. He looked aloof and educated — more like a banker
than your ordinary jailer.

"Well, Sheriff," he says, giving no more than half a look
at Jude as he was struggling to stanch the blood, but being
in handcuffs couldn't, "I'd like to congratulate you on bringing in the Lambkin."

"Thanks, Warden. Thanks."

"I'd *like* to see you get that three-hundred-dollar reward."

"It will come in handy. And Lamb here has sworn (I got it in writing) that I, and nobody else, got him. And I got him, and the money — alone."

Warden said, and each time he was emphasizing "like" more obviously, "I'd *like* to commend such an able, active man for doing his duty. But, I'm afraid I cannot. 'Fraid you didn't get your man, nor reward money either."

"I don't quite get you."

"This fellow isn't Ruby Lambkin, no matter what he says. He's an impostor."

"Look here. I got proof and plenty of it. He confessed and signed his confession."

"You can get any man who isn't a real born hero to confess to about anything — if you kick him in the face." (So he seen what Burnap had done out there in the yard.) "What you're forgetting is that I was jailer over to Woodstock before I got appointed here. We had Ruby for four or five days. I know what he looks like, as you know your wife. That's not him. Besides, I could have two other men here in this office within half an hour that also have had time to study on him — and back me up."

For the first time he looked square at Jude. "If you wish to bring assault and battery charges against Sheriff Burnap, you have the right, and witnesses. Now, Mr. Sheriff, you satisfied this man is innocent?"

Burnap said he wasn't. He showed all those affidavits and such. The Warden agreed to hold Jude forty-eight hours on "suspicion," to give Burnap time to prove himself right.

Warden told Burnap that, as for all those false-swearing people up to Norwich, they needed their heads put under a pump. People were seeing too many Ruby Lambkins. This loose use of imagination was getting in the way of catching the genuine article. He hadn't thought the High Sheriff of Windsor County would lose his head too.

Jude was treated like a guest. A doctor came to fix his face for him, free for nothing. He put ointment on the chafing caused by those too-tight irons. Jude slept in the house of one of the turnkeys, within the yard, not in a cell. And he slept in a real bed. It did take him all of that forty-eight hours to get freshed-up again, after all he had been through.

One thing rankled in him. The Warden had called him "impostor." That's what he had been, no matter how inadvertently.

Word got out fast onto the street and up and down the river towns that this weren't the real Ruby Lambkin. It was either a poor innocent gentleman, a most respectable limner by trade, who had been brutally used by Burnap; or it was a no-account, fiddling fellow caught impersonating his betters. The papers took the former attitude. And in a highfalutin language, they certainly made sport of Burnap.

Mr. Sharp paid for my victuals and lodgement (such as it was). He was doing a smart trade, selling off his assorted Lambkin ballads on street corners and taverns, fast as he could hand them out. I found out (now I was dependent on him) he was a touch parsimonious. He got all his food for himself (and now for me too) by scrounging for it. Yet I wouldn't of thought to leave him, nor Windsor, until I saw Jude walking out the prison.

We were waiting for him at the prison gates at the hour set for his release. Waiting there also for him was a group of gentlemen in high hats and frock coats, all just alike, as I remember them after so many years. They were leading citizens obviously. When Jude did come out they just brushed Sharp and me aside and tipped their hats to Jude, all alike and as one man. Their spokesman said they had come to "escort him" and to apologize for the rough treatment he had received in Vermont — some such talk. They had balled up around Jude and were walking down the main street. Mr. Sharp and I tailed along after.

They didn't apologize any, but they escorted him all right, and they took him to the exact center of the bridge over the Connecticut, right to where Vermont ends and New Hampshire begins.

"Mister," said one of them, "don't you never come back to Vermont — ever again. It's a little state and, like a little chimney, it gets hot easy. Hot as Hell. Too hot to hold you. We, a body of the better citizens of Vermont, are getting where we don't much care whether you are Ruby Lambkin or not. We just don't fancy your looks. Maybe there are a baker's dozen of you lanky, dark young fellows, all out impersonating each other, and half drowning poor helpless old invalids, and making improper advances to respectable matrons. Now git."

They turned on their heels like one heel, and marched back off that bridge.

I certainly understand now how they felt. Think of the waste of money! Every militiaman called out was paid a little somewhat. Those factory girls had been given a half holiday and took a whole one. Dartmouth just about cleaned out of students. Norwich cadets sent on a fool's errand. No sensible community could stomach such goings-on.

We stood, leaning against the guard rail, just looking at each other. Jude's face had now had time to really swell and blacken and one eye was closed up. He tried to laugh it off. And whatever was I doing here? Why weren't I up to Hanover — where I belonged?

We walked off the bridge and into New Hampshire. It was pleasant by the riverbank and we sat there for some time, to make plans. Mr. Sharp had cold johnnycake and a moldy cheese and a bottle of "herbal tonic" guaranteed to grow hair on anything, but mostly alcohol. The long grass was nice to lie in, and the sunshine felt good. We lay in a row there, with hats over our faces for sunshades. Considering Mr. Sharp's natural curiosity and his born gabbiness, at first he was considerate and didn't question too much.

He told us the head of that delegation of respectable citizens was Johnny Fessenden's father from White River. We hadn't known that.

Jude said he had to figure out what next. Everything he owned was up at Faucett's — including all his money, for except for pocket change we kept our money in a secret box he had contrived below the whipstock. Neither he nor I had a cent. Although he wouldn't admit that no matter how many citizens of how great respectability told him to keep out of Vermont, he was intending to obey them — still, at the moment, he had "lost his taste" for Norwich. If he showed up up there, with this terrible black eye, people would think either Mr. Faucett had given it to him or Emma had, defending her virtue — if any. It was decided I was to go back, pay up what he owed to Faucett's, get the microscope and so on back to Dr. Dwight, and say his and my farewells to everybody, then drive down and meet with Jude.

Mr. Sharp had held on to his consuming curiosity pretty well until now but, "Aren't you wishing to see Mrs. F. again?"

Jude sat up. "No," says he, "she's nothing to me. Never was and never could be." Then, I couldn't believe my ears, "Fat old fool — and bone-lazy to boot."

Now "fat old fool" isn't, to my way of thinking, the language of love. You can call a woman worse words (but I will not soil my pen with them) and still love her. But not "old," I maintain, nor "fat." Fool, maybe.

Then Jude flopped over to rest easy on his back for a while, and he politely inquired of Mr. Sharp as to how his business had been going. It had been "scrumptious," says Sharp. And now he had been figuring out a new one based on recent events. While I went to Norwich, he'd be hitting for Claremont, because there was a journeyman printer there

that would print up his new ballad — the one he was working
on now. And he could get to selling it, striking while the
iron was hot. And although it wasn't completed, and he
might have to hum some, would we like to hear it?

Jude put his hat firmly over his face and said he didn't
care if he did. I think his suspicions were aroused as to what
it was about.

Mr. Sharp didn't stand up and make a public spectacle of
himself as usual. He sang and hummed, lying flat on his back,
pausing now and then to explain a hiatus, or take another
pull at that herbal tonic. He announced the title, "The Cruel
Husband." And was Jude sure he'd like to hear it?

"Somewhat," said Jude, real cagey. "But not much."

> " 'Twas on the bright Connecticut
> And midmost of the year . . . "

"What's midmost?" Jude interrupted. "Don't you mean
early September?"

"Midmost sounds good. You like the start of it?"

"Not particularly."

Soon enough Sharp was singing:

> "Oh, roll me to the river,
> The old man sayeth.
> And Ruby Lambkin
> Rolled him
> And pushed him to his death."

"Inaccurate," says Jude. "For he didn't die."

"True facts come out later."

"Well, anyways," said Jude, relaxing, "I like it fine. Go
ahead."

"But when he hit the water . . . Blessed if I haven't forgotten just how it goes in here.

> "And his arms began to work,
> And his legs began to fly . . . "

Mr. Sharp went on and on with it. Then back again to correct it. Jude was captious and interfering, and yet indifferent. He was insisting Mr. Sharp had ought to stick to facts — he had used his imagination too much. That was about like the kettle calling the pot black. Both seemed real easy-tempered. Mr. Sharp said proudly (and it turned out factually) that what really had transpired wasn't going to matter any more, for he, now, this very minute, was deciding what it was people were going to believe. And what you believed was more important than what happened anywhere. He went on to say, for instance, that if people "believed" God was in his Heaven looking out for them, why then, God was. And if they believed the Devil was out back of the woodpile, waiting for them dark nights, why then, there he was. He could prove it. Or take Jude's line of work. He'd paint up a young woman, say real pretty, and she aged or passed on. Nothing much else left of her, but wouldn't her descendants forever believe she was just like Jude done her? And so, in a way, there she was — always real pretty, and most appealing young.

It is funny that sitting there along the east bank of the Connecticut River was the first time I heard what I suppose is the most famous ballad New England ever produced. Certain things got changed, the title for instance. It is always called nowadays "Lena Linkmouse," and that river has been everything from the Shenandoah to the Oregon. It has passed through too many lumber camps, gone too far to sea, up and down the Chisholm Trail too often, been sung over too many times in soldier camps (both the blue and the gray) to come out as innocent as it began. Mr. Sharp shouldn't be blamed for the impure stanzas added by others. I'd like to state they were not part of the original composition.

Some things never did change. That gorgeous rollicking tune he set it to (or concocted). The name of the "hero" was always Ruby Lambkin (and that, in the end, was just about all that was "believed" and existed of him). The woman was always fat and her name was Lena Linkmouse. I think Sharp figured it, there was no such family name and so no hurt feelings apt to arise. Likewise, Linkmouse rhymes with both spouse and house.

So it was fair on in the afternoon when we got up from there and started each in our own direction. Jude was moving on to Charlestown. Three years before he had been there too briefly. He felt the place a good, rich, almost unworked field. He'd be dug in somewhere waiting for me. I could ask about. Sharp was heading for Claremont. He had given Jude a loan — which was contrary to all his feeling, being a real suspicious little man. He trusted Jude as much as anybody, but he trusted nobody much.

. . . .

Forty

. . . .

I WAS AWAY four days. I found Jude and Mr. Sharp sitting on the stoop before the hotel. It had a highfalutin name. Like The King Charles. Although Sharp had got his "Cruel Husband" all printed up and was raring to go, he wouldn't have dared leave before I came along with Goldie, the chaise, and the ready cash. And then, would you believe it? — he charged Jude for all those scraps of food people had given to us when I was dependent on his charity, for, as he said, he'd been the one that had procured them.

Now he had his money he weren't waiting for longer than I could report on the situation up around Norwich. What of the Sheriff? I couldn't tell him a thing. Ruby reappeared? No, he hadn't — far as I knew.

"Did you see Mrs. F?" as he always called her.

"Naturally. And she told me she wasn't charging anything — not even for all you had writ up against yourself on that slate."

"Nothing at all?" Jude exclaimed, "for room, board for me, bait for my horse for over three weeks?"

"She said you had been so put upon while there she figured that you had earned it."

"True enough," said Jude, "but that was a very decent action — for a fundamentally indecent woman." For it seems to me, after that evening at Kitchen Corner, when Emma stood up and so falsely incriminated him, he never had again a good word for her.

Now he was adding, with a barkish laugh, "How's smuggling?"

"I didn't inquire."

Sharp asked if Mr. Faucett was looking pretty good.

I told them how he'd lost his wheelchair, so he had no choice but keep on his legs — such as they were, and that wasn't much. And I guessed he lost his wits somewhat, and most surprising, his bad temper and his filthy language. He was after Mr. Poke if sometime he had a minute to spare, would he be so kind as to fish up his wheelchair for him? That wasn't how he used to talk. He'd lost his popgun too in the river and, seemingly, his taste for shooting songbirds.

"Improved?" asked Jude.

"In a way he had, but . . . "

"Nuts, is he?"

"Nuts — just about." And the way now he was teetering about that slippery, slimy riverbank, gazing in to see hide or hair of his wheelchair, did look like (Mr. Poke had told me) he'd fall in and really drown, about any time now.

I will add here what I didn't learn until Jude and I were on the Barrier a month later. He did fall in and Emma married the imp.

Mr. Sharp didn't like the idea that Ruby had drove the poor old man out of his wits, by the dunking he'd given him. He didn't like it that if Mr. Faucett did fall in and drown even if at a later date, Ruby might be considered morally responsible. He was shaking his head and making a ticking noise with his tongue against his teeth.

"What you ticking about, Mr. Sharp?" Jude asked.

"Everybody likes it Ruby cured the poor, paralyzed old husband — don't want him to have driven the old fool nuts. And if Mr. Faucett should drown, why that just about leaves Ruby a taker of human life. And as soon as Ruby does take a human life — why, then the jig is up."

"Glad you're admitting it is a jig."

"Sure it is a jig. And it seems just right now — I'm having a premonition and seeing the handwriting on the wall. It's only as long as he stays sort of *innocent* people want to hear of him. Tick, tick. He has to be guileful and guileless. Can't put it plainer than that."

"Not so in real life?" Jude asked him.

"Not especially. I've been watching him. He began by stealing odd things and linen from the line. Went from there to stealing dogs. Then horses, silver spoons, holdups on the road, breaking houses, church silver . . . That was just as far as he could go. I was afraid it might be a little mite too far. People were so pleased how he got that hundred dollars out of Johnny Fessenden, they were in a forgiving mood. Now I'm dreading that he take the next step — and go too far. For if he takes the next (I'm referring to human life), he'll just destroy himself."

"Good," says Jude, who was being no politer to Mr. Sharp than when I left. "Can't wait for the bottom to drop out of him, personally."

"It will," says Sharp mournfully. "Soon as there's one drop of blood upon his hands. Mark my words, for I feel it coming."

He left us then, with the money owing paid back and his pack full of "Cruel Husbands." I sat there on the stoop of the King Charles thinking idly, "Well, there goes Phineas Sharp . . . " I should of said, "There goes Lena Linkmouse, starting out on her nefarious way through the length and breadth of these United States. And when we all are dead and gone she'll be still going strong."

. . . .

Forty-one

. . . .

Ruby WAS TAKEN, when he was taken, with no fuss at all. He was betrayed by three flatboat men, companions of his.

Perhaps you know how, when the Connecticut River gets to Bellows Falls, the whole thing narrows up, pulls itself together and goes jumping down a gorge, smashing at the black-toothed rocks, banging at the sides of its bed. Only one person ever went over those falls and lived, and she was drunk — a Abenaki squaw. Her canoe was smashed. No boat ever made it, therefore there was this boat canal. First thing like it in America. Eight locks to it.

The flatboat got into one of those basins and stopped, for it had been decided to turn Ruby over to authority. He had been hid up real cute in their cargo of hides, wool and potash. But now he had a congestion of the lights; pneumonia, people would call it today. He was off his head, weak and harmless as a kitten. I guess his friends figured it he'd die just as easy in jail as on a boat and they might as well get the money on him — no difference to him. Beyond doubt they had been long acquainted with him and not only had been hiding him long spells at a time, but selling off stolen goods for him.

So the captain ran up into town and came back with a constable and soon a good many other authorities and a doctor. It was decided to leave him lay where he was. The gentlemen from Bellows Falls got on the flatboat too, and it was commanded to float down to Brattleboro, where there was a fine, breakproof jail. The one at Bellows Falls wasn't much to brag about. Even if Ruby died, they wanted him locked up good.

We got word of all this where we were at Charlestown across the river from Brattleboro. You'd of thought it was the President of the United States that was ailing by the way people and the newspapers took on. Daily reports — where there was a daily paper. One day he was doing a little better, setting up and taking nourishment. Next, the doctors were shaking their heads and looking grave.

There was some indignation as to the way he was taken, sold by his treacherous "friends." People were saying he weighed about one hundred and ninety and he went like so much beef for around a dollar-thirty a pound. Put like that it did sound real despicable.

As a fact, it was doubtless the flatboat men's decision to turn him in that saved his life, although that didn't amount to much when you added up the score. Even with the best care he barely scraped through. At first the doctors wouldn't permit anyone to question him. And he was permitted female

nursing. For his day hours, Nurse Rachael Morrison, a good
ripe sixty. For his nighttime nurse, Florence Duddey, and
she had five children. These women looked like a wise choice,
but at least Nurse Duddey didn't so prove, and I have my
suspicions of Nurse Morrison as well. Ruby could twist
women. From cradle to grave he twisted them. I haven't
dwelt on this side of his nature much as it reflects no credit
to the good sense and dignity of New England womanhood,
and besides, I don't think those tales were correct. This
delicate care of him did start a precedent, prejudicial to
holding him as soon as he began to strengthen. This he did
a sight faster than anticipated.

Of course, Jude was interested in all this, but not too much
so. I felt he didn't feel connected with Ruby any more. May
have been the fine September weather we were having. Not
like those muggy, hot, unthinking days of August. He was
selling plenty of pictures. Then he got an order to do an
overmantel for the local antiquary, Jonathan P. Peabody.

In his young days Squire Peabody had done all the work
(tanning) he had a mind to. Now he was working even
harder, digging up Charlestown's past. For here at Charlestown had stood old Fort Number Four, gone for two hundred years. But just where had it stood? Some said up on
Main Street. Some said riverside. The whole town was
trembling with excitement. A man would find an arrowhead
by the river and say that proved the site. Then someone else
dug up a skull on Main Street and, until it was admitted to be
the skull of a calf, was insisting this proved the site of the fort.

But the problem of where the Johnson Garrison had stood
was known and agreed on. It was the destruction of this house
Squire Peabody asked Jude to paint. Overmantels, as I think
I said earlier, were falling out of fashion, yet Jude did enjoy
to do them. Had space enough to move about in. Under
Squire Peabody's direction he went to work with a will.

We lived in Squire's house and did our work there. He

was planning when he passed on to give this house and all that was in it to the Charlestown Historical Society. Already he had crammed it full of everything from King Paugus's samp bowl to the first feather bed made from the feathers of the first flock of geese. He had the biggest kidney-stone ever passed in that district. He had stuffed catamounts and a drum that had rolled at Yorktown, and lots of books on ancient life hereabout, and records. Jude dove into the spirit of the place and read up on everything.

It seems these Johnsons were making merry (August, 1754) over flip and watermelons when the Indians surprised them and carried off seven of them captives to Canada. It was tough on Mrs. Johnson, who was in the family way. Jude got in all these facts very nice. As for his Indians, you could feel the unmitigated horror of them, and hear their devilish screechings. You could all but smell the varmints. I've been attacked by living ones out west and I can say they weren't a patch on these Jude painted up. Jude certainly enjoyed this job and put his back into it.

Not far south was Walpole. It too had its antiquarian spirit, and great local pride. They couldn't bear to think of Charlestown's bloody beginnings being thus permanently and publicly recorded, and their ancient sufferings neglected. No sooner had Jude completed the destruction of the Johnson Garrison up here, then he was to go to Walpole and do his durndest with the Indian attack on their Kilburn family. There was great antiquarian rivalry between those two peaceful, pretty towns.

By the way, the Indians never did take the Kilburn family's garrison. Those Kilburns were not the sort to be enjoying flip and watermelons just the wrong time, nor their women so light-minded as to get in the family way just before a long walk for Canada. Jude got sort of fond of those carefree Johnsons, so he never did do quite so well with the smug, forethinking Kilburns. He gave them all pursed-up mouths that looked like they had never bitten into a watermelon in their lives. And of course (being so wise), they had known the Indians might be on them and hadn't had a drop of anything more foolish than well water for days, and their stomachs were so sour even that had curdled on them.

But that picture too was giving the completest satisfaction when a squabble arose between those two towns. Charlestown (led by Squire Peabody) was saying no more than forty Indians had ever attacked the Kilburn Garrison. Walpole said, no, it was four hundred Indians. They got so het up on this point they bade Jude fix the proper number forever in his picture. He was to paint in all four hundred of them — no back views nor profiles allowed. Every Indian had to have a full face on him and a feather and be countable. I kept count for Jude. He wasn't happy about their insistence on this point. He said it peppered up the whole background, and it did.

You can see that we were busy, happy and profitably employed. September was just about ending. Then something happened across the river, over to Brattleboro, that broke up this antiquarian interlude. Worse yet, it reunited a little something in Jude with Ruby Lambkin once more.

For some time Ruby had been out of bed and well enough to be questioned. From all over New Hampshire and Vermont sheriffs and such, and private parties, were coming to ask him where he had sold that horse, or hidden such and such silver spoons, and so on. And clergymen were flocking to him to get to work on his soul — if any.

Smokey Burnap naturally came down from Windsor County. He was determined he'd learn from Ruby the fate of that church silver. Naturally, a man of his importance was permitted to go to Ruby's cell and to question him alone.

Nobody believed Ruby attacked him. He was again in handcuffs and still weak as cambric tea. Also, everyone who had had contact with him, ministers, nurses, turnkeys, and

general public, all agreed he had shown nothing but the
gentlest manners to them, never offering violence by tongue
or deed. The clergy and those two fool women were the
loudest in his defense. That fellow must have had a real
winning way with him.

Smokey Burnap stomped out, and then it was discovered
that Ruby was lying unconscious on the stone floor of his cell,
in a pool of blood. Burnap had smashed at his face again and
again, choking off his windpipe with his left hand so he
couldn't holler. Ruby was terribly bunged up.

There was great indignation against Burnap, but the jail
officials (considering Burnap was an official too) decided to
accept the Sheriff's story — Ruby had sprung on him and he
had acted in self-defense. They hoped to shut the whole
thing up. They couldn't shut up those two nurses. And now
it was causing criticism that two nurses were still being paid
out of tax money to care for a man out of all danger. So
the officials fired the nurses. This made things worse. Now
people were saying these kind, very devoted (and extremely
vocal) women were being fired so other sheriffs, and such,
could beat up Ruby if he didn't care to tell what he had done
with his loot. So it was agreed Nurse Morrison and Nurse
Duddey could visit him, just about as it pleased them — day
or night. The clergy had been doing that right along.

Speaking of Ruby's "Christian humility," as the clergy
were, the first thing he said when he regained consciousness
was that he was going to "cut out Burnap's heart." I call that
rough talk from a repentant sinner.

The cruelty Burnap had actually done Jude — that is, kicking him in the face when he fell in the prison yard at Windsor
— had never haunted Jude as had the cruelty he had feared
from him, and never suffered. I am referring to that long
night alone with him at Kitchen Corners — and every moment Jude had expected the blow to fall, and he in handcuffs
powerless to defend himself. That imaginary blow that had

never fallen, now I see, was worse than the actual kick. Suddenly Jude was for tossing aside all our pleasures and profit at Charlestown and Walpole and was set on getting to Brattleboro to tell what he knew of Burnap's brutality. Of course, it would have to be of the kick — the Warden at Windsor had witnessed it. No law court would consider being hurt by an imaginary blow worth talking about.

He got surprisingly excited about all this, and wanted to talk about Burnap, Ruby and himself all the time, even to the antiquaries who were a derned sight more interested in Indian cruelties all that time back than what was going on over to Brattleboro today. The last sixty-two Indians he fairly shot in — a blotch for a face and a slash of red for a feather. Then on to the next. He got going so hard he overshot the mark, or I lost count. For if that picture still exists and you ever get to Walpole and count up, you'll find there are four hundred and six of them, all told.

We put up at Brattleboro House. It was near the prison and was headquarters for everybody come to question or to pray at Ruby. Likewise, it was here Nurse Duddey habitually stopped, after her call on the prisoner, to have a mug of ale in the ladies' parlor. Ladies didn't go much to the barroom and so all the sloppy-minded and sentimental and half-witted beings hereabouts were like to congregate there too, at around three. She was there pretty punctually every day and fairly gooed out the latest information about that rascal. We saw her there. She was a big, motherly-looking woman; sloppy gray hair and a fresh pink skin — one elbow on the table and her ale in her hand, shaking her head over that "poor, helpless boy" and how Burnap's attack on him had just about sent him back to death's door. There were other stories about Burnap's cruelties and considerable talk of getting up a petition for his removal. Jude, of course, found ready ears to hear him and, as it was common knowledge that there was

somewhere about a limner who had been confused for their
hero, they were all pleased to meet him. Ruby's luster did
lend a certain shine to Jude wherever he went these days. He
enjoyed that to the hilt. Although that trip from Norwich to
Windsor had been too much of a good thing, even for him, he
never forgot the weary disgust in the warden's voice when he
had called him an "impostor." Next day Jude tried to locate
the proper authority to tell his tale to. Seemingly there wasn't
any. They were going on the theory, least said, soonest
mended — a mistake politicians often make.

Jude was making no effort to get work and then, in a queer
way, an order came. He had a letter from Squire Peabody.
He began by saying how much a portrait of King Paugus
would mean today and he realized that in, say two hundred
more years, a portrait of our "contemporary Robin Hood"
might be equally interesting. If Jude could get permission,
and wouldn't charge more than five dollars, he would engage
for a portrait of Ruby Lambkin. This pedantic confusing of
Robin Hood and Ruby shows how far even highly educated
men were taken in by all the loose talk going about. Ruby
was no Robin Hood.

Jude tried and tried. He couldn't get permission. The trial
would be coming along in a week now. He could carry
pencil, paper to that if he wished. I suppose they were fearful that an appealing likeness of Lambkin would arouse even
more sympathy with him. They wished no more fat of that
sort in the fire. Now I think they were right.

As I've said, nobody ever had broken Brattleboro jail.
Then Ruby broke it, and he had a woman to help him. That
was part of his tradition and I thought how it would please
Mr. Sharp, although the motherly Nurse Duddey was not
what one would consider Ruby Lambkin's meat. And she did
time for it too.

Weeks before, she had given him a file. He had filed off his irons. He filed the bars at his window and he chinked up cracks with chewed bread. He was no hurry to be leaving. He had to see Burnap first.

His cell gave on a lumberyard — sixteen-foot drop into it. He noticed that the master of the yard habitually hung up work clothes and such in the yard. I suppose he was too proud to be seen on the streets in the humble attire of his trade, being so come up in the world. Of course, nighttime would be best.

So Ruby was all ready to depart and yet he waited and waited, biding his evil time. Through one of the clergymen, he had sent word to Burnap that now he was ready to tell where he had hid up that church silver, for he was repenting of his bad deeds and now he saw that this communion service was an offense against God as well as man. His conscience pricked him like he couldn't sleep nights. He would tell Burnap where it was, but no one else, and no witnesses could be present.

Burnap came. Nobody will ever know just what happened. Warden said he had forbidden it that Burnap ever again see him alone; the man told off to be present didn't get his orders, and so on. Of course Burnap knew that Ruby had swore to cut out his heart.

There was no sound of a struggle, yet Burnap was of powerful physique, by nature wary, and had in a way been warned. Yet Ruby did it.

He had a poor, wretched knife, such as would be allowed a prisoner to cut up his meat. This he had sharpened and sharpened with his file — it was like a stiletto. He got that in Burnap's throat.

Then he settled down to do like he said he would, although now any moment someone might walk in on him and good sense would dictate the window, the drop, and the get-away. No time at all to waste. But he preferred to risk it, stay where he was and do just what he wanted. I guess he did what he wanted and when he wanted to, more consistently than any man I ever knew.

What he did next, the mess he made, speaks better for his persistent and misguided enthusiasm than for good sense or any anatomical knowledge. He broke his knife finally against a rib and gave up. That cell looked like a slaughterhouse, and Burnap as though he had exploded. Then Ruby left.

Mr. Sharp had said as soon as he took a human life the jig was up. I'm not sure it would of been, the life being that of Burnap. But mutilating the dead was something else again. By the way people carried on you'd of thought it was the worse offense.

So right there and then, that night over to Brattleboro, the bottom, so to speak, did fall out of Ruby Lambkin. The man who throwed down that broken knife, kicked off his irons and jerked out the sawed-through bars, dropped into the lumber-yard, put on the master's clothes and escaped, wasn't ever quite him again.

Someone else. Maybe just Reuben Lamb like some poor woman named him twenty-four or five years before. Maybe Lamb the Murderer, like they soon began to call him. But Ruby Lambkin lay just as dead beside the mutilated body as Burnap was himself.

Forty-two

W<small>E HEARD YELLING</small> and alarm bells, horses galloping, and tollings from all the church steeples. So we guessed Ruby had squeaked out. Although we were in bed, we were up out of it, hauling pants on over nightshirts, heading for downstairs. Every other guest at Brattleboro House was affected the same way, except ladies put on skirts and shawls.

There in the ladies' parlor was Nurse Duddey, enjoying her last nightcap of ale for some time. The constable came and took her away. She was crying.

An hour later the doctor staggered in for a couple of quick brandies. He looked like he needed them. He said he had never in all his life seen anything so unprofessional as the mess Ruby had made of Burnap. Obviously the man hadn't known where to turn to find so common an organ as a heart. He thought anatomy should be taught in the public schools.

Jude should now have crossed back into New Hampshire. There was still plenty of work for him to do under the elms of those pretty towns. He tossed all that away. He said he was blamed tired of the very name of Ruby Lambkin. He was hitting out west from here, to the other side of the Green Mountains — Bennington, for a fact. He'd been to Bennington five years back. He said it wasn't on the Connecticut nor a tributary of the same. Completely different watershed, and he'd bet over there nobody had ever heard of Ruby Lambkin.

He spoke a little desperately. Fact is, he didn't care where he went so it was pretty far off, peaceful, and he could rest up and get his head screwed on a little tighter. His degrading longings for Emma, his indignation at Mr. Faucett had undermined him. Now Ruby's murder of Burnap was the last straw on the camel's back.

Maybe what bothered him was this. Ruby Lambkin had forced his attention to the fact he weren't a great one for getting things done. I suppose men of a contemplative nature are apt to look enviously at men of no more than action. Jude couldn't help but of noticed, while he was only pondering on what he'd like to do, Ruby came along and did it for him.

He told me, during that trip over to Bennington, that if he had been his own grandfather he might actually believe that he and Ruby were two parts of the same personality. He said people, only that far back, could believe such nonsense. He, being the child of a more factual generation, could not. Yet I'll swear half the people heard him telling of Mrs. Casserine and her litter of fox cubs at Canaan had believed him, and some of those who heard about how he had given Ruby (or vice versa) a lift on the Canaan road had believed that.

Phineas Sharp would of said that what you want to believe you do, and sometimes that turns out to be truer than truth.

So we were in the mountains, and it was a mountain road we traveled by. Every valley had a rushing stream to it — which might or might not be well bridged. Then, after the dip down, we'd haul and zigzag up, up and over the great granite shoulder of the next mountain and from there, behold below us the next wild valley. And stretching out about us, forests, cliffs, gorges, and distant heights going on and on like frozen waves to sea.

The air was like crystal, and like wine to drink. The coloring-up had not begun in earnest yet. But here and there, and

in the swamps mostly, there was red, like fire burning — as if
someone had dropped a slow match. And the rest of the great
forest stood ready to catch on fire from these first few spots.

We got up our last rocky barrier and into Bennington.
Thus we were over the Green Mountains into a soft rolling
land. New York State was no more than four or five miles
away. It was surprising after all the wilderness we had traveled through to see again rich farmlands, big barns, fat cattle,
well-built houses.

The white church stood up handsome, white and light,
against the pale blue sky. It was a genuine beauty. About it
were white marble gravestones, crowding up to the picket
fence like they wanted to look out. They had cherubs and
angels, grapes and death'sheads on them, and all were cut
from marble. We had passed out of the slate country into the
marble land. You often can guess things like that by no more
than gravestones.

So we were out of the Connecticut Valley. I guess the
brooks hereabout head for the Hudson. We were almost out
of New England itself, but if Jude figured we had passed out
of what you might call the Ruby Lambkin belt he missed his
guess.

As I said, he'd been here before, some years back, but the
hostler who came out to take Goldie when we stopped before the Catamount Tavern gave him a suspicious look, as
though to say, You may be Mr. Rebough, the limner, like
you are telling me or you may be Lamb the Murderer; anyhow you two have got yourselves so mixed up I don't care
for the sight of either of you.

On the other hand, Mr. Bigger, the landlord, was apologizing to Jude (who he remembered well) for the whole State
of Vermont and the indignities Jude had suffered at the hands
of this "Hill of Worms." It came out that Mr. Sharp had
been even here with his ballads and befuddling tales. Ruby

was just about as well known a character here as back where
we came from.

Yet one thing we noticed. People round here were terribly
afraid of him. Men slept with guns to hand; women were
scared of being left alone, even in broad daylight. It was like
the old days of the Indians. When night came you could almost hear doors and shutters being locked, barred and bolted.
It was like that, I guess, in all the towns for far around. For
it was Lamb the Murderer that was loose upon them now
(where would he strike next?). And for the first time I heard
Burnap's name mentioned with pity and respect.

We were no more than settled in well at Bennington before
news came of activities possibly proving him to be over the
state line, into Massachusetts. The flatboat I mentioned
earlier came nosing in towards the canal at Turners Falls,
then carelessly went aground and blocked the entry. The lock
keeper, in a tearing rage, finally boarded it to find why it
weren't behaving properly. The captain and one man were
on it but incapable of sensible navigation because someone
had cut their throats. The third fellow was never located —
dead or alive.

It looked like Ruby had revenged himself upon his be-
trayers, and people said now he had got that reward money
for himself. Or maybe the missing flatboat man had killed
his fellows, taken it, and beat it. Yet fact was that money
hadn't been paid out yet. You know how slow authority is
about coughing up hard cash. Now they decided to hold on
to it a mite longer.

We stayed around Bennington for no more than two weeks.
Jude didn't seem quite himself to me — or perhaps he was
more his own self than usual. He began talking to me much
freer than previously. More man to man. But he was sort of
listless and lazy and real trifling when it came to dusting
around and finding sitters and such for himself. He didn't

unpack one canvas or even pin up his trade card. Mr. Bigger would of liked him to do a regular inn sign, for the Catamount still had no more stylish sign before it than a moldy old stuffed catamount. Jude wasn't interested.

For his own amusement (there was no money in it), he started several times to paint a picture of the white marble gravestones beside the white church, crowding up to peer out at live passers-by. He told me if he could only get it just right he'd be painting man's fear of death, and the loneliness of it, and the longing of the dead for the living. Many of these stones had open mouths on them. Cut in the marble were words for them to be saying. "As I am now, so you shall be . . . " "Memento Mori" and "Oh, Relentless Death." Yet even this work was no more than sketchings and experiments in different shades in white. The real thing he was going to do "sometime." Not now. Nothing was now. Everything was "sometime."

He was listless even with the people we got to know about the Catamount. He'd start out being sociable and then just give up, and sit there, dumb as a mouse in a cheese. I don't remember he even tried to tell but one story, and that he weakened on and never did get to the end. It was when there were a number of the local gentlemen and a party of four or five travelers off the stage and we were all sitting out a cozy evening by the big fire. The fall winds were blowing about by now and tankards of hot flip were more in demand than mugs of cold cider.

Talk was of the cold and the winter coming on and those men were boasting that wherever they were from was the coldest spot in Vermont. One man told how where he came from it was so cold one winter the conversation froze up — and what it sounded like, come spring, and everything said all winter thawing out suddenly. Naturally Jude, being from Hampton, Connecticut (a pleasant, warmish spot as New

England goes), hadn't much to say until he bethought him of his travels.

He said some years back he had been far up into New Hampshire, almost to Canada. Real rough, stony, backwoods sort of place. Biggest hills, or mountains, you ever did see. And up there the winters lay six months of every year.

That trip had not profited him any. There wasn't a person up there with a spare cent for a plug of tobacco, much less the necessarily considerable sum for a likeness. They were real poor and worked hard during their brief summer to set by food and fodder for themselves and their beasts to take them through the next winter — let alone providing for the hired man. So it had become a custom thereabout, when harvest was done with and everyone had ate a good Thanksgiving dinner, to freeze up the hired man until next spring in time for ploughing. Such gentlemen as were farmers present would recognize the fact hired men eat plenty.

"Fact," said one man who was a prosperous breeder of Morgan horses. "And ever since I was a shaver, I've heard tell how, further north from wherever you are at the moment, they freeze up the hired man. You seen it with your own eyes?"

"No, mister," said Jude. "No I haven't. Don't travel wintertimes personally, and if I did I'd sure keep out of northern New Hampshire. But I've talked to plenty who have seen it done. Common knowledge up around there. There's an art to it. They have to wait for a dry day and cold — a fifteen-below day. For the freezing process must be quick. And by the same method they freeze up not only mince pies and such, like us, but a powerful stock of provender. Well, the right day comes and they ladle out the liquor to the hired man like it was well water, so by sundown (and the house timbers cracking with the cold) he passes out cold, for they have been removing from him all his outer garments and gone as far with his inner as decency permits. They lay him outside the door. For that first night somebody stays by him, being fearful of wolves and other varmints. Morning comes and he is stiff like an icicle, and just about as brittle. It takes mighty thoughtful handling not to break pieces off him when he is in that state.

"They lift him carefully and lay him in the shed along with the rest of the cordwood — although some folks prefer to stand him up against the wall, and if he froze up with his lower jaw hanging, it makes a nice hook to hang a lantern on. And some put him in a pine box, lined with hemlock, and bury him in a drift — danger of that method is they might forget him.

"Sometimes it happens up there, just as I guess around here (I know it does to home), the young lady of the family falls in love with the hired man. Name of Sprigg — Susanna Sprigg, I believe. She understood the custom but, seeing it applied to the gentleman of her choice, she found she didn't care for it and she couldn't figure out how she could ever get through that long, black, cold winter without him. She pondered and pondered and waited for a day when all the folks were abroad. She was determined to thaw him out. There isn't any way to do it, gentlemen, but wait for spring and let nature take its course. Sudden thawing produces shock and shock results in death. She figured it that if only she could hang him up in the chimney it would be no more shocking to his system than the coming of spring. Miss Sprigg was a real powerful girl with plenty of heft to her. Fact is, he weren't so much more than a runt. And so, taking the most elegant care not to drop him nor bust him up in any way (I've told you how brittle are these living corpses), she inched him into the house, got him way up the chimney, hanging on the ham hooks. Pa and Ma came home, likewise younger brothers and older sisters. She didn't tell a soul what she had done. She sat waiting to see what would happen."

There was a pause — so long I began to feel a touch nervous.

"Yeh?" said the horse breeder. "And then what?"

I'm recording this story partly because this is the only time when I was present that he started one and couldn't finish it. And it is an indication that something had gone real wrong with him. He'd got that fellow hanging on the ham hooks and his girl awaiting for him down below and it looked like he'd have to think fast or leave them there like that forever. This failure of his was part and parcel of the same thing as his not being able to get any painting done — just then.

"I guess," says he, dipping his face in and out of his flip tankard, making an effort to think out what next, "you've all heard this old chestnut before. I can read it on your faces and I apologize for carrying the tale thus far, and thank you for your courtesy in not shutting me up. But I won't trespass further on your good nature."

I was on to him all right. And he'd got them sitting on their seat-edges, bug-eyed as a parcel of children. But he wouldn't go on. Couldn't. He was stuck.

Then it was like Heaven opening up and he saw his escape, for Mrs. Bigger and her oldest daughter were standing modest at the door, waiting, I guess, for a pause in the conversation to come in and say supper's ready.

And Jude was blessing himself and, in a whisper to the gentlemen, admitting he hadn't guessed ladies to be present and of course they would understand (they knowing the story so well) why he could not finish it.

So Mrs. Bigger came in and told us supper was on the table, never understanding, I suppose, the look of gratitude in Jude's eyes.

• • • • • • • • • • • • •

Forty-three

• • • • • • • • • • • • •

OF COURSE Phineas Sharp and his loose talk had caused Jude embarrassments. People around Bennington naturally didn't feel favorable toward Mr. Sharp.

Then he came strolling back into town, with his pack on his back and his sidewise glancings. He came humming, for I heard him. Jude and I were in that graveyard. We peered out at him, just like those stones themselves. Jude didn't hallo at him, so I guess he may have felt some resentment. Letting him pass so close to us, not knowing we were looking at him, was, I guess, a betrayal of friendship.

By nature, as well as by trade, Mr. Sharp was a sleeper in barns and ditches, and it cost him little or naught. In spite of the happy-go-lucky, money-come, money-go angle to his hat, smiles and stride, he did like to save his pennies. But having heard Jude was put up at the best tavern in town (which was part of Jude's selling habits), Sharp was willing to pay the price for a night at the Catamount, merely for the pleasure of his society.

When Jude and I got back there we found Mr. Bigger had refused to accommodate him, on the grounds of rascality. And if there weren't poor little Mr. Sharp sitting disconsolate on the grass of the narrow common before that house! There was no professional reason why just before us two he should appear happy and carefree just then, and he didn't.

Of course Jude told him Mr. Bigger had got things wrong. In fact, Jude had liked being confused with Ruby Lambkin. He had *loved* it — never realized his own potentialities before. As for that trip from Norwich to Windsor — that had been the proudest day of his life. Especially those girls at White River. This talk cheered Mr. Sharp up considerably.

"I've been setting here in the cold," says he, "this hour-long, waiting and hoping to hear you say some such thing. If I have done you the harm landlord says I have, I want to apologize. But if I haven't, I'd rather not."

"Don't."

"Now I must be going on."

Jude offered him one third the bed with him and me, and likewise a new tune out of Mr. Bigger. Mr. Sharp shook his head; feelings had been hurt.

"Where you heading for now?" Jude asked him, "and at this time of day?"

"I'm heading for Troy town or Albany. Leastwise the Hudson River and a boat to take me to New York. From there I'll take a boat south, for I like to go south wintertimes — like those there birds." He pointed at a great convocation of grackles noisy in the trees above us. "I don't hole up for winter like you, and woodchucks, rattlesnakes and such," and he prodded a sharp elbow in Jude's ribs to indicate he'd made a joke.

Then he talked of the South, and Negroes singing in the fields and quarters, and gentry singing in great white houses, and mockingbirds singing in chinaberry trees. The Southland people, he said, wanted different songs to sing than people up north, and he had to carry a different line of goods to please them. The gentry (and their slaves could no more afford to buy from him than the mockingbirds) were fond of young people dying for love. You could even have rose bushes growing from their graves and entwining — old things like that nobody would listen to in Yankee land. Yankees like best to hear of clever folk who got things done. Well, like Ruby Lambkin. But being clever wasn't a genteel quality. Nor getting things done either. Ruby wouldn't go over good in the South.

Jude interrupted him, that being the only way to get a word in edgewise. "Hear more of him? Any news since perhaps he was around Turners Falls and perhaps killed those flatboat men?"

"He may of been, and may not of been the fellow who tried to break a bank in Greenfield, Mass. Nobody got him and he got nothing either. Nobody even got a good look at him."

"Why they thinking it was he?"

"This would-be bank robber was disturbed on the point of gettin' in a window. Nighttime. Somebody shot at him. President of the bank, I guess. He jumped down and beat it. Shot back. So people think the robber being armed and so vicious, it can't be anyone else."

"You think people have changed? Now they want him vicious and armed?"

"Oh, those are just Massachusetts people — always did think they were a thought too law-abiding and serious-minded for their own good. No Ruby Lambkin could of sprung up among them — a Lamb the Murderer could of."

"Guess he did murder Burnap all right, and I certainly know how he felt. As for the flatboat men — they did save his life, people say."

"He thought they had the money."

"You think he killed them for it?"

Mr. Sharp considered a long time. "No, I don't. But Reuben Lamb might of — I'm no authority on Reuben Lamb."

"I can't see much future for him hereabouts. Why don't he go west, or Canada, or south if he has any sense. Think he has any?"

"Well, no. Not what you'd call real good horse sense. For Ruby Lambkin always did as pleased him. No sensible man does that."

Mr. Sharp was referring to Ruby Lambkin always in the past tense — like he was dead. After all, Mr. Sharp had had quite a hand in the making of him. I guess he could decide when he was done for. According to him he died when Burnap died. They two together on the stone floor of Brattleboro jail.

He was on his feet now, adjusting his straps on his shoulders. He wasn't pretending anything, not even to being fresh as a daisy when he was dog-tired.

The sun was going down and the color coming up. All to the west it was crimson and gold and clouds floating through, like great gray fishes with gilt edges to their stomachs.

It was whist and still in town and lights going on in the Catamount behind us. We could hear people laughing from inside. Sharp turned his head, a little longing-like. Jude again offered him a piece of our bed, although we had done that for him at Grafton to our sorrow — he had kept us awake all night with his wiggling and talk.

"You ever plan to retire, Mr. Sharp, off the road?" Jude asked.

"No," says he, "I took to the road early and I'll die upon it late." We were walking along with him toward the western road for York state. "Not as my father died," he added ruefully. "He died in a workhouse. Was a shoemaker. Shoemakers have always been singing men. So was he." We were walking slowly and he was silent for a long time — for him. He said, for no particular reason, and at last perfectly honest, "I'm sixty-four."

Nobody could of guessed it, although you always knew he wasn't near so young as he looked. "What's more, when I die there will be no more like me coming on."

To cheer him up Jude said he guessed there never had been or ever would be anyone like him.

"No," says Sharp. "My trade's done. Pianofortes and music stores. Sheet music. Music books. I'm the tail-end of the last. People, learned people, have told me there have always been singing men upon the road since the beginning of time. But I know they will not last on into time to come. If I had a son, or a grandson rather, I'd never learn him my trade."

We had come to the edge of the high ridge on which Bennington sits. Below us was the great valley into York State. The road he would follow on dipping and appearing and disappearing across it.

"Ballad singers and broadside men are done for," he said. "If I had a lad to plan for I'd set him to work early in one of these here factories before he ever got the smell of freedom in his nostrils — soon as he was housebroke. That's the future." We weren't contradicting him.

"I hope," says Sharp, real melancholy, "whoever finds my body will bury it beside the road. No pauper's grave for me — in behind the workhouse cow shed, like my pa. Tewksbury, Mass., by the way. I've come to a good many conclusions, first and last, me alone a good deal and with time for thinking."

"What, for instance?"

"What we long for is more important than what we have. Like the ass in the fable (you remember?) with the bundle of hay hung before him. That's what keeps us going too. Illusions keep us going — even though they aren't, and never were, no more than dried grass and pretty parching if you get them. But you never do."

He was kicking at a stone with one of his restless feet. "This here free life on the road — perhaps that was my illusion. Too late to go back, try again and find out. But I feel called upon to give you advice, Jude — and you a young fellow just starting out, and me real aging and looking for a grave to rest in — I'd say this. 'Get off the road. You got a nice house and a nice family. Stay put.' "

He had called Jude "Jude" for the first time — not Mr. Rebough, as previously. It was his way of admitting there was some thirty-odd years in the difference in their ages. Jude rose to it and as they shook hands for parting he called him "Phineas," but it sounded awkward, and you knew he wouldn't when they met again. If ever.

We stood watching him dipping off that high ridge, disappearing on that road and reappearing. It was getting dusky-dark, but we could still see him hitting it up fast now, and going good. You never could believe how old he was, but now you knew, saying how young he seemed didn't change the fact any — for all his youthfulness was just one more of those illusions of his.

Jude and I didn't say so, but we felt guilty-like watching him. There had been those times when we had been real irked with him, and he did talk too much but, by and large, he was a wonderful man.

Naturally I never saw Mr. Sharp again. He was certainly right — he was the last of his trade I ever met. But one thing he, nor me, nor Jude ever guessed was this: Jude was just about the tail-end of his trade too. Not the last of people like H. H. Hooper, who called themselves artists and had studios. But he was among the last of the traveling limners, for already (unbeknownst to any of us) that Frenchman, name of Daguerre, had done his work. Before you could guess it the itinerant limner was clean off the road and the daguerreotypist and the tintype men were on it. They were taking better likenesses and for less money than even Jude. So Jude Rebough's trade, as well as Phineas Sharp's, was already dying off, and soon to be dead as the dodo.

. . . .

Forty-four

. . . .

W̲ᴇ ᴛᴏᴏᴋ ɴᴏ ᴍᴏɴᴇʏ ɪɴ at Bennington and we paid out plenty. Jude wasn't up to scratch. He hadn't unpacked and offered for sale any of those faceless portraits he had prepared, although I think he could of found buyers in plenty. I'd urge him, but he'd say things like this: "Eddy, do you remember what Henery Hooper said about them? Cart before the horse, and all that? I wish I could always begin face first, like I did for Evelina — that was nice." He weren't satisfied with the portraits he had been doing, and almost like he knew (as he certainly didn't) about those chemical and mechanical processes that had already been completed way off in France. Perhaps he was at one of those pauses that sometimes comes to a man when he is trying to free himself from the past (and that would include Emma), and not yet ready to step ahead into the future. Then, not being able to go either forward or back, comes that sickening, unrooted pause.

Although listless, apathetic, and not even able to finish off that story he started on, he was also restless. Suddenly he wanted to get up and out of here. He knew just where — North Adams, Massachusetts, some miles south of here. The day he made this decision, and told Mr. Bigger we'd be paying up and be leaving next morning, he was already sneezing, shivering and saying his throat hurt him.

He looked too sick to travel, even when we were sitting in the chaise before the Catamount, and Mr. and Mrs. Bigger were urging him to wait on until after that cold was under control. There had been a lot of those real heavy colds around these parts this fall. Lots of them went into the lungs — like Jude's and Ruby's did.

So we were heading south, and soon were crossing the state line into Massachusetts. Although we had been going south, more or less, ever since we left Norwich, Vermont, this was the time I really felt we were heading home. That road goes up and down, but because they run a three-times-a-week stage on it, it was good. And it weren't a cold day, but Jude was shivering and there was no wrapping him up to warm him. Next moment he was sweaty-hot. First and last time I ever saw him with bright red cheeks. They became him marvelously, but made him seem a changeling to me. And he was chatty as a monkey — or Mr. Sharp.

He talked to a considerable extent about Emma, and not lovingly and not respectfully. Perhaps more frankly than a man of his delicacy would of in his completely right mind to a boy of fourteen. For I had had a birthday. Birthdays were a thing we paid no heed to, in those days. He had considerable to say of Ruby Lambkin, laughing about him mostly, and not referring to him as "Lamb the Murderer" or, worse yet, "Lamb the Ghoul" as people were these days. He felt he *had* to meet him. Once again he was insisting he *had* to ask him if he too had trouble shaving the cleft in his chin. He wondered if Ruby felt the same way about him. He had always had a feeling Ruby knew just where he was and what doing. Did I see those there bushes shaking? Weren't there a man behind it? What did I think? Suppose it were Ruby? Had we time to turn about and whip up Goldie? Or had we better continue on our course and act nonchalant? Then I'd begin to shiver and sweat too. We'd be seeing before us a

bridge of sorts. What if Ruby were hidden under it? What
if he popped up out of it at us? Then Jude would give what
I can only describe as a hollow laugh. "Yep," he'd say, "that
old Lambkin he knows where we are. Lonely road passing
from Bennington to Williamstown. And Eddy, I'm believing
he knows where we keep our cash — hid up in that secret
hole I fixed at the base of the whip-stock. Maybe he sold his
soul to the Devil for such knowledge, but *he* knows. Drat
him for a bad egg."

He got me so furred up my hands were trembling on the
reins, for why couldn't Lamb (being a murderer) kill us both
off, right here — go off with Goldie, tell folk he was that
poor honest limner who had been so confused with Lambkin,
keep on driving to beyond where any word of him had pene-
trated? I weren't so scared to die — what scared me was the
ghosts Jude and I would make. Two more of those curst
murdered travelers on the roads of New England, stopping
passers-by, pointing to our slashed throats, trying to lead
people (and they wouldn't follow) to our secret graves.

I tried to get him to stop at Williamstown. It was so
pleasant, something like Hanover and, seemingly, the college
there was inhabited by the same young gentlemen as inhabited Dartmouth. No. He insisted on North Adams.

We were in the chasm the Hoosic River makes, and the
forest stupendous about us, and wild as in Indian days. The
ledges were dripping green with moss and the maidenhair
trembled to the roaring of the water. And then if there
weren't a clearing and, of a sudden, a factory and girls looking
out, their hands all the time busy with their work. And there
were boardinghouses built for them, and they had tried to
make it a touch homey, like girls do. I mean they had grown
bean vines up about the doorways, and there was girls' wash
out on the lines. By that wash you could figure what good
wages they got — some of those drawers had lace on them. Of

course it was the water power that had brought the girls here.

We came into North Adams but at first we couldn't get up Main Street, nor to the hotel. Whole place jammed with horses — forty or fifty of them, Morgans mostly, and beauties. Two men had been sent out by a Boston stage company to go through country parts and buy for them. Summertime they had been going from farm to farm in New Hampshire and Vermont buying and buying, but now they had got their herd so big they could scarce manage them, even with country boys hired in extra to help. The boys had their dogs, of course. You can't drive horses like cattle, so they were cutting loose and scampering seems like all over North Adams. Boys yelling and dogs barking and women trying to keep them out of the flower beds and flapping aprons at them horses; manes and tails flying, flying hoofs and heaving flanks, whinnying and snorting. They, with the mountains about them and the trees coloring up, and that narrow little white town — it was, all in all, one of the prettiest sights I ever did see.

Now here is a strange fact. Later I was to see the great herds of truly wild horses on our western plains. A herd consisting of hundreds upon hundreds of them. But in those great open spaces they never seemed half so wild as these hand-fetched-up Morgans just gone temporarily wild, and running crazy through a New England town. Even Jude stopped his talking, to watch I suppose, for it was half an hour we sat there in the chaise, waiting for the men and boys to get the horses penned up. But the fact was, he had fallen asleep.

I got up to the hotel stoop. It had a big one running the whole length of its front, roofed over in what was then a new style, and later would be called a piazza. All the stable boys and such were out helping with the deluge of horses. I hitched Goldie and started in to inquire into accommodations. Nailed beside the front door was this sign:

Hawkers, peddlers and mountebanks
Methodist Ministers, not accommodated
Others please wipe their feet and
COME IN

I didn't know what to do. It worried me to think of taking him further, but I didn't know how seriously this sign should be taken. Maybe a joke. Wasn't sure whether or not an itinerant limner was exactly a peddler or not. Mitty thought so.

So I went to the clerk at the desk and I said I had a sick gentleman with me, and required accommodations of the very best. Because I was so set on it that we wouldn't be refused, because he was a peddler of sorts, I said that of course Mr. Rebough of Hampton, Connecticut, was in a position to pay for all the comfort a place like this had to offer. It was pretty elegant here but I looked about it like it wasn't in the least what a gentleman of his magnificence was used to.

"Sick gentleman, eh?" said the clerk, jumping like a trout to a fly. In those days, and maybe now, it was a common thing for the well-to-do to come, along the fall of the year, to the Berkshires to take the air as at other times they went to spas to take the water. There was plenty of money in it for the hotel and tavern keepers. So the clerk himself was running out to assist, seeing all the boys were off after horses, and called Dr. Raymond out of the barroom. I heard the clerk whisper to him, "Very rich — ought to be something for both of us in this . . . . " Well, they got him in. Jude was breathing hard and dopy and the doctor, to make conversation, I suppose, and to sound important, was talking about a consumption. All Jude ever had was a hard cold. The chambermaid was running for hot-water jugs and the landlord's pretty wife sort of supervising and warming blankets and fetching him milk and brandy — everything Dr. Raymond suggested. Jude liked the fuss. They certainly made him comfortable.

Dr. Raymond, by the way, was no country man. He had come out three years back, with an elderly lady also in search of health, from Boston — a lady so wealthy she could afford to take with her her personal physician. She had either died or been cured but he had seen the possibilities of the place and stayed on. For invalids and semi-invalids did come, and most of them were real well-to-do. Yet the two local doctors didn't suit them. Dr. Cott was a sight better at handling, say, a lime burner who had fallen into his kiln or a woodsman who had hit himself with his axe, than this fancier trade which he tended to laugh at. And old Dr. Roper was a terrible dirty man and usually drunk but the best-liked man in North Adams. There was a place all right for Dr. Raymond living here at the hotel. I never could quite figure him. He was no quack. He was very learned, yet he did have certain quackish ways to him. He had a pointed black beard and rather Italianate ways. He had two pastimes. He collected and pressed flowers, like Jude, and he sketched and water-colored, somewhat also like Jude. So when he found these were the pastimes of his patient (I dursen't let on Jude painted for dollars and cents) it made a pleasing bond.

Long before then, of course, I had told Jude what I had done to him, being fearful of that sign and he so wobbly I dursen't be real honest.

"Well," he says, "I'm not good for anything else but a gentleman of leisure. Forget it, Eddy. You done well by me. How you say I made all this money?"

"Inherited," says I, "and investing in ships at sea and so on. They've been quizzing me."

"Well, I don't look like I had inherited *much*. Just a little, maybe shrewd investor. That might be me. But anyhow, it's rather restful to feel so rich — for once." He wasn't mad with me at all.

First supper he ate downstairs the landlord himself waited on him. We didn't go to the barroom first. Jude ordered wine to go with our victuals, and the landlord was afraid it wasn't up to his standards, and so on.

Being sick has a refining effect upon the appearance of most of us. Jude started out spare and contemplative-looking, and after five days in bed he came out looking almost too genteel to feed himself. And he spoke languidly (that's how he still felt), and neater and nicer than I thought he knew how to. There always was something of the actor to him.

We sat out on that long stoop considerable. He with a plaid shawl over his knees, and about his shoulders a beaver cape Dr. Raymond lent him. I bet he got it from that first wealthy woman patient of his. It was a woman's cape. He coughed a lot. Seems as if every respectable man and woman in the place were stopping to enquire as to his health and telling him how the air of the Barrier would cure him of whatever ailed him. Nobody seemed to know what he was supposed to recover from, nor he himself. I know now it was the dumps. No medical word for it.

We drove out, he and me. All around and about us was the beauty of the fall — burning like fire upon the mountains, orange and salmon-pink, yellow, crimson, and pale, lost colors you hardly noticed at first, but the longer you looked the more beautiful they became. And the color burned up and up and up. And some days you'd think it was finer in the sunshine, and next know it was never so fine as when seen through mist. Next day rain and shine off and on and the shadow of clouds crossing the great valleys and the sun suddenly sending down a finger to point at one special spot. That was finest of all.

Fall, standing there on the New England hills like an army with banners fighting a sort of rear-guard action so summer can slip off south, like Sharp, and the birds, and the flowers, to warm long days. Yet fall has always been defeated. Winter comes seeping and creeping in — not fighting quite fair. Yet every year fall stands up to fight him and goes down at

last to the cold gray and the burned-out ash colors, he lying
dead, as it were, on our fields and forests and our roadsides
and our farmlands. He don't go south ever. Not New England fall.

Sometimes we'd tie Goldie and walk — halfway up Gray-
lock one day, pausing to talk to the charcoal burners or the
lime burners, and the toothpick-legged silly sheep following
us, because they thought we were carrying salt to them. The
sheep baa-ed at us, and the red squirrel and the blue jay made
our music. Cider presses too. The vicinity about was famed
for its apple brandy.

The mountains and the color and the cold rolled about us.
The maples were losing their fire and the oaks had begun.
It was rough, burly weather for the most part. We ate and
slept good.

Naturally, the businessmen of North Adams had thought
that as Mr. Rebough had done to date well in his investments
they might tap him for some more. I heard a lot of that talk,
sitting on the stoop. This place was in a predicament. Their
natural resources and their water power were terrific, but
they had no navigable river. No cheap way to get their
produce out. Trapped like that. For instance, most of their
marble was burned for lime. Marble was too bulky for horses.
And their great forests were burned for charcoal. And of
course they had to make their cider into brandy. Cloth wasn't
too bulky for them to be able to make a profit, even if it had
to go out on horses. The town was divided. Half of them
believed a canal through Hoosac Mountain was the answer.
They had had an engineer in and he said Mount Hoosac
could be tunneled. This would be the greatest engineering
feat ever attempted in the world. Half were betting their
bottom dollars on a railroad. I'd never even seen one in those
days. I didn't quite believe in them. Canals I'd seen, so
naturally I thought the canal men made sense. But the rail-

road men were right, for canals and rivermen (and the songs
they sang) and the great strong horses on the towpath — all
that were just as much on the point of departure as ballad
singers and itinerant limners.

We'd been there for over two weeks. They had made me
up a bed in a corner of his big room. When I woke he was
already up and almost dressed, and he had already rung and
the chambermaid had brought him up hot water. He was
standing at the mirror by his washstand shaving, silhouetted
against the light. There was not much of it as yet. Before he
spoke to me I could feel a stillness from him. He didn't say
anything, as he often did when shaving, about wondering if
Ruby had trouble with the cleft in his chin too. He was
wrapped up in himself. "Eddy," he said, "I feel like painting
today." He sighed and added, "Yep," and went on shaving
and thinking. Then he said, "After breakfast I'm going to
fetch in the canvas I was working on way back last spring."

"Emma," says I.

"You might call it that. Or, on the other hand, you
mightn't. I don't know, nor care either, but . . ."

I feel I should tell more of how it was he painted her face
in at the last. But it was as if all this dawdling, his inability
to work or finish a story, that bad cold even, the long walks
and the heavy sleeping, the fact that we were terribly cut off
from everybody else by my inadvertently putting him in a
false light — as if everything, the most unrelated things that
had happened for the last month, had had a purpose to it:
only to fit him for this one task. Part of him, the most important part of him, was lying low all the time — waiting and
waiting, knowing the exact moment had not yet come. And
now that secret part of him nudged him and told him that it
was now or never.

He got to work. Of course he had those pencil sketches of
her in one of his books. I'm not sure he used them much. It
was the memory of her he needed most. Nobody could of

painted like that in cold blood. No. It was like fate on him. The witches made poppets to stick pins in, and he had to paint Emma to rid himself of her — different purpose, but part of the same thing.

We scarce spoke to each other but he looked self-confident, for he knew now he was going to do it, and do it right.

It didn't take him long. Two days — and yet I've seen him slap in a face in two hours, so you might call it long.

He painted her with compassion, and yet still with longing and at least the memory of love, or something worse. Maybe he felt some shame as he painted her, but there was no shame across her lovely face. Whatever she had done she wouldn't have felt any, so she was beguiling and soulless — a pagan goddess. But he had proved no pagan man.

So Emma leaned forward out her window, forever enticing and effortless. She leaned from out that house, always, I know, in Jude's mind an evil house — with the bad old man whooping it up for someone to roll him out so he might shoot songbirds, and the wounded catbird buzzing all afternoon long, and Silas Poke in the kitchen up to what no one but the Devil ever knew, and the smugglers and rivermen on the Connecticut behind the house. Even Ruby Lambkin cast his bright shadow across it.

I've said Emma's skin had freckles, so he got a golden glow to her. Her great gray eyes stared straight out at you — mermaid eyes he said they were. And that is as good a word for them as any.

Either because of or in spite of the witch's brew that picture had come out of, and it had magic to it, when done he knew it was good. So did I.

"Hip-hop couldn't of done you," he said to it. "I could. So I did do you. And you are done with. All through with you — Mrs. Emma. What's more, you never were anything but a poor, unthinking creature."

This picture he signed — only one that summer he did

sign, except Evelina — I had noticed he had signed that.

Although it was obvious to me he cared naught for anyone's opinion except his own in regards to this particular portrait, he decided to have a punch party here in his great chamber, somewhat in honor of this fine thing, somewhat in recognition of the many courtesies the gentry of the place had extended to him (and the opportunity to invest in their schemes). I knew we would be leaving now, and soon.

When eighteen or twenty of them, ladies and gentlemen both, had arrived and everyone had had a glass of wine punch and a sweet biscuit, Jude pulled the shawl back from off the picture on its easel.

"You understand, ladies and gentlemen," said he, "this isn't exactly a portrait of a real person. Something I have had in my head to do for some years."

It glowed there, in russets and yellows, and copper and bronze, and green enough; blue too. I doubt if one person in the room there had ever seen a picture so light and bright. He didn't paint shadows ever (like Hip-hop). His things never were muddy-looking. As I said earlier, it was a little like drawing in paint. Maybe he shouldn't have. I've been told nobody ought. But why oughtn't they? Far as I'm concerned the answer was right there.

Those people looked and looked, like they couldn't believe their eyes. If they had been real knowing about painting they might of laughed. These country people weren't so wise — or a lot wiser.

Then, first thing, Dr. Raymond (after all, he was a Boston man of considerable learning and clever enough with his brushes himself) was clearing his throat and saying he didn't wish to insult Mr. Rebough — he knew painting was just a pastime of his and of course he never sold his work for cash, but . . . There was a look in his eye — a covetous look. He had to have it. Jude looked just the right amount surprised to think of taking spot cash for it. It ended up this way: three

men there — Dr. Raymond, our landlord, and one of those
railroad "cranks" as we thought him then, but well-to-do in the
lime business, all set their hearts on her. And when I say set
their hearts, that's just what I mean. Except for Dr. Raymond
they were real ignorant of the art that went into it. It was the
gorgeousness of the color and perhaps, more than anything,
the easy triumphant beauty of the woman. I guess they had
looked long enough at the sort of buttoned-up beauty of your
average Yankee woman. So often they are pretty as wild
flowers in their youth, but scrawny and bilious-looking at
middle age. Yankee women don't often mellow into beauty,
for that mellowing process takes more time and sitting than
they want to give.

It ended this way: they daren't offer a wealthy gentleman
chicken feed. It was me they approached — would my uncle
be persuaded to part with it and so on, and for how much,
and all that. Guess Jude had had a bad effect on me, for I
was picking up some of that play-acting came so natural to
him, and, incidentally, I was fearfully ashamed that I had
run up such bills on him. It ended this way: the landlord
bought it for one hundred dollars to hang in the barroom,
where the other two could sit and look at it all they wanted.
As you know, this was twenty times as much as he was used to
getting. Our stay at North Adams paid off good. And here's
a sad thing — if he had been needful of the money he'd of
got five dollars, as usual. For to him that hath shall be given,
and so on. I've seen that happen over and over.

Now, looking back at the situation over many years, I can
see how it was Jude had to paint Emma to get rid of her.
And having done so, he had also to be rid even of his painted
image of her. She was hung there over the bar before we left.
She did look good there, with the pewter tankards hanging
about her and the fragrance of rum toddy rising up about her
— for she herself had been a tavernkeeper. Seemed right she
should be right there, looking just like that, enticing cus-

tomers for one more drink. Although, fact is, she was in life a touch too lazy to be bothered — and her guests took as pleased them and wrote it on that slate, or were waited upon by Mr. Poke. She was too easygoing.

I'd like to think of her there like that forever. But the landlady (Jude and I both heard her) did say to her husband, and exactly in Mitty's tone of voice, "A mite fleshy — isn't she?" So I don't know. I wish I knew.

If ever there was an example of Phineas Sharp's philosophy — that is, that the dream of a thing is more important than the substance of it, it was right there in that picture. Now it never mattered that Emma was going to go right on aging (and she was old enough to start with), and it didn't matter if she was to have undying fame as "Lena Linkmouse" — a real part of her Jude had got down in paint. As long as that picture lasts, she lasts, if you see what I mean.

• • • • • • • • • • • • • •

Forty-five

• • • • • • • • • • • • • •

It was the last of October. Fall had burned down to ash and embers. Now the trunks of the birches stood out like long white stitches against a somber tapestry. And now it was more than a white wisp of mist old Greylock wore on his forehead. It was snow up there. On Hoosac and on Mount Williams was snow too. So fall, like I tried to say earlier, had fought his rearguard action and, as always, been defeated and he lay dead where he had fought.

Other signs winter was seeping in on us. One day late we were walking up Main Street and it was twilight. The new moon was tossed up against the pale apple-green sky like a fingernail paring. There was no breath of a breeze to blow the cold out the valley. Not a vapor of mist offen the river to blanket the last of the flowers from the hard settling-in of the cold.

It would be "black frost tonight." You felt it like a whisper through the valley, as if the words were in so many people's minds it could carry from one to next without speech. "Black frost tonight."

Then we saw what Jude was telling me was the Festival of the Little Old Ladies of New England. I don't mean that no young person or posy-minded man might not go out to cut what flowers he might before the frost killed all. But this I remember: what we saw behind white picket fences and stone walls and out in front gardens and in back gardens were little old women, huddled up in red shawls, or with crocheted fascinators about their bent little old backs. Each one alone. They moved silent through their gardens with the scissors of Atrope in their gnarled old hands. Clip, clip, clip. Rank marigolds and cat-faced pansies, sweet clove pinks (clip, clip, clip). Mignonette and fragrant stock, verbena, velvet dahlias and five o'clocks, so the last flowers lay in the old women's baskets, or perhaps in a hiked-up apron. For it would be "black frost tonight."

The sun down and they back in their houses again. How cold it was! And so still and clear. And with the coming of the cold, Orion came closer. He bestrode the frosty sky. The stars in his belt glittered. All the stars in the Heaven trembled with the cold.

We were leaving now. Early next morning, but no need to call us. It would be a Tuesday morning we'd be going, and on that day the mail coach from Greenfield would come in at dawn. First was the bugle sounding from the top of Hoosac Mountain. It was there the heavy horses, rented out in Florida to help lug the coach up the east face of the mountain, would be put off. The horn sounded again. The hotel was all confusion and bustle. Next was the clatter of hooves and the rattle of wheels right up the main street of the town. Before the coach swayed to a stop, the mail was going off and the mail was going on. And the four tired horses, wrapped in the mist of their own breath and sweat, were being taken out and the four fresh ones were being backed in and tackled, and they were raring and fighting the hostlers to be off.

I've ridden in many a steam car since, and they go mighty fast, but nothing ever seemed to go so fast as a first-class mail coach. Of certain coaching lines in New England at the same period the less said the better.

The shivery-cold passengers, and blue-nosed at that, were huddling for the dining room. As usual, one lady was so jounced up it was more a question of keeping down what she had taken in night before, at Athol, than taking any more aboard.

We were dressed and ready to go, except for breakfast which we knew we wouldn't get until the mail coach was off again. We stood in the dark dawn watching the driver gulping hot toddy and eating about a dozen doughnuts, but not getting off his box. He had on a caped greatcoat and a red muffler. His name was Will Fellowes and he was a well-known character in those parts. He was so important up there, on his throne so to speak, most people hardly dared more than stand and admire him — as speechless as Jude and me. The head stableman was well enough acquainted to durst say, "Will, what's your news — if any?"

Will Fellowes blew his nose in the old-fashioned airy manner without benefit of any handkerchief. He reached in one pocket to his greatcoat and pulled out a pistol. He reached in other pocket and pulled out its mate. "Well, they warned me. And you see that fellow there?" He pointed to a young man that didn't look like much. "He's given me for a guard. He's armed too. I sit front and he sits in back and he's guaranteed to be able to hit a barn door at fifteen paces. Ain't you, Pardee?"

Pardee smiled limply and said, yes, he wasn't sure but he could.

"What you fooling around with weapons for, Will?"

"Oh . . . Company just thought I hadn't enough to do. It's that murdering monster, that Lamb who cuts people up. Well, he tried a break — to break a bank night before last in Springfield. Five or six saw him and shot at him, but they couldn't fetch him down. It was him all right. And the company got the idea he may try for a mail coach, and . . ." His voice rose to a roar, "Boy! Boy! Take up the slack on that nigh leader's tug chain. Damn fool," he muttered, "damn fool . . ."

The horses were frantic to be off, rearing against the hostlers that held them. Will Fellowes too thought enough time had been wasted. He let out his voice. "Coach loaded and off — you get a wiggle on in there," and out slunk the passengers, half fed and still shaky with the cold. The driver who carried the United States mail permitted no dawdling from passengers.

I guess we ate up what those passengers had paid for and then never given time to enjoy. We sat to a long table with four or five others. Two had come in from Greenfield. It was agreed that it was shocking if the country was so lawless, mail coaches had to go armed, also that Lamb must be getting low in funds. Seems this was the second time he had tried to pull off a big job and had failed on it. With these Massachusetts men there was no Lambkin fable (as you might call it). Massachusetts has always taken law-abiding pretty serious. They never would of had any use for Ruby Lambkin at his best. Sharp had been right about that.

It is often like that. One section of the country's meat
is the next section's poison. I doubt if Billy the Kid would
of seemed like great shakes to the police force of New York
City where he was born. You remember Phineas Sharp
maintaining that Ruby existed because people longed for
him? And I, having lived through all that Billy the Kid
nonsense, will say the same of him. But these here North
Adams businessmen weren't longing for any Lambkin.
All they longed for was a tunnel through Hoosac Mountain.

We went out of North Adams by the road the coach had
come in on. The eastern slope is a sight steeper than the
western but it was fine wild country. At the foot of Hoosac
was a boy beside the road. He was minding two heavy spare
horses and Goldie nickered at them. They were already
harnessed, waiting to be hitched up to the next vehicle that
would hire them. The coaches always did, and heavy
wagons and well-to-do people wishing to spare their own
horseflesh. I think they were the biggest horses I ever saw,
strawberry roan with white ruffles on their feet, Roman
noses and short backs.

The boy minding them was a Negro boy, and no more
than ten. He was sort of sylvan-looking, if you know what
I mean, with soft, velvet deer-eyes. Seeing we looked
friendly and were ready to visit with him, he was ready
to visit with us.

He had an abandoned charcoal burner's hut where he
kept food for himself and for his horses, and a place to sleep
nights. Seeing we looked chilly, he built up a fire on his
marble hearth, for marble was so common thereabouts it
was used for hearths in huts even. He had fine manners, far
better than your average Yankee boy, and was so at ease
with strangers you could guess he had been well treated.
Jude was so taken with him he gave him all the spare food
we had with us, except the jug of hard cider that he was
too young for.

There weren't many Negroes in New England except in the cities. It seemed strange finding this little fledgling one, that looked like he oughtn't be out of the nest yet, all alone, and yet so unlonely and unscared tucked off like this in the great depths of the forest.

He told us his mother, four years back, had run away from a bad master in one of those wicked slave states. She got to Florida (we were in Florida township, Massachusetts) with her two little boys by the so-called underground. She died there. The two small boys came on the town. It was worked out thisaway: one brother stayed with the minister and did odd jobs and got schooling, while other brother was left out here with the town-owned spare horses. They took turns about. And even here in his hut he had study books with him. These boys had been given the last name of Florida, having none of their own, and being sort of wards of that town. I think our boy was called Paul Florida. I've often wondered what happened to those two boys, and if there is still a Negro family up around there called Florida. I never think of them but I wish them well. If living, they must be real old men by now.

. . . .

Forty-six

. . . .

WE KNEW winter would come early and be full-sized when it came. Wasps and hornets were building their winter nests high up off the ground, so they foretold to us the snows would be deep. And the wasps were sealing in an extra supply of spiders in their mud nests to give themselves a little somewhat to nibble on if the snows lingered long. There were terrific thick husks on the corn. And thicker than average coats on horses and cattle. I swear Goldie's coat was two inches deep. Chipmunks too knew they'd need big, bushy tails to keep their little noses warm this winter. So they grew them.

Muskrats were out along the shallows of the ponds building the biggest, warmest huts they knew how. Woodchucks and raccoons were putting on layers of fat, so as to have enough stored right on their own bones to feed them in their sleeping, all winter long.

The geese flew south ten days ahead of themselves.

All the beasts knew what was coming. We knew enough to look at them and learn.

And if golden rod is especially deep yellow, and the bright berries of the sumac especially red; if beech and oak trees hang on to more leaves than usual, and the cat-tails show inordinate long heads — those things too are a sign of deep snow, heavy cold, early winter and late spring.

The woods looked bare. Corn was shocked and standing on the tawny stubble fields. Orange pumpkins dotted about the shocks. Scarecrows still stood guarding, but now there was nothing for them to guard.

Crows were out gleaning, looking like blown bits of charred paper. And talking all the time — like crows talk.

Far above, the lonely hawk floating. Harvest is over. It is the lonesomest time of the year.

All over New England, man, beast, vegetation, and houses were getting ready to withstand the siege of winter.

The Governor had proclaimed a Thursday late in November was to be our Thanksgiving Day. We would be home by then. After that I was to go to Waltham. It seemed fitting to me that I was to have a chance to bow my head over Mitty's bright red and white checked tablecloth, and the turkey and the cranberry, and the four kinds of pie, and the giblet gravy and hot bread, and give thanks to God for the kindness and loving care I had received from the Pratts and Jude Rebough during eight years of my life. I had never thought of such a thing other Thanksgivings. Now I knew I would. For one thing, I was older now. For another, I was leaving them.

We passed through Turners Falls and Millers Falls, Farley and Erving. Jude was in no lingering mood. He might have found sitters for some of those faceless canvases of his, but he was turning against them. I guess he was about through with that way of painting. So Hip-hop had really gotten under his skin.

We did spend, I think, four days in Orange, which is not much of a place any way you figure it. They had no house of public entertainment open there. Night was coming down. It had drizzled all day and now the drizzle was beginning to freeze to ice upon us.

The blacksmith, at whose warm shop we stopped to inquire, told us that a Mrs. Leander Avery had been licensed by the town to put up travelers. From where we sat in the chaise we could see the house he pointed at. It looked not too bad. But he said he couldn't recommend it.

"Why not," says Jude.

"She's off her rocker."

"How far off?"

"That, mister," says the blacksmith, "depends on your own standards." And he added gallantly that he himself was so far off he considered Mrs. Avery pretty close to normal, at least for human standards — any horse with no more sense than she had, ought to be locked up.

Jude always had a considerable understanding of goofers because, as he said to me, he was a little goofy himself. He never laughed at them like most people, even decent people, did in those benighted days.

"What kind of bats," he asked, "has she in her belfry?"

"Baby bats," says the kind smith, real compassionate.

He told us Mrs. Avery had had, in all, three children. But she had proved unable to keep any of them going long. When the third baby died, about eight years back, they had had to use force — the minister and the undertaker, half the town — to pry it loose from her, and she yelling like a hyena. That was the time her mind really broke, although he had known her in school as Rose Pearley and she hadn't had her head screwed on too tight even then. She had never accepted the fact that those children were dead and buried. For instance, she had never once gone to the grave-yard to look at the three pretty little white marble lambs her husband had set up over those tiny graves. But she was a neat housewife, and a woman of good character. The town fathers had licensed her, hoping to buck her up some. They hadn't bucked her up any.

He told us he must warn us her house gave some travelers the creeps. Travelers had been known to jump up and out of there in the middle of the night and in their nightclothes, jibbering that the place was haunted.

"Little folk haunt it?"

"Yeh, little folk."

Mrs. Avery did look in a maze all right. Like a sleep-walker. She could do well by us without really looking at us, nor saying much, nor seeming to listen to us. You knew right off she was listening to other voices than ours. For in-stance, in the middle of making up our bed she lifted her head to listen. You knew she had heard a baby cry, so of course she had to leave us to tend to it.

She was gray-haired under her neat white house-cap and had a wet, unwholesome looking gray skin, and a sort of loony smile, and her teeth were terrible.

At supper that night we noticed how she ate and ate and ate, not because she wanted to but, like other nursing women, just putting down the victuals from a sense of duty. Her husband, a powerful-looking, real silent man, just came home long enough to eat and be gone. He did tell us that he was going back to his shoe shop, for he and some other men were figuring to go ahead into water-power shoemaking (all except the hand binding and finishing). That man stayed to home no more than he could help. Then she listened and she heard a baby cry, so she excused herself, unbuttoning the front of her dress as she shot out of the kitchen.

That night we heard her going to the room next ours again and again — once singing. It was a lullabye I could remember my own mother singing. I had never thought of it or heard it from that day to this day. It goes: "Hush, hush, the waves are rolling in. White with foam, white with foam. Father toils amid the din, while baby sleeps at home." She hoped next morning we hadn't been awakened everytime she got up to go to the children, but she couldn't keep their cradles in the room with herself and Mr. Avery. They made Mr. Avery nervous. I should think they might have.

Mr. Avery, by the way, stayed to his shoe shop about eighteen hours a day. And I don't blame him.

There was a high-chair in the kitchen, pretty much scuffed up. Jude told Mrs. Avery he was a painter by trade and he'd be pleased to touch it up for her. It was the first thing he had said to her she had really listened to. It was black and gold banded, like so much country pine furniture at that time. He told her she was to pick what color he was to put on next. At first she couldn't seem to make up her mind, although she did seem (for her) real interested. I guess she hadn't made as important a decision for years. Her caring for her house, husband, guests, and phantom babies had all become automatic. She got almost pink in the face over it, but she got it out finally. She'd like the chair white.

We got the scraping done and the first coat on. While waiting for the white lead to dry, Jude began offering to put a few flowers on the back. He drew out little pansies and forget-me-nots and tiny moss roses, as we were sitting at the kitchen table. She was to choose what sort of a nose-gay she wanted.

Then, for no apparent reason, she began telling us all about those children. None of them had lived long enough to know much more than their own mother (so she did know they were dead). She told us of how they had been wrested from her, and they crying and she crying (so I guess she thought they were still alive). And then if she didn't hear one of them, and she was modestly excusing herself and hastening to it.

No reasonable person could of made sense out of her. She was a poor, gentle soul and she touched Jude's heart and, as he said, he was far enough off the common course so he could understand those who (like her) were further yet.

He certainly got her to talking. She forgot the eleven o'clock feeding and I guess the two o'clock. Those little phantoms were getting weaned real fast. He was making her describe to him what they had looked like, for he said if she could, he'd paint their pictures for her, he being in the trade. No mention of money.

Although he usually sold about three pictures of deceased babies to bereaved mothers, this year it happened we hadn't sold a one. I fetched them in and set them up on kitchen chairs.

She knew right away which was which.

"Why . . . That's Rosalie." She got pretty excited. "And this here is Rosamund — that means rose of the world," she added shyly. "And the one with the violets bunched in her hand — that's Rosalind." She went on talking a lot about them, but actually she couldn't describe them, more than they all had curly yellow hair and pink faces.

Jude told me it was the pink faces gave him the idea, for he painted them all alive. He'd slap on the paint and Mrs. Avery'd clap her hands. And he'd laugh and she'd laugh. It was the closest I've ever been to confinement in a crazy house. Those wreaths of wild flowers he had already done were delicate as gossamer and ever so pretty. What he was doing now was terrible. For, to please her, he was getting them too alive for their few months of age. And too grinny. But the more they smiled, the more she smiled back at them.

I don't know whether this fooling of Jude had any lasting effect, but she was talking naturally as anybody. Suddenly she wanted us to walk up to the graveyard with her. She wanted to show us their graves. She never had been there once, but she knew where the family lot was. There were big, bare old maples about it. We had to kneel, us three, and dig in the heaps of still-colored piled leaves to find the gravestones. They were set almost flush to the ground. Three little white marble lambs. Pretty, innocent little things in a row. I noticed the children had died fourteen, twelve and eight years ago. Each was the "beloved daughter of Leander and Rose Avery." There was a little thin sunshine on us, and the dry leaves and the graves. We sat there some time. Jude and Mrs. Avery talked quite a long time about death, and about life too.

Next day we took the Athol road. Jude told me that while I had been to the barn, hitching up, Mr. Avery had come to him and said hard cash was scarce as hen's teeth for him just that moment. He was just about scraping the barrel to put the cash into that new scheme of shoe manufacturing which now, by the way, was incorporated as the Orange Shoe Company. So he gave Jude a handful of stock certificates. Jude didn't care much for just pieces of paper, but he was pleased by this taciturn man's gratitude.

One reason I have told this occurrence is to show how little a man in his line of trade can figure where the money is really coming from. If he kept that stock in that company I'll bet he was paid for three days' work more than the entire rest of a year's work. For it went up and up.

In a way, the same thing was true of that picture he did of Emma. He had no thought of raising money on it. Emma was about the finest piece of painting he ever did that I saw. Those three babies, about the worst. He hadn't done either job for money, yet they certainly paid off.

. . . .

Forty-seven

. . . .

THERE ARE SEVERAL Brookfields lying between where we were (Orange) and where we were heading for (Worcester). It was on to dusky when we came into the biggest of them. Jude was telling me of how here it was, and long time ago, Bathsheba Spooner with the help of a young lover and two hired-in British soldiers dumped her husband in the well. Yet to this day, Phineas Sharp was peddling "Ding-Dong-Dell — Spooner's in the Well," and Professor Paracelsus had a wax-work of the bloody deed. It had been sheer tragic horror back in the old days when done. But now it had been mouthed over by so many and so pulled out of its original shape, people were sort of fond of the horrid deed. He had been here before and actually the first thing a Brookfield man wanted to show you was the well where Mr. Spooner got up-ended. He guessed they were prouder of Mrs. Spooner than of anyone else Brookfield had ever nurtured, and . . .

Then we saw folk running and yelling. The doors to the shed wherein was the town fire pump were swung open, and same time the church-steeple bell began the infernal clinkerty-clong-clong by which the fire society and every other able-bodied man was summoned to help. It was suppertime. Men came a-running, with a piece of pie in one hand and a fire bucket in the other. One had stopped to fill his bucket with nice Baldwin apples. Seemed like everyone was chewing on something, but they got there fast.

We stopped where they were, for some of these men would expect and want a ride to the scene of disaster. Anybody with a horse to hand was supposed to give fire fighters a lift.

It wasn't for no fire. We made out through all the bawling and clinkerty-clonging that three men had cornered "Lamb the Murderer" in "Old Man Turnbull's barn," so these men were tossing aside their leather buckets and yelling for weapons. Some got pitchforks and scythes. Some butchering knives, axes, pistols and fowling pieces too — but most of them were those primitive weapons that may not be so lethal, but seem so much more savage. And to us, innocent by-standers as it were, it wasn't "Lend your rig, mister?" for they clean put us out on the ground and we saw four or five of them jumping aboard and whipping up Goldie, which surprised and terrified her so she was off on a canter. That's more than she would ever have done for Jude or me. So one after another, farm wagons and the doctor's rig, just about anything on wheels and to hand, was "commandeered" and racing for Old Man Turnbull's barn and the capture, or better yet, annihilation of that hated criminal.

We followed after, wishing of course to keep an eye on our

property. The mile of road from the center of town to Turnbull's was all over people, excited and happy mostly, and
determined to help set up a tight ring round the barn, and
to see the fun anyway. Jude and I were dog-trotting it, without too much wind left in us for talking. But Jude said,
"They are just as happy as though they were going to a
hanging."

We did pick up a little of what had been happening. Three
days before, at Leicester, some hunters had come on an
abandoned mill. Noting it had signs of someone camping out
there and thinking it might be Lamb, they approached slyly
and — if there he wasn't! They called on him to surrender.
He left fast, running like a deer, but bouncing and weaving
like a hunted fox so they couldn't get good aim at him. They
shot and shot at him. No use. He may have shot back at
them. They swore he was armed.

Now he had got to Brookfield and tried the same thing —
lying very low, stealing no more than his daily food, but this
time nested in a barn loft with plenty of eggs or milk, shorts
or oats, right to hand for the picking up. I didn't hear how
Turnbull guessed he had this dangerous guest. He guessed
and, sort of sly-like got the constable. So Ruby (as I still
thought of him), seeing Turnbull with a squirrel gun,
constable with a pistol, hired man with a meat axe, all
converging on the barn, thought first to light out — thought
better, and dove back into the barn again; all three saw him
good. That's when word was sent to sound the alarm bells
and get everybody out that could walk that far. That's about
what came. Would you believe it? — some of those women
had babies in their arms, and some had brought their knitting.
There was a real old gentleman got there on two canes — took
him an hour and a half, but he got there.

It is terrible to see some several hundred people out to
corner and kill the one, no matter how evil the one is. The
one against the many always wears a crown of glory, even if it

is made up of Hell-fire and sulphur. I've even felt it (just a touch of it) out west when we've hunted down and treed, say, a marauding, sheep-killing devil of an old catamount. There is the moment always when you feel it. The men, the horses, the dogs and the guns on one side — and the brave old cat fighting it out to the last. Sure, we get his hide — but he's got the glory. Can't see how some men feel so big about it. But of course it has to be done. Like this too. Somebody had got to kill Ruby Lambkin. But Jude and me, he being young by nature and me young in years, weren't wishful to be standing by, like the rest of those gap-mouths, squealing for his blood.

Goldie, being one of the first arrivals, we found hitched up pretty well towards the barnyard. All those wagons and rigs that came late were hitched all wee-waw over the place, no order to it. We could no more have got her out without unhitching and moving about twenty other rigs then you can fetch out a bottom jackstraw. We did preserve, as you might say, a certain separateness and dignity by climbing into the chaise and just setting there. Jude had a big bottle of hard cider under the seat. I think he thought we both needed some stimulant to take us through the nasty scene we were about to witness. Seems incredible, but those fire fighters, in no more than a mile and Goldie running best she knew how and the chaise all the way on one wheel, had found it and emptied that bottle. Jude was so mad he swore. He didn't often.

"There are some things," says Jude, "no man should be asked to see cold-sober. A hanging's one of them."

"You think they'll hang him?"

"No. Those people that say he is armed and will shoot it out — I think they are right. He won't be taken alive. But mark my words. He dies here."

The fact was soon apparent that nobody wanted to go inside that barn and give Ruby the chance to drill him, although it would of been a help because as soon as he fired, the other men would know where he was. I think in the West some man would have done this, for western men take terrible pride in their physical courage, even when it leads to no more than infantile showing off. Yankees aren't like that. Yet I'll say this for Massachusetts men: there has never been a lynching — no, nor serious mob action in the entire history of their old state. So they boast. I'll bet you anywhere else except in New England those hundreds of milling and excited people packed in too tight would of cooked up a real ugly mob spirit. Those Yankees didn't, being of too highly an individualistic temperament.

It looked like stalemate. There was a tight cordon now about that whole barn. A mouse couldn't of gone through it, yet nobody had a mind to go in after him and be a real hero. No sirreee! They'd rather just sit until they had starved him out I guess.

So the sun went down and the moon came up. It was the Hunter's Moon. Even now more and more people were arriving, because the alarm had spread to other Brookfields by now. Then, of a sudden, the whole picture changed. We heard the crackling and roaring first. Next saw the licking of the orange flames. There had been some irresponsible talk of "burning him out." Perhaps now it was dark some imbecile had done so. Perhaps Ruby fired the barn himself, knowing he was trapped and deciding he'd sooner die by fire than noose.

When a barn starts like that it's done for. And as the smoke belched and billowed about us we heard the frightened crying and stamping and pitiful moaning of the beasts.

Here is a funny thing: not a man among them had the courage to go in that barn after Ruby. Heroic action like that wasn't along the line of their trade. But now farm animals were in danger they were all ready to rush in to get them out

— for every man of them was a farmer, and the horse scream-ing in fear of flame and the moaning cow and the frightened sobbing of the sheep awoke them to sheer heroism. For this was their trade.

Many of those men got badly scorched. It looked like the ridgepole would collapse, for the north gable was sagging, get-ting ready to fall. Everyone risked their lives, but every animal was got out — even the horses which, as usual, made a deal of trouble. Even the cats and rats came pouring out with no help from anybody. But Ruby didn't come. He'd of been shot down if he had. Men were waiting for him, guns in hand.

Then the ridgepole broke and the sparks flew up, just as old Job had noted them thousands of years before. Jude softly recited those words. I think it was one of Job's friends said them to him, one Eliphaz, and an extremely observant man, "Yet man is born unto trouble, as the sparks fly upward . . . I would seek unto God, and unto God would I commit my cause." We both doft our hats for that, feeling how no clergyman seemed to be of a mind to say a few words over Ruby's infernal grave. So we said them.

We waited until the heat was beginning to abate from us, for Goldie had been hitched too close to the barnyard for her or our comfort, and the orange light began to die down. Now it seemed for the first time we were seeing the moon again, she so cold and inhuman, with a sort of an expression as though saying men come and go but look at me — I go on forever. For it is good to look at the moon in time of personal sorrow. Makes both you and your pains seem no account.

And Jude and I both felt pain. It seemed a terrible death for a man to die, and right before your face and eyes. But as Jude said, his suffering was over now and if taken alive it would be just beginning. It was better this way, surely.

And so no more of Ruby Lambkin, except the songs and

the tales of him and maybe a handful of charred bone at the
bottom of Old Man Turnbull's barn cellar-hole. Jude was
guessing souvenir hunters would be digging for them in the
charred embers before they had even cooled off.

It had been like seeing a living human being cast into Hell.
I suppose this was a fitting ending of Lamb the Murderer, if
not for the larky and happy young Ruby Lambkin.

Now, somehow, the wagons and such were straightening
out and leaving. We put on the hats we had dofted in respect
for his passing and with considerable difficulty managed to
worm the chaise out of there.

. . . .

Forty-eight

. . . .

Oᴸᴅ ᴍᴀɴ Tᴜʀɴʙᴜʟʟ got the reward. Since Burnap's murder this had climbed to $500. This was fair enough. He had
his barn to rebuild, and all those frolicksome folk that had
roosted all over his property had done considerable unavoid-
able damage. Judging by the way Jude's cider disappeared,
I guess they had helped themselves freely to what they might
have considered needful around the old man's place too.
Then too, it was Mr. Turnbull that had spotted Lamb.

Jude was right in one thing: the souvenir hunters got
into that still smoking cellar-hole before the coroner and his
jury. The charred bones collected for these gentlemen to
sit on didn't amount to much. In fact they were so few,
people were saying Lamb, being of an infernal nature, had

just evaporated, or Split Foot had come for him and fired the barn by mistake. I sort of liked hearing people talk about him like that. It did connect him once again with Ruby Lambkin.

One thing was certain: he'd make as fine a ghost to go out haunting lonely roads as New England had produced in these later days. Jude and I like to think of him, nimble and limber-like, happy and mischievous, and real beguiling too, tricking the tricksters, outsmarting the law. But he ought to haunt (if he knew what was good for him) those gullible, pretty towns both sides the Connecticut River — the upper half of that river.

As we headed for Leicester Jude talked sensibly of his future plans. He was going to set up a nice interior-painting business — just like Mitty had thought would be proper for him. It would support him just as well as all those painted-up-in-advance portraits he had been doing. Somehow they were apt to turn out so bad (did I remember Captain and Mrs. Dolliver?) that he thought he could take as much satisfaction in just honest coloring walls. All of them had made Hip-hop squirm. He was getting to feel the same way about them himself.

But spare time he'd do as he always had done — paint "overmantels" for the heck of it, even if he couldn't sell them. And he talked of several he had in mind — the white, peering gravestones of Bennington, the old ladies of New England cutting the last flowers before frost, and I think some more. He got pretty excited about these.

His mind turned to Leaf. Mitty was bringing her up too strict. He'd got to step in and take more responsibility for her. She did cry too easy and was too high-strung and shy.

"You used to like tagging me when you were her age, Eddy, while I went out sketching."

"Sure I did."

"Mitty won't like it, but I'll be taking her, seeing how

you are leaving us. For I don't want Leaf to grow up to be
a knitting-minded woman. And she's got what I don't think
you ever had, a little somewhat of a gift. If she prove so,
I'll teach her what I can, and see to it that later she has the
best masters. Not so ignorant of my own trade as I am.
Hip-hop brought that home to me."

Then he went on to tell of the horrors of his training
at the hands of that monster in human form, Julian Parker
Cove of Worcester, Mass.

I'm ashamed to say I felt jealous of Leaf, and she his own
child and ever so like him and me no more than a stranger
after all, and without even that "little somewhat of a gift."

I knew what was right and proper and it disgusted me
then, and it still disgusts me now, that I could of been
jealous of his own child. Yet thinking about him and Leaf
together did more to reconcile me to Waltham, Uncle Gore
and the harness trade than any one thing. And after that
the West for me! There is a plain somewhere between
Brookfield and Leicester. As he talked I was gazing at the
plain. There were buffaloes and Indians on it, in my mind's
eye.

And next we were coming down off Dead Horse Hill in
Leicester, striking right for the heart of Worcester, although
no more than six months before Jude had sworn to me
he'd never enter that town again.

"You too old to thumb your nose for me at Worcester?"
he asked.

"I guess I am too old."

"Guess you are."

Worcester is the county seat. Before us was the white
church and the courthouse. Back of them the common and
the old graves. And back of that the market and the
farmer's wagons, for it was market day.

"I'm going to drive the whole demmed length of their
demmed Main Street," says Jude. "I'm going to bow left

and right and tipping my hat like a governor seeking re-election. For I ain't scared of anybody, no not I, and no-body's scared of me." And he told me to sit up straight and he certainly was sitting up straight himself. "This place," he was saying to me, "was Hell for me when I was a boy — an overworked, underfed, real put-upon boy at that. But now I'm that boy no more. Don't mind if I do take a gander at it."

And, "Look-a-there, Eddy. Here's old School Street where that demon Cove had his workshop." We halted to look down the street at it. It wasn't a painting shop any more. It had grown to a really big coach-making establishment. But the old name was up above it. "Julian Parker Cove. Maker of Coaches for Horse and Steam." No wonder some of those coaches looked very queer to me.

We were still gazing down School Street, which being a side street had no sidewalks. Three gentlemen, coming from behind us, I guess, found our blocking the entry to the street irritating. They had prosperous backs and the look of men with money to invest. One of them turned, glanced back to see who was so in the way.

Jude and he looked at each other, and then stared hard. Jude said, "Mr. Cove, isn't it?"

The other gentlemen paused to look up at us, and wait for him. Mr. Cove looked real pleased but a little vague. He came right up to Jude, hand out, "Why . . . if it isn't . . . Now give me a pause for thought . . . Never forget a face . . . Don't tell me and I'll get it. I've seen that face before."

I hadn't expected to see Jude shaking hands with him, but he was.

"I've got it! Josh, or Jove, or — no, not Jules. Weren't you apprenticed to me once? Now you may tell me your name."

"Jude Rebough," he said, "once again."

"Well, if this isn't a happy occasion. I do appreciate your

stopping to look me up. Gentlemen," he turned to his friends, "if this isn't one of my old boys."

Jude handed him one of his trade cards. "Smartest apprentice I ever had. And you can say for me, can't you, Josh — I taught you good?"

"You did. You taught me good."

Mr. Cove was a rather big musty-looking old man, bags under his eyes and a deflated-looking double chin. I mean he had no fat on him to fill it. He didn't look especially evil, but sort of sick and therefore pathetic.

"Well, Judah — for I can't stand on formality with one of my old boys — how long you going to be in Worcester? Mrs. Cove would be delighted if you'd dine with us. And I could recommend you to the ladies and gentlemen of my acquaintance."

Jude was too dumbfounded to say much but a thank-you-kindly. He looked a touch subdued.

"This gentleman," Mr. Cove addressed his companions, taking an arm-length squint at Jude's trade card to get the name right, "this Mr. Degow, was the most gifted lad I ever had the pleasure to teach. I was always telling him and insisting on it that he go ahead into free-hand, for he certainly was born a cut above just lining coach wheels." Then, turning to Jude, he said most feelingly, "Job, my boy, the Lord blessed you with extraordinary competence. While teaching you I felt I was working in the Lord's own vineyard." Then back to his friends with, "Didn't seem right to hold a lad who had already surpassed his own master in his chosen field of free-hand to the completion of his indenture. But I did hate to see him leave me, Mrs. Cove too. Always had a soft spot for Judas."

Well, all I can say for this meeting is that the divergence of what each man remembered as "the truth" would of given Phineas Sharp a good laugh. I guess Mr. Cove had never admitted even to himself that an apprentice had struck him.

When he got up off that floor he had told his wife he had slipped on the soapsuds. Or another possibility is that Jude had been riding his imagination on too loose a rein through the years. Jude did look a little abashed — like a man who has been bragging that he was the worst boy in school and then meets his old master who humiliates him by saying he never gave him a moment's worry.

So we did drive the whole length of Worcester Main Street. The thing I remember best next to Mr. Cove, and yet related to him, was the preparations being made for the railroad. Mr. Cove was making the coaches for steam, as I said. But we saw hundreds of men, foreign men mostly, working with pickaxes and shovels and dump carts and wheelbarrows on what they called "the line." By another year the steam cars would run all the way from Boston to Worcester. And as for old Blackstone Canal, they had begun to fill that already. Those Worcester men had guts. For they say it was the same men as had financed the canal that now were filling it and financing the railroad, betting their money on steam.

Three years later I rode on those steam cars, only to Worcester, for they still went no further west than that. I was going west and of course I thought of Jude and me marveling to see all those men working on the line. And we were naturally wondering if a thing like that would prove practical, or would it just be a fad. Neither of us had felt convinced that steam and iron could take the place of horses and water routes.

. . . .

Forty-nine

. . . .

I WROTE EARLIER how Hampton was the hub of a charmed circle of everybody's "knowledge." That close to home they knew him and they knew me and it would of been hard, ever, to persuade them we were anywise different from what they thought we were.

Like they knew I had used to stammer. Nobody up, say, at Dr. Dwight's knew. I never had stammered at any of them up there.

And they "knew" Jude too. They weren't going to mistake him for a rich young gentleman, in search of his health (like North Adams) who painted for the fun of it. Nobody hereabouts, like Johnny Fessenden, would think they were held up if Submit Pratt's husband asked them what time it was. No sheriff would boast how he was going to take off his hide and nail it to his barn door, like Burnap. Girls wouldn't squeak and squeal, "My, ain't he the handsome fellow," like those girls of White River. No one would suspect him of pushing elderly invalids in rivers, and then seducing their wives. Even that coffin-shaped box we had to the back of the chaise — everybody so close to home knew about what was in it. They never had thought how he might be a body snatcher. On the other hand, nobody was going to ask if we fixed clocks.

We hit back into that "charmed circle" at about Thompson, Connecticut. On our way out from home, last May, we had encountered Mitty's old relatives, "Cousin" Deacon Thatcher and "Cousin" Mrs. Deacon Thatcher. And if they weren't right there in the gutter before their house, outside the bristling white picket fence! They were burning leaves. They both had rakes in their hands and the identical rectangular steel-rimmed spectacles, these resting upon long noses that were useful to them for squinting down at things like Jude and me.

"We got to do it," Jude says to me. "They'd be pretty hurt if we don't stop the night with them. Don't know why Mitty cherishes these old harpies but she does, so here goes." He stopped the chaise.

They were as unwelcoming as before and as suspicious of Jude and his trade. It wasn't until Jude was picking up the reins and saying we'd be pushing on that Mrs. Deacon said that if we had a mind to we could step in.

Thing I remember best about this stop was that it was the last night away from home, and that Deacon asked me suddenly how my stammer was and, if Jude hadn't answered up for me, I'd still be sitting there trying to say it didn't bother me any more.

After supper we were still setting by the kitchen table. We knew we were to hear again about the leaky calf-weaner Deacon had bit on thirty-one years ago next August. Or he'd be reading to us of the dangers of peddling, out of Bible Society tracts. Then Mrs. Deacon asked Jude a little slyly if whether on his travels he had heard of any good new cure for rats. And the way she looked you could guess she was scared silly of them, and likewise had them in her house but was ashamed to admit it. Like most people that have fleas don't like to talk about it.

Jude settled back to enjoy himself, for I guess he'd rather

listen to himself talking than good words out of Deacon. No
new ways, says he, but on this summer's travels he and Eddy
had had additional proof that old ways were best.

It didn't surprise me any any more that he was saying all
this had happened up to Fairlee, Vermont (a place we never
got to). A farmer up there, name of Scattergoods or Doolittle
— one of those trifling-sounding names — had had a most
terrible visitation of rats.

There had been no more than a few mice, just enough to
pick up dropped crumbs and keep the place neat, and the cats
from getting lazy, and then came the rats — big and rough-
looking, with teeth like chisels on them. Bigger than the cats.
So the cats up and moved out. And the old hound dog soon
after.

The rats took over. They gnawed up everything. Went
through the oak paneling in the best room; set up a bowling
alley in the garret and they bowled all night; went through
hogsheads to get at the molasses and the rum barrels to get at
the rum — they spilt more than they drank. They prospered
and they multiplied and they hung in festoons from the ceiling hooks carrying hams and seed corn. They ate the beds
down to stumps. Looked like they'd begin on the family next.
So, obviously, the family or the rats had better move out.

Those Thatchers were getting to look real nervous.

Jude asked them if they had ever heard of belling the lead
rat. Of course they had. You take a thimble, and you put a
tiny clapper in it. You catch the lead rat. Turn him loose
with this bell on and he leaves, all the other rats after him.

Only problem of course is — how do you tell the leader?
Mr. and Mrs. Deacon were sitting on the edges of their
straight chairs saying they "wanted to know," and "Tut, tut."

Those Doolittles figured it this way: As the rats had come
like an army they'd watch out for the most military-looking
one among them. Sure enough, there was one that strikingly

resembled old Andy Jackson — stringy-looking, but tall and earnest. And he had the same sort of pompadour. But they, being good Republicans, naturally couldn't vote for any Andy Jackson. But perhaps the leader was political? (They had seen those rascals digging in the pork barrel.) And they had observed one of them often standing on the cracker barrel making speeches. He had a beetling forehead and a blazing eye. In other words, he did resemble old Dan'l Webster. Should they try to catch and bell him?

Or perhaps it was the grizzled old lady rat — looked just like the wife of the old Squire up to Fairlee and she always seemed to be having last word at everything, and so high-bred and tony she looked down on Old Hickory and Mr. Webster both.

Then there was one of those rats forever at the Good Book. (Tut, tut, tut — this time from Deacon.) He'd got the gilt and leather offen it, and had gone straight through Genesis, Exodus, Leviticus, but was bogging down in Numbers — just like a lot of other clergymen (tut, tut, tut — but Jude went right ahead overriding their finer feelings). For even if that rat was so pious and learned, and labored ever so diligently in the Vineyard of the Lord, you couldn't say anybody was paying any heed to him. Might of — in the godly, good old days. Not now. No.

He was so firm on that point they could hardly manage more than a feeble "I want to know."

What of the power of money — in these late degenerate days? For one of those rats had put his mind right on the accumulation of great wealth — was always hiding buttons and such in a hole. He went on accumulating and accumulating and getting thinner and meaner all the time.

So the Doolittles figured they had plenty of candidates, but not one beyond-reasonable-doubt people's choice.

Then one morning, mincing along the kitchen floor, was

the prettiest little she-rat you ever did see — honey-colored fur, amber eyes. Had a little straw bonnet on her, with blue beau-catchers a-streaming behind. Soon as Dan'l Webster saw *that* he jumped right off his cracker barrel in the middle of a peroration. General Jackson stopped parading his troops, furred up his pompadour and cleared his throat. The clergyman forgot where he had got to in the Good Book. There weren't a pair of masculine whiskers weren't twitching. And those beady eyes brightened. So first, all the men among them indicated they were ready to go wherever she went. And the lady rats (madder than hornets) would be going after their men. That little hussy weren't hard to catch — thumb and forefinger did it. The little bell looked ever so nice on her. They opened the door. She tossed her head and tinkled her tiny bell, and left. And every dern last rat after her.

"And the *moral* of all this?" says Cousin Deacon Thatcher, a touch threateningly. Mrs. Deacon was clicking her rockers at us, and her false teeth. They didn't like his story. No, not any of it.

"No moral to it," says Jude. "Just a fact. Youth and beauty are terrible powerful components of life — for good or ill."

"If I ever thought," says Mrs. Deacon, "a hussy in a blue beau-catcher was a greater leader of sensible people than a man of God . . ."

"But they weren't sensible people. They were rats," Jude defended himself.

You see that story didn't go down too good, but it saved us from hearing about leaky calf-weaners and being read to from out of Bible Society tracts.

Jude told me one reason it didn't go so good was because it wasn't sinful enough. What they liked was good hot sin, right off the griddle, spiced with plenty of detail. He hadn't been able to think of any such on the spur of the moment. All he had done was best he could.

Fifty

Nᴇxᴛ ᴅᴀʏ was a Wednesday. I remember that because next day after was Thanksgiving day.

It was a somber, sad, dark day — naked trees, close low skies. And it was cold and looked to snow. There was cat-ice on the roads, and yet it was a happy day. You kept seeing people drawing up before houses — young folks with children in red mittens, and the old people's doors open to welcome them. Out came whiffs of cooking. Herbs from turkey stuffing, spice from puddings and pies, hot bread rising, coffee being ground, and turnips and onions boiling — for it don't hurt them any to be cooked up day before. Turkey giblets, too, get cooked Wednesday, but the turkey itself usually goes into the brick oven at about midnight. So there was a happiness in the air with laughter and hugging and kissing. Everybody was calling out happily to passersby like us — people who knew us saying how we'd be home for Thanksgiving.

People by and large ate good in New England. Even the real poor got baskets from the well-to-do. But women have been known to burst into tears first time they see a little rich girl with a basket on her arm saying that Mama knew they hadn't got enough to feast on — and here was the pope's nose and the neck, and the first batch of gravy that came out too greasy and the pumpkin pie that got dropped. Why tears? Well, for some people this may be the first realization that everybody knows how poor they've got. Yankees are terrible proud people, by and large.

Some who have no turkey and not even an old hen to spare send their young men out shooting, to bring home whatever they can pick up. Maybe a partridge or a brace of wild ducks. Perhaps a rabbit or a coon. There were no deer left in Connecticut. We saw several of these hunters out with their guns — out on the bare fields or mucking around in the swamps. When we got to Abington Four Corners there was one of them sort of gived out and discouraged, sitting on a wood pile, gun in hand, but no game in his bag. Head down — looked like his family would have no more than corn meal and salt pork in their pot next day.

I've said that Mitty had too many relatives. Among the nicest she had was the Colton P. Squireses living right here. It was on their wood pile the discouraged hunter was sitting. Those Squireses owned sawmills and timber land and were more lumber dealers than farmers.

Mrs. Squires was pleasant and comfortable as an old shoe, and had the same sort of good looks — if you get my meaning. She was out before her house in a plaid shawl, for she had heard wheels and thought it might be her married daughter from Pomfret and her family pulling in for the holiday. It was largely the young people who visit the old on Thanksgiving.

There was considerable of the milk of human kindness in her by nature, and a lot of bounce left in her, considering her years. So we paused to pass the time of day with her, not getting out of the chaise however.

Then she told us how we might shorten the distance from Abington to Hampton. She said her husband and two sons had been lumbering in what's called "the Old Colony tract" (for this stretch had been in the family back to colony days). Half that timber was being taken out to Truman Fisher's sawmill over to Hampton and half they were sledging back to their own mill at Abington. That meant there was a first-class path right through Old Colony tract — not town road but better than passable. We were to continue like we were for about a half mile. Turn right at Blaise's. If we didn't know Blaise's we could recognize it because they had a pet raccoon. As they also had hunting dogs, the coon was kept chained to the roof of a red shed. And that shed leaned against the house in such a way Mrs. Blaise could feed the coon from her second-story bedroom window.

By now the disconsolate hunter had taken up his gun and drifted away. Mrs. Squires seemed distressed she hadn't given him anything. "Poor fellow," says she. "If you overtake him, Jude, will you tell him to come back here? I might let him have the old rooster, but . . . And I'll tell him how to cook it nice so it will soften up in the pot."

Jude said, "I know. You put a brick in the pot along with the rooster, and when you can stick a fork in the brick the bird is done."

Then she was determined to send Mitty a very special kind of mince pie she had been trying a new receipt on and so forth. So at last we left her.

We got to Blaise's. There was the red shed and the raccoon. It had its little rubbery hands pressed against that second-story window. The hunting dogs were sitting down below and scratching and resting. They weren't baying that coon, but they hadn't completely lost all interest.

Leading off from town road was the short cut. It circled the Blaise barnyard, kept on going across stubble and soon hit into woodlands.

"Looks all right," says Jude.

But believe me, it looked lonely. Suddenly I didn't want to. I can't figure why I was so set against it to this day. But I felt something up my spine. I felt a premonition.

I said I was sure we'd break an axle on it, get stuck in the mud. A few snowflakes fell. I said there was a big storm coming and we'd lose our way.

He said it would save us a mile. I think he was longing for his wife and children and home again. He pulled at Goldie's right rein and clucked at her. She wouldn't budge. "Well," he admitted, "they do say horses always know the short cuts. But Goldie never does like anything new."

"She knows she won't like it. And don't you think town road would be surer?"

He didn't think so. He slapped her back with the reins and clucked hard at her. So she, like me, gave up.

We crossed the bare field with its scarecrow and the crows, and we came into the woods. I felt like we were being watched all the time, and a feeling of fatality. Something was going to happen to us from which we could not escape. Like in a dream.

Some of those woods had been cut so far back they had grown up into pretty heavy second growth. Some had never been cut, and some as recently as last winter. There was an awful lot of hard wood, and they bare now. There wasn't so much as the rustle of a leaf. Not a bird spoke.

Naturally swamps were dry now, but the Squireses had put down corduroy in a number of spots. Goldie wouldn't cross such unless I led her.

That was what I was doing when I noted, before her feet, coming up through the corduroy, the pitchers of the sidesaddle plant. They were still green. But the rain that had filled them had frozen some. I touched one and it snapped off — was as brittle as glass.

I called Jude to come see. He and me knelt there, with the snow coming down a flake at a time, and Goldie peering over our shoulders. Jude wanted to see what insects those plants had been eating when death came to them. Suddenly Goldie snorted. She had seen somebody behind us. We

were on our feet in a flash. You might say he was our disconsolate hunter that Mrs. Squires had thought to give her
old rooster to.

Jude and he stood looking each other right in the eye.
Jude said slowly, not thinking these were words he and I
might die for, "I guess you're Ruby Lambkin." He should of
pretended not to know him.

"I guess. You the limner?"

"Jude Rebough."

Ruby laughed.

Those two men did look surprisingly like. More alike
than most brothers. They had those wide square-chinned
faces, eyes a bit opener and larger than most men. Such
faces I call tomcat faces. But Ruby was neater-featured than
Jude and, because he was better built and considerably
heavier, he looked shorter. Likewise, there was no gangling
to that man. I've had to take other people's word for it
as to what Ruby looked like in his heyday. I only saw him
with my own eyes this once — and he at his worst. But somehow he had managed to keep himself shaved. And even now
you could feel he took pride in himself.

Those who had been likening him to a catamount weren't
too far off. There was a sort of still danger about him, like
he was about to pounce. He was standing stock-still but
you knew if he moved he'd move fast. Someone had knocked
out his front upper teeth since the last printed description
of him had been made. This made the eye teeth, in contrast to the bare gums between, wicked-looking like carnivore's. Most of all, looking at him you felt that he was
dangerous.

Jude said curiously, "How you get out that burning
barn?"

Ruby shrugged real nonchalant, pleased to have a chance
at bragging how smart he was. He and Jude didn't have
the same mannerisms.

"Nothing to that. I just walked out of there with a pig under each arm. Everybody so glad to see those pigs, didn't look too hard at me. Then I kept going."

"You set the fire?"

"Naturally. Farmers always lose their heads if a barn catches. Them were no more than farmers."

"Then being dead has had considerable advantage for you."

"Considerable, but . . ." and a look came on his face so fierce and murderous it was terrifying, "anybody that knows I'm not might get the money offered away from that fool farmer." His eyes prodded straight at Jude. "Reward don't tempt you any?"

"Me? No, not any."

"And I ain't no murderer," he burst out. "I killed Burnap in self-defense."

"Nobody could 'murder' a thing like Burnap," says Jude to pacify him. "No more than you could 'murder' a weasel. Look-a-here you and I see eye to eye on that score."

"And people durst hold it against me I didn't cut him up too good. I figured it this way. When he saw I was going to get him, his heart was dropping down into his boots."

"Why," says Jude, real considerate of his feelings (and he had better be), "you looked for his heart just about where I'd of looked. And by the way, I'm no informer — if that's what's eating you."

"Ain't eaten by anything," he boasted, "except . . ."

"What?"

"Victuals." As he said this word his face changed. He only looked hungry and trusting. We had about our usual amount of bread and cheese with us, but at Worcester we'd bought store candy for treats and fine tea for Mitty and a loaf of crystallized sugar for Dorinda. Likewise, we had Mrs. Squires's mince pie. We had a bottle of real West Indy rum for Tite and Labe.

If feeding that fellow would keep him off our necks, you bet we'd feed him. And he wanted a fire, to boil up the tea on and toast his bread and cheese. I guess he'd been living for a month on little more than the raw eggs he'd been swiping. He did fetch out three eggs from his back pocket and I boiled them along with the tea. The snow was still drifting in slowly. He wanted a blanket or something to sit on. We got him that. He thought of everything for his own comfort, and I'll admit for ours too. Goldie's even. It was he suggested I slip her nose bag on her.

In spite of his friendliness there weren't a moment when we didn't feel he might decide just to kill us, and us the only ones in the world knew he was alive, and go off with all the money he must of guessed we'd been accumulating. It was for the money he'd lain in wait for us, when he overheard Mrs. Squires give us that information about the short cut. But now it was like he was too courteous to bring up so vulgar a subject among friends. Jude handled him just right. If he hadn't, I guess our bones would be resting yet in Old Colony Tract near by those sidesaddle plants, for every moment was touch and go with that fellow.

We were at the mercy, not of any good sense or reasoned decision, but of his whims and hunches. He always had done just what he felt like when he felt like it, at the spur of the moment. I don't think he had ever "decided" to do anything. Just did what came along.

A lot of his lawbreaking and so on had been real whimsical, like his plaguing so at Burnap — weren't any real money in it for him. My guess is he always had been a little skee-gee. That doesn't mean he wasn't smart and tricky, for he was, but good sense and he weren't acquainted.

One other fact colored our meeting with him. He was pretty sociable by nature. He had been most terribly alone ever since he had killed off Burnap. He must of felt in need of friends, someone to boast to, sit and eat with — someone to listen to him and chat with and drink rum. He drank most the rum. Yet there was something real attractive about him.

He wanted to tell Jude quite a lot. For instance, that he had not killed those three flatboat men who had either saved his life by turning him over to jail and medical help, or had cashed in on him. Take your choice. As for Burnap — he and Jude saw alike. And on Johnny Fessenden alike. Jude told him of the antiquary of Charlestown who had asked him to do up a likeness of him. This flattered Ruby no end. He began boasting of his success with women to Jude. Real nasty talk, but certainly it held your interest.

"When you got to Faucett's — you remember Faucett's up to Norwich?"

"Sure I remember."

"I've heard a lot of talk ... "

" 'Cruel Husband'?"

"I've heard that sung."

"All true facts, every word of it. But I didn't know that damn fool old 'possum could swim."

"Yeh . . . But Emma, was she real glad to see you?"

"Emma? Who she? Sort of scraggly little woman, was she? Sharp elbows?"

"No. She came full-size."

"Well, women," he confided, "they are all so demmed easy and all so much alike a man can't always remember which is which."

Jude should of been above prodding at him, jogging him into remembering his own lechery. But he did more than satisfy his own low curiosity, for he was putting Ruby into a nice friendly frame of mind.

Ruby was saying how it was "soft sawder" that did it. "The softer the sawder, the harder they fall." We had not only to listen to his advice on such matters but hear how he encompassed the virtue (if he did) of Nurse Florence Duddey up to Windsor Prison — she the one that gave him the file.

And about three or four widows and a peck of farm girls, etc. Jude wanted to get him back to Emma Faucett.

"Why didn't you say Mrs. Faucett in the first place," Ruby demanded. "You mean that feather-bed lady, with pumpkin hair? Sort of refined?"

And that was all Jude got to satisfy what I must admit was his ungentlemanly curiosity.

The snow was settling down, whitening everything. The wind wasn't blowing any, but it was getting dark there in the woods. We weren't more than halfway through Old Colony Tract. But we dursen't suggest going until he said so.

Goldie was tossing at her feedbag, spilling out the last oats. I thought how next spring they'd shoot up green between the logs of the corduroy, longside the sidesaddle plants. I'd walk along here. By the green oats I'd know the very spot. Then I remembered next spring I'd be in Waltham.

I guess Ruby must have felt he'd better find a quiet barn to hole up in for the night. Maybe back to Blaise's. Now at last he got down to what you might call business. He did it this way: "Mr. Rebough," says he, "I hate to ask it of a friend, but I could use a loan. Haven't saved much against a rainy day. I'm on my way, hoofing it for New London. That was what I was figuring on when I saw you there to Abington. And I'll take a boat to anywheres. If a man has cash on him no questions are asked, so if I had a little cash . . ."

"Of course," says Jude. He'd known this was coming.

"Mr. Rebough, I guess you've been pretty diligent all summer."

"I got some spare cash."

"I'm not holding you up at no pistol point. This ain't no highway robbery. I'm only inquiring . . . where's your wallet?"

"Would fifty do you?"

"That would do me fine."

"Eddy carries the wallet for us," Jude said. "Eddy will you

fork out fifty dollars for this gentleman?" Nothing was being said about our spare cash — hid up like I told you in the whipstock.

"And the fact is, Mr. Lambkin, this isn't no loan. I call this fifty, well, a recognition of the fact you did a lot of little things for me — so to speak. Things I might of done for myself, if I had been a touch more agile. I'd be pleased to give ten dollars to anybody got you out of that infernal blazing barn. You did it. That's ten dollars. I'd give, say, five dollars for making a bigger fool than he was born, even, out of the no-account Johnny Fessenden. As for rolling Francis Faucett in the river — that's worth ten again to me."

"What you give me for killing Burnap for you?"

Ruby was catching right on to the idea.

Jude hesitated. "Five," says he firmly.

"And for gutting him for you?"

"Not a red cent. I disapproved of that, by and large." And again that danger sign in the man's eye. Jude had played with fire when he refused to pay him for the mess he made of Burnap, but he went on real easy, "Eddy — where we got to now?"

"Ten and five and ten and five more," I said. "That's thirty."

"Thirty won't suffice," said Ruby sharply.

"Then twenty is for that ride from Norwich to Windsor jail I took in your name. It was a pleasant ride, by and large."

"I seen it," says Ruby, "from the flatboat I was on."

"And I'm giving you my wallet too, as a keepsake from me to you."

Ruby laughed. He had an easy laugh. He was up on his feet and our bonfire was about out. More snow had fallen than you'd of thought.

"And why don't you go west," Jude asked him, seeing him about to go. He didn't say "and behave yourself." He certainly wasted his breath on a lot of things — like those rats that so offended the Thatchers — but he weren't so simple as to suggest anything like Ruby Lambkin was ever going to reform.

Ruby must of known we had a lot more money on us. He didn't ask for it. But he did say how, as long as we were so near home and there would be plenty of food waiting for us there, he'd take the rest of the victuals. Likewise, he'd "borrow" Jude's heavy overcoat. He got that, and he picked up the blanket we had been sitting on without so much as "by your leave."

We got into the chaise. He stood a moment at the step, hat pulled down and overcoat collar turned up. He mumbled something at us — I never was sure what. Next moment he was gone. There was something eerie about him, but it may have been the circumstances under which we met.

Nowadays I'd go so far as to say Jude showed a lack of public spirit not reporting Lambkin — and the reward would of come in handy. What he promised Ruby he promised under duress — nothing against a man breaking a promise like that. Even if you could call that fifty dollars a "gift," Ruby certainly did steal his overcoat and blanket. So Jude didn't do right, leaving that immoral rapscallion loose upon the world. But he was like that. He thought spiders and their webs beautiful and he liked snakes, so maybe you shouldn't expect a reasonable judgment from him on a thing like Ruby Lambkin. And he never could of painted so good if he had been like other people — like what I am now, for instance.

I've been a tower of respectability to Wichita, Kansas, and a pillar of the First Baptist Church out here so long, maybe it's my judgment that is warped.

. . . .

Fifty-one

. . . .

IT WEREN'T until we saw Mr. Truman Fisher's sawmill, set up on Broke-Axle Brook, we felt really out of the woods — figuratively and factually speaking. We turned left there, and over the bridge and soon were on Hampton Main Street. The town lay under its first blanketing of snow. No more was falling, and, judging by the way the moon was fighting to come out, no more would fall tonight. But it was the writing on the wall — winter had come.

People, by and large, talk too much about the horrors of New England winter. It's real pleasant — if you have made proper preparations for it ahead of time, like you ought. For farmers there is not much more than stock feeding, chores and wood cutting. If you've got things fixed right there is more time for sitting and neighborliness in winter than any other season. The great fires are burning then, and chestnuts or apples to roast, and hot flip or grog — suit yourself — or corn to pop. And time for chat and stories and to read books too. Tite was always reading away in Gibbon — every winter.

The ring of skates on the dark ice of our lonely ponds. Or maybe pickerel fishing, and the red bobs bobbing mean you've hooked one — and if that ain't the grandfather of all pickerels ever caught in Snailers Pond you give up. But your fingers are so stiff, you lose holt on the slippery thing and it's gone flop through the hole in the ice, free again. Nobody will ever believe how big it really was. That's the sort of disappointment a man may remember for over sixty years.

Breaking the roads was fun. All over New England hundreds — no, I guess thousands — of oxen breaking the roads. Farmers, like the Pratts, boasted more of the strength of their oxen than any one thing. As breaking the roads was a community effort, that was the time to prove it. I've seen so many as thirty yoke hitched to one "leveler," and the oxen strong as sin and slower than cold molasses moving through drifts higher than their shoulders. No man not on snowshoes could get through. And no horse. But the oxen could. And every farmhouse you passed by everybody was inviting the men and boys in to warm up and "wet their whistles," and the tiredest yoke would be taken off and left there. The fresh yoke tackled on in front — if they were powerful as well as fresh. I've seen big boys in tears because their "Bright" and "Star" have been voted out as worthless. And Tite Pratt came home tipsy and singing Hallelujah when one of his yokes, name of Narses and Orestes (they two eunuchs he'd been reading of in Gibbon) held, by common consent, first place for four miles.

In the lumbering parts of New England, of course, there was tree felling and log snaking to be done. For the logs had to be hauled to some flow of water (like Merrimack or Connecticut) big enough to float them down come spring. We had lumbering, like the Squireses, but nothing like what they had north of us.

I liked wintertime to be in the barn. It was so warm and smelly, and the beasts more dependent on man and more affectionate, cozy and safe. I never did know what the big sheep farmers did with their sheep up in the country of the sheep craze. I think they left them out. And thinking of them I could almost see the dark, silent bodies of the hunting wolves and the twitch of the catamount tail, and she about to pounce.

Yet when I think of winter in New England it is the hearth fires I think of most, and the fragrance of wood smoke. Every wood that burns has its different smell. Some, for instance, smell so terrible, nobody'd burn them unless ignorant or freezing to death. In some sections, of course, they burn more pine than others or more chestnut or oak. I guess everywhere poor people burn white birch. It costs naught. Not even much labor. Although a pretty thing, most people look down on it for a weed. But as I remember it, wherever yellow birch grows it is cherished for the sweet incense of its smoke. That's why, coming up along Hampton Main Street, we smelt yellow birch burning, for it was holiday season and the best weren't too good. It never did give much heat.

Pine Hill was before us, with its topknot of stunted pines. The moon was out now and shining on it. We rounded that. We took our own lane in, rounding Pine Hill. Then we saw before us Pratt Farm. It looked broad and handsome and well kept up. And it was. We were listening for Brutus to announce us. They were expecting us some time this night and had set lamps to windows to welcome us, or Mitty may have been afraid we'd miss it in the dark and drive by. There was even a barn lantern hanging by the barn door. Inside the house we knew Laban would of finished drawing the turkey, and Mitty had it stuffed and sewed up. Tite would be regulating the heat in the brick oven so it would be just right at midnight — which is the time to pop in "the alderman in chains" as we called our turkeys, because of the link sausages over them.

Jude said, "Something has happened to Brutus." We saw his kennel with its frosting of snow. No dog. If living, he'd be barking at anyone driving up this time of night and on recognizing Jude, would be roaring and growling with rage.

"If I'm correct in my deductions," said Jude, "and that Brutus has gone to his reward, I'll shed no tears."

Then we saw a strange and lovely thing. In the angle between the house and barn, in and out the moonlight and the lantern light, the foxes were playing.

So Tite hadn't got him a new dog yet. Brutus must of just died. Those derned little red rascals wouldn't darse to carry on so if they smelt a dog. They knew Brute was dead, and had gathered, so to speak, to dance upon his grave.

They hadn't come chicken hunting. You could almost see them laughing, but they knew enough not to laugh out loud. It was all secret and silent — and mysterious, for foxes don't travel together. I suppose they were litter mates and parents. One big one (and I think it was Old Split Foot himself) went up backwards on his hind legs and jigged it there. They were dancing a pattern on the light snow and we too were about ready to laugh, thinking of Tite's consternation next morning when he went out for early chores and saw all those pretty slender prints of fox feet lying on the fresh snow like chains. We sat there, holding our breath, to watch them. Then Goldie, longing for her friends and her own stall, whinnied. There wasn't a fox in sight, but doors were flying open. We heard excited voices calling our names. We had gone far and seen much but it was nice to be home again. He perhaps forever, and me for no more than five days.